A Bright
Young Thing

Also available by Brianne Moore

All Stirred Up

A Bright Young Thing

A Novel

BRIANNE MOORE

alcove
press

Copyright © 2021 by Brianne Moore

Published in the United States by Alcove Press, an imprint of The Quick Brown Fox & Company LLC.

Alcove Press and its logo are trademarks of The Quick Brown Fox & Company LLC.

Library of Congress Catalog-in-Publication data available upon request.

ISBN (hardcover): 978-1-64385-533-2
ISBN (ebook): 978-1-64385-534-9

Cover design by Lynn Andreozzi

Printed in the United States.

www.alcovepress.com

Alcove Press
34 West 27th St., 10th Floor
New York, NY 10001

First Edition: September 2021

10 9 8 7 6 5 4 3 2 1

For my parents, who were always happy to listen to my stories

Chapter One

Orphanhood came suddenly on a glass-clear day in February 1930. It was the first dry day that week, so my parents decided to take the new Delage out for a drive.

"Time to stretch her legs," Father said. "We may go have a wander around Rockingham Castle. You should come along and get some roses in those cheeks."

He ruffled the top of my head, and I ducked and playfully swatted him away. How many hundreds of times had I been hauled off to Rockingham over the years? Even my father could only make the place sound interesting so many times. Anyway, I had a cold to recover from and a poem that wanted writing. So, I stayed behind.

"Just an hour or two," they said. They kissed me on the cheek, urged me to get some rest, and were gone. Replaced, seemingly in a blink, by Officer Anson (poor man, only his second week on the job). Helmet in hand, pale, stammering that there had been an accident. That half a mile outside Market Harborough, Mother had cut the wheel too sharply and sent the car tumbling down an embankment.

I stared at him as he stood, sweating, in front of the fire. His blue wool uniform was too tight and cut into his neck. He ran a finger around the collar every now and then and shifted his weight. Funny the things you remember at times like this.

"It's a tricky corner, that, very tricky," he jabbered, unnerved by my blank face and silence. "I've seen plenty of drivers get into trouble there—even men!" He chuckled and received in reply a long, slow blink. The fire snapped twice, sending sparks toward the chimney, and yet I felt chilly. The carriage clock on the mantelpiece hammered out its ticks, further fraying Anson's nerves. He cleared his throat, looked down at the helmet he was still holding, as if unsure what to do with it. "They're sure it was quick, miss. I—I'm very sorry, miss. They were good sorts, your parents. Always had a kind word." Frowning in concern, he bent to peer into my face. "Is there . . . anyone else we should notify?"

"Notify?" The word had no meaning. Not a thing he'd said after "I'm sorry to have to inform you there's been an accident" had actually penetrated the thick shroud that almost immediately wrapped itself around me. All I could hear was the crunch of collapsing metal. The oddly musical breaking of glass as a distant car somersaulted over dead grass and mud. But no, my parents weren't dead. Of course they weren't. I had that new poem to show them. It would make Father laugh.

Anson had run out of things to say, and the clock filled the silence. Finally, a voice that was not my own, but that of some frigid automaton driven by a lifetime of the right sort of training, thanked the hapless man for all his trouble. "I realize this must have been difficult for you," the voice concluded.

He seemed puzzled. Probably wondering why I hadn't broken down, wailed, sobbed, cursed the fates. Isn't that what women did when met with tragedy? He hadn't seen enough sudden grief to know that some bodies, when shocked, self-anesthetize. He would come to know it, but for the moment he clapped his helmet back on his head and made his escape, probably thinking "the quality" were a strange lot indeed.

Once he was gone, I threw my poem into the fire and retreated to my room. The shroud thickened and settled, swaddling me layer by layer in a protective cocoon in which I felt nothing. It was a relief, that.

This was the first great shock of my life. There would be others—so many others—in the coming months. They would bruise and toughen and soften me all at once. But this first, this greatest, seemed more than I could bear. How *could* one bear such a thing? A cataclysm that opened the earth beneath you? Left you scrabbling for a handhold as you stared into the darkness that was so eager to eat you alive, and wondering, just for a little while, if it would be easier to simply let go and let the void take you?

How do you bear the silence that follows the death?

I stayed shut away, unable to face a house that was still full of my parents. Beyond my door, Father's aftershave lingered. His artifact collections gathered dust. The seedlings Mother and I had planted were just beginning to sprout.

Aunt Elinor came from London and made all the arrangements so efficiently, it was as if she'd been planning for this moment for years. Not even the death of her only sister could shock *her* into a torpor.

Friends came to coddle and care for me, to try to lift me out of my stupor. But I would not lift. I drifted through the funeral service in a somnambulant daze. Afterward, I was parked by the fire in the drawing room to receive the usual platitudes: "Such a *shame*! Such a lovely couple—and in the *prime* of their lives." And, when they thought I couldn't hear, "Astra will be *quite* the catch now, won't she?" Appraising eyes roamed the rooms, picking up on the new furnishings, thick-pile carpets, and streamlined sculptures that spoke of wealth and style and a careless sort of spending.

I might still be there, among the curio cabinets and cream velveteen, if not for Father. One fine day in April, Mr. Edgry, our family solicitor, rolled up the drive and informed me that if I didn't make a change to my living standards soon, I wouldn't have a penny to my name by July.

"What sort of change do you mean?" I asked, my cottoned-up brain struggling to make sense of the ledgers and papers before me.

"Economics, my dear," he answered, leaning back in the chair he'd assigned himself (Father's leather armchair, naturally). "Economies *must* be made. Serious ones."

"Well, I suppose we could do without a housemaid," I suggested.

He regarded me across the expanse of Father's desk with a mixture of pity and contempt. "You don't seem to understand," he said, carefully enunciating every word.

"The under-gardener too, then," I offered, though I was loathe to lose garden staff. "Perhaps the butler?"

Beside me, Aunt El made a mortified noise, quickly strangled with a harsh cough.

Edgry closed his eyes as his face steadily reddened. His blood-sausage fingers clenched his lapels. I had the disturbing sense he was trying very hard not to throttle me. He slowly rose, looming over me.

"The housemaid must go, *and* the under-gardener, *and* the butler, *and the house*!" He snatched a handful of bills and waved it at me. "Don't you understand? You can't afford any of it. Your Father lost it all. You have *nothing*."

Those words—you have *nothing*—somehow penetrated the cocoon I'd been sheltering in. They tore right through it—*riiiiip*—and light and air flooded in, stripping the last comforting threads away and shaking, slapping me awake. Everything was too loud and too bright: the tweeting of the robins in the stone birdbath just outside hammered at my skull, and the brilliant blue of the morning glories stung my eyes.

Something began expanding in my chest, ballooning so massively it would surely blow me to pieces. Instead, it traveled upward into my throat and came out not as tears, as expected, but as hysterical laughter.

Edgry was so startled he leaned away, as if he thought I might suddenly be a danger to him. Aunt El, in horror, hissed: "Astra, control yourself!"

And then the tears came. I'd laughed hard enough for my sides to hurt, but the laughter vanished just as soon as it had come, and I exploded into loud, messy sobs that utterly defeated the handkerchief Aunt El shoved toward me.

"H-how could this happen?" I gasped. *"How?"*

"Millions of people all over the world are asking themselves that question." Edgry pushed away from the desk and paraded angrily around the room. "The fact of the matter is, Astra, your Father, God rest him, was a fool. No sense at all, that man. And then of course he started to get desperate when your mother—"

Another noise from Aunt Elinor interrupted him—a bizarre sound this time, like a goose being throttled while playing a trumpet. Edgry glanced at her, then cleared his throat and pressed on, circumnavigating the room as he spoke.

"Well, you know how it is. Plenty out there in the same pickle you're in, my dear. At least you still have something of worth." He waved his arm at the walls as he came to a stop at the window overlooking the garden. After a few moments' silence, he turned to me, hands clasped behind his back, and said, "The best thing you can do is to sell up. Go live with your aunt and cousin, pay off the debts, and put away anything left."

Aunt El stifled another cough and agreed. "Yes, of course you must come stay with Toby and me." Though I could practically see her calculating the cost of housing another person.

"Sell Hensley?" With everything that had happened, I would lose my home as well? Leave the echoes of my parents behind and let them become the property of strangers? And that was even assuming I *could* sell it. I didn't know anyone who was buying places like Hensley. Most people were getting rid of them. "I'm *not* selling the house. The Davieses have been here for a century. My mother built those gardens." I gestured to the flowery expanse beyond the French windows. "There must be something else I can do."

I grabbed a ledger and scanned it, wishing I'd been better prepared for this sort of thing. But my governess had said, "What does a girl need sums for? You'll scare off your suitors." And Mother had smiled and promised to teach me what I needed to know "when the time came." Had that time not come and gone? I was twenty-three years old—what had she been waiting for?

"What's this?" I asked, pointing to an entry for Vandemark Rubber. It looked like the only thing in the ledger that didn't have a minus sign next to it.

Edgry huffed and flopped back down into the chair. "I told your father not to get mixed up in that, but he never listened to me," he said. "'Helping a friend,' he called it, and gave that fool enough money to buy a twenty-five percent stake in the company."

"Well, it couldn't have been *such* a bad idea," I pointed out. "It's making money."

His face darkened. "Not for long, I'm sure. It's owned by the Ponsonby-Lewises."

My cousin, Toby, who up until now had been content to recline on a sofa and watch the show, groaned.

"There's nothing wrong with the Ponsonby-Lewises, Tobias!" his mother snapped. "They're a fine family. And sit up like an adult, for heaven's sake!"

"They aren't fine at all, Mums," Toby countered, slowly rising and giving me a pitying look. "They're an *old* family, and that's not the same thing. I knew their son and believe me: this is a family whose tree hasn't branched enough."

"What are some of these others, then?" I asked, again turning to the ledger and hoping for a miracle. "Who's this Clarence Ha—"

"Never mind that. It was something that didn't work out, just like the rest of them." Edgry snatched away the ledger and snapped it shut. After tucking it away in his satchel, he folded his hands over his belly and glared at me.

"If you're determined to be foolish about this and hold onto the place, you'll have to let it to someone," he said. "You don't have the money to keep it up; you can hardly even pay the servants. Your father was about to start mortgaging it just to keep you all afloat. Get a tenant until you can find a man who can afford to help you keep it."

Even through my confusion, I resented that last bit. Was it so outrageous that I find a way to keep up my own house?

And so, the house was let. I was surprised, given the state of things, that we found someone. But though millions suffer, there will always be some people with money. The one we found was a flash theatrical producer who wanted his family out of London so he could continue his affair with a promising young actress from the chorus line of *Rio Rita*.

"They agreed to a generous price," Edgry told me in a tone that still indicated disapproval. "Between that and what comes in from Vandemark Rubber, you should have an income of around a thousand pounds a year. Do try not to spend it all on hats, will you?"

So, to London, with its tarry air stinking of motor oil, coal, and manure. London, with its cacophony of noise: the clatter and crash of traffic and trains, tooting horns and bleating whistles, bellowing newsboys and beggars and buskers—all clamoring for money and attention. Streets that darkened prematurely, hiding tramps and pickpockets hovering just outside the ghostly ring of light cast by globe-shaped lamps.

To Aunt El's house on Gertrude Street, one in a row of staid, respectable homes. White stucco on the ground floor and brick above. Inside: decor that had been very popular the year Prince Albert died.

I arrived on a clammy day in November and took in my new surroundings: the saints and crosses, threadbare carpets, heavy furniture, and light-smothering draperies. And I thought, *I need to go home.*

But to go home, I needed money.

How far would a thousand pounds a year stretch? What did I need? What could I trim and set aside? It had taken this disaster for me to realize I didn't know what the simplest things cost. And I needed to know because economies, as Edgry had said, would have to be made. So the day after my arrival, I sat down and, using one of Mother's account books as a sort of guide, attempted a budget. Two hours later, this was what I had:

Income: £1,000/year
Projected Expenditures:
    Lady's Maid: £65–100
    Clothes:
    Entertainment: free, with the right friends
    Card games: £100–200 (?)
    Travel: variable

Just like Edgry's ledgers, Mother's accounts were a mystery to me: pages and pages of pounds and pence and who was paid and who was owed, but nothing to suggest money was coming in. How was she paying for these things? And what *were* some of them? I puzzled over entries for something called "Rosedale": the rather princely sum of 50 pounds paid promptly the first of every month, going back as far as the ledger did. It was nearly the only thing paid on time. And more recently, "Dr. H" appeared, accompanied by amounts so large my stomach actually knotted.

But that was the least of it. There were huge sums that I knew could be attributed to me. To the things I needed to be a fashionable young lady. Dressmakers and travel expenses and gifts for friends who were getting married or having babies. I almost cried at the sight of them. Where to even begin?

As I gaped at the ledger, Toby strolled in, glanced at my work (if you could call it that), tsked, and commented, "Grim stuff, old girl." He patted me on the shoulder and eased over to the window to claw back the layers of curtains and starched net. A feeble finger of sunlight penetrated the gloom for all of ten seconds before retreating behind a passing cloud.

Toby sighed and turned his attention to the sofa, pummeling cushions that, under the pressure of nearly half a century's worth of bottoms, had redistributed most of their plump to the outermost edges, as if the stuffing were trying to flee.

"You may," he continued, "have to start buying your frocks *from the shops*. And—dare I say it?—you might need to trade your holiday in Cannes for a week in Biarritz instead." He tossed me a cheeky smile before giving up on the sofa assault and stretching across the cushions with a wince.

"Hardly the time for jokes!" I rubbed my forehead as the deep pulsations of an impending headache began. How much did aspirin cost? Could I still afford headaches?

"Au contraire, my dear. The bleak times make for the best jokes. Gallows humor and all that. Something about dreadful situations brings out the cleverness in people."

"Not me." I put my pen aside and slumped in the chair, feeling defeated.

"Oh, give it time, darling. Once the dust has settled, I'm sure you'll come up with something." Toby drew a tortoiseshell cigarette case from his pocket and scrutinized the contents before selecting one.

"I'll have to, won't I?" I said, shaking my head as he offered me the case. "No, thank you. A whole one will make me jittery. I'll draw off yours."

Toby's eyebrows rose. "You're lucky I'm a generous soul." He struck a match, lit the cigarette, took a drag, and leaned back, eyes closed, slowly exhaling the smoke. He smiled, a private, satisfied sort of smile and then handed the cigarette to me. I took a quick puff and returned it.

Toby mournfully shook his head as he accepted the cigarette. "You have to learn to appreciate things."

"You know how your mother feels about girls smoking," I reminded him, glancing toward the door to make sure Aunt Elinor hadn't suddenly appeared, summoned by sin. "And that's just what I need—to have her toss me out."

"Nonsense, Mother would never do that. Throwing over the orphaned niece would put her hopelessly behind in the sainthood stakes." Toby took another careful drag of the cigarette and began absently rubbing his left knee. "You're assured of a roof over your head for the time being, at least."

"But not the roof I want. How can I find enough money to save Hensley when I don't so much as know the cost of a hairpin?"

"It's less than a thousand pounds. You should be safe there."

"But what about everything else? It's not the individual things—it's all of it together. And just look at this! I'm hopeless." I waved the budget in the air, then tossed it back onto the writing desk and began attacking the fire with the poker. Angry sparks shot upward and out, spattering and hissing on the hearth.

Toby sat up and eased away before he got singed. "There, there," he soothed. "No need to burn the house down over it. Why don't you do as Edgry said and find a nice, rich young man to marry you? I'm sure you could find someone. You're not so decrepit."

"Oh thank you very much. But I've reviewed my current offerings, and they aren't promising. No, I'll just have to get *myself* out of this mess."

"Well, you might be at risk of a matching, whether you want it or not," he warned. "Mother's got *plans*. She's been after me to invite friends 'round to throw at you."

"Bachelors bouncing around like tennis balls," I groaned.

"And you joyfully swatting them away!" he chortled. "I think that might be rather entertaining. I may sell tickets!"

"Ahh, we've found the way to make my fortune at last," I declared. Then, more seriously, "How long before she starts serving in earnest?"

"I give her fifteen minutes the next time she sees you."

"Goodness!" I sank back into the armchair. "She *is* desperate to get rid of me."

Toby waved his cigarette case. "No. She's just of the generation that thinks the only thing for a girl to do is to marry well and quickly, before the bloom's off the rose."

"If that's how she feels, then why did she wait so long herself?"

Toby struck a match and lit the cigarette. "She was waiting for the right man to sweep her off her feet."

We laughed, both at the idea of Aunt El being swept and of pliant, colorless Augustus Weyburn doing the sweeping. My uncle's death had probably been the most dramatic thing to ever happen to him, and even then he went as quietly as he lived: choking to death on a grape. Poor man.

Toby gave me the cigarette, and I puffed away for a moment, thinking.

"There is Vandemark Rubber," I mused. "That's something. I spoke with Mr. Ponsonby-Lewis, and he said the business was going quite well.

They make tires, he said, and they've got an exclusive contract with Mr. Porter to supply his automobile factory."

"Not sure I'd take P-L senior's word for it," Toby warned. "He's a bit . . . off. A few years ago he got it into his head to create a line of green chickens, and when breeding them that way didn't work, he just had his flock dyed."

I paused. "All right, he may be a bit eccentric," I allowed. "But he seemed confident. Maybe I could work on Mr. Porter. Convince him to increase his order or something. I could charm him."

Toby chuckled. "Yes, I daresay you could."

I stood and examined myself in the spotty mirror over the fireplace, assessing my qualities. I was fortunate as far as looks went. Like both of my parents, I was tall and willowy, with Father's dark eyes and heart-shaped face and Mother's chestnut-colored hair. It fell to just below my ears, in carefully arranged waves and pin curls. My lips could, perhaps, be a little rounder, but lipstick could fix that.

I sighed. Was this all I could do? Become someone's decorative wife or simper to an old man?

In disgust, I threw the remains of the cigarette into the fire, watching the coals eagerly consume the last of it. "It isn't fair, Toby, that things should be so hard." I turned and leaned against the mantelpiece, arms crossed, scowling. "You men can always go out and . . . I don't know, discover something or build a railway somewhere."

He laughed. "Can we indeed?"

"You can. And you do. You're all *usefully* educated."

He threw back his head and laughed. "No, my dear, you have it quite wrong: the more expensive the education, the more *useless* it is. I spent most of my schooldays on Latin verbs, and what good is that? I can assure you, very little has ever been accomplished purely by saying '*veni vidi vici*' properly."

"That's still more than I can do. The sum total of my education was curtseying, music, and penmanship. I know how to properly address a duchess but don't know the price of a packet of tea."

"Surely that's in the ledger somewhere?"

"The thing is practically written in code." My eyes moved toward it. "You don't know what 'Rosedale' or 'Dr. H' are, do you?"

Toby shrugged and shook his head.

"Well, I think they have the Davieses to thank for *their* holiday in Cannes."

I turned back to the fire, clutched the mantelpiece, closed my eyes, and silently counted to ten. It was a soothing technique my mother had taught me.

"And if that doesn't calm you, imagine a flower slowly unfurling," she'd said.

I heard the flutter of paper as Toby picked up the budget. A moment after, he said, "Perhaps you could do without the lady's maid."

I shook my head. "No, I can't. It's not respectable for me to travel alone, now I don't have Mother to accompany me. And every heiress I know got one as soon as she was able. It'll be a dead giveaway if I don't have one."

"Would it? No one cares if a man doesn't have a valet." He shrugged and lit another cigarette.

"Of course they do; they just don't make quite as much of a thing of it. If I don't have a maid, everyone will start to wonder why, and then they'll guess I'm hard up."

Only those with titles and great names to hide behind could be poor and still receive invitations to everything. Others who fell on hard times quietly slipped out of the social circle and were forgotten. A family I knew had once owned three mills near Leicester, but they'd shut down, one by one, and then the family had simply disappeared. Sold up and went somewhere without so much as a goodbye. I'd heard the eldest daughter was working as a waitress, but I was sure that couldn't be true, because Effie was as clumsy as she was stupid. At the time, I hadn't felt much pity for them—they were a brash and spendthrift lot—but now I was thinking of them a little more kindly. But that was really the best one could hope for: pity. And I would *not* be an object of pity.

"Suit yourself." Toby examined me critically. "Probably for the best: you're starting to look like a woman who does her own hair." He shuddered.

"Beastly creature!" I lobbed a needlepoint cushion at him. "Make it up to me by helping me persuade your mother this is a good idea. We'll need to do it soon too. I've already placed the advertisement for the post and need to have someone hired by the time I go to Gryden Hall in two weeks."

"Gryden!" He flinched. "Bit of a mixed blessing, that."

"I know. But I need to start getting out, and Cecilia's just dyyyying to see me! That's how she put it in the letter, too—lots of extra 'y's'."

He chuckled. "Sounds like her. She probably can't wait to see a friendly face after having been trapped out in the godforsaken countryside with that sister of hers." Toby gave me a warning look. "Tread carefully, my dear."

"I can manage Millicent. She's the least of my worries."

"It's not just her you have to worry about. They'll all be staring you down, all weekend long. Couldn't you have found a more relaxed event for your return to public life? Weren't there any drawing rooms at Buckingham Palace?"

"Not a single one. Everyone's off hunting, the king included."

He rolled his eyes. "Yes, of course. They've all run off to stand around in the damp and deliver England from the scourge of grouse." He shuddered again.

"Well, anyway, Cee says that Joyce and David will be there too. It feels like years since I last saw Joyce."

"Ahh, still married, then? There's a wager I've lost."

I had run out of cushions to throw, so I just settled for a glare. "Yes, still married, *and* enjoying it. At least, I haven't heard any complaints from Joyce, and you know I would have if she had any."

"She does speak her mind," he agreed. "Must be the American in her." The clock on the mantelpiece chimed the hour. "Ahh, teatime. Gird your loins, Mums will be here any moment. But perhaps talk of this lady's maid will distract her from the bachelors." He stretched back out on the sofa, grinning.

With a sharp cough and a terse: "Hasn't Jeffries brought the tea yet?" Aunt Elinor announced her arrival.

"Ahh," Toby crowed. "Speak of the devil!"

His mother paused in the doorway, the very picture of Severe: spear-straight posture, tightly scraped back dark hair, high-necked, floor-length black dress.

My spine stiffened as soon as I saw her, but Toby drawled: "Afternoon, Mums."

"Tobias!" his mother gasped. "You're smoking!" Her hand reflexively clutched the cross she wore around her neck.

"Am I?" He glanced at the cigarette in his hand. "Why, yes, I believe you're right."

"You know I abhor smoking, Tobias! The smell never leaves the furniture. Put it out this very moment." Aunt Elinor sailed over to an armchair and settled on its edge, coughing once more as soon as she had landed.

"Terribly sorry, Mums," Toby said. "But since the damage has probably already been done, may I finish my ciggie?"

"You may not, and don't use slang. And sit up *straight*!"

Toby sighed, handed the cigarette off to me, and hauled himself into a sitting position. I smiled sympathetically as I tossed the cigarette into the fire, resisting the urge to sneak a final drag.

"I'll be hungry now," Toby fretted. "Hope Jeffries brings the tea soon."

Right on cue, the door opened and the butler entered, magisterially wheeling a cumbersome tea cart laden with the teapot and a single plate of bread and butter sandwiches. He eased awkwardly around my piano, which had been jammed into the overstuffed room and was already proving a trial for anyone expecting a clear path through the door.

Toby groaned, "Bread and butter! Can't we have cake or something, Mother?"

"I don't see why we should eat extravagantly when it's only the three of us. Plain food is good for the soul, don't you agree, Astra?"

"I'm sure it is, Aunt Elinor. Nothing like a penitent's diet to consider one's sins."

She pulled out a handkerchief and coughed into it as I began pouring the tea.

"You really should see someone about that cough," I commented, handing her a cup.

She waved a hand at me even as she coughed again. "Never mind that. Come and sit by me, dear, we need to have a talk."

Toby raised his eyebrows and looked pointedly at the clock as I took a seat next to his mother. "She's quick off the mark: that was under five minutes," he murmured.

Aunt El set her teacup aside, took both my hands, and smiled in a way she probably meant to seem kind, but which actually felt slightly menacing. Smiles did not come naturally to her.

"Now, Astra, it's been some months since your tragedy, and of course it's entirely proper that you took plenty of time to mourn your parents. But now you must start considering practical matters. I don't need to remind you how dire your situation is . . . "

No, she certainly did not.

"And while I'm content for you to be here, you can't expect to stay indefinitely."

"Don't you feel welcome, my dear?" Toby asked with a half smile.

Aunt El continued: "The best thing for a girl in your position is to secure herself a husband."

"Ah! You see, Astra, what did I tell you?" Toby crowed.

"What are you going on about?" Aunt El asked sharply.

"Nothing at all." He winked at me and smirked into his teacup.

"Well, there it is, dear," she said, turning back to me. "Now, since you show no urgency in the matter, despite having been introduced to any number of excellent young men, it seems to have fallen to me to find someone suitable." She sighed, as though put out by this inconvenience.

I tried not to look too horrified, but dear lord, what sort of man would Aunt Elinor consider an appropriate life partner? Probably someone like—God help me—*her*.

She scowled. "Don't look at me like that, young lady! You children nowadays think you have all the time in the world to do what you want, but you simply don't. You must start thinking seriously about this; you're leaving things rather late."

"You can't have it both ways, Mums," Toby piped up. "Either Astra's a child or she's socially ancient. You have to choose one."

"It's foolish of you to sit by and expect suitable men to keep appearing," Aunt El told me, ignoring her son. "All of your friends are starting to snap them up. Why not Lord Beckworth? His mother's gone off to France, and now I hear the poor man's quite lonely."

"He can get a Labrador, then," I suggested tersely. "What does he need me for?"

"I wouldn't subject an animal as intelligent as a Labrador to life with Ducky," said Toby. "I think they have laws now against animal cruelty."

"There's nothing wrong with Lord Beckworth, Tobias!" his mother snapped.

"Nothing at all, Mums. But mark my words: when we were at school he definitely wasn't one of the finest minds of his generation, and, like this sofa, he hasn't improved with age. No, Mums, keep your desperate bachelors: nobody's good enough for our Astra." Toby made a gallant half bow, twirling a sandwich in the air. I giggled.

"For heaven's sake, Tobias, be serious!" Aunt Elinor snapped. "There must be some friend of yours Astra hasn't been introduced to yet."

"If she hasn't been introduced to him, there's probably a *very* good reason."

"Oh, come now, they can't all be idiots," she huffed.

"Of course they are, Mother. But they're the finest idiots in Britain. One must have standards."

"You're being deliberately difficult," she snarled.

Toby shrugged. "Maybe Astra doesn't want to be married."

"Of *course* she wants to be married. What else is there for her to do?"

"I've been thinking about that," I said. "I'm trying to work some things out, just . . ." I went and picked up the ledger. "You don't know what Rosedale is? Or Dr. H?"

Somehow, she managed to stiffen further. "Never mind about any of that," she said in a tone so chilly I actually shivered. "We have important matters to settle. My friend Mrs. Jeffries has a box at that new Noel Coward play next weekend. I'll ask her to invite you and Lord Beckworth along. And you've accepted Lady Cecilia's invitation to Gryden Hall?"

"I have," I confirmed warily.

"Good. I'm sure there'll be some worthwhile young men there. Lord Hampton wouldn't miss out on that shooting. He was *so* solicitous after your parents' funeral. I'm sure you could make some inroads if you just tried."

Toby shook his head. "Mustard's spoken for, mother," he informed her. "Jossie Bfyddlye told me all about it last week."

"What?" she cried, aghast. "Lord Hampton *engaged*? That can't be correct, I would have heard."

"It only just happened, Jossie said. But he had it right from the horse's mouth after Mustard had one drink too many. He never could keep secrets, old Mustard. Not when he's spifflicated, anyway."

"Who's the lucky girl?" I asked, pleased for Hampton.

"Belinda Avery."

"What? Lord and Lady Crayle's girl?" Aunt El exploded. "That plain little bit of nothing! What an absolute *waste* of a coronet!" She bit a sandwich in half with such rage I was sure she imagined it was Belinda's head.

"I say good for him," I declared. "She's a nice girl, and that's just what he needs." I didn't want Hampton anyway, despite his future dukedom. He was sweet, but he wasn't for me.

Aunt El sighed and raised her eyes skyward, clenching the cross once again. Having evidently prayed for patience, she released the cross and leveled her eyes at me. "Now, Astra, about Lord Beckworth . . . "

"I promise I'll give him some serious thought if you agree to just one thing."

Her eyes narrowed to slits. "What's that?"

"Allow me to hire a lady's maid."

I braced for her reaction. Unsurprisingly, she looked at me as though I'd just proposed something utterly outrageous.

"A lady's maid! You must be joking!"

"Not a bit. Even the most hard-up people keep personal servants. No man wants to marry a pauper," I added slyly. "And anyway, the expense won't be too great. I could probably get one quite cheaply with things the way they are right now."

"Don't talk about money, Astra—it's common," said Aunt El.

"Astra must have a maid, there's no question about it," Toby piped up.

"Of course you'd say that," Aunt El huffed. "You've always taken her side."

"Well, she's always right. It seems a good policy to back the person who's always correct. Let her have the maid, Mother. She's right about it being a dead giveaway if she doesn't have one—see how frumpy she's looking lately! No man wants a frump either."

"I'll contribute to the cost of her upkeep, of course," I added. "Shall we say"—I grappled for what seemed a reasonable amount—"two pounds two shillings a month?"

She turned to me in horror. "*Two pounds two shillings?* What do you intend to feed this person, caviar and Montrachet? One and one should be more than sufficient."

"One and one it is, then."

At least now I knew the cost of a bread-and-butter diet. Not much, but certainly a start.

Chapter Two

❧

"You have a whisky-and-soda look about you," Toby observed, wandering into the drawing room the following week and finding me drooping amid piles of neatly penned and lightly perfumed reference letters. He cocked his head and scrutinized me. "But I can't quite tell if you need one or you've already had five."

"I need one—desperately!" I croaked, swallowing an aspirin (half a crown for a packet of fifty; I'd decided they were worth the investment).

"Right you are." Toby popped off to his father's now unused study, where he kept some necessities locked in an out-of-the-way cabinet.

It was feeble of me to feel so done in after a day of interviewing maids—I mean, it's not exactly going down the mines, is it? But having never hired before, I had no idea it'd be such a performance on my part. Most of them had interviewed *me*, barely settling down on the edge of the armchair before delivering rapid-fire questions about afternoons off and my expectations as far as hairdressing and seamstressing went. My stammered responses seemed to disappoint them, or maybe *I* disappointed them, with my obvious naivete. Still, with pursed lips they'd passed me their references and were gone, one after the other, blending into a faceless stream of lacquered marcel waves and sensible shoes.

Toby returned with the promised restorative and handed it over. "Shall we drink to your new maid, or does the search continue?"

"The search, thankfully, is concluded. Here's to Miss Angela Reilly."

We simultaneously raised our glasses, then sipped.

"What makes her so special?" Toby asked as I handed over her references.

"I'm not sure, really." Certainly Reilly wasn't the sort of person to stand out: She had colorless, homely looks that were neither bad enough nor good enough to be memorable. Her dull, straw-colored hair hung lifelessly in a wispy chin-length bob, blending almost perfectly with her sallow skin. She had watery, washed-out blue eyes and a skinny frame, like a girl who'd stopped developing almost as soon as she'd begun. Unlike the others, she'd asked no questions, just sat quietly, hands folded in her lap, feet crossed at the ankles, as flat and contained as a plank. She hadn't seemed put off by my fumbling inquiries, simply answered them quietly and succinctly in the drawn-out vowels of the East Midlands. I found that accent comforting: it reminded me of home. Her withdrawn demeanor was also appealing. I didn't want a gossipy maid.

"She's jumped around," Toby observed, glancing over her list of past employers.

Well, yes, there was that. She'd explained that one lady she'd worked for had died, and some of the others "just weren't quite the right fit." It nagged, but any concern was outweighed by her extremely affordable price and the experience she brought to the position. I told myself she'd just been unlucky.

"It's nothing to worry about," I reassured Toby. "She hasn't done anything terrible, or she wouldn't have any references to show me." I moved over to the piano and started up a nocturne. Toby shrugged and took up his usual place on the sofa.

"So," he said a few minutes later, a wicked glint in his eye, "how was your night at the theater?"

"The *play* was delightful. It's a good thing your mother didn't come, though. It probably would have finished her off. It's about divorced people, and the love scene in the second act was decidedly racy."

"Is it? I'll have to catch a matinee. Did it put Ducky in the mood to whisper sweet nothings in your ear?"

"Hardly. He slept through that bit." I stopped playing long enough to act it out for Toby, slowly nodding, nodding, then jerking awake and apologizing a little too loudly.

"Poor lad." Toby laughed. "I almost wish I'd been there to see it."

"Yes, poor man. The theater's not the place for him." I ran my hands over the keys for a moment. "I shouldn't make fun," I said quietly. "He's nice, and I'm sure he'll make someone a wonderful husband someday. Just not me."

"Good for you. Most girls seem to have such low standards nowadays. I've seen men who can barely string three words together get snapped up and marched to the altar before they can say, 'How d'ye do?'"

"Well, what do you expect when we girls are supposed to find husbands within two years of our debut?" I asked him. "Did you make the best choices at twenty?"

"No, certainly not," he chuckled. "I don't think I make the best choices *now*, which is why I've avoided matrimony thus far. It helps that I have no great name and no money. Girls want a title or an income. Preferably both."

"The men aren't much different," I pointed out.

"True, true. So, are you back to working out how you'll make your fortune?"

"Oh, I've sorted that out already. I'll just go and play piano at the Gaiety," I joked.

He smiled a little. "Well, you do have your writing."

"Nobody's going to pay me for those silly little poems and stories."

"Try something more ambitious, then," he suggested. "Surely there's room in the literary milieu for some new blood."

"I'm sure there is; I just don't know that my blood is up to the task. Or my brain. I haven't written anything in months. Too distracted."

"It might do you some good to get back to something you enjoy. Take your mind off Rosedale and the mysterious Dr. H."

I sighed. "Hard not to think of that. I made some inquiries about Dr. H, but there are dozens of them registered and I don't know where to begin. And who knows who or what Rosedale is?"

"Shame your mother didn't keep a diary."

"No," I said slowly, my brain finally starting (after all those months) to grasp something useful. "She didn't, but Father did."

Toby gave me a "there you are, then" sort of look. I'll admit, the thought of having a project, something I might actually be able to accomplish, ignited an excited tingle deep in my belly. Of course, if I'd known then what I would end up uncovering, I might not have been so enthusiastic. Would I have chosen not to know, if I had had some sense, some second sight of what was to come? Would I have simply pushed the ledger aside and avoided all that pain and confusion and the strengthening that comes with it?

No, I don't think I would have.

"I'll see about finding the diary after Gryden," I decided.

"If you survive!" he said, laughing. "Take my advice: Watch your step, and if Millicent gets her claws out, shoot straight."

*   *   *

The local train puffed into Gryden Crossing exactly ten minutes late and just barely managed not to overrun the platform. As usual, I took that as the driver's mild protest at having to stop there at all. Most trains pass the place by, but the Marquess had the influence to make the local trains stop whenever there was a house party. I was the only guest who alighted that afternoon, and I felt the harsh stares of my fellow passengers, and their silent curses at the delay, however brief.

The station master (a handyman on the estate pressed into service for the day) had woken from his between-trains doze long enough to join Adams, the chauffeur, on the platform. They looked so smart in their uniforms, standing at attention, that I felt almost like royalty being greeted by an honor guard.

"Welcome to Gryden Crossing," the stationmaster said, stepping forward with a little bow, a greeting he used for every guest, be they duke or law clerk.

"Thank you, Mr. Sheldon. How are your wife and children?"

He beamed at me for remembering. "All very well, very well indeed, miss." He scurried away to help Reilly with the luggage. With a deafening blast of the whistle and a shower of soot, the train sluggishly chugged away.

It was a clammy sort of day—overcast, with a clinging mist that clouded the ground. As I settled into the back of the Bentley, sliding into place on leather seats soft as velvet, the chauffeur spread a thick woolen blanket over my lap.

"Can't have you catching a chill," he said, tucking me in with all the care of a nursemaid.

"Thank you, Adams," I said.

He tipped his hat and climbed into the front seat beside Reilly as Mr. Sheldon secured the luggage and smacked the rump of the car twice to indicate we were ready.

We sailed along the narrow roads, hemmed in on both sides by intricately woven hedgerows, hoping we didn't meet a farm cart coming the other way. I snuggled down beneath my tartan rug as we reached the intricately scrolled wrought-iron gates of Gryden Hall. Then, down an avenue of ancient oaks that led straight to the Hall, a Palladian mansion made of biscuit-colored stone that looked warm, even on days like this.

The Marquess of Caddonfoot, stately and silver-haired, stood on the columned front porch, flanked by his daughters, greeting his guests. To his left was Cecilia: golden as a daffodil and plump as a cozy armchair. The very picture of her father in his youth, if portraits are to be believed. In the hostess's spot was Millicent, who presumably took after her mother. She certainly didn't resemble anyone else in her family, in looks or temperament. Toweringly tall, pole-thin, and black-haired, she struck me as a younger, more menacing version of Aunt El. As I climbed out of the car, she pursed her lips, stood up a little straighter, and looked ready to do battle. It was going to be a long weekend.

Lord Caddonfoot stepped forward with a warm smile and sandwiched one of my hands between his. "Astra, you're very welcome. You look quite well, my dear."

"You're too kind, sir. I'm doing very well, thank you."

"I'm so glad to hear it. You've been most missed here." He glanced over his shoulder at Cecilia, who beamed back, and Millicent, who offered up a nearly invisible upward flick of her thin lips.

"And I have missed all of you," I replied, grinning at Cee.

Caddonfoot smiled at me again, then said, "Why don't you show Astra to her room, Ladybird? I'm sure she's tired and wants to refresh herself before tea."

Cee bobbed forward, grabbed my hand, and rushed us inside, where we were greeted with a wag and a bark by her West Highland terrier, Ivanhoe.

"Oh, darling, I'm so happy to see you," Cee squealed, embracing me while Ivanhoe wove between our legs, unable to contain himself. "It's been dull as dried bones around here, but now I have you *and* Joyce, and we'll have a lovely time! Oh, but darling: How are you? *Really?* I'm so sorry I haven't been to see you in so long, but Millicent and I have been doing the country rounds, and I haven't been able to get up to London for *ages*."

"It's all right, Cee. I'm fine. Really."

Cee held both my hands and looked me full in the face for a long moment, trying to work out if I was lying to her, though if I were going to pour out my grief to any friend, it would be to Cecilia. She'd been the first to come to Hensley after my parents died and had spent those early days sitting with me for hours, gently coaxing me to eat "just a little, darling." The day of the funeral, it was she who led me to the dressing table, sat me down, and whispered, "Let's get you ready, then, shall we?"

I met her searching look with as bright a smile as I could manage. It seemed to be enough, and she hooked her arm around my waist as we drifted toward the stairs.

"I suppose it's good you're staying with your aunt and Toby just now. It's a good thing to have company, I think. And a change of scenery. If you hadn't gone there I probably would have dragged you here, no matter what Millicent said about it. But she's been such a bear about everything lately, and turning herself inside out over this weekend. When she heard I invited Ducky Beckworth, she nearly pitched a teapot at me."

"Lord Beckworth? I didn't know you were friends with him."

Cecilia stopped and looked puzzled. Ivanhoe, dashing ahead, paused on the landing and barked for us to hurry up. "Well, yes, I've met him a few times, and he stayed here once before, but I asked him here for you," she said. "Your aunt told me it would cheer you up, since you've been seeing a lot of him in London lately." She broke into a smile and her eyes shone. "I can see why that would make you happy: he is awfully handsome, isn't he?"

"My aunt's been exaggerating, Cee. He and I are only friends."

"Oh. Well, I'm sure he'll enjoy the shooting, at least. The gamekeeper says the pigeons are first rate this year. Oh, darling, I've got lots and lots to tell you. You're up in the blue bedroom, as usual."

Ivanhoe led the way, slipping into the room moments before we reached it. The very aptly named blue room is cozy and would be lovely if the late marchioness had been less fond of wide-eyed china shepherd-esses. They cluttered every available surface. The place oozed with their saccharine sap.

"Just as I remember it," I said.

Cecilia seated herself on the bed. "We're going to give you a wonderful weekend, dearest, I promise. I've fixed it all up so you can enjoy yourself."

I leaned over and kissed her on the forehead. "You're lovely, Cee."

"Oh, Astra, I want you to be happy."

I squeezed her hand, thinking of how she'd allowed me to cling to her during that awful time. "I know. And I'm sure I will be. It's hard not to be happy around you."

Cecilia grinned and blushed. "Everyone has to contribute something to the world, I suppose. We've got a nice batch here for the weekend. Lord Hampton and Belinda Avery arrived around lunchtime—did you hear they're engaged? I'm so pleased for them. It was a bit of a surprise, that, because he and Millicent were, well, spending a fair bit of time together, and she seemed to think it was all sewn up, but then Mustard spotted darling Belinda across the grandstand at the Derby, and there you are! Such a fairytale, don't you think?" She paused to sigh, then continued, "Joyce and David and Mr. Porter should be here any minute. And there's one more guest, but I'm keeping him a secret."

"Wicked creature," I teased her.

Cecilia smiled mischievously and bounced back onto her feet. "You'll thank me when you meet him. I'd better go down and greet people, or Millicent'll have my head. There'll be tea in the south drawing room at the usual time. Come on, Ivey."

She whisked around the door, followed by the yapping dog, and was almost immediately replaced by Reilly, who began unpacking while I scrubbed off the soot and dust of travel. As I returned from the bathroom, a silver-and-blue Rolls Royce came crunching down the drive and drew to a smart halt at the front door. The driver opened the passenger door, and after a brief struggle, G. P. Ranigan Porter managed to compress his bulk enough to disembark. He was followed by his son-in-law, David Bradbury, and finally Joyce, his only child, thickly wrapped in satiny black sables that matched her hair.

Joyce, Cecilia, David's sister Laura, and I had known each other since our braids-and-pinafore days. Our parents had dispatched us all to the same boarding school to complete what passed for a girl's education. Joyce, newly arrived from America, still had her brash accent (no trace of it now—she'd acclimated better than her father had), which almost immediately made her a target of Millicent's mockery. Millicent was two years ahead of us, her reputation so fierce we all gave her *and* Cecilia a wide berth. But one day not long after our first term began, I was in the local tuck shop and noticed Cecilia staring longingly at the bag of toffees I'd just bought.

"Would you like one?" I'd offered, holding the bag out toward her. She couldn't have looked more grateful if she'd been the Little Match Girl and I'd handed her a roast dinner with all the trimmings.

"Oh, *thank you*," she'd breathed, digging her hand into the little white bag and drawing out a toffee.

As she went to put it in her mouth, however, Millicent had swooped down, snatched it out of her hand, and screeched, "You can't have that, Cecilia—it's *bad* for you!" And then, outrageously, she'd tried to grab my bag of sweets.

"What are you doing? Get your own!" I'd shouted as the other girls in the shop stopped to watch the show. Millicent had had a dangerous look about her, but I wasn't going to let her get away with sweet snatching. Just when it seemed a real fight was imminent, in came our deputy headmistress.

"What's going on here?" she'd asked, expressing the full force of schoolroom authority in one raised eyebrow and a crisp tone of voice.

"That one's taking sweets from the other girls," the shop's proprietor had answered. He'd winked at Cecilia and me as he pointed to Millicent, who was outraged.

"Millicent, return to school immediately," Miss had ordered her. Millicent had looked even *more* outraged, but she'd had no choice and flounced out.

And so Cecilia became my constant companion, and Millicent my enemy. She'd tried to get me into trouble after that by making it seem as if I was cheating, and I had to admit, she did an excellent job copying my handwriting. But she hadn't counted on Laura, who had an older sibling and was wise to such nasty tricks. She saw what Millicent was doing and informed on her, pointing out that I, the spelling champion of our year, would never misspell "importance," whereas Millicent did so every time she wrote it. Forgery included. Millicent was nearly expelled. And Laura and Joyce joined Cee and I to create a tight-knit little foursome that not even Laura's marriage and subsequent uprooting to America had broken. I only hoped that my change in situation didn't end up being the thing that scattered us.

*   *   *

I emerged at half past four and saw Joyce and David stepping out of a room three doors down. Joyce had divested herself of the sables, revealing a royal blue suit I'd recently seen (and coveted) in *Vogue*. Her hair, I noticed, was different than it had been a year ago, and was also right out of *Vogue*. David, on the other hand, still looked the same: medium height and build, nice face, ready smile. I couldn't help noticing his tie matched his wife's suit.

"Here you are, Astra!" Joyce cried. "I was half afraid you wouldn't come, and I'd have nobody besides David to talk to."

"Oh, thank you very much," he said, amused.

"You're a cruel woman," I teased, embracing her.

"We're married now; I can abuse him at will," Joyce responded, linking arms with David and smiling wickedly up at him as we moved off down the hall.

"Is that a rule that cuts both ways?" he asked, smiling just as wickedly back.

"Not at all, my dear. You'll just make me cry. Is that what you want?" Her eyes rounded and moistened, and her chin trembled slightly.

David laughed. "No, never," he said, and kissed her.

"Good boy," she purred. "Astra, did Cee tell you Jeremy was coming?"

"Jeremy who?"

"Oh dear, I've spoiled the surprise. Jeremy Harris. You remember him: horrid little boy who used to come over to Wotting Park to play with David and ruin our tea parties."

"We did no such thing!" David protested.

"You did, and worse!" Joyce insisted. "And now you'll be making up for it for the rest of your life. Ha!"

"I don't remember him," I replied. I had vague flashes of a blond boy playing at war with David and kidnapping one of Cee's dolls, but that was all.

"You'll remember him *now*, I promise," said Joyce. "He's back from a stint in the navy and is *quite* the spectacular specimen of a man. I've half a mind to divorce David and take Jem for myself, but I've decided to be generous and leave him for you."

"How thoughtful," I said drily.

"Well, divorce is expensive and a bother, and the Bradburys don't need another scandal, do they?" She squeezed David's arm without looking up at him, and so failed to notice that he was not amused by the turn the conversation had taken.

"If he's such an ideal man, I'm sure I'll have stiff competition," I noted as we wound down the staircase.

"Oh, don't be silly, you'd certainly outshine all these silly geese, and you'd make a marvelous countess. He's an earl, by the way—did I tell you that? *Very grand*," Joyce whispered with a slight roll of her eyes. "Not much money, but that's all right: when you look like he does and have a title to boot, that sort of thing tends to fix itself. I'll set it all up for you. I need a new project anyway."

"Please don't, Joyce," I begged.

"It's not just for *me*, darling—you could use the distraction, surely. After the year you've had . . ." She clucked her tongue. "I'm sorry again we couldn't get back earlier."

"It's all right. I wouldn't have wanted you to interrupt something as nice as your honeymoon for something as sad as a funeral."

They'd been in California that week. Part of the around-the-world honeymoon Joyce had planned down to the last detail. But she had kept up a steady stream of telegraphs and sent a bouquet so massive it had nearly dwarfed the caskets.

"Well, most of it was nice," Joyce allowed. "Spending those few days with Laura was a terrible mistake. She kept coming to wake us up at dawn to run rings around Central Park. Did I tell you she's going to be some sort of fitness instructor?"

"That doesn't surprise me."

"Anyway, after three days we had to go to the Waldorf. And even then she kept coming by and trying to ring our room. It's almost as if she doesn't know what a honeymoon's for. And if anyone should know that sort of thing, it's her."

I cleared my throat, noticing David looking uncomfortable, and asked, "Well, aside from that, I'm glad it was a good trip. Did you see everything you wanted to?"

"And then some." She exchanged looks with her husband. "I took loads of films with the camera Daddy gave us. I'll show them to you on your next visit."

"Can't wait," I said, feeling uneasy for some reason. "Speaking of your father, I saw he came along this weekend."

"Of *course* he did. You know Daddy can never resist a shooting weekend. It's just so perfectly British. He went and got new tweeds and everything, even though I've told him time and again that nobody gets new tweeds. Even David tried to convince him that old tweeds are a badge of honor, but of course Daddy doesn't listen to David." She huffed as David briefly scowled. "Poor Daddy," Joyce sighed. "He tries *so* hard but never manages to get it quite right. And then they all titter behind his back." Her face darkened.

"Not everyone," David protested.

"Not *you*, of course. You're not allowed," she said to him.

The poor man practically threw up his arms in defeat.

"Millicent will have something nasty to say about those tweeds," she said.

I reached over and squeezed her hand, hoping that would calm her "Who cares what Millicent thinks?"

"That's the spirit!" Joyce agreed, brightening. "I'm declaring here and now that we're not going to let that cow spoil our first weekend together in a year. We're going to laugh and gossip, and you, Astra, are going to flirt outrageously with Jeremy, because I'm not going to see him carried off by some wan, overbred daughter of the aristocracy."

We stepped into the double-cube drawing room, a space that always seemed to be glowing, thanks to the warm golden damask that covered the walls and most of the furnishings. Today, the fireplaces on both ends of the room were blazing away, fighting the damp cold seeping around the French windows that opened onto the formal gardens.

In the far corner, Lord Caddonfoot was presenting Mr. Porter to Lord Hampton and Belinda Avery. Belinda, a sweet chipmunk-cheeked creature, was smiling at Porter as she shook his beefy hand. Her fiancé, Hampton, was grinning adoringly at her. When I stepped into the room, he glanced up and his expression changed to a friendly smile, which I returned.

Porter also looked up and grinned when he saw me, eyes swiftly running me up and down. He stood out in the room, and not in a good way: while the other men wore the country uniform of plain ties and subdued plaids, Porter's black-and-white checked jacket was just a little too loud, his lemon-yellow waistcoat and tie too bright, his shoes too shiny. He was standing by the fire, and beads of sweat gathered on his forehead. Millicent, making bored small talk with Beckworth by the piano, shot disgusted looks Porter's way. Beckworth seemed as eager to escape the conversation as she did, and kept looking longingly at the refreshment table just out of reach.

An arm snaked around my waist, and I turned to see Cecilia beaming at me.

"How do you like the gathering, darling? Will they keep you amused?"

"Of course they will, Cee. It's sweet of you to be so concerned about me."

"Well, someone has to look after you," Cecilia said staunchly, guiding me to the tea table. "Come and have some tea—you must be famished." She began arranging a plate.

Millicent, meanwhile, abandoned Beckworth to speak to someone else, leaving him free to assault the scones. He bounded over with a nervous smile.

"Hello, Ducky," Cecilia greeted him brightly. "You must be famished too."

"Oh yes, yes quite," he agreed.

"Well, let's fix that. Cream? Jam? Oh dear, Millicent's glaring at me, I'd better see what she wants." She handed me my plate and flitted off.

Beckworth smiled anxiously as he loaded a scone with so much cream and jam he nearly doubled its size. I smiled back. He has the sort

of face that invites smiles: imploring, round puppy-dog eyes and a gener-
ally pleasant look, though he is, perhaps, a little weak-chinned.

"So nice to see you again, Miss Davies," he said.

"And you, Lord Beckworth. And quite a surprise."

"Yes, yes, a surprise for me too. Lady Cecilia was nice enough to
invite me. Awfully kind of her: I was starting to get a bit lonely rattling around the house. It's just me now that Mother's gone to France to
work on her paintings. She does . . . abstract something or other. Lots
of shapes. I don't really pretend to understand it. Probably too clever by
half for me." He laughed almost apologetically. "Anyway, just me. Very
quiet."

"You poor thing," I said, softening. "But I suppose there's always
your club."

"Yes, yes, there is that. And the chaps there are always very nice
about inviting me to join in their card games, even though I'm a really
terrible player." He laughed again, and the hand that was holding his
plate of food jerked. The scone went sailing, flew apart, and landed on
the carpet. Jam-side down, of course. Ivanhoe leapt on it.

"Oh, Lord Beckworth, you've lost your scone!" Cecilia cried. She
rushed over and knelt to move the dog aside as Beckworth bent to
retrieve the scone, apologizing.

"So sorry! Now look what I've done, I've spoiled your carpet—"

"It's nothing, no trouble at all—Ivey, let go! Let's get you another
one . . ."

I stood there awkwardly, looking down at the tops of their heads and
wondering if they'd even notice if I wandered off. I decided to chance it
and turned to leave, only to nearly run straight into Joyce's father.

Like his daughter, Porter had small, gunmetal-blue eyes and a long,
straight nose; what was left of his hair was black (dyed, I guessed, noting
the unnatural uniformity of the color). That hair seemed to be easing its
way down his head, leaving a shining dome on top and an increasingly
luxuriant beard below. He smelled of Macassar oil and a touch too much
eau de cologne.

"Good afternoon, Miss Davies," he greeted me, his eyes once again
taking me in from crown to heel. "You're looking so . . . tall."

"Thank you, Mr. Porter," I answered uncertainly. "You seem well."

"Oh yes, I've been traveling," he explained, puffing out his chest slightly. "It always . . . *invigorates* me."

"Oh?" The way he was looking at me, I suddenly had an inkling what it was like to be Red Riding Hood in those last few moments before she and her granny were devoured.

Vandemark Rubber, I reminded myself. *Hensley.*

I simpered and giggled and said, "Well, we should all take a page out of your book, sir. Though you have been very much missed while you were away."

"Not nearly as missed as I'm sure you were," he responded.

"You're too kind, Mr. Porter."

"Ahh, hello there, Mr. Porter," said Beckworth, climbing to his feet with the now lopsided scone back on his plate. "How's business?"

Porter's smile and eyes hardened. "Hardly a subject for mixed company, lad."

"Oh." Beckworth deflated. "Yes, yes, of course. So sorry to have interrupted."

"Ducky, let's get you another scone, shall we?" Cecilia said, gently tugging Beckworth toward the table.

I sighed inwardly. So much for talking up Vandemark with Porter this weekend.

"You must be happy to have Joyce back again," I commented in an effort to steer the conversation in a more cheerful direction. "She and David have been gone so long."

"Indeed." His eyes flickered to his daughter and her husband. They were standing beneath a portrait of the first marchioness, who didn't seem to approve of whatever they were talking about. "It's nice to have Joyce back. I think she's finding being a wife something of an adjustment, though. She was always quite headstrong."

"I'm sure she'll adapt soon enough," I said. "She just needs a new project to keep her mind occupied."

"I thought of putting her in charge of my New Year's Eve party," he confided.

"I'm sure she'd love that."

"I do hope we'll see you there."

"I wouldn't miss it."

Something about the leering look he gave me made me shudder, and I covered it by taking a step closer to the fire and sipping my tea.

"This damp cold," I murmured.

"Do you need something to warm you?" he asked.

Cecilia paused on her way to Belinda. "Do you need a shawl, Astra? I'll get you one." She bounded out of the room before I could answer.

"I hope we'll be seeing much more of you," Porter said. "Joyce hopes, I mean. She's missed you terribly."

"She's such a dear to be concerned about me."

"We were all concerned. Terrible thing. But you seem to have gathered yourself quite well. It's one of the things I love most about the English: they do soldier on."

"Yes, we do that, don't we?" I responded tightly as the backs of my eyes prickled.

"And you couldn't stay locked up forever, pretty little lady like you." He grinned again and chucked me under the chin. The gesture was so shockingly intimate I instinctively took a step away from him. His smile disappeared. He blinked in confusion.

"Here you are," Cee sang, reappearing and draping me in a thick tartan shawl. "Nice and toasty warm."

"You're a darling, Cee." I drew it around me, welcoming the extra layers in between myself and Porter. It made me feel safer, and I regained my composure.

"Are you keeping her cheered, Mr. Porter?" Cecilia asked him, waggling her finger in the man's direction. "No long faces here."

"He's doing a marvelous job, Cecilia. I doubt even you could do better."

Porter seemed to relax.

"Oh, Astra, do come look at Belinda's ring. I've never seen a lovelier one. You don't mind if I steal her, sir, do you?"

"Not at all." Porter answered. "I hope we have a chance to speak again, Miss Davies."

"I'm sure we will, sir," I answered with a smile. "We have the whole weekend."

Chapter Three

꧅

First night dinner—now the real test begins. The arrival tea is nothing: we're greeting fellow guests and getting the lay of the land. Meanwhile, below stairs, the maids and valets are hard at work on our behalf. Whispering secrets and trading information. The clever ones give little but gain much. We all want those to be *our* servants.

As soon as we scurry back to our rooms, we're provided with the tittle-tattle we need to make snap judgments over the cocktails, begin judging harshly by the fish course, and retire into hissing gossip circles over the brandy and coffee.

"Will it be a quiet weekend, do you think?" I asked Reilly (oh, these little codes we spoke in). "Or should we expect some trouble and strife?"

She took her time answering, concentrating instead on tugging my blue charmeuse dress into place.

"This seems to be a peaceful and well-run household, miss. I'm sure it will be an enjoyable weekend for everyone."

I studied her face as she fussed with my neckline, wondering if she was concealing things from me. Holding on to some shiny little nugget of information for such a time as it might be useful. If so, she gave no sign of it. Perhaps we were just a dully respectable lot. Or maybe people were better at hiding things nowadays than they were in our parents' time, when delicious scandals abounded. Or perhaps Reilly wasn't one of those clever servants. Whatever it was, I was being sent downstairs unarmed and vulnerable. A shell-less turtle in a fox's den.

But you can't show weakness. I pasted on a brilliant smile, put my shoulders back, and processed into the drawing room, hoping I exuded the confidence of a princess.

As soon as I appeared, Cecilia hopped to, snatched a drink from a footman's tray, and descended on me.

"Lovely dress, darling. Is it from Vionnet's new collection?" she asked, handing the drink over.

"Why, yes it is," I lied. It was an old dress of mine, cleverly made over by Reilly.

"I thought so." Cecilia turned me this way and that to have a look. "You should really try Schiaparelli—you've got the perfect figure for her gowns. Millicent and I were talking about going to Paris soon to see the new designs; you should come. It feels like such a long time since we were there last."

"I'll think about it, Cee." How long did I have before people wondered why I always excused myself from these pricey jaunts?

"I heard Joyce completely ruined my surprise and told you about Lord Dunreaven coming." Cecilia pouted. "He arrived very late, the naughty thing. I thought Millicent was going to have a stroke. I half suspect he's the reason she planned this party in the first place. We've been seeing a lot of him during the country rounds. I mentioned you when we were at the Wetherbys last month, and he seemed *very* interested."

"Did he indeed? I don't see why."

"Men always like a pretty woman with money," Joyce explained, coming up behind us. "I should know."

"Joyce, what a terrible thing to say! David didn't marry you because of that," Cecilia protested.

Joyce shrugged and sipped her drink. "I'm sure it didn't hurt. Nor would it with Jeremy."

"Oh, Joyce," Cee said, rolling her eyes, "he's not so *very* poor. Come on, let's go talk to Belinda. I don't want her feeling neglected."

Belinda had her fiancé at her beck and call and didn't seem neglected in the least, but she was only too eager to recount the story of how she became engaged. ("He gave me a wee kitten, and the ring was tied around its neck with a pink satin ribbon!"

"Oh," Cee gushed, "*so* romantic!"

"Yes, yes, very," Beckworth agreed, nodding energetically and sloshing part of his drink.

The meaningless murmur of our chat was abruptly strangled when Millicent, positioned right next to the door, unexpectedly shrieked, *"Dunny!"*

Poor Beckworth jumped, losing the rest of his martini. The rest of us swiveled toward the doorway.

There stood perhaps the most beautiful man I'd ever seen.

The Earl of Dunreaven was perfectly proportioned: tall, but not gangly, with strong shoulders and a tapering waist. He had wavy, champagne-colored hair, a firm jaw, and full lips that were now forming a polite smile, though I sensed Millicent's greeting had startled him as much as it had Beckworth. His skin was just a touch darker than that of the other men. I imagined it was the result of years spent walking the decks of ships patrolling the warmer corners of the Empire.

Still a naval man in bearing, if not by profession, he held himself perfectly straight, but not stiffly. If he found it awkward to be made the center of attention, he didn't show it. He returned our stares with a pleasant—if not particularly warm—smile as his eyes flickered over everyone in the room, swiftly taking us all in. Was it my imagination, or did his gaze seem to linger slightly longer on me?

"I hope you'll all forgive me," he apologized. "I didn't mean to make an entrance."

Millicent laughed throatily as she reached over and twined her arm through his. "Dunny," she purred with a Cheshire cat–like smile, "you are a naughty thing, arriving so late. You're lucky we didn't start without you; we were just about to go through."

He turned his attention and smile fully on her, making her simper in a way I hadn't thought possible.

"You should have gone. I'm disgracefully tardy," he said as Lord Caddonfoot joined them.

"How are you, my boy?" Caddonfoot greeted him heartily with a handshake.

"Very well, sir. I must apologize for my late arrival. Car trouble."

"Poor thing." Millicent stroked Dunreaven's arm. "You'll want a nice hot meal. Shall we go through?"

He glanced at me once more as she steered him toward the dining room. I hoped no one else noticed my cheeks warming, but

Millicent's eyes narrowed. "Keep away!" they seemed to warn. "He's *mine*!"

Unfortunately (for her) the seating at dinner put me almost directly across from Dunreaven, who was sitting to his hostess's right. He smiled at me as I sat, and Millicent looked murderous.

Beckworth popped into the chair next to me and immediately began chattering. "There should be good shooting, I hope. There was last time, wasn't there, David? Even *I* almost managed to get something. Of course, David's much better than I."

"Well, Jem'll give me a run for my money this weekend, won't you, Jem?" David said to Dunreaven.

"We'll have to wait and see," Dunreaven answered modestly.

"Oh, I'm sure you'll kill the most birds tomorrow. You're by far the best shot," Millicent purred.

"I'm much better at fishing, really," said Beckworth. "Did I ever tell you about that salmon I caught last year up in Scotland?"

Dunreaven's eyes flickered up to Beckworth for a moment, then back down to his plate. He smiled to himself.

"Do you fish, Miss Davies?" Beckworth asked.

"No," I replied, "I'm afraid not."

"Oh." He looked disappointed and seemed at a loss as to what to talk about.

"Do you shoot?" Dunreaven asked me.

"I can if I have to, but it's not my sport of choice."

"And what is your sport of choice?" he inquired, leaning in just a little, as if he were actually interested in my answer and not just making polite conversation.

"Yes, what do you like to hunt, if you can't stomach blood sports?" Millicent wondered, smirking.

"I never said I couldn't stomach them, just that they weren't my preferred form of recreation," I responded. "Believe me, I can strike a mortal wound as well as anyone else here, when it's called for."

Dunreaven chuckled.

"From what I heard, Hensley isn't much good for shooting or fishing," Millicent said silkily. "Too small, I think. More of a little family home than an estate. The way Cecilia describes it, it sounds like a nice little cottage."

"It's certainly more than that," Cecilia protested.

Joyce flicked a glare Millicent's way.

I forced a smile. "Hensley has many charms," I said, trying to keep my tone pleasant. It wouldn't do to burst into tears before the game course.

"It's such a beautiful place," Cecilia seconded. "The gardens are lovely."

"My mother's pride and joy," I managed to force out around the egg-sized lump taking over my throat. I bowed my head, closed my eyes, and tried to imagine that flower slowly unfurling, as Mother had taught me. When I looked up again a moment later, I caught Dunreaven watching. His head was cocked the tiniest bit, eyes narrowed almost imperceptibly, as if he were trying to work me out. Goose pimples broke out up and down my arms.

Millicent looked over at him. Her eyes flashed dangerously.

"It must be nice to have something that reminds you of your mother," said Beckworth kindly. "I do so love a good garden. I hope to see it someday."

"Perhaps Astra will invite us all sometime soon, to repay our hospitality here," Millicent suggested in a honeyed voice.

"I would love to, but unfortunately I have tenants living there now," I said, a little sharply. "All those memories: I thought it best to get away for a little while."

"What a pity," Millicent drawled.

I picked up a spoon and lightly tapped "cow" on the table in Morse code. It was a skill Laura had picked up from David and passed along to the rest of us while we were at school. Joyce snorted. Dunreaven's eyes flickered back up to mine, and a little half smile crept over his face.

Lord Caddonfoot steered the conversation on to other things. I looked down at the chives wilting in my consommé, swallowed hard, and tried not to think of home.

* * *

"Why don't we have a game of bridge?" Joyce suggested when the gentlemen joined the ladies in the drawing room after dinner. "Who'll play?"

There were too many volunteers, so we drew cards to see who would play first, and I came up the loser.

"Bad luck, Astra," Millicent smirked, taking her seat opposite Dunreaven.

"No matter," I said airily.

"Lucky for us, though," said Cecilia. "Won't you play for us, Astra?"

"If you insist." I seated myself at the piano and launched into a song.

"What *is* that?" Millicent asked a few moments in, her voice thick with disgust.

"Gershwin," Dunreaven answered for me. "Isn't that right?"

I nodded.

"*Gershwin?*" Millicent rolled her eyes. "I might have known music like *that* would come from a name like *that*." She sniffed, shuffling her cards around. "All the music nowadays seems to come from people who are only half a step away from barbarity. Is that noise all we have to offer the world now? What will our descendants think when they look back on what we call culture? Where is our Mozart? Our Chopin?"

"Our Mahler?" I added slyly.

Millicent looked suspicions but nevertheless said, "Precisely."

"Gustav Mahler was a Jew," Joyce tightly informed her.

"That's a rich bet," David commented, watching his wife's play.

"Don't fuss—I can afford it," she replied.

"Can't you play something civilized, Astra?" Millicent snapped. "This isn't a jazz club, you know."

If it were, I'd be getting paid for providing the entertainment, I thought acidly, but I obediently segued into my favorite Mahler nocturne.

"That's a bit better," Millicent condescended.

Dunreaven, now playing as the dummy, set his cards down. He strolled over to the piano and leaned gracefully against it.

"Astra Davies," he murmured.

"Lord Dunreaven," I returned without pausing in my playing.

"It's been a long time. I hardly recognized you without your braids."

"Well, little girls have a tendency to grow up. And we get rid of the braids because little boys tug on them."

He laughed. "Surely I never did that!"

"You surely did. *And* you kidnapped Cecilia's doll once and made her cry. Cee, not the doll. You and David held her for ransom in some pirate game. The doll, not Cee."

"What an awful little boy," he murmured. "I feel like I should do penance."

"You should. Fifteen tea parties and maybe we'll call it even."

He chuckled. "I'd rather something more grown up. Perhaps some dances?"

"I'm sure Cecilia would be delighted. But you'd have to ask her." I changed to a light waltz with a cheeky smile.

His eyes (green, I noticed, with amber flecks) flashed momentarily, and he grinned. "So, what else has changed, aside from your hair?"

"So many things."

"Fortunately, we have all weekend for you to tell me."

"Don't you have some birds to shoot?" I asked. "And there are other guests here I may want to spend time talking to."

His eyes moved toward Beckworth, deep in a conversation about fishing with Cee and Lord Caddonfoot. "You're right, that was presumptuous of me," Dunreaven agreed. "I'll have to work for your attention, then."

"Anything worth having takes a little effort."

His smile widened, and I very nearly missed a note. "And you think your full attention is worth the effort?"

"Don't you?"

"Fishing for a compliment?"

"Like I said at dinner, I don't fish."

"You know," he said warmly, "when Joyce and Cecilia talked you up, I thought they must be exaggerating, but that doesn't seem to be the case."

"I'm sure that's not true," I said, laughing. "What did they say?"

"Quite a lot about your dazzling wit and charm."

"Doesn't sound like Joyce. Must have been Cee."

He shrugged. "It's possible I'm embellishing from my own observations."

"You're too kind, Lord Dunreaven. I'll end up being a disappointment."

"A disappointment? You could never be a disappointment!" Cecilia cried, plopping down on the bench next to me. "She's lovely and clever, isn't she, Jeremy?"

"Don't force him, Cee—it's not fair," I protested.

"I can assure you, I don't need to be forced," Dunreaven replied.

"Jeremy, we need you back!" Millicent shrilled.

"I think I'll step out, if you don't mind," he replied. "Mr. Porter, would you care to take my place?"

"Then Astra can take mine," Millicent said, slapping her cards down on the table. "It was a terrible hand, that. Dunny, do be a gentleman and make me forget all about it."

"Astra, did you still want to play?" Joyce called.

"Yes, thank you," I said, though I was a little disappointed to have to end my time with Dunreaven already. "Excuse me, Cee, Lord Dunreaven."

Millicent smirked as I took her seat at the table. She slipped her arm proprietarily through Dunreaven's and steered him firmly away.

* * *

Reilly was just tucking the hot water bottle between the sheets when I returned to my room. I'd left some of the others downstairs, finishing coffees and one last round of cards. Millicent had dragged Dunreaven to the portrait gallery to see a Canova bust of some long-dead relative. They hadn't yet returned by the time I collected my winnings (enough to cover the staff tips for the weekend, thankfully) and headed upstairs.

"Pleasant evening, miss?" Reilly asked as she helped me out of my dress, slip, and corselet, and into a nightgown.

"Pleasant enough." I sat down at the dressing table and smeared on cold cream while Reilly hung up my dress and began setting my hair.

"I hear Lord Dunreaven has arrived," said Reilly.

"Yes, that's right. Created quite the stir. Do you know anything about him?"

"The housemaids say he's handsome." She paused to wrap a curl around her finger and pin it tightly to the side of my head. "Mr. Bradbury's man says his lordship comes from an old family with an estate called Midbourne down in Sussex. His father died in the war, and his mother passed away quite recently."

"Oh? Poor man," I said with some feeling.

"Perhaps that's why Lady Millicent's so determined to make sure he enjoys himself this weekend." Reilly sprayed the curls with a sugar-water setting solution.

"How sweet of her to be so attentive," I remarked sourly. "She truly is all heart."

"Yes, miss. That's *certainly* what they say downstairs."

She straightened everything on the dressing table, setting combs and brushes in rigid rows, like silverware at a state banquet. "Will you be needing anything else, miss?"

"No, thank you. Could you please come back around seven?"

"Of course, miss. Goodnight, miss."

As soon as the door closed behind her, I reached into the top drawer of the dressing table and retrieved and lit a cigarette. I puffed away while I thought.

If I couldn't talk business with Porter, I'd have to work on ingratiating myself instead. See if I could make a friend of him, and then approach. The way he'd been behaving toward me suggested that keeping the line between "friend" and . . . something else entirely . . . might be challenging. But then, what was life without a challenge? And what other hope did I have? How much longer would I let those strangers sleep in our beds and spill coffee on our rugs while I moldered away at Aunt El's?

I remembered an old school acquaintance once telling me she'd got herself a "sugar daddy."

"He'll do anything for me!" she'd said, laughing. "These sweet old fellows, they love a bit of attention from a bright young thing."

A bit of attention: I could give Mr. Porter that.

I stood, tossing the cigarette into the fire, and strolled over to the bedside table. Cee had stacked a few novels for me to read, and I flipped open the first one. It was the latest Agatha Christie—*Murder at the Vicarage*. Perfect for a country weekend. Cee's such a marvelous hostess; she thinks of everything.

I settled into bed with it and was just getting to a juicy bit when a knock made me jump so violently I kicked the hot water bottle right out of the bed. The strange thing was, whoever it was wasn't knocking on the door, like any normal, civilized person, but on the *wall*. It took me a moment to recognize the pattern: Morse code.

Intrigued, I abandoned the book and pressed my ear against the wall, trying to make out what was being tapped. L-O-V-E-L-Y. I drew away and stared at the flocked paper, wondering who else in the house besides me, Cecilia, David, and Joyce knew Morse. I was fairly certain it wasn't any of them.

The tapping stopped, and I rushed toward the door to try to catch my mysterious knocker. But in my hurry I crashed into a table and sent it, me, and six china figurines tumbling. When I stood up, I immediately put my foot down on a doe-eyed boy playing the pan pipes. Cursing and hopping and swearing vengeance on all Crown Derby figurines forever, I gave the pursuit up as lost, retrieved my hot water bottle, and decided it was time to turn in.

Chapter Four

〜

Reilly breezed in the following morning at seven o'clock on the dot and handed me a cup of tea. Without so much as a raised eyebrow, she righted the side table I'd knocked over the previous night and began restoring the figurines to their rightful places.

"I'm sorry about that, Reilly," I said, feeling ashamed and thinking of my mother scolding me whenever I left things lying about.

"Servants aren't slaves, Astra," she'd say. *"They're not here to wait on you hand and foot. Don't be so helpless."*

"No trouble, miss." Reilly finished with the figurines and moved on to the wardrobe, selecting breakfast-appropriate attire while I drank my tea and steeled myself for the day to come.

The men would be off shooting just after breakfast, leaving us ladies to entertain ourselves until lunchtime. I could probably duck Millicent for most of the morning, but unless I skipped breakfast, there was no way to avoid facing her over the bacon and eggs: unmarried girls weren't allowed to have breakfast in bed.

"So, how are things downstairs?" I asked as I finished my tea and slid out of bed. "Are you all settled in and comfortable?"

Again with the codes. What I really meant was: *Have the others started to trust you enough to share anything useful?*

"Quite settled, miss, thank you." Reilly paused, then: "Lady Millicent's maid has been *particularly* friendly."

I gave her a sharp look as she started helping me out of the night-gown and into some lingerie. Her face, as always, was unreadable. "Is that so? Fishing about, is she?"

"Yes, miss. But I shouldn't worry, if I were you. She and I seem to have very similar interests. I believe I could make a friend of her."

Well, I thought, as she fastened my all-in-one and pulled a slip over my head, *that would be handy.* Someone so close to Millicent could provide highly valuable weaponry with which to stock my defensive arsenal. But this sort of move was hardly without risk.

"Don't try too hard," I advised. "We're only here for a few days, after all. Probably best we keep our heads down instead of encouraging her to strike first."

"Of course, miss." She zipped my skirt and held up a cardigan.

Once I was suitably suited up, I headed downstairs and was rudely greeted by the sound of Porter bellowing, "That's not good enough, goddamn it!" into the poor, defenseless telephone. "I need those tires and this is the *third time* the order's been late!"

He paused to smile and wave cheerfully at me as I passed. I returned the greeting even as my brain shifted to panic. Tires? This wasn't about Vandemark, was it?

I couldn't very well loiter, so I swallowed and continued on to the dining room.

Millicent was already there, helping herself to food at the sideboard. David was making good headway on a heaped plate while, across from him, Belinda toyed with a slice of toast.

As I poured myself some coffee, I felt Millicent's gimlet eye boring into me. I pushed my other concerns away and turned to face her with a forced smile.

"Wearing blue today, I see," she said. Quietly, so the others wouldn't overhear. "What a *bold* choice. Most women steer clear of the colors that make them look sallow."

"And yet I see you're wearing green," I returned, unable to stop myself.

She smirked and slithered off, taking the seat at the head of the table. I spared a moment to roll my eyes before collecting some eggs and grilled tomatoes and seating myself next to Belinda. I greeted David with a smile (genuine, this time) as I did so.

"Morning, Astra," he said. "Joyce sends her love."

"Breakfasting upstairs, I take it? I don't blame her." I quickly glanced at Millicent, and David smirked. "Are you excited about the shooting?" I asked him.

"It's a perfect day for it," he replied, nodding toward the sunlit park.

I turned to Belinda. "We've hardly had a chance to catch up since our arrival," I said with an ingratiating smile. She seemed surprised by my chummy tone, and well she might: we were, after all, only nodding acquaintances. But she seemed sweet, and she'd be a duchess someday, so it couldn't hurt to try to be better friends with her.

"No, I suppose not," she said. "You've been busy with Cee and Mrs. Bradbury."

"Oh yes, well, Joyce and Cee and I have known each other since we were practically babies. I'm sorry—I suppose you feel a little left out."

"It's all right, I understand," she said, not the slightest trace of malice in her chirpy tone. "Besides, I have my Georgy." A dreamy look that reminded me of the china shepherdesses came over her face.

"It's wonderful to see two people so in love," I gushed. "I only hope I can be as lucky as you someday."

"I don't deserve my luck," said Belinda, sighing. "I don't think anyone else could be as lucky as me, because there's no other Georgy in the world, is there?"

"No, unfortunately not."

"But then, everyone has *their* Georgy, don't they?"

"We can only hope so."

I was starting to think it was a bit too early for so much saccharine and prayed for deliverance. It came in the forms of Beckworth and Dunreaven, who rode another wave of Porter's expletives into the dining room.

"I'm on a bloody *shooting weekend*, damn you! Don't telephone me again!"

"I say!" Beckworth tittered. "I think we're all awake now."

Dunreaven chuckled and patted him on the shoulder, giving me a 'well, *there's* a thing' look as the two men made their way to the sideboard.

"Good morning, Dunny," Millicent trilled.

"Good morning," Dunreaven answered politely, making his way to the empty seat to my right. Beckworth turned away from the food with an excited grin, sloshing his coffee, only to find me hemmed in by Belinda and Dunreaven. His face drooped and he dragged himself off to sit next to David.

Millicent frowned, then turned to David "How is marriage, David?" she asked him. "Does that wife of yours still let you fly, or are you permanently grounded now?"

"Joyce is splendid," he replied.

"Tell Lady Millicent how Joyce arranged for you to meet Lindbergh on your honeymoon," Dunreaven prompted as he dug into his kippers.

David glared at him but nonetheless obeyed, launching into a very detailed account of their luncheon together that Millicent was forced to pretend to listen to.

"I hope you had a pleasant night, Miss Davies," said Dunreaven.

"I survived without permanent injury," I answered. "Though I can't say the same for one or two china figurines. How was your Canova expedition?"

He smiled. "It's a fine bust."

"So I hear."

He took a minute or two to drink his coffee while looking at me thoughtfully and then said, "Astra's a very unusual name. Wherever did your parents hear it?"

"My mother said a family friend used the word in conversation and she liked it." I shrugged. "I used to hate it, but now I like that it sets me apart from the multitudes."

"Indeed. Starlike: one in a million."

"Please, Lord Dunreaven, one in a billion," I responded playfully.

He chuckled. "Quite right. And are you a lucky star?"

"Wish on me and perhaps you'll find out."

"Then I wish more girls were like you."

"And I wish more men would stop referring to us as 'girls,'" I retorted.

He leaned away from me slightly, brows raised. "My mistake. I wish more *ladies* were like you."

"That's much better," Belinda told him, nodding emphatically.

"But that's not a term that can be used universally," Millicent interjected, cutting off David's in-depth description of pecan pie. "A woman isn't necessarily born a lady."

"Some are," I reminded *Lady* Millicent.

Something flickered in her eyes: the look of a hungry fox that has just lured a wounded rabbit into the glen. "That's right," she agreed silkily. "*Some* are."

The table had gone silent. The air between the two of us thickened. It was the sweet shop all over again. Where on earth was Miss?

"Well," Belinda spoke up tentatively, "Some are born to it, and some learn."

Millicent responded with a look and a tone that Edgry would have applauded. "No, *dear*. It's not the sort of thing that can be learnt. You either *are* or you're *not*. It's quite confusing, I know, because we're all so democratic nowadays that everyone mixes together. You have dukes sitting down to dinner with bankers. Lords enjoying their shooting with . . ." Her eyes flickered, for a mere instant, toward the door through which we could still hear Porter's muffled shouts. Millicent sighed. "Sometimes I feel like we've let our standards slip too far. Perhaps we ought to take stock and close the gates to the more common sort. Make Society something to truly look up to again, instead of something anyone can join if they spend enough or manipulate the right people."

I swallowed hard at the implication that I'd only become friends with Cee in order to get a leg up socially. And I equally resented her suggestion that Joyce and Porter had merely bought their way in. I glanced up and caught David's eye and could tell he wasn't too happy about it either. But before either of us could say anything, Millicent went on:

"What do the lords here think? Should we not be more exclusive? Wouldn't you rather be reassured that the women around you are true ladies instead of the granddaughters of vicars on one side and . . . what was it? Buttons on the other?"

Her eyes were boring into me now; I could feel it. There was a silence so heavy I felt the weight of it on my chest, pressing *hard*, and I struggled to breathe normally. I was aware of everyone else staring at me, waiting to see how I would respond. I didn't trust myself to speak, or move, afraid I'd either rile her further or stab her to death with a grapefruit spoon. As tempting as that was, my life was already complicated enough.

I set my face into a cool mask and turned to look at her. "Boots, actually. And it was my great-great-grandfather Davies. Without him, the soldiers would have had to fight barefoot at Waterloo."

"Then we owe him a debt of gratitude," said Dunreaven, with a brief smile my way. I noticed, despite the smile, that a muscle along his jaw-line kept appearing and then fading away, as if he were clenching and unclenching his teeth. "David, do you think we'll bag more grouse than we did at Holkham last month? I've got a fiver that says we do."

*   *   *

Breakfast broke up soon after. The men gathered to leave for the first drive, and I fled for the sanctuary of my bedroom. I would have liked nothing more than to hurl one of the figurines across the room and watch it splinter against the wall. Imagine that wall was Millicent's head, and the shards were burrowing into her skull, wiping the smug look right off her face.

But Reilly was there, laying out my tweeds, and it wouldn't do to make a scene.

Instead, I snatched the nail file off the dressing table and began dis-integrating my left thumbnail. Reilly looked up, cocked an eyebrow, and stepped back from the carefully arranged clothes.

"I have everything all ready for you, miss."

I responded with a smile so brittle it nearly cracked. "Excellent. Thank you. Could you come back around twelve, please?"

"Of course, miss."

The sound of shouting men and barking dogs just below my window indicated the guns were ready to leave. Reilly began gathering things that needed to be taken downstairs as, with a brisk knock, Joyce strode in.

"What an absolute beast that creature is! David told me all about it." She took my shoulders, holding me at arm's length. "Darling, are you all right? God, she's awful, isn't she? Do you want me to poison her tea? I'll do it, you know."

"That's sweet of you, Joyce," I said, feeling a bit better already.

Reilly arched her brow again and slipped out, probably hoping to get the whole story from one of the footmen.

"And I've had words with David," Joyce continued. "I can't believe he didn't speak up for you. He says he was too stunned, but that's no excuse. What a mouse! My father would never have just stood by. I told David he'll be lucky if I don't make him sleep in the dressing room tonight."

"Don't do that, Joyce, it's not his fault."

"Well, he has to learn! No woman wants a timid husband. What if Millicent turns the guns on me someday?"

I laughed. "She'd have to be suicidal."

The door flew open and Cecilia and Ivanhoe rushed in.

"I swear I'll never speak to Millicent again!" Cee declared, throwing her arms around my neck and nearly strangling me in a hug. "You poor, poor thing! Insulting you like that! And on your first outing after a bereavement!"

"You're both overreacting!" I cried. "But it's very kind of you to be concerned. I think we all know there's no love lost between myself and Millicent."

"She's just annoyed because she expected to have Dunreaven all to herself," Cecilia told me. "But she can hardly hope to out-charm you."

"You're very flattering, Cee. And your sister can ease her mind because I'm not interested in pursuing Lord Dunreaven."

"Why not?" Joyce asked indignantly, as if I'd somehow insulted her by rejecting her husband's friend.

"Oh, really, as though I haven't had a difficult enough year already. The last thing I need just now is Millicent gunning for me." I had more than enough to occupy my mind without piling all that on as well. And a penniless lord was no good to me at all, even if he did look like Gary Cooper.

Cecilia patted my shoulder while making sympathetic whimpering noises. "Poor Astra. You've had *such* a time of it. But wouldn't a little romance help? At least then the whole year won't have been one long misery."

"You sound like Toby." I chuckled. "And there are other ways besides romance for me to find happiness."

Cecilia and Ivanhoe cocked their heads, as if this answer perplexed them.

"Don't worry about Millicent—she's just being mean because she's sour about Hampton and Belinda," Cecilia reassured me. "Do you want me to poison her tea?"

"I already offered," Joyce told her.

"I think we all need an adventure," Cecilia said decisively. "What about Paris, as I suggested? Paris in the spring! It'll be wonderful, Astra—say you'll do it!"

"I'll see."

Cecilia, clearly understanding that to mean "yes," bounced up and down, clapping her hands and squealing. "Oh, we're going to have a wonderful time!"

Hoping to steer the conversation away from this trip, I asked, "Were either of you knocking on my wall last night?"

They both looked at me like I'd lost my mind.

"Knocking on your wall?" Joyce repeated.

"Someone was. In Morse code."

"Well, it certainly wasn't me, and it wasn't David. I can definitely vouch for *his* whereabouts last night."

Cecilia's eyes lit up. "Ooh, a mystery! What were they saying?"

"Lovely," I answered.

Cee and Joyce swapped a meaningful look.

"Astra," said Joyce, "Surely you know—"

"A secret admirer!" Cee cut in. "How perfectly, wonderfully, beautifully romantic. It'll be a lovely story to tell your children someday."

I was starting to be sorry I'd brought it up. "It's probably nothing. Maybe I was hearing things. The book was playing on my imagination."

"Maybe it was a ghost," Joyce joked. "Some poor dead relative of Cee's, pining away for a lost love."

Cecilia and I laughed. Ivanhoe yapped and jumped around in a circle.

"Shall we go downstairs?" I suggested. "I think Ivey needs more room to roam."

"Yes, all right," Joyce agreed, eyeing a clutch of figurines. "I always feel like I'm being watched when I'm in this room, and after what Astra's just said, that goes double."

"Millicent's finalizing menus with the cook, so we should be safe in the drawing room for an hour or so," Cecilia reported.

"She's the one who should worry about being safe," said Joyce as she processed out.

I moved to follow her, but Cecilia took my arm and drew me back into the room, closing the door.

"I didn't want to say anything in front of Joyce," Cee whispered, eyes darting here and there, as if she expected ears to pop right out of the walls, "but I've heard something about your maid, and I think you should know about it."

"About Reilly? What is it?" Good lord, we'd only been in the house a *day*. What could she have possibly done to upset someone already?

"Well, it's the housemaid, Emma. When she was helping me get dressed this morning, she said that Reilly . . . well, that Reilly was making advances to three of the footmen." Her cheeks pinkened. "Emma said she overheard Reilly telling them to come to her room."

"All of them?"

Cecilia was well and truly blushing now. She spread her hands in a helpless gesture. "I'm sure this is all a misunderstanding, but you may want to have a word with Reilly. It seems that her attempts at friendship might be going over a little *too* well."

"Yes, of course," I responded automatically. But how, exactly, does one broach such a subject? This was yet another bit of my education that had been overlooked.

"And of course I've asked Emma not to breathe a word to anyone, especially Millicent," Cecilia added.

That hadn't even occurred to me. Just the thought of it made my stomach clench. I doubted having a notorious maid would make me very popular with hostesses.

"That's sweet of you, Cee. Thank you."

"Emma won't say anything—she loves me," Cecilia reassured me. "Oh, I'm sorry, darling! I wanted you to have a nice weekend, and look what's happened."

"It's all right. It's just a bit of a surprise." I tried to smile and took her hand. "Come on, or Joyce will think we're talking about her behind her back."

* * *

At half past twelve, we ladies motored out to the luncheon site: a stone folly located halfway between the house and the site of that morning's avian bloodbath. The folly, shaped like a ruined castle, had been built by the first Lord Caddonfoot at the height of the craze for useless structures. Cee, of course, loved it and thought the folly was the most romantic spot in England. I guessed we had her to thank for having our lunch there.

As we disembarked, the wet-dog stench of tweeds announced the imminent arrival of the gentlemen. They appeared, trailing beaters and retrievers, everyone looking muddy and triumphant.

"An excellent morning!" Lord Caddonfoot reported.

"Hooray, Papa!" Cecilia crowed, clapping. "And everyone else!"

Urged on by the Marquess, the overexcited dogs bounded toward the guests. They barked and swirled around our legs, sniffing at the table despite the shouts of the head gamekeeper and anxious waving of the footmen. Caddonfoot laughed and patted the nearest dog on the head.

"Who bagged the most, then?" Joyce asked David.

"Jeremy, of course," he answered. "As we all predicted."

"I think you, Lord Caddonfoot, and I were evenly matched, David," Dunreaven countered.

"Don't be so modest!" said David, lightly shouldering his friend. "You probably shot half of the birds we bagged."

I glanced at the truck where the birds were hanging. "Very impressive. The pheasants of England will fear your name forevermore."

Dunreaven grinned, and to my annoyance, I felt a swift tingle shoot up my spine. Fortunately, we were all distracted by a nearby Labrador. Throwing caution to the wind, it lunged for a game terrine, leaving a pair of muddy paw prints on the damask tablecloth. Millicent bellowed, *"Out!"* and everything on four legs scurried away.

"I'm sure I winged that last bird you got," Porter grumbled.

"I think you're quite right about that, sir," Dunreaven agreed.

The footmen collected themselves, swept away the stained tablecloth, and poured drinks as we descended on the table.

I slipped into a seat beside Porter and smiled sweetly at him. Perhaps if he was in a good mood, he'd be a bit more forgiving of that late shipment. "It was kind of you to give Lord Dunreaven that bird. Most other men would have taken full credit for the kill, even if they had only just winged it. I hope you've enjoyed your morning."

"I have, thank you. Looking forward to this afternoon." He leaned toward me and dropped his voice. "No more winging: clear, straight shots the whole way!"

"Good for you, sir!"

The footmen began passing around plates of oysters, and Porter rubbed his hands together. "Shooting always gives me an appetite."

"All that fresh air," I said, nodding. "My father used to say it was the best thing for a good appetite and a healthy glow. Oh, Mr. Porter, are these new tweeds?" I delicately plucked at his sleeve. "They're simply splendid. Not many men can really pull off this year's cut, but you certainly do."

"Well, thank you very much, Miss Davies." He sat up a little straighter, puffing out his chest before diving into his oysters.

"Still prefer fishing?" I asked Beckworth, who was seated on my other side, looking flushed and quite proud of himself.

"I think so, but shooting may win me over yet—I've had a good day today. I got five on my own."

"Five? That's wonderful!" squealed Cecilia. "You should come back here more often. Gryden seems to bring you luck."

Beckworth grinned and blushed darker.

"Of course, it's really about the sport, not how much you come away with," said Caddonfoot.

"It's always about how much you come home with," Porter countered, mopping at some oyster juice dribbling down his beard. "Why do anything if you get nothing?"

Millicent pursed her lips. "I suppose one can't expect everyone to appreciate the finer points of these things."

Porter slurped down his last oyster. "I'm sure you don't mean me, Lady Millicent." He gestured to his shell-strewn plate. "As you can see, I appreciate *many* fine things." He winked at me, and I smiled back.

Across the table, Joyce frowned ever so slightly, but I ignored it and said to Porter, "I'm so glad that distressing phone call this morning didn't affect your sport.'

He shrugged as the oysters were replaced with a steaming curry. "Nothing to worry about, just a small business matter. But this is not the place for that sort of talk. Business in the City, not in the drawing room, I always say. I've noticed refined ladies tend to find such conversation quite dull indeed, as they should."

"Oh, don't stop yourself on my account," I told him with a sickly smile directed at Millicent. "As we all know, I'm really quite common."

Across the table, Dunreaven ducked a smile behind his napkin. Something in his eyes seemed to say, *Well done,* but I might have just been imagining it.

"'Common' is certainly not a word I'd ever use to describe you, Miss Davies," was Porter's oily reply.

"No, no, certainly not," Beckworth chimed in. "*Certainly* not."

"So many gallants rushing to your aid, Astra," Millicent observed. "Dunny, would you care to weigh in?"

"Miss Davies has plenty of supporters already; I'd only overcrowd the field."

"You have to be bold, Jeremy," Joyce urged. "Were you this timid when you were piloting ships? Thank heavens we haven't had another war."

"Thank heavens indeed," Dunreaven agreed. "I prefer a quieter life now. I find it's much nicer piloting sailboats."

"You should take Astra sailing. She loves it, don't you, Astra?" Joyce's glance screamed, *Now's your chance!*

Dunreaven turned an inquisitive look my way. "You sail?"

"I do, but I haven't been out in years. My grandfather, *the vicar,* was quite keen and used to take me off to Lulworth Cove. We'd explore the caves and he'd tell me all about the smugglers who used to use them."

"Family stories?" Millicent suggested.

"Sailing's in the blood," I continued, ignoring her. "My father's people came over on the ships with William the Conqueror." Father had loved telling that story.

"The last great Davies," Millicent said, sniffing.

"I sail too," Beckworth piped up. "Well, I punt, at least."

"Oh, do you? How lovely! I've always wanted to be punted," Cecilia breathed.

Dunreaven concealed another smile as Millicent hissed, "Honestly, Cecilia!"

"I'd be happy to take you sometime, when you're next in the neighborhood," Beckworth offered with his usual puppy-like eagerness. He then glanced over at me, blushed again, and somehow managed to somersault a fork over his left shoulder.

"I used to take your mother punting, my last year at Cambridge," Caddonfoot recalled, smiling at his daughters. "We'd pack a picnic, and I'd sing to her the whole way to our secret picnic spot." His smile turned wistful, and he looked off into the distance.

Cecilia sighed dreamily. "*So* lovely."

"I bought pearls for my wife," said Porter, nodding toward Joyce. "Same ones I gave you for your wedding. Seemed to do the trick."

"And your father, Miss Davies?" asked Dunreaven. "Pearls or punting for him?"

"Neither," I answered quietly. "It was flowers. Lilies every morning, and something different every afternoon." The lilies had become a tradition: Mother received her daily bouquet by ten o'clock whenever we were in London.

I saw my mother, giggling and glowing as she received that delivery, only too happy to once again detail every bouquet Father had sent.

"It's perfect," she'd say, "because we met at the Chelsea Flower Show."

Only a year ago, Father had confessed that he'd arranged that meeting after seeing her enraptured by *Madame Butterfly* at Covent Garden. It was our secret.

"These lovely romantic gestures," Joyce mused. "Does anyone do them anymore?"

"Surely some do," said Dunreaven.

"Georgy does!" Belinda piped up. "He's done the most wonderful things for me."

"He's the outlier, then," Joyce commented. She seemed unaware of the indignant looks David was shooting her. "Although apparently Astra's got a secret admirer."

I glared at her as Dunreaven said: "Is that so? How very *lovely*."

I looked up sharply and he smiled. A secret, knowing little smile. Of course! How stupid of me not to realize that the naval officer would know Morse code.

"A secret admirer? How thrilling! What's he done?" Belinda asked.

Joyce had a coy look on her face, and her eyes were moving between Dunreaven and me. "Someone's been knock, knock, knocking at her chamber wall."

If she expected something dramatic, she was cheated. The only response from Dunreaven was a mildly interested expression as he asked the nearest footman for more Waldorf salad.

"As I said, it was probably just the wind," I said. "Or a ghost."

"Well, we should all be so lucky to have someone make the effort for us, even a dead person," Joyce sighed.

Millicent didn't seem to think so: she was practically smoldering.

Caddonfoot roused himself and cleared his throat. "All this talk of romance," he said in a thick voice. "The young men will be too misty-eyed to line up their shots properly. Gentlemen, what do you all think of moving to the near meadow for the afternoon drive?"

* * *

The ladies were invited to join the afternoon shoot to cheer the men on, but like Toby, I've never enjoyed being damp and deafened. Instead, I took a long walk and returned to the house to thaw before tea.

I rang for Reilly and was just taking off my hat when I noticed a torn slip of paper lying on my pillow. Setting my things aside, I reached over and picked it up.

A beautiful head lies here. I dream about it every night.

Behind me, the door opened and Reilly came in.

"Welcome back, miss. Have you had a pleasant afternoon?"

"I have, thank you," I answered distractedly. "Do you know who this is from?" I held out the paper.

"No, miss. I didn't put it there. Would you like me to draw you a bath?"

"In a moment. We need to have a talk first." I tossed the paper onto the dressing table and turned to face her, arms crossed.

But I still had absolutely no idea what to say.

"Yes, miss?" she prompted after a very long silence.

"Well, it's just . . . It seems the maid, Emma, has . . ." I closed my eyes and tried to gather my thoughts. "Reilly, I've heard some things about how you've been conducting yourself with the male servants here, and I'm afraid it really must stop."

She looked puzzled. "Miss?"

"Well, really, Reilly, a little flirtation is one thing, but going after three men, all at the same time, is quite another. Inviting them to your room! Your behavior reflects on me, and I do need to think about my own reputation. Just, please, be more circumspect."

She blinked for a few moments, then said, "Of course, miss. I'm very sorry."

"It's all right. Just . . . please bear all this in mind."

"Yes, miss. I'll draw that bath for you now, miss."

I nodded, pleased with how well I'd handled the matter.

A few minutes later I was happily slipping into the steaming water, letting the heat and the smell of rose oil ease my tension. My mind wandered, skipping from Porter shouting into the telephone to Edgry sneering at me. From columns of numbers in ledgers to Millicent glaring and Dunreaven chuckling. Memories and fantasies jumbled together, and I saw my father smiling fondly at my mother when she wasn't looking and gently brushing a hand over her hair, not seeming to mind that it had begun to thin and lose its luster. And then I imagined Lord Dunreaven skimming his fingers along my shoulders and neck, leaning forward and whispering, "One in a billion," into my ear, so close I could feel the heat of his breath.

I started, sloshing water over the side of the tub. I must have dozed off. Ivanhoe had nosed his way in, hopped up on a chair beside the bathtub, and was snuffling at my ear. When I came to, he sat back on his haunches and cocked his head, as if to say, "Now what were *you* thinking of?"

"Can a girl not have any privacy?" I wondered as I hauled myself out of the water and reached for the warmed towel and my dressing gown. I padded down the hall back to my room, with Ivanhoe following; opened the door; and discovered Millicent, in full teatime splendor, standing next to my bed.

I yelped. Ivanhoe whimpered and scurried out. "Did Reilly let you in here?"

She arched an eyebrow. "I hardly need that creature to give me permission to enter a room in my own home."

"That *creature?*"

"We need to discuss this maid of yours, Astra," she informed me.

Oh, dear Lord. I closed my eyes and hastily counted back from ten.

"What about her?" I asked, trying to keep my tone even.

"I've heard some disturbing things. Mrs. Bletchett is very upset."

"Mrs. B—?"

"The housekeeper!"

"Oh. Emma spoke to her, then?" How like Cecilia to have too much faith in someone.

Millicent frowned. "Emma? What does she have to do with this?"

"With . . . what?" Had Reilly actually managed to put *both* feet wrong in our first twenty-four hours here?

"The matter with your maid!"

"What matter is that?"

"What does Emma have to do with it?"

"I have no idea, Millicent. I don't even know what you're talking about."

"I'm talking about the *socialist propaganda* that was found in your maid's room during this morning's surprise inspection." Her eyes gleamed and her nostrils actually flared at the revelation.

I couldn't believe this. "She's a socialist as well?" I cried stupidly.

The language did not escape Millicent. Her eyes narrowed. "What do you mean, *as well?*"

"I mean . . . as well as all those other socialists out there. Like the government. Socialists, all of them. Propaganda, you say?"

"Pamphlets," she hissed. "Several of them. It looks like she was preparing to hand them around. She's clearly here to recruit."

"Oh."

"Is that all you have to say?" She advanced, but I refused to be cowed and stood my ground, wishing there was more between us than a padded satin dressing gown. Plate armor would have been my preference. Millicent paused just a few inches away and drew herself up to her full height, which was just above my own, unfortunately. "I can't have that sort of thing here. I have to consider the well-being of the other servants, not to mention my sister. They are all vulnerable and impressionable, and this way of thinking is an extremely dangerous road. That maid will have to go. Tonight."

There was a soft knock, and in came the woman of the hour herself, carrying a freshly polished pair of shoes. Millicent glared at her and made a strange sort of hissing sound before vacating.

"Well, this is just brilliant, Reilly!" I raged as she put the shoes down next to the bed and stood there, looking confused. "*Socialist pamphlets?* What next? Do you have any other secrets you'd like to share? Are you also the Grand Duchess Anastasia? Do you have the Hope Diamond secreted about your person?"

"No, miss."

"Do you want to tell me just what's going on here?"

She paused for a few moments, frowning. Then her expression smoothed out as everything fell into place.

"The pamphlets," she whispered, bringing her hands up to cover her face. "They aren't socialist, miss," she added more loudly a few moments later. She dropped her hands. "I think my intentions have been misunderstood."

"They definitely have." I took a deep breath. "Right, let's go back to the beginning: Is this what you were talking about with the footmen?"

"Yes, miss."

"How on earth did a housemaid mistake that for flirtation?"

Reilly shifted her weight from one foot to the other. "I think she misunderstood my suggestion we all join a movement together," she explained. "You see, Emma, she's . . . well . . ."

"Bit of an under-boiled egg?"

"You could say that, miss."

"What movement?" I asked, calming down a little now that at least one thing had been cleared up. "Is that what these pamphlets are about?"

She nodded. "It's nothing too bad, miss," she promised. "I'm trying to support—get support—for a petition to overturn the Trade Disputes and Trade Unions Act."

I blinked, feeling as stupid as Emma. "The what?"

The expression that crossed her face reminded me of a teacher who's just realized she'll have to spend a lot of time explaining something basic to an extremely slow pupil. It was a look that said, *Lord, give me strength!*

"All right, never mind that for now," I said, not quite ready for this so soon after having been subjected to Millicent's lecture. "Why didn't you explain all this earlier?"

"I'm sorry, miss. I just thought it might be easier this way. I thought the matter had been dealt with, and we could just put it behind us."

I sighed. "We have a serious problem, Reilly. Lady Millicent's ordered me to send you away immediately."

Her face instantly went sheet-white. "Oh, miss," she breathed. She looked terrified, as if she thought I was going to throw her out into the woods in the middle of the night.

I sagged onto the edge of the bed and in a gentler tone asked, "Have you approached others?"

"A few," she squeaked.

Now it was my turn for the *give me strength* expression. The clock in the hall began chiming half past three. I sighed. "I have to get ready to go down. This will all have to wait."

Reilly nodded and went to fetch my tea dress while I rubbed my temples. She paused in her preparations and handed me an aspirin, which I swallowed dry.

"I'm not at all happy about this, Reilly. Nobody likes hearing that their servants are causing disruption."

"No, miss."

"I don't like secrets. You should have told me what you intended to do before you made yourself a political activist," I added.

"Yes, miss."

"I'll have to think about all of this and see what can be done."

"Yes, miss."

I turned to the dressing table to fetch a comb. Only then did I notice the note I'd found on my pillow was gone.

* * *

I could feel Millicent's eyes boring into me even as I listened to Beckworth natter on about every detail of the last drive (he very nearly managed to shoot *three more birds*) and talked to Belinda about her wedding plans.

The sear of Millicent's gaze was so distracting it was a relief when her voice finally whipped across the room: "I hope you've sent that Bolshevik packing, Astra."

I turned toward her, prepared for battle. "I don't think that's necessary. I've spoken with her, and she's learned her lesson."

Millicent smirked. "Oh, there's so much you don't know about running an important household," she purred. "Hensley is such a little place, I can't expect you to know the finer points of managing a large staff."

"You're quite right, Millicent," I agreed. "Our servants were too busy to waste their time gossiping and making trouble."

Her lips thinned briefly, then stretched back into a smile. "I think all servants need a firm hand. Don't you agree, Dunny?" She laid a hand on Dunreaven's arm.

"I don't feel sufficiently informed to offer an opinion on the matter," he replied.

"Now, now, Millicent," Cecilia placated, fluttering around like a nervous butterfly, "there's no need to make a scene. It's not something to get worked up about anyway. It's clearly just a misunderstanding."

Millicent glowered at her sister. "It's difficult to misunderstand socialist propaganda, Cecilia."

Cecilia reeled. "She's a socialist as well?"

"Yes, Cee, just like the government," I swiftly agreed.

She looked completely lost, and now Joyce was giving me a *you'll explain this later* frown.

"I say, a socialist," Hampton murmured. "She's not going to take us to a cellar in the middle of the night and gun us down, is she?" He laughed shakily at his own joke, but no one else joined in.

"She very well might." Millicent nodded vigorously. "That's what they do, these *socialists*. Murdering their betters in cold blood!"

"I don't think that's quite true," said David. "Don't most of them just want more equality?"

"How very American of them," Joyce commented with a thin smile. "No wonder the aristocracy hates it."

"They want to be handed everything," said Millicent. "It doesn't matter if they've earned it or not. They want everything taken from everyone else, gathered together, and then handed to them. They're lazy."

"What have you earned?" I asked her before I could stop myself. "Did you buy that portrait? Or that chair? With money you earned yourself?"

"I certainly earn my keep," she icily informed me.

"Yes, so you keep reminding me. Running this household, so very *efficiently*."

Cecilia made a frightened little squeaking noise, but Joyce's eyes were beginning to gleam with delight at the show.

"We can't all be like you, Astra, putting our feet up and letting other people do the hard work," said Millicent, glancing at Dunreaven to gauge his reaction. He seemed to be particularly fascinated by the *Evening Standard*, so she got nothing from him.

"Steady on," Beckworth murmured.

"Oh, here come your defenders again," she crowed. "Perhaps one of them will marry you and see how well your liberal views work when you're mistress of his house."

"I'm not interested in marrying a man who's looking for a housekeeper," I snapped. "You can have him. Apparently you have the requisite skills. Though apparently that hasn't been enough to secure you a husband so far."

Dunreaven's eyes flickered up from the newspaper, and he gave me a warning look. *Ease off, here be dragons.* But too late now.

Millicent's entire face sucked inward in momentary rage, then she shrilled, "Father! Astra's maid has been passing around seditious materials below stairs and upsetting the other servants. She needs to be gone from the house, don't you agree?"

Poor Caddonfoot, roused from his doze by the fire on the other side of the room, snuffled, blinked, and said: "What? What's this? Astra's . . . maid?"

"It's nothing at all, Daddy—go back to sleep," Cee implored.

"Yes, it's nothing. Millicent's just in a sniping mood," Joyce added.

"Oh, right," he mumbled as he dropped back off.

* * *

I took to the garden to stomp and smoke my rage out in the gathering twilight. The stars were just appearing, and I paused to look up and pick out Andromeda and Cassiopeia, winking back at me. Andromeda had faced far worse trials than I: her own parents had chained her up as a sacrifice to a sea monster. When held up against that, my own situation seemed ridiculous. But to be lectured about being lazy and useless by someone who had never earned a thing in her life! It made me want to hit something.

I puffed at my cigarette for a while, then looked down from the stars and saw Lord Dunreaven coming my way.

"I felt like a bit of fresh air," he explained as he approached.

"You've had nothing but fresh air all day. You're saturated with the stuff."

"You can never have too much. I hear it gives you a good appetite and a glowing complexion."

I couldn't help but smile just a little.

"I'm sorry, would you rather be alone?" he asked.

"No, it's all right."

He, too, looked skyward. "Poor Cassiopeia, chained to her throne for all eternity."

"That's what happens when you upset the Nereids. Few things seemed to rile the old gods more than boasting you were better than them."

He chuckled. "They were a very human lot."

"Frighteningly so. All our frailties and squabbles paired with immense power."

"All the better to remember not to upset them, then."

"Have you come out to lecture me?" I asked sharply.

"I wouldn't dream of it."

"Good."

My cigarette had burned down, and I stamped it out in the grass. From an inner pocket, Dunreaven retrieved a silver cigarette case decorated with a raised design of a sailboat. He flipped it open, held it toward me, then struck a match. As I leaned in to light my cigarette, I took the opportunity to study him more closely.

"Your eyes aren't green," I observed as he waved out the tiny flame. "I thought they were, last night, but they're not. I think they're hazel."

"I am not what I first appear," he told me as he lit a cigarette for himself.

"Oh? Are you a spy? Some kind of imposter?"

He smiled and the tip of his cigarette glowed. "Would you be more interested if I were?"

"Perhaps. I could write a novel about you, to fill my hours."

"You couldn't simply put a seafaring earl in your novel?"

"Literature is already full of earls and sailors."

"It's also full of spies and imposters."

"True. But there are few spies and imposters who are also earls. With hazel eyes. Are you a socialist as well? That would make things really interesting."

He shook his head. "I hate to disappoint you, but no."

"Pity. So much for your literary immortality."

"I'm sure the world is richer for that."

I laughed.

A mist was creeping in, and I blamed that and the fact I was dressed in a bit of gossamer nothing for the goose pimples breaking out over my arms. I must have shivered, because Dunreaven suddenly put his cigarette in his mouth, removed his jacket, and draped it over my shoulders. I should have handed it back immediately, like a proper young lady. But it was still cozy warm from his body and smelled like woodsmoke and aftershave and something else I couldn't quite identify—could it be sea spray, or was I imagining that?—so instead I found myself snuggling in and thanking him.

We walked a few moments in silence, then he asked, "Will you keep the maid?"

"Do you think I should get rid of her?" I countered.

"It's not my decision."

"That doesn't stop most people from airing an opinion."

He chuckled. "I'm not 'most people.'"

"No, indeed. Most people wouldn't have gone knocking on a young lady's wall in the middle of the night."

"You've found me out!" he cheered.

"You made it quite obvious at lunch."

"It was never meant to be a great mystery."

"Wasn't it? Would you care to explain yourself? Or had the brandy and the fine Canova bust gone to your head?" I waved him on with the hand that held my cigarette.

"You strike me as the sort of woman who appreciates someone who does things a little out of the ordinary." He grinned quite beautifully. "You enjoyed it didn't you?"

I smiled blandly. "I admit nothing."

"You will make me work for it!" he said, laughing.

"Of course! Aren't I worth the effort?"

He took a long drag of his cigarette, making the end glow bright. "Very." He stamped the finished cigarette out. "Now, is your maid worth it? All the trouble with Lady Millicent, I mean." He indicated the house with a jerk of his head.

I sighed. "She's an excellent maid, and it's a difficult time for anyone to be unemployed. I would be sorry to lose her."

"Well," he said, "if she does the job she's been hired for and you get on with her, then I say you should keep her, and let her believe what she wants. Just warn her about making waves in certain households."

"My, my, a liberal-minded aristocrat. I feel like I've just seen a unicorn!"

"I told you, I'm not what I first appear."

"Are you an eligible earl?"

"I suppose I am."

"Then you are exactly what you *first* appear. It's the second and subsequent glances that count."

"And do I warrant a second glance?"

We had nearly reached the house, which saved me from answering. I tossed the cigarette away, shrugged out of the jacket and handed it back to him. "Thank you for the company, but if Millicent sees us coming back in together, she'll have *me* taken to a cellar and shot tonight. So do be a gentleman and take another turn around the garden while I go in."

He took the jacket, bowed low, and sauntered off.

* * *

The dressing gong rang just as I reached my room. Reilly was already there, setting out jewelry and fussing with my dress. As soon as she saw me, she stopped what she was doing and stood waiting for me to either fire her or start getting ready.

"Should we start with my hair?" I suggested, sliding onto the bench at the dressing table.

Out of the corner of my eye, I saw her sag slightly with relief. She sprayed a comb with a little perfume before working it through my hair, then fetched a curling iron warming on the radiator.

"Have you always been political?" I asked as she got to work reviving my waves.

"No, miss," she answered with a soft laugh. "If you had asked me five years ago, I don't know if I could have named my own member of Parliament."

"What turned you into such a firebrand, then?"

She bit her lip as she focused on twirling a piece of hair just so around the iron. "The mines and the strike," she finally answered. Off my questioning look, she went on, "Where I grew up, most of the men went down the mines. Sent underground as young as twelve to breathe the dust and the muck and break themselves with the haulin'." Her accent was starting to thicken as she became more agitated. Letters dropped like flies. "I've known many gone down that way, come up coughin' black 'n blood till 'e couldna speak mor'n three words together. There's no sun on 'em, and when they're 'urt, there's no help. One lad who died in an explosion, 'is family was given three hundred 'n fifty pounds as compensation."

I gaped. *"Three-hundred and fifty pounds?"* I might not know what stockings cost, but I was sure a human life was worth far more than that. And here I was, complaining about only having a thousand a year.

"Those that live do no better," Reilly continued. "Their pay's gone from six quid a week to less 'n four. So, they went on strike. You know there was a strike?"

"Yes, of course." It was four years ago, but I still remembered people complaining about it. One neighbor of ours wailed about being unable to get to London for a shopping trip because all the transport workers had walked out. Others looked on the strike as a lark: a bit of a break from the routine of visits and parties. The boys temporarily took over driving buses, and the girls posed for photographs while punching tickets and serving tea to strikebreaking workers.

"They didn't want trouble," Reilly insisted, "but it was the only way to get anyone's attention. But the strike didn't do nothin', and to keep their jobs the miners 'ad to take *longer* hours and *worse* pay." She jabbed a pin into my hair a little too viciously, but it seemed wrong for me to wince. "My oldest brother 'as five little 'uns and can hardly afford to feed 'em. They cry because they're 'ungry. I send what I can, but . . ." She shook her head. "The government passed a law that restricts strike action and picketin', so nothin'll ever change, not so long as the law's there. That's the law I want repealed."

"But you just said the strike didn't work," I pointed out.

"Not this time, but maybe the next time or the next," she said hopefully. "We 'ave to keep tryin', miss."

I sat for a while in silence, absorbing that. Despite my sheltered upbringing, I wasn't entirely unaware of the difficulties people were facing. Just the other day, I'd put a few coins in a cup held by a one-legged man I had come across near Oxford Street. In his other hand he'd held a sign: "War veteran. Please help." There were three medals, polished to a sunbeam shine, pinned to his chest.

He was hardly alone. On trips to Leicester I'd seen plenty of people in the streets, begging. Some were in rags, while others had clearly dressed in their best, hoping that looking "respectable" would earn them more pity. But no matter what they wore, they all had the same look in their eyes. A hopelessness and despair. I noticed there seemed to be more of them in the last few years. I'd assumed these were the unfortunate unemployed. I hadn't realized that even people with jobs couldn't make ends meet.

And to think of women complaining about spoiled shopping trips while the children of their husbands' employees cried from hunger! It actually gave me a bitter taste in my mouth. "I think perhaps you do need to do something," I murmured, angrily tapping a lipstick against the polished surface of the dressing table. "Someone has to."

Reilly's watery eyes widened, as if she were shocked by that response.

I swiveled to face her. "Is there anything else I need to know? Now is the time for you to be completely honest with me."

"I—" her eyes darted and she turned a little pale. "I was arrested, miss," she said in a rush, flinching, as if she expected me to start battering her.

"Arrested? What for?"

"I went to a rally and things got . . . overheated," she explained. "I hit a policeman with my umbrella, and he arrested me. I know I shouldnae 'ave done it, and I was sorry."

"I'm sure you were," I said. "Does all of this have anything to do with you changing jobs so often in the last two years?"

She hung her head and nodded. "My first mistress died, as I told you. I was at the second place when I was arrested. They found out because I was locked up overnight. My mistress was a kind lady, so she agreed to write me a reference and not say anything, but I had to go. At the next place they didn't take kindly to me talkin' to the other servants about unions. It were three months after that afore I saw your advertisement. I was nearly out of savings, and they wouldn't let me have unemployment because I turned down a job as a skivvy."

"And if you ran out of money, where would you go?"

Reilly shrugged and blinked fast, as though trying to hold back tears.

"Besides your former mistress, does anyone know about your arrest? Anyone who might talk to, say, Lady Millicent any time soon?"

She shook her head.

I tapped the lipstick again, thinking, then decided. "I'm not going to fire you, Reilly. But I think for the remainder of our time here you'd better keep to yourself and avoid mentioning petitions. And I should warn you that my aunt is not liberal-minded, so if she hears about you talking unions in her household, she may insist I send you on your way. What you do in your own time is your business, of course, but for everyone's comfort, it may be best to remain subtle while we're in London. Agreed?"

Reilly nodded.

"Right, then." I stopped abusing the lipstick and started applying it. "There's the second dressing gong now; I'd better hurry."

"Yes, miss."

Chapter Five

~

"Home again, head still firmly attached!" Toby crowed as I came in, trailing Reilly and the cab driver with the luggage. "The weekend must have gone better than I expected."

"It passed without human bloodshed," I confirmed.

He handed me a lit cigarette and ushered me into the drawing room. "Mother's gone to feed and lecture the Great Unwashed, so feel free to savor that ciggie."

I sank into an armchair and took a satisfying drag.

Toby lit a cigarette of his own and reclined on the sofa. "Right, then. Full report, if you please."

I sighed. "Well, Millicent's on the warpath; Joyce's father kept looking at me like I was a pear tart with extra custard; I made friends with Belinda Avery; and the men bagged more than fifteen hundred birds."

Toby laughed. "Not a bad time all around, then."

"I suppose not."

"And how's Ducky? Did he find a pair of brain cells to rub together, or were you stuck with just the one all weekend?"

"Don't be cruel, Toby."

Toby gave me a *look*. "You're not softening up, are you? I refuse to pull crackers with that man every Christmas for the rest of my life."

"Don't be ridiculous. I'm certainly not galloping down the aisle with him. Someone should, though. Aunt El's right: he's lonely. He needs a nice girl who wants to fill his house with children and fawn over him."

"Cecilia, then," he said, laughing. "Or Belinda."

I sat up, astonished. "Toby, that's brilliant!"

"Is it? I'm fairly sure that's the first and the last time anyone will say that to me."

"No, really, Toby, that's an excellent idea: Cee and Beckworth!"

He laughed. "Becoming a matchmaker now, are we?"

"Hardly. I think I'll stop at just this match."

"Still not interested in one of your own? I thought the arrival of *that* suggested otherwise." He pointed to a large vase filled with lilies and asters on a side table. I tossed the finished cigarette into the fire and walked over to the bouquet.

"What've you done with the card?" I asked.

"As if I'd steal a card from you. There wasn't one."

"More secret admirer nonsense?" I rolled my eyes and returned to the chair.

Toby examined me for a moment, then handed over another cigarette. "Are you going to tell me who they're from?"

"Lord Dunreaven, almost certainly. He favors secret messages."

Toby frowned. "Dunreaven? The name's familiar: give me a clue?"

"Earl in the royal navy. A literal golden boy."

He mulled that over, then brightened. "Oh, Jeremy! Is he back on dry land? Good for him. I thought the sea would have swallowed him up, like all the other men in his family. I'm glad Poseidon spat him back out. We were at St. Dunstan's together, you know. He was always good about defending the smaller boys from bullies. Knew how to throw a good punch when necessary. I wish he'd followed the rest of us to Harrow, I could have used the help."

"Isn't abuse part of the experience? Makes a man out of you and all that?"

"Well, it didn't work for me. When that failed, Mother thought that Father dying would somehow provide motivation, but, well, I doubt the grindstone suffered for lack of my nose." He smiled cheekily at me. "So, Dunreaven's sending you messages and flowers, then? Mother will be over the moon when she hears!"

"Will she? Joyce says he doesn't have much money."

"And what is 'not much money' to Joyce?" Toby snorted. "Most of the grand old families are hard up anyway, especially if they lost someone in the war and had to pay all those death duties. Nobody really minds if a lord is penniless; he can trade on his title."

"Lords are luckier than I, then," I observed tersely. "Please don't say anything to your mother, Toby. I don't need her nagging about this. It was nothing, just a bit of flirtation, if even that." I hoped he couldn't see my cheeks pinkening at the memory of that warm, sea-spiced jacket wrapping around me. "And anyway, Millicent seems to have staked a claim, and it's best that I not get further entangled with that one."

"No, indeed. And on that note, were you going to tell me about Comrade Reilly, or were you hoping to keep that all to yourself?" He grinned wickedly as I gaped.

"Who told you about that?" I demanded.

"Millicent did, of course." He retrieved an envelope from his inner pocket and held it out. "This arrived in the evening post yesterday. You're lucky the maid collected it. I'd never have been able to pry that out of Jeffries's hands."

I yanked the note out of the envelope.

Dear Mrs. Weyburn,

I feel it my duty to inform you that a most unsuitable person has been employed by your niece and is now living under your roof . . .

"Good lord," I murmured, leaving the sofa to put the note in the fire. Any residual thought of firing Reilly evaporated with it. Millicent would surely render her unemployable, and I couldn't very well condemn the poor woman to a life of poverty.

"*Is* she a socialist?" Toby asked. "Reilly, I mean."

"No, she just wants to see the decent thing done. I can't fault her for that."

"Suppose not. Hopefully Millicent will be too distracted going after Dunreaven to send these notes to every home you visit."

"One can only hope." I finished my cigarette and stood. "Now I've caught you up on the gossip, I have some work to do."

Toby laughed. "Better you than I!"

* * *

While I was away, the butler had brought some boxes of my parents' things down from the attic and stacked them next to the baize-topped desk in Uncle Augustus's study. This was a sad room, as neglected as my uncle's memory. It smelled stale and felt stuffy, and there was a fuzzy blanket of dust over everything. The only piece of furniture that showed signs of having been touched in the last decade was the walnut cabinet, tucked away in a corner, where Toby kept his drinks. The room was all dark green and dark wood, hunting prints and reproduction busts of famous thinkers. I wondered if my uncle used to sit here, looking at those and reflecting on his shortcomings.

I sighed and threw open the curtains, raising a choking cloud of dust, then knelt and began sifting.

What a packrat my mother had been. It seemed like she'd kept everything, even dried-up posies from dances long past, each one marked with a date on a cream-colored card. One had initials as well: *M.E.C.* There were photo albums, three tarnished silver christening cups, babies' lace caps, and birth certificates.

And finally, buried underneath a silk scarf and Mother's empty perfume bottles (still smelling faintly of Bellodgia), I found my father's black leather diary.

My heart beat harder as I sat, breathing in the ghostly perfume, turning the book in my hands. I brushed my fingers over the name stamped on the front in gold letters. How many times had I seen Father at his desk, scribbling away in this? I'd wondered what he wrote about, but had never dared sneak a look. Somehow, that had seemed like a terrible violation. Even now, I found myself hesitating. Reluctant, still, to intrude. I even looked guiltily over my shoulder before lifting the cover, as if the spirit of my father would be standing there, shaking his head and saying, "You disappoint me, Starling."

But there was no one there, of course. So I opened it and carefully turned the leaves. Perhaps I was expecting something dramatic, but it mostly seemed to be the brief, banal notes one would expect from a respectable, semi-fashionable gentleman.

Sunny today. Wondering if the agapanthus needs dividing. Ask Lillian.

But then:

11 March: Astra's friends all away now. Miss the noise already.
Lillian off to Rosedale this week, so it'll be even quieter.
London for me, perhaps?

Rosedale. *Rosedale!* A place, then. But what sort of place? Not the home of one of Mother's friends, or anyone else we knew. A town? A village?

I stood up, scanned the bookshelves, and pulled down an atlas. A glance at the index revealed no Rosedale. I thought about places my mother used to go and stay for any length of time. There were a few friends she'd visit, and her father (*the vicar*), down south. Maybe Rosedale was near one of them.

I turned back to the diary, hoping for more clues.

13 June: London—Edgry, lunch. Joined by a friend of his—
Hatry. He has an intriguing proposition.

Hatry. I remembered that name. That awful afternoon at Hensley. A quick glance and a half-formed question before Edgry yanked his ledger away.

1 September: London—Lillian, Dr. Hartleby

There he was, Dr. H. Like the ledger, the diary showed my mother and father visiting him regularly throughout the autumn. Nothing to indicate why, though.

Then:

20 September: Hatry arrested. Fraud. Investment gone.
30 September: London—Pearl

Pearl? Who on earth was *Pearl*? Now it was Rosedale, Hartleby, and *Pearl*? What next? What on earth had they been up to, my seemingly devoted, quiet parents?

I thought back to those months before the accident. Tried to recall some warning signs of change in them, but there was nothing. I'd been away most of that time, visiting friends. Attending dances and concerts while my father was dumping what money we had into some fraud and this Pearl creature. And every time I'd come home, he had greeted me with a twinkling eye and "Hullo, Starling. What sort of mischief have you been up to?"

I felt the bitter creep of bile even as I thought of it. Mischief indeed! What else had he been concealing? Were there things that he hadn't even dared consign to the diary?

I helped myself to a drink and returned to the drawing room. Toby was still lying on the sofa. I shoved the diary in his face, open to the first page that mentioned Pearl.

"Who's Pearl?" he asked mildly.

"I'd very much like to know that myself." I helped myself to one of his cigarettes as he slowly pulled himself upright and paged through the diary.

"Steady on, darling, I'm sure it's nothing to get worked up over. Your father wasn't the type to step out."

I thought of the man living at Hensley now, putting on a respectable front while squiring a chorus girl around London. Did all married men do that after a certain point?

"Maybe I don't know what type my father was at all," I spat, dropping like a sack of flour into the armchair. "Smiling and cheerful and all the while wasting money on useless ventures and keeping these little secrets."

"Everyone got swept up in that investment boom," Toby said with a sigh. "That's why the Crash made such a racket. Maybe Pearl was something else your father was looking into. I mean, do you really think he would be writing about meeting another woman in a diary he kept where your mother could easily find it?"

No, probably not. Father might have been foolish, but he wasn't completely stupid.

I threw back the remainder of the drink and took an agitated puff of the cigarette, trying to sort out the mess churning in my mind.

Toby raised an eyebrow. "You'll want to separate those two, you'll set yourself alight." He gently pried the glass out of my hand. "Listen, darling, discovering our parents' secrets is all part of growing up. Why, when I found that drinks cabinet in Father's study, it was fully stocked, bless him. Much as we may think otherwise, our parents are human. They'll have made mistakes and kept secrets just like the rest of us."

He took my hands and squeezed them. "You and I both know your parents were devoted. Barrett and Browning all over again. That diary is full of evidence of it. Your father could hardly bear to do anything without Aunt Lillian's input."

"But why didn't they ever want *my* input?" I wondered. "Why were they keeping these things from me? We could have managed it all together, and then I would have been prepared. They didn't trust me. It's as though I was still just a child to them."

"We're always children to our parents." Toby shrugged.

I sighed and flipped the diary open again: *Lillian off to Rosedale.*

Rosedale. Well, that was something I might be able to get to the bottom of. I stood, handed the cigarette to Toby, and went to the telephone in the hallway.

"Yes, can I have West Lulworth, please, or whatever exchange is nearest?" I asked the operator as Toby strolled over and leaned against the doorway of the drawing room.

"What're you doing?" he asked.

"Detective work," I answered.

"Lulworth here," an officious woman informed me.

"Can you connect me with Rosedale, please?"

The line crackled, then a polite voice said, "Good afternoon, Rosedale House."

My heart was beating so fast I was feeling a little lightheaded. "Good afternoon. My name is Astra Davies. I believe my mother, Lillian Davies, was known there?"

A pause. Then, "Yes, Miss Davies. May I say how sorry we all are for your loss."

"Thank you. That's very kind of you."

"Is this about Raymond's fees?"

Raymond?

"His—his fees?"

"Yes." The voice on the other end sounded uncomfortable. "It's only that they haven't been paid for some time now."

"Oh. I'm so sorry. I'll make sure everything's paid immediately." This Raymond, whoever he was, had been important to my mother. This was the only bill she'd paid promptly. I should respect her wishes. "Is he . . . well?"

"He's very well," the voice answered, sounding relieved to have the awkward conversation out of the way. "He'll be so happy to hear his sister was asking after him."

"His *sister*?" I shrieked. My stomach doubled up, tangled itself, and then tried to leap into my throat. *Sister!*

Toby stood up straight, mouth agape.

"I'm sorry," I managed to say. "Just to be clear—did you just say that Raymond is my brother?"

"Oh yes . . ." The voice on the other end of the line seemed to have realized she'd blundered, but it was too late to go back now. "Yes. Raymond is Lillian Davies's son."

Chapter Six

❧

"A brother!" Toby breathed.

Two drinks each had done nothing to calm or order our minds, and now we were sitting side by side on the sofa, staring blankly ahead. What can one say after a thing like that? On top of everything else, my parents had been hiding a brother from me. Why on earth would they do such a thing?

We heard the front door open, and Aunt Elinor swirled in, complaining between coughs about the rudeness of the taxicab drivers and how intolerable the traffic was now.

"I've always said it: the automobile is a *curse*." She came into the drawing room and was met with a pair of pale, bewildered faces. "What's wrong with you two?"

"I've just telephoned Rosedale House," I announced.

Now she, too, was pale. Her eyes dilated and she sank into the armchair.

"No, no, you didn't," she murmured. "Dear God, you *did not*."

"I did. And they told me about Raymond." My shock was being replaced by a harsh, hot anger. "You knew about him, then?"

"Of course I knew!" she blazed. "I told Lillian not to get mixed up in the matter, but she never listened to me."

"Mixed up? He was her *son*!" I cried.

"Don't let anyone else hear you say that!" she bellowed. "Never! Do you know what that place is? A madhouse! He's a gibbering idiot. A blot on our lives. If anyone knew, none of us would be invited anywhere again. *You*, Astra, would *never* find a husband. 'Tainted blood,' they'll say. Even your mother, softhearted fool that she was, knew that. No one

77

else must know. You must forget all about it." She punctuated this with a hacking cough.

But I couldn't forget about it. How could I? Even if he was deranged, he was still my brother. And my responsibility.

The fees! In the shock that followed my telephone call I'd neglected to telephone Edgry and tell him to pay Rosedale's fees. I stood and moved toward the telephone.

"Where are you going?" Aunt El demanded, following me into the hallway.

"I need to speak to Edgry. The fees haven't been paid." I picked up the receiver.

"My dear"—Aunt Elinor snatched at the hand holding the receiver—"think for a moment. It is a great deal of money. It would be much better for all of us if you simply sent him to a public facility. He was your mother's burden. He shouldn't be yours." She tried smiling, attempting to ingratiate me.

I stared at her in shock. "He's my *brother*!" I cried. "He's not a pauper or an inconvenience to be disposed of!"

The smile vanished. "Do you want a future or don't you?" she shrilled. "Do you want to go back to Hensley or don't you?"

I paused, just for a moment, and considered that. Yes, paying these fees would make it harder for me to save money and go home. But I couldn't simply abandon this man to life in some lunatic asylum. God knows what those sorts of places were like. I imagined a Dickensian horror, all filthy cells and straightjackets and maggoty food.

I slipped my hand out of hers, looked her in the eye. Harnessed that chilly tone of mine. "The fees will be paid. He stays where he is."

She pursed her lips and her eyes blazed. "Foolish girl," she spat, coughing. "Foolish, willful, *wicked* girl!" She stomped upstairs.

*   *   *

There was a heavy feeling in the house after that, and Christmas was a dour affair, with no tree and few gifts or decorations ("Disgraceful waste of money," Aunt El sniffed). There was cake, though: a dense creation that looked like a brick and tasted like a punishment. We ate it anyway, and I played carols on the piano while Toby dozed and Aunt El knitted something useful and unlovely for a poor child. I had quietly sent a Christmas card to Rosedale, hoping Raymond would like the picture on the front, even if he didn't understand the meaning.

I was sorely in need of a distraction, so Porter's New Year's Eve fancy dress couldn't have come at a better time. Reilly and I managed to concoct a credible Queen of the Night disguise from a black velvet gown, a length of cheap black gauze and some spangles. The effect was striking: I glittered with every step.

Promptly at ten on New Year's Eve, Toby and I joined the throng streaming into Porter's grandiose palace on Park Lane. We flowed up the stairs and into the ballroom, which rose the entire height of the house and was designed for grand entrances. Guests strolled along the balcony that wrapped around the room, then processed down a sweeping gold and silver staircase to the main floor.

Toby and I paused on the balcony and looked at the throng below. The crème de la crème of the see-and-be-seen crowd was already dancing to the music of an orchestra concealed behind a wall of potted palms. Dowagers bunched and gossiped. Husbands wondered how long before they could escape to the leathered embrace of their clubs, so blissfully free of jazz and plotting women. Far above, Bacchus smirked from the skylight he adorned, surrounded by centaurs with pipes and naughty-looking putti.

It was a bright scene—bright as could be—and yet I couldn't help but feel there was a certain desperation to it all. That we were all dancing, drinking, laughing, calling for the band to play another tune, but *faster* and *louder*, so we could drown out the ominous scratching of the wolves at the door and the rumble of thunder in the distance.

Or maybe that was just me.

"Right, then." Toby helped himself to two champagne flutes from the tray of a passing footman and handed me one. "Here's to putting 1930 behind us."

I tried to set aside my dark turn of mind. "I'll certainly drink to that." We clinked and sipped, and I finally spotted Cee below, dressed as Maid Marion. As she looked up, I waved. Her bright smile increased its wattage and she bounded up the stairs, threading through couples attempting to make a dignified descent.

"Darling!" She threw her arms around me and kissed both cheeks. "Happy New Year! Oh, you look splendid, really spiffing. Hello, Toby, how are you?"

"Gracious lady." He bent over her hand. "The world is always that much brighter when you're near."

"Oh, you." She giggled and blushed. "Isn't this wonderful? Joyce has really outdone herself. She says there are going to be fireworks at midnight! Oh, and she promised Lord Dunreaven would be here." She smiled and nudged me.

I sipped my champagne with studied nonchalance even as I felt an unbidden thrill. But then I thought of Aunt El. *No one must know! Tainted blood, they'll say!* And Joyce, shrugging. *Not much money.* The champagne churned painfully in my stomach.

"There is some bad news, I'm afraid," Cee continued. "Millicent's decided to come. But we won't let it spoil our evening, will we? She's been in quite a good mood lately anyhow. Dunreaven came for tea yesterday and then took her for a walk in the park. She's preened over it ever since."

"I'm sure she has," I snorted, realizing, to my annoyance, that the mental image of Millicent and Dunreaven strolling arm in arm through Hyde Park irritated me.

"Oh, Astra," Cee chattered on, "You'll never guess who Lord Beckworth is dressed as: Robin Hood! Imagine that!" Her cheeks blossomed.

"Yes, *imagine that*," Toby parroted with a conspiratorial wink at me. That costume had been our doing, of course. As soon as Cee told me her costume, I had Toby suggest Robin Hood to Beckworth. "He'd been considering dressing as a rubber duck," Toby had reported. "I mean, *really*. You did the poor boy a favor, Astra."

"You two make the perfect pair, then," I said to Cecilia, who blushed deeper.

"He looks quite dashing," she admitted.

"Right. I must circulate. Ladies, if you'll excuse me." Toby gave us both an ingratiating smile before departing.

Cee and I linked arms and wound down the twinkling staircase. At the bottom, Joyce (as Cleopatra), David (Mark Antony), and Porter (Henry VIII) greeted guests.

"Ahh, lovely to see you, Astra." Joyce greeted me with a cheek kiss. "I'll tell Jeremy to look for the lady who dazzles tonight."

"Don't go telling him anything, Joyce," I said.

"Quite right, we should make him work for it," she agreed. "But not too hard, or it'll put him off. We'll talk later, Lovely—on to David and Daddy with you."

I shook hands with David, then faced Porter.

"What a beautiful sight." He enveloped my hand in a meaty paw weighted with rings. "You certainly have a sparkle about you, Miss Davies." He chuckled at his wit.

I tittered in return. "How charming of you to say so, sir. Thank you so much for the invitation. Marvelous party, as always."

"Joyce's doing, of course," he said. "It's good that someone here earns their keep." He glanced over his shoulder at David, who rolled his eyes. "But these things need a woman's touch, I feel." He leered, and I could feel my smile grow brittle. "You'll dance with me later, Miss Davies?" He just barely managed to make it a question.

"Oh, how kind of you."

He seemed satisfied with that and released me at last. Cee and I moved on. I saw Beckworth heading our way, tripping over his own feet in his haste.

"Cee, you need a dance," I insisted. "Don't you agree, Ducky?"

"Oh, I . . . yes, of course!" Beckworth agreed. "Lady Cecilia, would you, uh, do me the honor? Just to warn you, I tend to tread on toes now and again."

"You won't tread on hers," I reassured him. "Cee's an expert at making the roughest dancers look like Fred Astaire. Go on, Cee—don't waste the song."

"If you're sure you won't feel abandoned," she said, glancing from me to Beckworth even as her right foot started moving impatiently.

"Of course not. There are loads of people here for me to talk to. Go on!" I practically shoved her toward Beckworth, who took her hand and led her away.

As they dissolved into the crowd and I considered what to do next, a flash of yellow satin and jewels at the top of the staircase caught my eye. Millicent had arrived, pouffed and pomaded into Marie Antoinette. She paused, tapping a fan against her hooped-out skirts, looking down on everyone. A moment later, Lord Dunreaven appeared, dressed in a Russian folk costume: baggy black trousers tucked into knee-high boots and a royal blue velvet jacket trimmed in fur and embroidered in silver. A silver-blue silk sash with silver fringe was slung twice around his waist.

The sight of him, maddeningly, made my stomach jump in excitement.

Millicent simpered and took his arm so they could make their entrance together. Aunt El would have been shocked by such a display. I could practically hear her now:

"Surely they must be engaged, to arrive together so publicly? My word, the things young people get up to nowadays! It *never* would have been permitted in my day!"

I helped myself to another champagne and tried not to watch them make their grand entrance. What did I care who either of them arrived with? It wasn't going to spoil my evening. I was there to have a good time, and by God, I would!

I escaped into the adjoining dining room, which was dominated by an enormous gilded fountain spouting blood-red punch. A gaggle of young men gathered around it, daring each other to drinking contests and helping themselves to the astonishing array of food. One boy, drunker than the others and dressed as a jungle savage with a blacked-up face, grabbed a massive piece of pork pie and tried cramming it into his mouth all at once. I thought uncomfortably of Reilly's nieces and nephews, going to bed hungry.

"There's cake!" Toby announced, materializing with a laden plate. "What do you think, could we smuggle some of this back? Have you got any extra room in that dress?"

"Leave off, Toby!" I hissed.

"Oh, we've gone sparky. Don't frown at me, miss—you'll get wrinkles. What's got into you? Has Millicent oozed in?"

"She has, but it's not that."

"Well, whatever it is, don't let it spoil the evening. Here—" He put his plate aside and replaced my champagne with a glass filled with something grass-green. "Drink this and you'll forget all about Millicent. Drink two and you'll forget your own name."

I smiled and sipped the drink, which kicked like a mule. I took another tentative sip just as Dunreaven appeared in the doorway. His eyes swept the room, and he saw me and approached. "Good evening, Miss Davies."

"Good evening, Lord Dunreaven. I think you know my cousin, Toby Weyburn?" I gestured in Toby's direction.

Dunreaven shook Toby's hand, clearly trying to place him. "Oh!" He brightened. "Not Toby Weyburn from St. Dunstan's?"

"The very same." Toby seemed surprised to be remembered.

"It's good to see you again," Dunreaven said heartily. "We should catch up."

"How nice! Let's. But for now I think I'll stop third-wheeling and go make sure Buckoo Wallace doesn't drown himself in the punchbowl." Toby vanished and I discreetly set aside the lethal drink he'd given me.

Dunreaven turned his attention back to me. "Queen of the Night?"

"Well, that remains to be seen," I rejoined. "You look quite striking. You'll probably win first prize."

He responded with a self-deprecating smile. "I wondered if I'd overshot the mark. It was my father's costume. More suited to him. He enjoyed being stared at. I don't."

"People will stare at a titled bachelor no matter what he's wearing."

His mouth twitched. "I suppose so. Makes it devilish hard to know who really wants to spend time with Jeremy Harris, though."

"That'll be the ones who aren't staring," I told him.

"How very helpful you are, Miss Davies."

"I aim to be more use than ornament."

He smiled. "Well, you would have to be *very* useful indeed, then."

The way he was looking at me made the skin up and down my arms prickle. I swallowed hard and tried to think what to say next.

The boys over by the fountain howled over one of their comrades' feats, providing a welcome distraction.

"They're getting raucous early," I murmured, glancing over my shoulder at them.

Dunreaven followed my gaze and watched for a little while. "Everyone's looking for an escape," he commented. "This seems the perfect place to find it."

"I suppose." I gave him a questioning look. "What are you trying to escape?"

"Nothing!" He chuckled.

"Of course. You're trying to get into something, aren't you?" An arch smile and a glance toward Millicent, who was trapped in a ballroom conversation with the Dowager Duchess of Portland.

Before he could respond, one of the young men—sharp-featured, florid with drink, clenching a cigarette in an amber holder between two teeth—swung around the punchbowl, shouting "Miiiiissss Daaaavieeeeessssss!" He was dressed as d'Artagnan, and his actions knocked his curly wig askew, revealing sand-colored hair underneath.

He bounded over, took the cigarette holder out of his mouth, and said, "Freddie Ponsonby-Lewis."

"Not of the Vandemark Rubber family?" I responded.

"The same! The same!" Freddie grabbed my hand and pumped it vigorously. "We're in business together, you and I. Don't I feel the lucky one!"

In the background, I saw Toby grimacing.

"My, aren't you just the berries! You know, I thought most of the girls in New York were pretty, but by Jove, if you can't keep pace with most of 'em!" Freddie twirled me around so clumsily I nearly fell flat on my face. I was only saved by grabbing Dunreaven's arm and steadying myself. At the same time, he reached out and caught me by the waist, leaving his hand on the small of my back just a little longer than was strictly appropriate. I should have stepped away as soon as I had my balance, but I didn't.

"You're too kind," I said to Freddie, glancing at Dunreaven, who seemed to be trying very hard not to laugh. "And how did you find it there?"

"Brilliant place, really brilliant—just brimming with energy! Not like tired old London, ho ho! There's so much *pep* and *zip*! Everyone's doing *something*!"

"Are they? That's good to know," I said. "All we seem to hear about is how many people are out of work and how terrible it is."

"Oh yes, that." He shrugged and briefly struggled for something to say. "Well . . . even then people are doing something. Loads of them selling apples and things all over the city. You never go hungry there!"

I had no idea how to respond to that. Dunreaven certainly wasn't smiling now.

"And what brings you back?" I asked. "It doesn't sound like you missed London."

"Not a bit! But family, you know. Dad wants to concentrate on his chickens, so I'm running the business. Isn't that a pip?" He spread his arms wide in a "ta-da" stance.

I blinked at him in horror. My future—my ability to move home and support myself and take care of Raymond—was now going to hinge on *this person*?

"Oh, sorry chap," Freddie said, apparently only just noticing Dunreaven was there. "Pleased to meet you, Mr.—"

"*Lord* Dunreaven." Jeremy rose to his full height, looking down at Freddie the way he probably eyed up wayward midshipmen. It certainly had the same effect: Freddie looked cowed.

"Oh, right, then." Freddie nodded. "Well, if you're not going to claim this dance with Miss Davies, I will." He tried straightening his wig and held out a hand to me.

"So sorry, but I think I feel a twisted ankle coming on," I said.

Freddie's face puckered in confusion for a moment, then he smiled. "No trouble. The next one, then!"

"I'm afraid the next dance is claimed, old man," said Dunreaven, patting him on the shoulder. "Better luck next ball."

I glared at Toby, who finally extricated himself from the knot at the fountain and came over. "Come on, Freddie, you're only half in the bag. Let's see if we can get you *really* sozzled." He hooked an arm around Freddie's shoulders and led him away.

Dunreaven and I watched them go. I closed my eyes and thought of the flower opening while also counting back from ten.

"Might I presume to ask for the next dance?" Dunreaven asked, recalling me. "That is, if your ankle isn't bothering you too much."

"A miraculous recovery, it seems." I desperately needed the distraction. I took his arm and we returned to the ballroom just as the band shifted its tempo downward.

Dunreaven and I swept into the stream of dancers. "Are you all right?" he asked. "He seemed to upset you." He nodded toward the dining room and Freddie.

"Oh yes, I'm perfectly fine." I gave him a bright smile he didn't seem to believe.

"Are you really in business with him?"

"Not for long, I hope." We danced in silence for a little while. I noticed he smelled faintly of lemon, with a spicy-musky undertone that reminded me of bay leaves.

"What you said earlier," he began. "I think there may have been a misunderstanding. You don't think Lady Millicent and I arrived together, do you?"

"Didn't you? You came in together."

"That's just it. When I came in, she was waiting at the top of the staircase. She took my arm and we came down. What was I to do? I couldn't very well toss her over the banister."

"Why not? In those hoops she probably would have just bounced."

He laughed.

"Anyway, you can come and go as you please with whomever you please. Makes no difference to me."

"Doesn't it?"

I swallowed hard and avoided the probing look he was giving me. "You should partner her next, or her nose will be well and truly out of joint. No more cozy teas."

"A shame. I was hoping to monopolize you for a little longer."

"And why should you want to do that?"

"Why do you think?" He grinned and I shivered a little. "But if our time here is to be so limited, could we meet again, elsewhere?"

I couldn't help myself. Perhaps the champagne or that drink Toby had given me had gone to my head. Or perhaps the warmth of Dunreaven's arm around me was making me do foolish things. "I suppose you could pay me a visit at my aunt's."

His eyes flashed—an eager look, like someone just presented with a wonderful gift. "Will you be in tomorrow?"

Part of me screamed, *What are you doing? The last thing you need is more complications,* but I couldn't help it. I found myself saying, "I will."

The song ended. As couples dispersed or regrouped for the next dance, Millicent appeared beside us with a sickly sweet smile and dangerously glittering eyes.

"My, what a charming pair you make! You do enjoy your titled gentlemen, Astra!"

"I enjoy a good dance," I replied evenly. "All I'm after is a pleasant evening."

"And I'm sure you'll have *no* trouble finding a man to provide it."

Dunreaven's lips tightened.

"*You* might need a man to do it," I shot back. "I can manage on my own."

Toby appeared, flushed, lifting a glass and crowing: "Off with her head!"

Millicent scowled at him. "Is this that cousin of yours, Astra? The one who never gets invited anywhere?"

"Clearly not—I was invited here," Toby rejoined. "Though obviously they'll invite anyone." He gestured toward her.

"Toby, why don't we go catch up?" Dunreaven suggested, as Millicent made a brief lemon-sucking face before giving me a cool once-over.

"Is that costume your maid's doing?" she asked. "I'm surprised she didn't dress you all in red. Or have you come to your senses and sent your pinko packing?"

"She won't do that—Reilly's too good with hair," said Toby. "She might even be able to help you." He stepped back slightly with a pitying look. "Then again, probably not. Astra, can I steal you before Porter or Freddie come forth to claim their dances?"

"Yes, please do." I took his hand.

But before we could make ourselves scarce, Freddie came barreling out of the dining room alongside another young man, each of them carrying another friend piggyback style. The men getting the piggyback rides were urging their mounts on as if this were the Grand National.

"Tally ho! Over the hedge!" the boy Freddie was carrying shouted.

The foursome barreled straight through the dance floor, scattering Lindy-hopping couples. Millicent tutted in disgust. Toby chuckled, grabbed a glass of champagne from somewhere, and said, "I hope they invite Freddie again next year. This is the most fun I've had in ages!"

Chapter Seven

～

Although I didn't get to bed until dawn, I was still up early enough to enjoy a late breakfast in a blissfully quiet house—Aunt El and the butler were out, and Toby and the housemaid were both sleeping off sore heads. Once fed, I headed for the drawing room and sat down with Mother's ledger. After Freddie's performance the night before, it seemed more important than ever to fully come to grips with my finances.

I was ticking along quite well when I was interrupted by a soft knock on the door.

"Yes?" I called, a little irritably.

Reilly came in and announced, "The Earl of Dunreaven is here, miss."

"Bother," I muttered. I hadn't expected him to take me up on my invitation so quickly, and I was in no state to be receiving any guests. My hair was still twisted around pins and curlers, and I was wearing a cranberry wool skirt that was at least two years old, and a comfy but ancient gray wrap-front jumper. Not even any jewelry. At least I'd managed to get some lipstick on. Still, it was the sort of getup even a husband shouldn't see you in, according to the magazines I read.

"Miss?" Reilly whispered. "I could tell him you're not at home."

"No," I responded. "Not at home" was code for "Of course I'm at home; I just don't want to see *you*." It was a rebuff and a snub, and I didn't want to deliver either. After all, I *had* invited him. I gestured to my hair. "Help me with this, please?"

Reilly retrieved a comb from her pocket and pulled out hairpins with one hand while combing out curls with the other. In no time, I at least looked passable.

"Show him in, please." I stood, smoothing my skirt, making the best of things.

Dunreaven entered, perfectly turned out in a gray wool herringbone suit with a red carnation in his buttonhole and crisp, pressed pocket square. He was carrying a small posy of ruffly, scarlet ranunculus. I felt scruffier than ever beside him, but as soon as he saw me, a soft look came over his face. It was as if he *liked* seeing me this way.

"Good morning, Miss Davies. I hope I'm not intruding."

"Not at all, Lord Dunreaven. May I offer you some tea or coffee?"

"Thank you, no, I've had plenty of both already."

I nodded to Reilly, who withdrew.

"I must apologize: you've caught me unawares this morning," I admitted.

He shook his head. "No, I should be apologizing for coming so early and unannounced. But I brought a gift, in the hope I'll be forgiven." He held out the posy with a smile, and I accepted it. "I'll have you know I scoured Covent Garden for those this morning. There were white flowers everywhere, but I think red is more your color."

"You're too kind. That wasn't necessary." Nevertheless, I was touched.

"It most certainly was necessary! My grandmother used to tell me that one can arrive somewhere unannounced or empty-handed, but never both."

"What a very nice philosophy." I laughed. Setting the flowers down next to the ledger, I gestured for him to sit. "Please do have a seat, Lord Dunreaven. Sofa or armchair, it's your choice. They're equally uncomfortable."

"I'm sure I've felt worse," he reassured me, choosing the sofa.

I took the armchair. "We must thank the armed forces for making you all stoics."

"Yes, it does do that," he agreed. "A naval career offers many things: discipline, stoicism, and a chance to see the world, warts and all." I raised an eyebrow and he elaborated. "That is, to see the parts that aren't kept quite so tidy for the tourists." His face pinched momentarily. "You see things when you're off the beaten track. Things both beautiful and . . . less so."

I studied him for a moment. "Is that why you left the navy and came home?"

He shrugged. "I thought it might be nice to enjoy civilian life for a little while before I was called back into service."

"Is it really so bad?" My throat stuck at the thought of the misery wrought by the last war. I was very young, but I had certainly seen the results. Dozens of boys from the Hensley neighborhood had failed to return, or returned missing pieces of themselves—limbs, eyes, nerves. Every town and village had its memorial etched with row upon row of names. Cemeteries seemed overly full, and the second Sunday in November was now a day of black clothes and muffled bells.

"We'll be at war with someone," Dunreaven confirmed in a voice as somber as those bells. "India, Spain, Germany . . . I don't see how we can avoid it. All this unrest, it's bound to bubble over at some point. You can only placate people for so long."

I didn't like the idea of him going off to war. Or David or Beckworth or Hampton or any of the other men I knew. The thought of waterlogged trenches and ships blasted by torpedoes sent a chill through me. I needed to ease us away from this or risk bursting into tears.

"I should start traveling," I said in a falsely bright voice. "See the world while I still can."

Dunreaven seemed to rouse himself from a deep thought. He, too, brightened artificially. "I'm terribly sorry. What a dark subject I've brought up on a day that should be hopeful. Yes, do travel as much as you possibly can. It opens your eyes and mind in the most wonderful ways. And a change of scenery does everyone a bit of good."

"Mmm, an opportunity to get away from it all," I murmured without thinking.

He gave me an arch look. "And what do *you* want to escape from?"

"Secret admirers, Lord Dunreaven."

He laughed. "I thought ladies liked those sorts of things."

"Some ladies do," I allowed, "but I'm afraid I'm not one of them. I like a man who's not afraid to own his bouquets and mysterious notes."

He frowned. "I'll confess to the bouquet, but I don't know anything about notes."

"No? You didn't leave a note in my room at Gryden Hall?"

He chuckled. "As you well know, I prefer a more percussive form of communication. It sounds as though I have a rival."

"Then you'll both be disappointed, I'm afraid."

"Is that so? That's not something I'm accustomed to hearing."

"I'm sure it isn't. Your face and title must smooth the way enormously."

"Not always, clearly."

"One can't have everything. Weren't you taught that when you were young?"

A fleeting smile. "I was. And yet, I keep expecting things. Or hoping for them."

"'Hope springs eternal in the human breast,'" I quoted.

"It does. And what do you hope for, Miss Davies?"

"Peace. In all things."

"I very much hope you get it."

I sighed. "Right now, that seems unlikely."

"Oh?"

"If you had someone like Freddie in your life, would you expect a peaceful time?"

"I'm inclined to be optimistic about him. He's excitable and was enjoying himself overmuch. He's hardly the only one: half the men at the club were cradling pots of coffee and glasses of bicarb this morning. He may come all right in the end."

"How very generous you are to the boy." A bitter edge crept into my voice.

"Boy?" Dunreaven chuckled. "He must be close to my age. If he's a boy, then what am I?"

I laughed. "You? Why, you're a lord!"

"What, and is a lord not a man like other men?" he asked, clasping a hand dramatically to his breast. "If you prick us, do we not bleed?"

"Of course!" I answered spiritedly. "But the blood is blue."

"No, no, I assure you, my blood's as red as any other man's."

There was a devilry to his smile, and my heart sped up.

"I have a confession to make," he told me. "I came here today hoping to catch you off your guard, but now I see you're too clever for that."

I arched an eyebrow. "Do you want to rattle me?"

"Maybe a little," he responded, again with a roguish smile. "As I said last night, I want to get to know you. I thought it might be easier when you haven't had time to plan clever responses to fob me off."

Now both my eyebrows shot up. "Do you think that's how I spend my time? Anticipating what you'll say so I can bank my witty replies?"

"It seems to be what a lot of women do."

I narrowed my eyes. "You don't think much of the fairer sex, Lord Dunreaven."

"Quite the contrary, Miss Davies: I think about certain members a great deal."

"This is starting to sound dangerously like flirtation, Lord Dunreaven."

He leaned toward me, eyes gleaming. "Are you afraid you'll have to call Toby in to defend your honor?"

"I'm perfectly capable of defending it myself, thank you," I answered briskly.

"You are indeed," he agreed. "Where is Toby anyway? It's very quiet."

"Everyone is either out or nursing headaches," I explained. "Toby gave the staff a bottle of something nice. A way of thanking them for sticking it out for another year."

"Is it really so terrible?" he asked.

By way of answer, I gestured to the room.

He laughed. "I'm glad to know I wasn't wrong when I thought this didn't seem like your ideal surroundings."

"No, but it's not the sort of thing I have much control over. A girl can hardly live on her own and be considered respectable."

"Can she not?"

"Only if she's very careful. By which I mean she leads a very, very dull life."

"I should hate to wish that on you." He glanced at my piano. "Yours, I take it?"

I nodded as he walked over to it, running his hands gently along the smooth wooden curves as though he were getting a feel for it.

"A fine instrument," he declared. "May I?" He gestured to the keys. "Please do."

He seated himself. "What would you like to hear?"

"I always leave that up to the musician."

With a beguiling grin, he began playing "Stardust."

I chuckled once I recognized it. "You play well."

"Not nearly as well as you."

"It's expected of me. Boys and young men are given so much to do—you're meant to go out and accomplish things. But girls are only meant to *be* accomplished. At suitably feminine arts, of course. Dancing, painting, music. I'm a hopeless painter, so . . ."

"But not a hopeless dancer," he pointed out.

"You're too kind. I think some credit must go to the partner."

He smiled and inclined his head in acknowledgment of the compliment.

"Who taught you to play?" I asked. "It's an unusual talent for a man."

"My grandmother," Dunreaven explained as he stumbled over a few notes. "I used to spend a great deal of time at the dower house when I was young."

"Did you? I don't know many boys who want to spend their days with their grannies. She must have been quite a lady."

He took his time answering. "Yes, she was," he said with a ghost of a wistful smile. "It was peaceful there."

I sensed a hurt there. A deep bruise that struggled to heal. I felt an urge to reach out and comfort him, so strong I clasped my hands together, to control them. It wasn't for me to soothe him. That was the job of a lover.

I cast about for another topic of conversation. "Will you stay in London?"

"I'm afraid not. I'm back to Midbourne in three days."

"Yes, of course. Those large estates don't run themselves. You've got all those tenants and farmers and the like looking to you for direction. I don't envy you that. Most days I feel it's quite enough to try to manage my own life."

"We're in agreement, then." He had finished the song and now glanced out the nearby window, absently twisting a gold signet ring he wore on his right hand. Round and round and round it went.

"You'll wear a track," I warned, nodding toward the ring.

He stopped worrying it. "Not much escapes your notice."

"Nonsense—plenty of things do. Just not the really obvious ones. Though I suppose I should be a good little girl and keep quiet about the things I see."

He turned to me. "Is that what they tell you to do?"

"Oh yes. Secrets are ammunition. We need to build up our arsenal for later use."

"You all sound frightening." He crossed to the window and looked out on the dreary street.

"You needn't worry," I reassured him. "Everyone's too busy trying to impress you to want to winnow anything out."

He turned to me. "Not everyone."

"Well," I said, shrugging, "as I said, no one can have everything."

"That's a shame." He sighed, returning to the armchair. "Because this year I am resolved to settle down."

"Are you indeed?" I tried to keep my tone light. "Well, you'll have no shortage of takers eager to help you whip Midbourne into shape. In no time at all you'll be drowning in a sea of satin debutantes and their be-furred mothers. I hope you can hold your breath for a long time."

"I can. It's something else they taught us in the navy."

"Good. You'll need it. Once you make your intentions known, there will hardly be a girl in London who won't be chasing you down."

"Except you, it seems."

"Well," I said as blithely as I could manage, "my resolution is for 1931 to be far less complicated than 1930 was. I'd certainly like less upheaval, and nothing heaves one quite so much as a trip to the altar. Please don't take it personally. Besides," I added, crossing to the piano and tinkling out some Vivaldi, "Millicent's got her eye on you, and I'd really rather not draw down her fire on my head."

He watched me for a little while, then asked: "Has it always been like this between the two of you?"

"Like what?"

"Like a pair of tigresses circling each other."

"Gosh, you make us sound so exotic!"

He shook his head, bemused. "I admit it's entertaining, but it must be exhausting."

"It's not my doing. I'd be perfectly happy to be civil to her, but she won't have it. You saw how she was during the shooting weekend."

He sighed. "She did behave poorly."

"She's a good old-fashioned bully, and I have no patience for that. I'd heard you felt similarly."

He frowned and thought about that for a while. "I think you're a bit hard on her. She hasn't had an easy time of it, you know. It was very difficult when her mother died. Apparently her ladyship did not go quietly, and Millicent was there at the end."

I paused, the light tune suddenly seeming wrong. "I don't know anything about it," I admitted, abashed. "Cee was away when it happened and was told that her mother died of influenza. It was quick and she didn't suffer." I thought about how Millicent was before and after her mother's death and concluded, "But Millicent was always a bully."

"Still, we are all shaped by our tragedies, are we not?"

Oh, we are. I could already attest to that.

I began playing Chopin, and Dunreaven studied me in silence. Under his gaze I could feel a warmth creeping up the back of my neck.

"Are you working me out?" I asked.

"I wouldn't dare try! Puzzling you, I think, is a better way to phrase it."

"Have you got me puzzled out then?"

"No, not in the least. And I think I like it that way. There's an air of mystery." He smiled playfully, but I didn't respond in kind. I didn't like him sensing my secrets. He began to look uncomfortable and returned to the window.

I continued playing and left him with his thoughts for a while. As the song drew to a close I said, "Why don't you tell me about Midbourne?"

"Midbourne," he breathed, joining me at the piano, "is a fine old house that's stood the test of time and deserves to be taken care of. It needs a woman's touch."

I smirked. "Hence your resolution. You're definitely looking in the right place if what you want is a wife to make you a comfortable home. Most of us were educated to a decorative degree. We're excellent at choosing wallpapers and arranging flowers."

I left the piano and fetched a cigarette. "May I offer you one?" I held up the case.

"No, that's all right," Dunreaven said. "I'm sure I've taken up enough of your time today. I only wanted to wish you a happy New Year."

"And to rattle me," I said with a smile. "A happy New Year to you too, Lord Dunreaven. I hope you get everything you wish for."

* * *

I turned twenty-four on the eighteenth of January and expected little more than a paper-dry kiss from my aunt and a cheery "Getting old, now, aren't you?" from Toby. So I was a little surprised to receive a large, rectangular envelope in the afternoon post. Inside was a watercolor painting on thick cardstock and a note on Rosedale stationary.

Dear Miss Davies,

Raymond wanted to send you a little something to wish you a happy birthday. Many happy returns.

Sincerely, Jane Kitt

Raymond knew it was my birthday? And he painted? It hadn't occurred to me that he would have hobbies or interests—Aunt El made him seem incapable of doing much at all. Clearly, that wasn't the case.

Mother had been a painter. I'd always been sorry I had no talent for it. Was this something she was able to share with him? It touched me to think of the two of them, side by side, painting away in companionable silence or encouraging each other's work.

The picture was a little clumsy—like something a young child might produce—but so bright and cheerful it made me smile just to look at it. Raymond had painted me flowers. A row of stems with smeary blossoms on top. How did he know I loved flowers?

There wasn't time to ponder that further because all of a sudden Cee burst into the drawing room, squealing, "Happy birthday, darling!" and throwing her arms around me. Joyce followed at a more sedate pace, looking around in undisguised horror as I set Raymond's painting aside.

"God, this place," Joyce murmured. "It's just like your aunt, isn't it? Dark, narrow, and devoid of comfort."

"I don't know," said Cecilia, "it's rather quaint. Dickensian."

"Yes, Bleak House," Joyce rejoined.

"Joyce, for heaven's sake, don't be unkind!" Cee chided.

"I'm sorry," Joyce said, without a hint of contrition. "Happy birthday, Astra. I just can't imagine why you want to stay here."

"Oh," I said, kissing her cheek, "it's so lonely in the countryside, and buying a place in London seems such a bother."

Joyce rolled her eyes as she perched gingerly on the sofa. "Don't tell me about that. David's been so sulky about staying at Daddy's that I told him we should find a house of our own in Town. But it's *such* a bore looking at houses, and you can never find one that's just right, can you? Anyway, I've got my hands full with everything we're doing at Wotting. I practically had to gut the place."

"Oh, Astra, who sent flowers?" Cee asked, bouncing in her seat and pointing to the bouquet of roses that had arrived that morning.

"Just a friend."

"Friend indeed," said Joyce with a wicked look. "No friend sends roses." Before I could stop her, she walked over to the bouquet and picked up the card. She read through it, and her eyes drifted up to meet mine as she held up the card for Cecilia to see. "'Many happy returns— J.H.' In *Morse code*."

Cecilia clapped her hands over her mouth as her eyes widened in delight. "Oh, Astra, darling—*Jeremy!*"

"Don't tell Millicent," I pleaded.

Cecilia shook her head solemnly. "Our secret, darling. Oh, how marvelous!"

Joyce replaced the card and returned to her seat. "Well, I'm sure our gifts will pale in comparison, Cee, but let's find out, shall we? Jeffries? Bring forth the offerings!"

The door opened and the butler entered, carrying a covered basket at full arm's length. His head was turned away, as if it contained a pungent dragon. He set it down in front of me.

"Will that be all, miss?" he asked me, edging back toward the door.

"Yes, thank you, Jeffries."

"Open it up!" Cecilia urged as the basket rocked and whined. I lifted the lid and up popped the velvety, honey-brown head of a King Charles spaniel puppy.

"Oh, Joyce!" I cried, scooping up the little creature and cradling him. He licked my chin, then looked around the room and whimpered. "Is he one of Louly's?"

Joyce nodded, patting the puppy on his waggling rump. "The only boy of the lot. He's the perfect man: lovely to look at, doesn't answer back, and with proper training, will do whatever you want. Much better than a husband."

"Joyce, really," I chided. Joyce smiled a little mischievously. The puppy wiggled, so I put him down and let him explore. He had Blenheim coloring, all brown and pearly white, with a kissing spot on the top of his head and a freckle-like spattering of spots over his snout. Everything about him invited affection and cuddles.

"I adore him! Thank you so much," I gushed.

"Your aunt won't mind, I hope?" Cee asked tentatively.

"I'll win her over," I replied with more confidence than I felt. Reilly had been bad enough, but a dog? That would take a lot of persuading. And I sensed she was still sour with me over my Rosedale sleuthing.

"All right, Cee, your turn," Joyce invited.

Cee, bouncing up and down in her seat as if she were being electrocuted, produced a postcard with a flourish. On one side was a picture of the Eiffel Tower, and on the other a message:

Twenty-four, darling! You deserve a nice trip to Paris. My treat! We'll go for the spring shows and spend ourselves silly! I'll accept no refusals!—Cee

"Cecilia!" I gasped.

"Oh, darling," Cee reached over and grasped my hand, eyes shining, "we're going to Paris, the three of us. And I'll treat you to a few dresses too."

"Oh, Cee!"

"There, now!" She bounced to her feet. "Joyce and I have agreed that this is going to be your best birthday ever, so now we're taking you out to lunch at Claridge's. We'll toast your next year with a glass of fizz and have a good, thick slice of cake. Maybe if we ask nicely, they'll put a candle in yours."

I smiled at them, feeling my eyes sting a little. How lovely these two were! They didn't even know how much I needed this. Needed *something* good and unreservedly joyful, after my parents and Raymond and this mess with Vandemark Rubber.

I was stuck with that, by the way. When I asked Edgry about selling my share, he'd laughed and said I could try, but no one would buy it. Porter was talking about taking his business elsewhere, and Freddie's behavior at the ball proved he was too unstable to run anything. And the Ponsonby-Lewis family didn't have the money to buy me out. So I'd need to find a way to make this work. Somehow. I was starting to think it would take a miracle, and I've heard those are hard to come by.

"You're wonderful, both of you," I said warmly. "Really, really wonderful. Thank you so much for my gifts."

Near the window, the puppy growled and lifted his leg against one of the curtains.

"Oh dear," Joyce said mildly. "Now you'll have to get new ones. Shame. Let's go and leave the puppy in here. With any luck, your aunt will be forced to redecorate."

Chapter Eight

∾

The weather took a foul turn the day of our departure for France. By the time we reached the ferry at Dover, rain was sheeting down, and the Channel was waving white-capped fists of fury at the sky. A rough crossing, to say the least. And poor Joyce is a terrible sailor at the best of times. Lunch on the train afterward restored her, though, and by the time we arrived at the hotel, she was chattering away about the plans she'd made.

"Schiaparelli tomorrow morning, and then we're all going to see Josephine Baker because I want something to really shock David with when I get home," she explained as we strode into the lobby of the Ritz and the maids peeled off to check us in. "And we'll do Lanvin, and Chanel, of course. Oh, I say, is that Belinda?"

We all looked toward the staircase where, sure enough, Belinda Avery was perched, wide-eyed, drinking it all in.

"Belinda! Belinda!" Cee squealed.

Belinda jumped, searched us out, and her face lit up. "Oh! Oh!" she cried, bounding over. "Oh, I'm so happy to see some familiar faces!"

"At this time of year, with all the ateliers open? You'll be seeing nothing but familiar faces," I reassured her as we all took turns embracing.

"But you're the first, and it's so lovely to see you. Isn't this all too, too wonderful? Oh, girls, I'm here to buy my trousseau! We've set a date, Georgy and I: the twenty-third of May, at Rakesburn. And you're all going to be invited!"

Rakesburn. I perked up. That was just a few miles from Hensley.

Cee giggled and hopped, clapping, then threw her arms around Belinda again. "I'm so happy for you!"

"I'm sure Lord Hampton can't wait for the day," I added. "He must have been sad to see you go on this trip."

Belinda nodded vigorously. "Awfully sad, my poor little thing. I almost thought he'd cry, but he bore up and even came to the station to wave me off. I think Mama's put him in a bit of a state, and he was almost afraid of me going, as if Paris is simply full of prowling Frenchmen—it's not, is it? Not really? Anyhow, I reminded him that Lord Beckworth was here, so I'd have a friendly gentleman I could call on if I was ever in trouble. That made him feel much better. He likes old Ducky. But then, who doesn't?"

"Beckworth? He's coming to Paris?" Beside me, I could almost feel Cecilia's cheeks pinken with delight.

Belinda's eyes widened and she clapped a hand over her mouth, like a little girl who's just blurted out a friend's secret. "Oh, dear, I hope I didn't blunder. I thought you would know."

"He's just visiting his mother," Cee excused.

"Oh yes, I'm *sure* that's it," Joyce said as the maids rejoined us and porters began collecting our luggage. "We'd best be off to get settled, Belinda. See you soon!"

"Belinda's such a sweet little thing," Cecilia commented as we processed upstairs. "I think it'll be nice to have her around while we're here."

"A protégée for you, Cee," said Joyce. "And speaking of additions: when does Millicent arrive? I'd like to be prepared to evade her."

"Later today. But she won't be staying with us. She's always hated sharing."

"*Quel surprise,*" said Joyce. "I'll bet she had her own little corner in the nursery, marked off by a chalk line nobody could cross. Right-o, this is me." She, her maid, and the porters stopped at the door to her suite. "See you both for dinner."

Cee and I were just next door, in a Louis XV–style suite as pink, white, and gold as Cee herself.

"Do you like it, Astra?" Cee asked as I poked a head into my bedroom.

Did I like it? What wasn't to like? And *God*, how I needed this. Two weeks of pampering and an escape from all my wearying cares. "What a question! I love it, Cee!"

Cecilia beamed.

"Now, then," I said, settling down on a dainty sofa, "what's all this between you and Beckworth? Have you been hiding something?" I gave her a meaningful look, and she turned the color of the roses in the cut crystal vase next to her.

"No, not at all! Didn't you know he was coming to France?"

"Of course not. Why would I? He and I are friendly, but it sounds like there's a bit more to it between him and you." I smiled teasingly.

"Oh, well, it's just that Ducky and I had a lovely time dancing at Mr. Porter's ball, and we talked a bit there, and he asked if he might call on me, and I said it was all right because you said you wouldn't mind. You don't mind, do you, darling? Because of course I'll send him off if you do." Her face pinched in concern.

"Don't be silly, Cee, of course I don't."

"I told him we were coming to Paris, and he said he'd been thinking of coming over as well because he hadn't been to see his mother in a while. He asked if he might look in while we were here."

"Well I think it's marvelous that you and he have sparked so nicely. You make a charming couple," I declared.

A pearly smile broke through the blush, which went just a shade darker. "He *is* awfully nice. And so gentlemanly and attentive."

"Which is just what you deserve, you sweet thing." I rose and embraced her. "You're the dearest person I've ever known, and I want nothing more than to see you embarrassingly, deliriously happy. If he ever fails in that, just say so and Joyce and Laura and I will sort him out."

"Oh, Astra, I wish I could see you happy with someone," she breathed, squeezing my hand.

"I'm perfectly happy as I am. I'm rather enjoying my independence," I reassured her, though I couldn't help but feel the slightest twinge of envy. How wonderful it must be to be so perfectly happy just at the thought of someone. Unbidden, Dunreaven popped into my head, smiling devilishly. With some effort, I shoved him right back out again.

"But you'll want something else someday. Surely nobody wants to be on their own forever." Her face glowed and she clasped my hands. "You'll want a nice family and a cozy home and evenings in front of the fire with someone who adores you." She sighed and gazed dreamily out the nearest window, which overlooked the Place Vendôme.

"Perhaps I'll want that someday," I agreed, wishing my life was simple and straightforward, like hers. But everything around me was such a snarl, I couldn't even imagine throwing a romance into it. "Today, I'm perfectly happy with you and Joyce and this beautiful place and the prospect of two wonderful weeks."

"It *will* be perfect, Astra!" Cee promised. "And if it's not, well, we'll just have to try again. That's what the autumn shows are for, isn't it?"

*　*　*

Cecilia had wrangled excellent seats at Schiaparelli's select showing, where the chicness of the showroom was exceeded only by the smart clientele. Europe's titled families had sent along their most fashionable young members to see and judge, and to be seen and judged in their turn. It was as thrilling as it was frightening.

"They do know how to do things nicely," Joyce commented, with a sweep of the room that swiftly appraised all she saw.

"But of course, darling," I said, as a waiter approached with flutes of champagne. "This is Paris!"

"And we may as well enjoy it while we can." Joyce sighed. "It feels like soon we won't be able to travel anywhere at all. So many countries simply losing their minds—poor France will end up quite isolated if it doesn't run mad as well."

"Oh, let's not think of that," Cee begged. "This is meant to be a nice holiday."

"Quite right," Joyce agreed. "Now, I don't know about you two, but I intend to spend recklessly. Do you think skirts will be shorter this season, or keep dropping? Much farther down and we'll be back in our grandmothers' day. Astra's aunt will be the height of fashion!"

On the opposite side of the runway, Millicent perched on a gilt chair, like a buzzard ready to pick over the offerings. She greeted her sister with a curt nod.

A hidden chamber orchestra began to play, and models strolled down the runway. A hundred pairs of eyes ate up the details, some filing them away to be passed along to slightly more cost-effective dressmakers later.

"Conservative this year," Joyce observed partway through.

"I don't think so. They're just finding new ways to be daring," I countered, admiring a silk evening gown the color of rubies. The material flowed and shimmered like water, draping suggestively over the body of the woman wearing it, and the deep plunge at the back was almost shocking.

"You must try that one on, Astra," Cecilia decided. "It's perfect for you."

"All right." There was no harm in trying, was there?

As soon as the show finished, the *vendeuses* descended, ready for rich sales.

"Miss Davies will try Rose Red," Cecilia told one of them in French, indicating me. "And I'd like these, please." She pointed to the clothes she'd circled on her list. The *vendeuse* looked expectantly at me, and I handed her a list with just a few things marked, mostly for form's sake. She glanced at it and gave me a raised-eyebrow appraisal that seemed very French indeed.

"You should really try more, Astra. You're here to enjoy yourself," Joyce urged.

I shrugged. "I only saw a few things I liked. And I don't want to spend my whole budget on the first day."

"Budget?" Joyce seemed confused by the very idea. She handed her own list over to the *vendeuse*, who sped off to arrange the fitting rooms. I noticed that Millicent had gathered no fewer than three *vendeuses* around her. They were smiling and fawning so much she must be spending a fortune.

"Anyone would think she was buying a trousseau," Joyce smirked, following my gaze. "And doesn't she wish!"

A young woman in a simple but perfectly fitted suit appeared at Joyce's elbow and led us down a hallway, lined with mirrors, to three fitting rooms grouped at the end.

In my room, the evening gown and a few day dresses waited, along with a fitter wearing a tape measure around her neck like a scarf. I couldn't resist: the gown came first. The fitter helped me into it, then gently patted and tugged here and there to make the garment lie properly. Once she was satisfied, she turned me to face the looking-glass.

It was deceptively simple, this gown: sleeveless, floor-length, and bias cut, so it hugged the curves in all the right places. The neckline skimmed my collarbones in front and plunged into a spine-baring drape in the back. Long, triangular silk chiffon accents spread from the waist to the hem of the short train. The rich silk lay on my body like paint, and the shade of red brought out my coloring and the chestnut shine in my hair. It was, without a doubt, the most beautiful thing I'd ever put on.

"Are you ready in there?" Cecilia called.

"Yes."

Cecilia slipped in, wearing a fluttering, ruffled white dress.

"Oh, it's perfect on you, darling. Didn't I tell you?" Cecilia cried. "Just the right color. You'll positively stop traffic in that!"

"Gathering at Astra's today?" said Joyce, sweeping in. "Oh, that was simply made for you, Astra. You must have it. Doesn't even need changing or much fitting: you could have it as-is. Maybe just a slightly longer train . . ."

"Yes, you have to have it," Cecilia seconded.

Like Adam with the apple, I was sorely tempted. Didn't I deserve some sort of treat after the year I'd had?

"How much is this?" I asked the *vendeuse* who was hovering at the edges of the peach velvet curtains embracing my fitting room.

"Thirty thousand francs, Mademoiselle."

I swallowed hard. That was more than £250.

"It's a steal. Buy it, Astra," Joyce ordered.

It had been stupid of me to even ask the price—I knew all along I couldn't afford it. But now I felt a little stuck. "Oh, I don't know." I shrugged and tried to look like I didn't care. "Not sure it's really my color."

Joyce and Cecilia gaped.

"But it's *perfect*!" Cecilia repeated, gesturing at my reflection. "Just look at yourself. It's lovely, just like it was made for you!"

"Really, Astra, don't quibble with perfection," added Joyce. "Treat yourself."

"I don't know that I want to spend so much on one dress." I hoped my desperation didn't show. "It's irresponsible. Aunt El has been after me about my spending lately."

Joyce frowned. "What business is it of your aunt's what you do with your own money?"

Cecilia pursed her lips and said, "I'll pay for the dress."

"You can't do that," I gestured for the fitter to help me out of it. She stepped forward reluctantly as the *vendeuse* muttered in French. Whatever she said earned her a sharp look from Cecilia, which shut the woman right up.

"Don't argue with me," said Cecilia. "I want to treat you. It's your birthday."

"What's all this?" Millicent poked her head in. "Honestly, Cecilia, you can be heard shrieking clear down the hallway. What are you buying now?"

"A gift for Astra," Cee answered stoutly.

Millicent cocked an eyebrow. "Surely Astra can afford her own clothes?"

"It's a birthday gift," Cecilia insisted.

"You do live well at my family's expense," Millicent said to me. "I can't wait to see what Astra gives you for *your* birthday, Cecilia. Excuse me, ladies."

As she left, I realized I'd been gritting my teeth. My jaw ached in protest as I relaxed it.

"Ignore her," said Joyce. "The dress is perfect; you must have it." She, too slipped out, followed by Cecilia, who smiled nervously at me before leaving.

So the dress would be mine after all, which made me feel just a little giddy. I made an appointment to come back to be fitted and discuss any changes I wanted made to it, then dressed and returned to the showroom to wait for Joyce and Cee.

While pretending to be fascinated by a collection of new-season hats, I sensed Millicent slithering up behind me. I faced her with an empty smile, hoping I wasn't about to be turned to stone.

"Afternoon, Millicent. How are you finding Paris?"

Instead of answering, she studied me coolly. "You're quite good at taking things from other people, aren't you?" she finally observed.

"Not at all. That seems to be your area of expertise."

One corner of her mouth quirked upward. "I suppose you're referring to that grubby little note of yours?"

"So you admit you took it?" I was surprised she'd confessed so easily.

"I'm amazed you would even bring that up," she said, lips fluttering once again. "No well-bred woman would ever be so forthright about carrying on with an engaged man. And with his *darling* fiancée under the same roof!" She clucked and shook her head. "But what else should one expect from someone like you?"

I rolled my eyes. "Millicent, you're talking utter nonsense."

"Nonsense? Then Lord Hampton was *not* already engaged to Belinda Avery when you received his note?" She crossed her arms and smirked like she thought she'd just won something.

"*Lord Hampton*? You think *he* wrote the note?" I burst out laughing. "What an absurd accusation! Everyone with eyes or ears knows he's absolutely gaga over Belinda. Why on earth would he be sending love notes to me?"

Millicent sniffed. "Some men simply can't help themselves when there's a young woman *throwing* herself at him. And the way you were behaving that weekend—" Her nostrils flared, and she made a disgusted noise. "There wasn't a man safe. I'm surprised you didn't try getting your claws into the footmen. But then, I've noticed many young women tend to run wild and forget how to properly behave once their mother's gone."

"Is that *your* excuse?" I retorted.

Her nostrils flared again, now in genuine rage, but she kept herself in check.

"You'll want to watch your step," she warned. "I still have the note."

"What good is an unsigned note? How could you even know it's from Hampton?"

"The handwriting matches his message in our guest book exactly," she announced, pulling herself to her full height and looking down on me in triumph.

"Aren't you a regular Miss Marple," I sneered. "You'll have quite the career ahead of you, once your spinsterhood is established." Her eyes flashed, but I wasn't done. "Who would you show the note to? Belinda? She's so mad for Hampton she'd probably forgive him instantly, and then she'd *hate* you. That's if she believed you to begin with."

"Oh, she'll believe me. I'll make her believe me. And she'll thank me for it too. You're quite correct, she probably would forgive Hampton. But she'd *never* forgive you. And what would everyone else say or do once word of this started trickling out? They'd excuse him—he's a man, we expect them to wander off the path now and again. But it's quite different for ladies, isn't it? What would Cecilia say, if she knew her best friend was a homewrecker? What would your aunt say?"

She had me there. I could call her bluff—how many people would believe the proof, even if they had it right in front of them?—but I'd only be provoking her to give it a try. And it would only take one or two people to believe it for the damage to be done, especially if one of those people was Belinda. And that would be it: no more invitations. *A harlot,* they'd whisper. *No shame, no shame at all. Lord knows what she'd do to get ahead.* There was no escaping that kind of reputation. And Aunt El would be apoplectic. I was already in her bad books.

"What do you want, Millicent?" I spat, not wanting to appear defeated.

But she grinned, realizing she'd won this battle. "I want you to go back to swimming in your own pond. Lord Dunreaven is not for the likes of you."

"This has the stench of desperation about it, " I scoffed. "If you want Dunreaven, have him. I'm not in this game; I'm merely a spectator."

Her eyes narrowed as she studied me. "You are a devious woman," she declared.

"Me? *You're* the one resorting to blackmail!"

"Are you two fighting nicely?" Joyce asked, strolling over. Cee hovered in the background, looking anxious. "I hate to interrupt, but Astra has terribly interesting things to do today. Millicent, that dress you had on earlier was perfectly hideous. I do hope you bought it. Come on, Astra." She slipped her arm through mine and led me away.

* * *

The encounter with Millicent put such a dampener on the day that I couldn't even face an afternoon of shopping. I begged off and instead spent the time smoking and wandering the streets, turning things over in my mind and marveling at how my life had become such a bewildering mess in such a short period of time.

Had Hampton really sent me a love note? I found it hard to believe. He and I were friendly, but I'd never detected anything greater than mild warmth from him. And he'd hardly spoken two words to me that weekend at Gryden, so enamored of Belinda was he.

But then, some young men do panic when faced with matrimony, and look to sow some wild oats. And what was it Aunt El had said? *He was so solicitous at your parents' funeral. I'm sure you could make some inroads if you just tried.*

Perhaps Millicent had it wrong, and someone else had sent the note. But who? It could have been anyone. Even Millicent herself, trying to trap me.

Not that it mattered. All that was necessary was for a few people to believe I was carrying on with him, and I was done for. Flung out into the frigid night just as surely as I would have been if they found out about my financial status. And Millicent knew that, of course. She could dangle this over my head for years.

I sat down on a bench next to the Seine for a little while, watching the water flow by. A soothing moment, it put me in mind of childhood excursions I had taken with my grandfather in his little sailboat. My frantic mind began to settle.

There was a young artist nearby, sketching away with some pastels. Watching him work made me think of Mother, with her paints and easel, out in the garden on a fine day. And then I thought of Raymond, taking to his art as enthusiastically as she had. What would become of him if I were disgraced? There would be little hope of me being able to promote Vandemark Rubber if no one would speak with me. I would have to sell Hensley or keep tenants in the house to maintain the income I needed to pay Rosedale's fees. It was either that or consign Raymond to the terrors and upheaval of removing him from the only home he'd ever known. That was unthinkable.

So, galling as it was, I'd have to do what Millicent wanted. For now.

Arranged around the artist were his other drawings, and I impulsively bought one—a field of wildflowers—to send to my brother.

The light was deepening, and the artist began packing up his things. Time to go back and dress for dinner. As I reached the hotel, I met Beckworth coming out just as I was about to go in.

"Oh, Miss Davies! Nearly missed you!" he greeted me.

"Hello, Ducky. When did you arrive?"

"In Paris? Just two hours ago. I came to France to see my mother and . . ." He ducked his head and blushed. "Sorry to impose, but you aren't busy just now, are you?"

"No, not at all."

We strolled toward the Tuileries in silence for a while. It was a blustery evening. The wind whipped and plucked the skirts and overcoats of passers-by as they scurried toward the warm embrace of family and lovers. I watched them come and go, wondering about their lives while Beckworth bit his lip and fumbled his walking stick. He finally blurted out: "You must think I'm a terrible bounder."

"Why on earth should I think that?" I asked, genuinely puzzled.

"It's just." He stopped and sighed. "I-I have to confess, I came to France to see someone besides my mother."

I smiled warmly. "Yes, I know."

He looked startled. "Did you? I—it's just that I know your aunt had thought that you and I . . . That is, certain people thought that, well, that you and I might . . ." He took a deep breath and looked everywhere but at me.

I reached out and patted his arm. "Certain people thought we would get on and should be acquainted, and they were quite right," I said. "I hope I can always count on you as a *friend*, Ducky."

He looked up at me and visibly sagged with relief. The concerned furrow vanished from his forehead, and he grinned instead, a genuinely happy expression free from any anxiety. I could see now why Cee found him so handsome.

"Of course you can, Miss Davies, of course!" he said. "You know you—you're really cracking! A really good egg!"

"What a sweet thing to say! You're quite eggy yourself, Ducky."

He laughed.

"May I offer you a bit of advice?" I asked.

He nodded vigorously.

"Lady Cecilia is a true old-fashioned romantic, and I happen to know that she would absolutely *puddle* if she received gifts from a secret admirer. It doesn't have to be anything grand: a bouquet of flowers with a nice note would probably do the trick. Maybe pop a bit of poetry onto the note. Shakespeare's sonnets, something like that."

He nodded again, already mulling it over. "Right. Right! I'll go do that now. Thank you!"

* * *

Our last evening in Paris—had the fortnight really gone so quickly? Rushing past in a glorious blur of beautiful things and food and friends and *Paris*. Even Millicent had failed to spoil things. But then, she seemed to be too busy cultivating Belinda to pay us much mind after that day at Schiaparelli's. We'd seen them together again and again, at fashionable shops and ateliers, where Millicent kept insisting that Belinda try on one unsuitable creation after another because:

"They're all the rage this season. Everyone will be wearing one!"

When she didn't have Belinda, the girls and I did, taking her to much better shops and charming cafés. I showed her Versailles, relating all the detailed history my father had once imparted to me as she soaked in its opulence, wide-eyed.

We'd arranged for a last-night dinner at Maxim's, but at tea Cecilia confessed that she'd invited Beckworth to come along. Not surprising at all, really. He'd come through beautifully after my suggestion, dispatching a daily bouquet of pink roses and baby's breath, accompanied by a note with a few lines of poetry, signed with a sweet pencil drawing of a duck. Cecilia absolutely melted every time they arrived. Of course I wasn't going to tag along to their dinner. So, at half past seven she found me in bed, lights dimmed, an icebag on my head.

"Darling, what's the matter?" Cecilia cried, gazing at me from the doorway.

I groaned theatrically. "Terrible headache. So sorry, Cee. You go on without me."

She hesitated, shifting her weight back and forth from one foot to the other. "I don't feel like I should leave you alone," she finally said.

"I have Reilly if I need anything. Go on and have a lovely time."

"All right," said Cecilia, clearly out of arguments. Or, perhaps, not all that eager to press the issue. "If you're sure. Feel better, dearest."

"I will. Have fun!"

As soon as I heard the suite door close behind her, I sprang up, threw the icebag aside, and turned on the lights. I'd have to order up some dinner—I was famished. As I reached for the telephone, however, the suite door opened, and Joyce poked her head in.

She raised an eyebrow. "Headache?" She slipped into the room, dressed to lounge in silk pajamas, her hair in a net.

"Yes. Really awful, but it went away just like that." I snapped my fingers. "What was your excuse?"

"Exhaustion. Ordering dinner? Don't bother—I already did. Hope you don't mind. We'll have a nice picnic up here and save Maxim's for next time." She settled down on a sofa and lit a cigarette, offering me one. I accepted. "So," she mused, "Cee and Beckworth, eh? Well, I suppose she could do worse. He's not as bad as I thought."

I joined her on the sofa. "They'll be good for each other. And if he's taken, my aunt will have to stop trying to throw us together. A win all around."

Joyce laughed. "I suppose that leaves you free to focus your energies elsewhere?" She sent a frank look over the trailing smoke of the cigarette.

"You're not starting in about Dunreaven again, are you?" I asked wearily. "We're friends. We get on. But there's nothing more to it."

"Friends?" She looked skeptical.

"Can a man and a woman not be friends?"

"Of course they can, but you and Dunreaven aren't friends. You're more like . . . *friends*." She leaned forward on the last word, eyes lidded, and exhaled it as if she were Mae West. "Honestly, I don't know why you're so resistant."

"I don't know why *you're* so *insistent*."

"Is it so wrong to want a project? I've got a husband, Cee seems on her way, the house is coming along. What am I to do with myself?" she wondered.

"Have a baby," I joked, finishing my cigarette and going for another.

Joyce responded with a short, mirthless laugh. "That is the natural progression, isn't it? No sooner have you taken off the veil and the orange blossom than people start staring at your middle." She stubbed out her cigarette, leaned back, and contemplated the ceiling. "Perhaps you're wise to be cautious. Men come out of the woodwork for an heiress. We're quite the prize, a quick ticket to fame and fortune. The matrimonial summit of Everest."

I exhaled smoke. "Something to be climbed and conquered? A mound for a man to stick a flag in?"

Joyce laughed. "Something like that."

"You do make marriage sound appealing, Joyce."

"Oh, it has its benefits. I can assure you, the act of love is everything it's made out to be, and more. And it's nice to have someone to warm your feet in bed in the wintertime. But honestly, Astra, I worry about you a bit. You seem so . . . unsettled."

"Of course I'm unsettled, look at the year I've had."

"Yes, yes, of course, but you know what I mean. Living with your aunt, refusing to treat yourself on this trip, holding Jeremy at arm's length—even though you clearly like him. And your behavior with my father . . ." She looked at me sharpish. "Is that it? Is that why you're only 'friends' with Jeremy?"

"What on earth are you talking about?" I asked her, completely baffled.

"Do you think I'm an idiot?" she asked. "I saw how you were with him at Gryden. So *very* charming. And he felt it too—he talked about you the whole way home. 'Oh, that nice Miss Davies, we really should have her to stay sometime soon, don't you think, Joyce?' 'Oh, Joyce, what sort of music does Miss Davies like? Make sure the band plays it at the party!'" She rolled her eyes.

"I certainly didn't mean for him to take it quite . . . like that," I explained, suddenly feeling a little desperate. "I was trying to be nice to him since I know you were worried about Millicent upsetting him."

"Well, you were *very* nice indeed." She was silent for a little while, then sighed, "If you want him, I suppose it's all right. Better you than some little nitwit who'll give him a son and cut me out of the inheritance completely."

"That would never happen, Joyce. And thank you for the invitation, but I'm not interested in being your stepmother."

"Thank God for that! But you must admit, Astra, you are a bit odd nowadays. You just seem . . . I don't know—stuck, right when you should really be getting out there and living." She gestured expansively with her hands, as if she were scooping up the suite and all of Paris with it.

"Can one be both stuck and unsettled?" I wondered.

She waggled a finger. "I won't be distracted by your quibbling, young lady. I only wonder if you haven't gone off on your own because you need someone to attach to and provide some stability. If that's the case, I want you attached to the proper person."

"Like a climbing ivy," I observed. "And you think Dunreaven's a good trellis?"

"Why not? He's practically the perfect man."

"Indeed, almost too good to be true." I stubbed out the cigarette. "Joyce, I need a quiet and simple life just now, and there's nothing quiet about a romance with one of the Season's most eligible bachelors. And the last thing I need is Millicent shifting to all-out war. The occasional skirmish is bad enough."

Joyce frowned. "Why are you so worried about her? If you married Jeremy, what possible threat could she pose to you?"

I had to admit, she had me there. I'd been so concerned with the here and now I hadn't considered that. But of course, Millicent wasn't the only thing coming between Dunreaven and me.

Joyce suddenly took my hand. "Astra, is there anything you want to tell me?"

Oh, if only I could. But what would she say if I spilled my secrets? How would she react to my poverty? To Raymond? Impossible to tell. The risk was too great.

I smiled brightly. "No, Joyce. I'm fine."

Joyce looked skeptically at me as she went for another cigarette. "All empty." She sighed and stood. "I'll go get some more. If the food comes, don't start without me."

She was only gone a few moments before someone knocked quietly. Reilly emerged from my bedroom to answer, but it wasn't the expected waiter. It was a man from Schiaparelli's with my dress.

"Just in time! *Merci*," I said as Reilly held out her arms for the gown.

The man, however, wouldn't hand it over to her. Keeping a pleasant smile firmly anchored, he said: "I'm sorry, Mademoiselle, but I must ask for payment first."

Taken aback, I said, "It's supposed to be on Lady Cecilia Tyburn's account."

The man looked slightly uncomfortable, despite the smile. "I'm sorry, but the dress was taken off the account, and we were told not to put it back on," he explained.

"By Lady Millicent?" I guessed. How could I have not anticipated this? Was I too distracted by everything else to realize that *of course* she'd force me to pay for a £250 evening gown I didn't need? Dear God, Edgry had been right: I'd just spent it all on clothes, and it was only March. My pretend headache suddenly became very real. My entire body felt like it had been dunked in ice water.

The man's smile strained further. "My hands are tied. I'm sorry."

"Will you take a check?" I asked miserably. I couldn't refuse to take the gown, because it was customized now.

"Of course, Mademoiselle," he said. "And," he added hesitantly, "please don't forget the fees for rushing the job."

"Of course not!" Was there no end to this? I hastily wrote the check out and handed it over, trying not to burst into tears. He relinquished the dress to Reilly, who gave me a quick, meaningful look before disappearing with it.

Joyce returned a few minutes later. "Have I missed anything?"

"Nothing you need to worry about," I answered as someone else knocked on the door. Reilly returned to open it, handing me the icebag and an aspirin as she passed. This time it was the waiter. He wheeled a cart stacked with silver-domed plates over to the table.

"Excellent," Joyce said, rubbing her hands in anticipation. "Come on, Astra. Don't let Millicent's bad humor ruin some perfectly good coquilles."

Chapter Nine

～

I returned to England a great deal poorer and thoroughly dejected, though I put on a brave face for the journey home. I didn't tell Cecilia what Millicent had done: I didn't want to spoil Cee's jubilant mood after her dinner with Beckworth.

At home, I found Toby in the drawing room, stretched out on the sofa and smoking, of course. He looked up, grinned, and greeted me with: "*Bonjour, ma cherie!* How was Paris? Did you bring me pastries?"

"Drink, Toby, drink!"

Realizing the situation was serious, he leapt up and fetched me a whisky, neat. I sank onto the sofa with it. Dandy, the little dog Joyce had given me, trotted over and whimpered, pawing at my leg.

"Poor darling," I murmured, reaching down to pet him.

"Poor *you*, apparently," said Toby, settling down to my left. "What's happened? You didn't accidentally get married or something while you were over there, did you? It's all right if you did—Paris, you know! We can probably get it annulled if we hop to it."

"Don't joke!" I blazed before gulping down the drink. "Millicent, she—she forced me to spend three hundred pounds on a dress!"

Toby goggled. "What? How?"

I gave him the highlights and he slowly exhaled into the sofa, shaking his head. "I'm not going to lecture you," he reassured me after a few moments' silence. "I'm sure you've already kicked yourself up and down a few hallways. But *really*, darling."

"I know! I *know*!"

My shrieking convinced Dandy he'd be safer underneath the piano.

Toby patted one of my hands. "I wouldn't worry too much," he soothed. "You'll just have to stay here a little longer."

The thought of that, and a look around the cramped room with its sad furniture and poky fire and *ugliness*, made me want to cry.

"There's more," I continued gloomily. "Millicent's blackmailing me."

"Oh my God! Does she know about Raymond?"

"No! Thankfully!" Who knows what damage—to me, him, and the rest of our family—she might do with *that* information? "Apparently Hampton left me a love note at Gryden, and now she's got it and is threatening to show it around."

Toby stared, so perplexed he couldn't formulate questions right away. "But—but Hampton's dizzy as a daisy over Belinda. Why is he sending you love notes?"

"I wish I knew."

He sighed again. "Sticky wicket," he admitted, shaking his head. We both brooded in silence for a while; then Toby perked up. "I've got something that may cheer you," he said. "I was housebound with a miserable cold while you were away, and I was so bored I had a nice woman from Edgry's office send over some of your father's papers to see if there was anything interesting there. And wouldn't you know it: I found Pearl!"

I straightened up. "You didn't!"

He nodded, crossed to the writing desk and pulled a sheet of paper out of the drawer. He unfolded it and handed it over. "Pearl Insurance Company" was stamped across the top in grand, curlicued letters. It was a policy insuring my mother's life for £5000, to be split between two beneficiaries: myself and Raymond Carlyle.

I stared at the paper for several minutes.

"Was this the only policy?" I finally asked as Toby resumed his seat.

"I'm afraid so."

"Why on earth would he insure Mother's life and not his own? What was—" Something occurred to me suddenly, and I went dead cold. "Toby, was she dying?"

My mind frantically rifled through the months leading up to the accident, picking out clues here and there. I must have been a fool—or unbelievably self-absorbed—not to have noticed. My mother had changed in subtle ways. She'd been quieter and had gone out less in the evenings. Her appetite had gone off, and her coloring too. She'd looked wan, and her clothes hung oddly on her frame.

Father, too, had been different. He was preoccupied and a little thinner. The hearty greetings he met me with had seemed forced. Or perhaps that was just the patina I was applying to the memories now.

I remembered Father inviting me along on that last drive, saying it would put roses in my cheeks. At the time I'd thought Mother needed the fresh air and the roses.

Dr. Hartleby. A last hope, perhaps, for two people desperate for a miracle. My father would have done anything, including driving himself into debt, to keep my mother from disappearing. I had never known them to spend more than a few nights apart. He had looked to Mother for everything. How would he have managed, without her?

And all that time, I'd been experimenting with cocktails, dancing all night, and careening about London with brash young men. Buying new dresses and hats and useless things I didn't need. Had my parents kept this secret because they didn't think that I, a frivolous creature who seemed to exist for no purpose at all, would be of use to them? Or did they like that their daughter was bright and giddy, and worry about permanently popping the bubbles of my effervescent life?

Toby's face, so triumphant a moment ago, was now pinched with sympathy. He patted me on the knee and sighed. "I'm sorry, old girl, but I don't know what was wrong with your mother. Does it really matter now?"

It mattered. All of this was at the heart of how my parents had felt about me. The real truths about my life.

I swallowed hard and looked back down at the paperwork. "Raymond Carlyle," I murmured. Why did Raymond have our mother's maiden name, not Davies?

As though he'd read my mind, Toby said, "I wondered about the name as well. Was he . . . born before she was married, do you think?"

So not just an insane brother, an illegitimate one as well? I closed my eyes and wished for deliverance from this mess. Why had I ever telephoned Rosedale? Why couldn't I be content to be ignorant?

"Was this policy ever paid out? Did you find anything else?" I asked, trying to focus on the task at hand.

"No. Everything else was about the investments that went bust."

"I'll have to go to the source, then. It's about time I had a word with Mr. Edgry."

*　*　*

Dressed in my most sensible suit and armed with some of the more interesting documents from my father's papers, I arrived at the offices of Billington, Phipps, and Edgry precisely on time for my appointment. A pleasant-looking secretary paused her typing just long enough to ask me to wait "for just a few minutes." Seated on a chair that seemed designed for maximum discomfort, I watched the minutes tick by on the secretary's desk clock. Tick, tick, tick. Ten, then fifteen. Just before twenty, something on her desk buzzed and she told me I could go in.

I had never been to Edgry's office, and my first impression was that it had been decorated entirely from the Pompous range of office and professional furnishings. Everything was dark, hard, and massive, from the blocky walnut desk with its green leather blotter to the looming bookshelves filled with desert-dry titles like *The Disposition of Shared Assets in the Third Generation, Volume IV.*

Edgry himself was making a great show of being busy, scribbling away at something and refusing to acknowledge me. If he thought that would put me off, he was wrong. I took a seat opposite the desk and waited.

At last, he returned the pen to its stand, folded his hands, and looked up, exasperated. "This is not convenient, Astra. What do you want?"

"I want to know more about this." I slid the insurance paperwork across the desk.

He glanced at it. "An insurance policy on your mother," he said, as if I were completely feeble-minded. "Possibly one of the few sensible things your father ever did."

"I know what it is," I icily informed him. "I want to know more about it. Is there only the one? Was it ever paid out?"

"I only know of the one, and yes, it was paid."

"When?"

"Two months after your parents died." He began shuffling papers around, trying to look busy while avoiding eye contact.

"So what happened to this money?" I asked.

"The bulk of it has been placed in trust." Again, the paper shuffling.

"What do you mean, *the bulk of it*?"

He moved on to fiddling with the banker's lamp on the desk. "Well, I took my fees, of course," he finally admitted.

"You *took your fees*?" My fingers twitched, and I wondered if a jury would convict me for pummeling him with *Principles of Property Law*.

"Yes! I'm not operating a charity, Astra. My services do cost money, you know!"

"Of course I understand that. But you can't simply help yourself, Mr. Edgry. I never gave you permission to do so."

"It's how things worked with your father," he said gruffly.

"Well, I am most assuredly not him. And you yourself have noted that things weren't working so well for him. Now, who told you to put that money in a trust?"

He shifted uncomfortably in his chair. "I discussed matters with your aunt, and we agreed that it was for the best that I manage the payment. After all, you were clearly incapable of making any decisions. We had a doctor who was willing to attest to it."

"Which doctor?"

"Dr. Anderson, from Market Harborough. He's known you all your life, and we know he can keep a secret." Another nervous shift in his seat. "Your aunt didn't want word of your . . . *indisposition* getting out. Between that and the . . . person at Rosedale and your father's endless foolishness, people would start to say your family was quite touched indeed." He tapped his forehead with one meaty finger.

A white heat started to build in my chest and threatened to boil up into my face. I tamped it down, afraid it might come out as tears. My eyes must have blazed pretty fiercely, though, because Edgry actually looked startled. "Neither you nor my aunt had any right to make these sorts of decisions," I said, concentrating on keeping my voice even. "My parents' estate was left to *me*, and I'm not under age or permanently incapacitated. You took advantage of my grief."

His face reddened. "You ungrateful child! You should be thanking me!"

"Did my father thank you for this?" I demanded, practically throwing another document at him. It was the details of my father's investment with Clarence Hatry, all prepared by Edgry. The amount was so huge I had actually struggled to breathe for a few moments after I first saw it. "Clarence Hatry was a friend of yours, wasn't he? Was Father grateful for that introduction?"

Most of the color drained from his face. "Who told you I was friends with Hatry?"

"Oh," I said, my head cocked in a mocking imitation of innocence, "was it a secret? My father didn't seem to think so. He mentioned your kind introduction in his diary."

Edgry breathed heavily and slumped.

"I know all about your chum and his fraud," I continued in a tone so chilly even I was shocked by it. "How many of your clients did you convince to invest with him?"

Edgry started to rise, waggling a finger at me, face reddening once again.

"Now, Clary . . . Clarence was a good prospect," he gabbled. "Your father was desperate for something so he could meet expenses and keep paying that Harley Street quack, so he was throwing money every which way. I was doing him a favor. Clary's always come right, always made money for his investors. It's not his fault that things went awry this time. It was those damned Americans, ruining things!"

He dropped into his swiveling desk chair, which swayed alarmingly at the sudden shock of his weight. I kept my face perfectly still, not wanting to give him any ground. He may have made me cry before, but not this time.

"How much money did *you* have invested with 'Clary'?" I asked with a sneer. Judging from the quick purse of his lips, I guessed it was quite a bit. "You steered clients toward an unsavory investor because he was your friend and you were in deep yourself. I think you've been covering some of your losses by helping yourself to 'fees' from my account and, I'll wager, others as well. Is that where my brother's part of the insurance payment went? Into your bank account? Is that why Rosedale's fees went unpaid?"

It was a complete shot in the dark. Perhaps Edgry sensed that, because after fumbling with the pen for another moment, he pulled himself together and looked down on me with the same expression he'd had that horrible day at my parents' house. That mixture of pity and contempt that said he just couldn't imagine what it was like to be such an imbecile. It made me want to smash his jowly face in with the banker's lamp, spatter those dull volumes with blood. At that moment, I would have enjoyed it. But I kept my face impassive even as I dug my nails into my thigh.

"I didn't take his money," he said tightly. "I'm not at liberty to tell you what arrangements were made. Client confidentiality, you know." He looked smug.

"Perhaps someone else can explain matters to me, then, since you have a conflict," I suggested. "Mr. Billington's always been very kind. He was at my parents' wedding, you know. Gave them a lovely silver pitcher which I still have. I'm sure he'd be *quite* interested to hear about all of this and could explain to poor, silly me how things work and why it's perfectly all right to defraud your clients." I paused, letting that sink in.

Edgry stared me down for several long moments, then deflated into the chair. Something surged through me, made my heart quicken and my face feel hot. I felt like I could do anything.

I continued in that cool voice—the same one poor Officer Anson had once encountered, "You will return your 'fees,' Mr. Edgry, and undo this trust you've put the money in. You have until Friday noon to get everything in order, or we'll be having a very different sort of meeting. Is that suitable? *Convenient* for you?"

I watched as he blustered for a minute. Then he grudgingly nodded.

I got to my feet and extended my hand with a frigid smile. "Good day, Mr. Edgry. So *very* sorry to have bothered you."

*   *   *

My heart was still going at a brisk gallop as I stepped outside. It wasn't until I was around the corner and half a block away that it fully sank in: I had just outmaneuvered Edgry. I had struck out on my own—I could do this! I had got my money back. I could manage. Perhaps I would save Hensley after all! Yes, of course I would. I *would*!

I put my chin up and smiled, then strode down the pavement as if I owned all of London.

I caught a bus back to Chelsea and, daringly, sat in the open top deck because it was a fine day and I wanted to enjoy it. I ignored the sideways glances of the men seated nearby and enjoyed the bird's-eye view of London.

The air was clearer than usual, and everyone seemed to want to be out. The pavement surged with people: nannies in uniform pushing prams, businessmen in suits dodging dashing children, ladies in the sorts of hats usually worn to impress female friends. Newsboys bawled the headlines ("Prince of Wales wins over South Africa! Rally in Konigsberg sees ex-Kaiser's son beaten with a truncheon!") and an organ-grinding busker entertained a crowd with his dancing monkey.

In the street, a choking mix of cars, trucks, and buses vied for space with dangerously weaving messengers on bicycles and plodding horse-drawn carts. One driver, standing on a stack of crates with the reins of a pair of coal-black drays held loosely in one hand, used his free hand to make a rude gesture to a driver who'd honked at him. Another double-decker, with a poster that screamed, "BOVRIL!" on the side of it, passed us going the other way. The conductor hung off the staircase spiraling toward the upper deck, and called out a greeting to his counterpart on my bus. There was a powerful hum to all of this, an energy that seemed to be both exciting and exhausting.

I alighted near Aunt El's, grateful for the relative peace of the neighborhood. As I rounded the corner onto Gertrude Street, I spotted Reilly, who'd had the afternoon off, standing in front of the house, talking and laughing with another woman. Not wanting to intrude, I slowed my pace. The other woman reached out and gently brushed something off Reilly's lapel, and Reilly smiled in a way that brightened and changed her whole face. Another few words, and the woman turned away and began walking in my direction as Reilly unlatched the black-iron gate and descended to the servants' entrance.

As the woman approached, I noticed she was a fair bit older than Reilly—probably close to forty, if not past it, and she had orange-red hair worn in a low chignon under a black cloche. She seemed familiar, but I couldn't place her. As we passed, she glanced at me and then swiftly turned her face away, as if she didn't want me to see her.

Strange though that behavior was, I didn't have time to dwell on it. As soon as I walked in, I was greeted by Dandy, waggling joyfully, and the butler, who informed me that Lord Hampton was waiting for me in the drawing room.

"He's been waiting for *some time*," he added emphatically, making it clear he disapproved of my having forced a future duke to wait for me. He'd tell Aunt El about it, and I'd take it on the nose over dinner. I thanked Jeffries and went into the drawing room.

"Oh, Miss Davies," Hampton said as soon as I appeared, "I'm sorry for coming by unannounced, but, well, it seems there's been a terrible misunderstanding."

"Has there indeed?" I checked to make sure no servants were nearby to listen in and closed the door. "Will you take a seat, Lord Hampton?"

"It seems," he explained as he lowered himself into one of the arm-chairs (and winced), "that a note I intended to have delivered to my darling Belinda at Gryden Hall went astray and wound up on your pillow instead."

"I see." That did make more sense than Hampton suddenly deciding he was in love with me. And to be honest, it was a relief to know that wasn't the case.

"It was a silly thing, really," he continued. "All that talk about romantic gestures—I thought Bin would be charmed if she found a little note when she returned to her room. I asked one of the footmen to deliver it while I was out for the afternoon drive, but it seems he delivered it to the wrong lady. I'm so sorry for any confusion."

"No worry, there's no real harm done," I lied. "I'm glad it's cleared up."

He smiled, but in a rather brittle manner. "Well, that's just it: I think a bit of harm *has* been done. You—you don't still have the note, do you?"

"No, I'm afraid not," I admitted. "It . . . went missing from my room."

"It was taken," he said, face darkening, "by Lady Millicent."

"Has she been to see you?" Surely Millicent wouldn't have the audacity to try to blackmail Lord Hampton as well?

He nodded. "She came to see me today, just before I came here. She warned me that she could show Bin-Bin the note at any time. And, of course, Bin knows my handwriting." His face pinched in helplessness and concern. "I think Lady Millicent's a bit put out about . . . Well, you see, she and I . . . that is to say, there was an expectation . . ."

"It's quite all right, Mustard, I don't need the details."

He nodded, then burst out, "Astra, I'm not quite sure what to do! If I lost my Bin-Bin . . ." He bit his lip as if he were afraid he'd start crying.

I reached over and patted him on the arm. "I wouldn't lose sleep over it. I doubt Millicent will do anything to scuttle your wedding at this point. She's worked too hard to become friends with Belinda." Millicent wouldn't have bothered to put in the effort for a mere Honorable Miss Avery. She wanted a duchess in her stable of friends. Then again, she was probably incredibly bitter over having lost Hampton to Belinda. Perhaps she saw all this as some twisted chance at revenge.

"You're sure?" he asked hopefully.

"As sure as one can be," I answered as brightly as I could manage. No use worrying the poor boy any more. "What did she want anyway?"

"Oh," he looked down at his hands, embarrassed. "Well, she wanted to be a bridesmaid, but I told her that was very much out of my hands. I think I've appeased her by giving her a reading. Cousin Gertrude will be very put out, but . . ." He shrugged helplessly.

"You can be sure that won't be the last thing she'll ask for," I sighed. "Even after you're married, she can hold this over you. And me." The thought filled me with a fierce rage. Would I ever be free of this terrible woman? "I'm so sorry, Mustard. I should have warned you. I never thought she'd go after you as well."

"What, then, she's threatened you too?"

I nodded. "She threatened to show the note around if I didn't dance to her tune."

Hampton's face hardened. "Well, I've never heard of a lady behaving in such a manner," he declared. "It's simply not . . . well, it's not all right at all, is it?"

"No, it's not. But I don't see what we can do about it just now." I might have been willing to do battle with Millicent for my own sake, but there were others to consider. "Would it help if I didn't come to the wedding, Mustard?" The thought saddened me: Going north for the wedding would give me a chance to see Hensley again, and that was a balm I sorely needed. And I was fond of Belinda and Hampton and wanted to see them on such a happy day.

Hampton thought for a moment, then set his jaw. "No, certainly not. Belinda wouldn't allow it. She's spoken endlessly of you and the other girls since you all returned from Paris. She's quite fond of you, and so am I. No, please do come, Astra. Unless, of course, you think it would all be too painful. I know Rakesburn is very close to Hensley."

"It's never painful seeing two people who love each other come together," I reassured him with a genuine smile. "I'm glad to see you happy, Mustard."

"I am the luckiest of men," he agreed. "And I'm sure your husband will say the same someday." He rose. "Afraid I must dash now. There are china patterns that need selecting, or so I'm told."

"Important indeed! I don't want to make you late for that. I'll show you out."

As I closed the front door behind him and turned, I spotted Reilly going up the stairs and called out, "Did you have a pleasant day, Reilly?"

She paused and turned. Still bright and smiling. "I did, miss. Thank you. Went to the flicks and saw the new Chaplin film."

"Did you and your friend enjoy it?" I asked pleasantly.

Her smile, it seemed, turned brittle. "Friend?"

"Yes. I thought I saw you speaking with a woman outside just a little while ago."

A long pause. "I don't know her, miss. She was just needing directions is all." She flickered a smile and hurried up the stairs.

Chapter Ten

It was a glorious May day, and I was going home. Nearly. The close of the month saw Toby and me on an afternoon train, puffing toward Leicestershire for Belinda's wedding.

I was happy to be going, but I couldn't have asked for a worse traveling companion. Toby, bundled in a sour-faced heap on the seat opposite mine, glared out the window as the green and pleasant land slipped past, taking civilization with it.

"The *countryside*," he snarled. "Dirt and wildlife and *fresh air*."

"You didn't have to come," I pointed out. "Nobody forced you onto the train. You simply couldn't be bothered to put up a fight."

It was his mother's doing. Jeffries had made a point of delivering both of our invitations during tea, when he knew Aunt El would be present.

"Good lord," Toby had exclaimed, "are they inviting everyone they've ever met?"

"You should be grateful for that, Tobias," his mother responded, practically giddy (well, as close to giddy as Aunt El ever got) at the prospect of her son being invited to a ducal wedding. "Astra, when you write your acceptance, please do one for Tobias as well. You'll word it much better than he will, I'm sure."

"Oh, Mums, no! It's in May! Who in their right mind is in the countryside in May?"

"Not another word!" she'd shrilled. "You will go, Tobias, and that's the end of it!"

He'd thrown me a pleading look, but I certainly wasn't going to argue with her. She was already cross with me because, after my meeting with Edgry, I'd asked her, as politely as I could manage, to please not decide what should be done with Raymond's and my money without consulting me.

"It was the best thing at the time," she'd responded irritably. "Really! You don't appreciate *anything* I do for you!"

Unsurprisingly, she was not inclined to help undo that trust she and Edgry had created.

"Your foolishness in Paris proves this was the best thing," she'd insisted. "What ridiculous things would you buy if you had all that money at your disposal?"

No amount of arguing that I had every intention of using the money responsibly persuaded her. Her heels were well dug in. And I didn't want to press the issue because heaven knows what she'd do if I annoyed her further. She was already taking every opportunity to shout and scold me, Dandy, and even Reilly. Not that Reilly seemed to mind: she had been in a very chipper mood the past few days. I think I actually heard her humming while she folded my blouses around sheets of tissue paper and slipped them into the suitcases.

Despite Aunt El, I'd been feeling somewhat optimistic. Edgry had duly returned his "fees," and I'd engaged a new lawyer. This man did not think I was an idiot and supplied me with regular reports detailing my income and expenditure, so at last I felt I was getting a much better grasp on my finances.

But then, I saw Freddie at Waterloo Station.

"*Tobyyyy! Miss Davieeeees!*" he'd bellowed down the platform.

"Oh, for heaven's sake," Toby had moaned. "They really *did* invite everyone."

"Going to the wedding?" Freddie had asked, bounding our way. "That's marvelous. There seem to be a lot of us going. It'll be quite the party!"

"How excellent," Toby had responded flatly.

"And I'll be claiming you for a dance at the ball right now, Miss Davies." Freddie'd waggled a finger at me. "No dancing out of it this time. Dancing out! Ho!"

He had followed us to our seats and plunked down next to me, chattering about all the excellent parties he'd been to and the ones he'd be missing because he "just had to go and stand by old Mustard when he takes the plunge and slaps on the ball and chain. It's just the right thing to do, isn't it? Besides, seems like all the pretty girls in London are going." He'd leered at me as he pulled out a flask.

"Your nobility is an example to us all, Freddie," Toby had darkly observed.

"I am a gentleman," Freddie had agreed, offering the flask to both Toby and me.

"It's a bit early," Toby had remarked as the train jerked out of the station.

"Well, it's five o'clock somewhere!" Freddie took a deep swig.

Toby had frowned. "Are you drowning your sorrows, Freddie? I've noticed you tend to jabber and drink when you're upset."

Freddie'd fiddled with the flask, then slid his eyes toward me with a brave smile. "You may as well hear it from me. Mr. Porter's taken his business elsewhere."

It was as if someone had thrown a bucket of ice water over me. I'd been afraid this day would come, but hearing it now, when everything else seemed like such a mess, made me truly feel like I was staring into an abyss. My stomach twisted several times. I'd gaped at Freddie. Even Toby's eyes had widened. "All of it?" I'd gasped.

Freddie's smile had turned a little desperate. He'd shrugged and nodded. "Sorry to say, but, you know, these things happen! My father's not been well and, uh, the running of the business has sort of fallen off a little. We were late on a few shipments . . . Ah well, can't be helped! Nothing's certain in business, eh? Maybe we'll find someone else."

Someone else to make a regular order that large? Someone else with a factory that needed supplying?

"Who else might that be, Freddie?" I'd wondered, hands twitching as I fought the urge to grab him by the lapels and shake him.

He'd shrugged again. "Dunno. Someone, maybe. Hopefully. And soon. Gosh, you know what? It's a little stuffy in here. Think I'll go to the bar car and have a snifter." Off he had stumbled.

Toby had sighed, then reached over and patted my shoulder. "Well," he'd said philosophically, "at least you still have your health."

As we disembarked, a frighteningly young man with lank black hair and hands jammed into the pockets of worn corduroy trousers ambled over and said, "Ye'll be the ones stayin' wi' th' 'orshaws, right?"

"Shouldn't you be in school?" Toby wondered.

The boy gave him a withering look and said, "This way." He led us to a cumbersome, black, cloth-topped touring car that reminded me of a hearse.

"What is that thing?" Toby asked.

"A Humber," the boy answered in a defeated tone.

We all climbed in. With some coaxing both physical and verbal ("Come on, girl, come on," as the boy eased on the clutch and the gas), the car wheezed itself onto the road, and we sped away at a thrilling fifteen miles an hour, bumping painfully over the untended ruts and potholes. The snail's pace gave Toby plenty of time to scowl at the countryside as we made our way to Elmswood, the home of a pair of sisters who had been friends with my aunt for years. I'd never met these ladies, but on her rare visits to Hensley, Aunt El would make a point of seeing them. Afterward, she would scold my mother for not including them in her social circle.

"Oh, lord, the *Horshaws*," Mother would say, rolling her eyes as soon as her sister's back was turned.

"That *house*," Father would agree, wincing.

Elmswood had been built by a merchant who did fairly well for himself in the Elizabethan age. Subsequent owners had added to it over the centuries, tacking on bits and pieces with absolutely no thought or respect for the building's original design. It looked like someone had cut apart pictures of other houses and stuck them together in a bizarre architectural collage. Dormer windows cut across the roof line, a brick extension with long sash windows stretched to one side, and the Humber wheezed to an exhausted stop beneath a heavy, Gothic-style porte cochere.

Toby and I climbed out while Reilly waited to be taken around the back with the luggage. The boy gave her a nudging look, however; then hopped down and shouldered through the front door with his hands full of cases and a hatbox. Reilly hesitated, throwing me a questioning glance. I shrugged. Down she came as well, picking up one of the remaining valises and trailing after us as we followed the boy inside.

The main hall was dim at floor level, but as our eyes adjusted, I saw it had a beautifully carved staircase that wrapped upward past a large diamond-paned window that probably would have made the place nice and bright if it wasn't north facing. At the foot of said staircase was a tiny gray-haired lady. Her face was spiderwebbed with creases, hands clasped in front of her, clenched to the white-knuckle point. Like my aunt, she was dressed well out of fashion, though in this lady's case she was only about ten years behind the times, in an ankle-length, blue-striped cotton dress. Her hair was parted rigidly down the middle and pulled back in a tight chignon at the nape of her neck.

The boy dumped the suitcases at her feet and stomped back out for the rest.

"You'll be Astra and Toby," the lady observed unnecessarily. "Welcome to Elmswood. I'm Alice Horshaw, but of course you must know that already. *Manifestum est.* I regret my sister, Bellephonica, cannot see you, but she's recovering from a great battle with influenza." She sighed. *"Brevis ipsa vita est sed malis fit longior."*

"Fit? Influenza? Oh dear, you won't want us here," said Toby disingenuously. "We'd better go back, Astra."

"I certainly hope it's not serious," I said, flinging an eye dagger his way.

"Aegroto, dum anima est, spes esse dicitur," she answered. "You need not worry, it's quite safe. The doctor has assured me she is no longer contagious."

Toby smiled tightly. "What a relief."

Alice looked me over and her face softened. "You look very much like your mother."

"Thank you," I responded, smiling.

Alice next glanced at Toby. "You look very much like your mother as well."

Toby tried, unsuccessfully, not to look offended.

"I shall show you to your rooms," Alice continued, turning and ascending the staircase. *"Excelsior!"*

Toby and I swapped sideways glances.

"What does that mean?" I whispered as we followed her up the stairs.

"How should I know? I'm not Caesar," he hissed back.

"I thought all you learned at school was Latin!"

"Yes, and who on earth remembers any of that? It's like algebra or dangling participles: the people who remember how to use it in adulthood are always the ones you avoid at parties."

"My sister's room," Alice announced, gesturing to the first door on the right at the top of the stairs. *"Noli ursam fodicare,"* she whispered.

"Right you are," Toby responded.

"Your room, Tobias," she said, indicating the room opposite her sister's. "And you, Astra, are at the other end of the hall, next to me."

"Lovely." I followed her to an unexpectedly pleasant bedroom, papered and upholstered in pale green toile. A carved four-poster took up most of the space, leaving just enough room for a wardrobe and a dainty lace-draped dressing table.

"I think—I hope—you will be comfortable here," said Alice, twisting her clasped hands as I got my bearings.

"Oh yes, certainly. Thank you," I reassured her.

My enthusiasm coaxed out a tiny smile and her hands stilled. "I am glad you and Tobias have chosen to stay with us," she informed me, with a quick nod. "Quite glad. We entertain little here. My sister . . . But after all, *homo sit naturaliter animal socialis*. So it's nice that you're here."

"Oh, thank you," I said a little uncertainly. "That's very kind. And I'm sorry if our visit disturbs your sister in any way."

Another smile, but a wry one this time. "It's for the best that she's bedridden just now," she told me. "She is not a natural hostess. Is there anything you need?"

"Where might I find writing paper?" I was hoping to send Freddie a note asking to meet when he was sober enough to discuss things rationally.

"In the library, just at the bottom of the stairs. We dine at seven o'clock promptly. Arthur will bring up the bags. I will leave you now."

And with that, she was gone.

* * *

The festivities got under way the following night, with a pre-wedding ball at Rakesburn. The last time I had been there was for a dinner the October before my parents died. I remembered my father being excited about some Flemish tapestries the duke had recently purchased, and my mother eating very little. At the time I thought it was nerves.

Tonight the house was lit up like a Christmas tree, and car after gleaming car was dropping passengers at the door before chugging away.

As the Humber lumbered forward, Toby pressed against the window, trying to make out the faces of fellow guests.

"Tommy and Sylvia Ruckle," he murmured as one glittering pair disembarked from a Bentley. "And the Arnold brothers," as the next car released a stream of tow-headed young men.

"How many are there?" I asked as one Arnold after another hopped out.

"I'm not sure. They all sort of blend together after a while." Toby answered. His mood was vastly improved, thanks, no doubt, to the splendid food on offer at Elmswood. We'd been treated to some delicious strawberry tarts at teatime. When asked, Alice had blushingly admitted she made the jam herself. She had glanced up toward her sister's room as she spoke, as if she were afraid of being scolded for bragging.

"Could you send a supply down to London?" Toby had hopefully asked her.

I'd been happy to discover that the newest part of the house contained a beautiful library. The long sash windows provided plenty of light, and it was quiet. The perfect spot to do some thinking about what to do now that Porter had abandoned Vandemark. Another client would need to be found, but who? Freddie couldn't be relied on to fix this; it would have to be me, but I had no idea where to begin. I wound up spending the afternoon looking out the window, thinking, and coming up with no solutions.

The car coughed and heaved itself to Rakesburn's entrance, drawing a few raised eyebrows from the Arnold clan. Arthur stepped out to open the door for us.

"Right, then," said Toby. "Once more into the fray!" He winked as he descended and gave me his hand.

I followed, carefully draping my train into place behind me, and now the Arnolds's eyebrows were rising for an entirely different reason. I was wearing the red dress from Paris, with pendulum-shaped diamond earrings my father had given Mother for a twentieth anniversary present, and combs in my hair that glittered with diamante swirls and foliage. Despite the long journey in the crawling car, I looked spectacular. Tommy Ruckle gave me an appreciative look as I passed by on Toby's arm, and Sylvia Ruckle responded with a good, sharp elbow to Tommy's ribs. His yelp followed us inside.

There was no doubt that a wedding was imminent. Thick ropes of white flowers, ivy, and ribbons were swagged up and down the front hall and the banisters of the stairs. Enormous urns spouted fountains of lilies that thickened the air and delivered a perfumed slap as soon as you entered. Toby blinked, his eyes watering at the smell.

But I breathed it in. Inhaled the heady atmosphere: rich flowers and tinkling laughter and softly glowing lights. Girls lifting gloved arms in greeting to their friends. Couples whispering, hands drifting surreptitiously around waists. Plans being made.

I soaked it up and decided, just for tonight, to forget about Millicent and Vandemark and all my other headaches, dive deep into the atmosphere, and enjoy myself.

Toby and I approached the bridal couple, who were lined up with both sets of parents between two urns, greeting guests as they arrived.

"Oh, Astra, how wonderful to see you!" Belinda gushed, clearly full of prenuptial euphoria. Her eyes glittered a little manically, and she was flushed. "Can you believe this is all really happening? I can't! It's like a dream—the most wonderful dream!" She sighed and laid her head on Hampton's shoulder.

He smiled at her. "I hope you never wake up from it," he said sweetly.

"No one deserves this more than you," I told Belinda warmly as the pressure of the crowd started moving me down the line. A quick clasp of Hampton's hand and a curtsey to the parents, and we were free. I left Toby lurking near a statue of Eros and dashed upstairs to freshen up.

As I was coming back down the hallway, combs settled, lipstick retouched, ready to make my entrance, someone grabbed my wrist and yanked me into a side corridor.

"I got your note," Freddie announced, pulling me much, much closer than was decent. His breath was like a breeze off a distillery.

"Freddie, what are you doing?" I gasped, trying to push and squirm away from him. His arms were like tentacles, wrapping themselves around me.

"You said you wanted to meet me. You were *most* insistent. So glad you're not upset about that business with Porter." He grinned and began swaying back and forth with me. "Let's be outrageous! Let's misbehave!" he sang tunelessly.

"I have no intention of misbehaving with you or anyone else!" I blazed, finally managing to wrench myself away from him. Two girls passing by in the main corridor took note of the scene, exchanged 'Oh, I *see*' looks, and hurried away. "Remember yourself, Freddie!" I growled. "Go sober up! We'll meet some other time."

He stepped back, befuddled. I smoothed my dress and was on my way.

The crowd of guests in the front hall seemed to have doubled in the time I'd been upstairs, and still more were arriving. I saw Cecilia making her way through the receiving line. Cee waved excitedly when she saw me; just ahead of her, Millicent glanced up too, and smirked, probably already anticipating a delightful weekend of making me miserable.

Well, if that's what she's after, she'll be disappointed.

Things might have seemed bleak just then, but I'd be *damned* if Millicent knew it.

I straightened my back, lifted my chin, and processed down the stairs like an empress. I concentrated on the cloying smell of the flowers and cast Millicent and Freddie from my mind. This would be a *good* weekend.

Toby was still next to the statue of Eros, but now he had company. He'd been joined by Dunreaven, looking more splendid than was strictly decent in white tie and tails. It was my first time seeing him since New Year's Day, and it gave me a thrill—much more so than I was expecting. My belly—and other parts—tingled, and I felt warm all over. Was he handsomer? Probably not, but you know what they say about absence and the heart.

I tried to remind myself that this was not the time for romantic entanglements. That my life was already a Gordian knot. He had no money and needed a rich wife. I needed to save Hensley and support my brother. And Millicent was ready to fight *very* dirty to secure a nobleman. But as I approached, both men looked up, and Dunreaven's deeply appreciative grin made any practical thought I'd ever had fly right out of my head. And suddenly, the cost of the dress seemed worth it.

"Look what you found," I said to Toby as I sashayed toward the men.

"I had nothing to do with it—he found me," Toby responded. "He's made an excellent show of being interested in what I've been doing with my life since our schooldays, but you're here now, so off I go. Ta now!" He melted into the crowd.

Once he was gone, Dunreaven smiled and said, "Why Miss Davies, if I may presume, you look simply splendid tonight. I'd say it was worth the trip north simply to see you in the famous Parisian gown." His eyes raked over me, eating me up. My ears and cheeks burned. "Lady Cecilia was right: it seems to have been made just for you."

"I suppose I shouldn't be surprised to find you're a discerning judge of ladies' fashion," I replied, as lightly as I could manage. "You really do seem to have been carefully constructed to be attractive to women."

He chuckled. "Stamped out in some factory?"

"No, not you. You're the work of an artist."

"Well, I've found that ladies nowadays have very high expectations."

"Some do. I'm sure there are plenty who would be happy just to see that face first thing every morning." I gestured to him with a teasing smile.

"I hope for more than that from a wife."

"Oh? And how goes your search for a spouse, then?"

"As you can see, I am unencumbered. So clearly the quest continues."

I tried not to let him see that pleased me, but I must not have been entirely successful, because his smile turned wry.

"Others, I hear, are having more luck." He nodded toward Beckworth and Cecilia, who were deep in conversation next to a potted ivy topiary. "Joyce says we all have you to thank for that."

I grinned at the sight of them and shrugged. "Not just me. Toby suggested it. And it wasn't really much effort. Just a gentle push from either direction to move them together, and they took care of the rest. She'll make him far happier than I would."

"And he'll make *her* far happier than he'd make *you*," Dunreaven added. He leaned a little closer and murmured, "Is it very wrong of me to admit I'm not sorry you won't become Lady Beckworth?"

His breath ticked my ear, and I shivered a little even as my whole upper body heated up. "Very wrong," I whispered back. "But I'll allow it, this once."

A devilish grin in response. Goose bumps up and down my arms.

"Shall we?" I gestured to the couples drifting toward the nearest drawing room.

"We shall." He offered me his arm. "May I have the pleasure?"

I took the arm and we joined the well-dressed tide.

The doors between two adjoining drawing rooms had been opened, creating a space large enough to dance. A few brave pairs were already swaying to the orchestra's staid tunes.

I saw Joyce chatting with a few acquaintances off to the side. As soon as she spotted us, she broke off the conversation and came bustling over with David.

"Oh, darling, how gorgeous you look," she greeted me with a kiss on both cheeks. "Doesn't she look delectable? David, don't answer that. Jeremy?"

"Quite edible," Dunreaven agreed with another appreciative look that brought back the tingle, stronger this time.

"How're those people you're staying with, Astra?" Joyce asked. "Friends of your aunt's, aren't they? Is it really awful? If it is, we may be able to squeeze you in with us."

"No, the lady's perfectly lovely," I assured her.

"Well, that's all right, then. And it's only for a few days anyhow. David, you'd better dance with me before it gets too crowded to move. Who hired this orchestra? So dull! Jeremy, twirl Astra around a few times, she's clearly dying for a go."

She and David moved off, and Dunreaven gave me a questioning look and nodded toward the dance floor. "May I presume? If you aren't otherwise engaged."

"You know very well I'm not engaged," I responded.

As we came together and he put his hand on the small of my back, I realized we were bare skin to bare skin, and now that tingle was becoming incredibly distracting. I couldn't help but notice that he, too, seemed to swallow a little hard. Trying to keep the conversation light, I asked, "How are you liking Leicestershire?"

"It's a beautiful part of the country. I'd like to see more of it."

"You should. It's certainly worth it."

"I've been told you grew up here. Could I persuade you to show me a little?"

"Possibly, if there's time." I looked up at him and noticed that his eyes were more blue than green tonight. For several long seconds I couldn't seem to look away. I felt the heat of his hand on the tender skin of my lower back. My chest tightened, and I forced myself to look over his left shoulder, focusing on the orchestra's bass player.

"I'm surprised you didn't spend today getting the lay of the land," I choked, sternly telling myself to get control. But the atmosphere of the party had thoroughly soaked in by that time. All the smiles and the heady flowers and Belinda's joyful laugh ringing over the music. The love and pure joy of finding someone who fits with you and makes you happy. I had let myself be swept up in it, this romantic riptide. It was pulling me farther and farther from the safety of the shore.

"I was occupied most of the day," he explained. "Lady Balsan had me over for tea and dinner."

"Lady Balsan? I don't think I know her." *Count back from ten . . .*

"Lady Cecilia's and Lady Millicent's aunt."

"Ahh, Sir Walter's wife!" How could I forget? She'd always looked down on us Davieses because Hensley had been built with money from trade. Didn't matter that we'd got out of said trade and settled into life as country gentry well before my father's father was born—Lady Balsan was the sort to think it took at least five generations to make a true gentleman. "Jumped up," she'd call us, to mutual acquaintances. Not that that kept her from hiring away one or two of our housemaids. Privately, I think what really bothered her was Mother always winning first prize at the annual village fete flower show.

"The bride and groom should feel honored: she hardly ever bothers to come to this part of the country," I commented. "But of course, Lady Balsan has a very compelling reason this weekend." I smiled up at him. "Tea *and* dinner. They're really putting it on. Just know they'll expect some sort of repayment for the hospitality."

"Oh? All my charms and sparkling personality aren't payment enough?"

I solemnly shook my head. "I'm afraid not. Nobody entertains a bachelor for free: they eat too much."

"Well," he chuckled, "I'm a moderate eater, so hopefully the price won't be too high."

I tsked. "Those are expensive ladies, and their time is costly." My smile turned kittenish. "It may very well cost you a ring or two."

"Is that so?" He laughed. "And will I be punished for failing to hold up my end of this bargain?"

"Most certainly! Prepare yourself for quite the battering, Lord Dunreaven."

"Fortunately my ship is a sturdy one and can survive an assault or two."

"But can it survive a full engagement?" I grinned playfully, and he smiled back.

"Is that a proposal?"

Touché. "You know very well it is not."

"Ahh, what a shame." He sighed dramatically. "Well, if the ladies press me, I shall have to inform them that I won't be bought by some scones and roast beef, no matter how deliciously prepared." He moved the hand on my back the tiniest bit, sending a thrilling electric jolt straight up my spine.

"They'll probably just redouble their efforts," I warned. "Millicent is dangerously close to being left on the shelf, and she won't stand for that."

"The shelf?" He shuddered. "That sounds grim."

"That's the way of it." I shrugged. "Everyone wants the new season's model: it's sleeker and shinier."

"I'm not sure that's true. Those in the know are aware that many things improve with age." He smiled impishly. "Are you not worried about being shelved yourself?"

"Not yet. I tell myself I have a year or two left before I'm declared a waste of tulle and effort."

"Perhaps I'll wait, then," he suggested.

"Oh no, don't do that. I'd hate to think of such a brilliant catch as you languishing on my account. I have things to do before I'm ready to settle down, and I can't guarantee they'll be done in the proper time."

He paused, then asked, "What sorts of things?"

"Grown-up things."

"I hear marriage is a grown-up thing."

"And yet girls are expected to go into it when they're virtually children." I sighed. "And some of the men are little better," I added, catching sight of Freddie in the crowd.

"You have it all sorted, then," Dunreaven said.

"Far from it, unfortunately."

The song ended. We drifted off the dance floor, along with Joyce and David, and were met by Cecilia and Beckworth.

"Astra, you look so, *so* perfect!" Cecilia gushed. "That dress is the best thing any of us got in Paris. Oh, isn't this exciting?" She looked around, wide-eyed. "It's too bad I've got to stay with Aunt Constance—it very nearly ruins the whole experience. She's so dull! And my cousin Emmy's turned into such an awful little girl. You know what she did yesterday? I took a second piece of cake at tea and she *oinked* at me. And she kept it up *all day today*. She hasn't said a single actual word to me, she just oinks all the time!"

Horrified, I glanced at Dunreaven, who grimaced and nodded in confirmation.

Joyce looked disgusted. "Your family breeds the most horrible little ticks, Cee. Not you, of course, but nearly everyone else. Are you sure you weren't left on the doorstep?"

"I do wonder sometimes," Cee sighed. "But Jeremy was nice enough to save me, weren't you, Jeremy? He told Emmy that fairies come out on full moons and transform children into animals, and if she wasn't careful she'd be turned into a pig herself. That quieted her down."

I grinned at him. "That was kind," I told him. "To Cee, that is."

"I owe repayment for the doll kidnapping, remember?" he replied. "And anyway, I hate bullies, as you know."

"Ahh!" Cee sighed, "Look! The bride and groom!" She applauded as Belinda and Hampton came in.

Belinda blushed, looked up at her future husband adoringly, and cooed, "Bliss."

Hampton beamed at her.

"Ohh." Cee melted, glancing at Beckworth, who grinned back. "So romantic!"

"And can you believe it?" Belinda breathed. "Georgy's parents are giving us this house for our very own. This whole beautiful place, with its lovely memories!"

"I can recommend some excellent people when you're ready to start doing it over," Joyce offered immediately.

David rolled his eyes and Belinda cocked her head, seeming confused.

"Why would I want to do it over?"

"She's joking, Belinda," I hastily reassured her before Joyce could respond.

Belinda tittered, then tugged on Hampton's hand. "Georgy, please dance with me. I don't think I can wait another moment!"

Hampton smiled obligingly and took her to the dance floor. The other couples melted back and applauded as the pair began their fox-trot. I watched them for a little while, happy to see two people so happy themselves, then turned back to find Millicent had inserted herself in their place.

"Astra," she greeted me, "what a pleasure it is to see you here."

"What a sweet thing to say, Millicent," I simpered. "I simply had to be here—I heard you were going to do a reading at the ceremony. However did you manage that?"

Her eyes flashed, then took me in from head to toe. "That dress is a *bold* choice," she commented. "Though I suppose scarlet is appropriate. So very eye-catching, that gown. Most ladies would be afraid of drawing all the attention away from the bride."

"No one could possibly outshine such a radiant bride," I answered sweetly.

Dunreaven was frowning, his eyes moving back and forth between us.

Millicent turned to him with a smile. "You promised me a dance, Dunny."

"Payment is owing," I teased him.

He gave me a warning look as he led Millicent away.

*   *   *

Considering we didn't get home until after three, I was up at the rather lark-like hour of nine to have Arthur drive me back to Rakesburn. Hampton had kindly offered me the pick of the stables, and within the quarter hour a pretty bay mare and I were on our way to Hensley.

Once clear of the stable yard, I gave the mare her head and had a good gallop over the fields. This was where my father had taught me to ride, on a fat gray pony named Almond. He showed me the paths to avoid ("too many tree roots down that one—you'll break your mount's legs and your neck") and the fields that offered a soft landing if I got into trouble. The gates and streams that could be safely jumped and the ones that hid ditches and rabbit warrens. And of course there were the secret spots where bluebells and violets grew in lush carpets, waiting for us to stop and gather a posy for Mother.

My current mount moved like a dancer, skimming the grass and nimbly leaping fences as if to say, *"Oh, this five-bar gate? It's nothing!"* Very different from Almond, who'd always been reluctant to go faster than a jerky trot. She died when I was thirteen, and we buried her at Hensley on a day much like this one: dazzlingly sunny with a slight breeze, the tropical smell of gorse and the promise of a brilliant summer in the air.

Mother's garden would be beautiful on a day like today. The wisteria would probably be in bloom, the roses just starting to open. Father would have opened the French windows in the library to catch the scent, then stood in the doorway, framed by morning glories, crowing, "Magnificent! When I die, I hope heaven is just like this."

"Don't be so morbid," Mother would chastise him.

I smiled, thinking of her in her floppy straw gardening hat and gauntlets, clucking over the plants as if they were errant children. Trimming and pruning and perfecting. She'd begun letting me help when I was six, and when I was ten, I was given a plot in her sacred space and created my own little garden, with her help.

"Someday you'll do this for your children," Mother had said as we planted a border of asters.

"We both will!" I'd told her.

The thought of it made my heart ache.

As I neared the house, I slowed to a trot and turned toward a gradual rise that gave the best views over the gardens. Hensley's roofline peeked over the hill. My stomach jumped at the sight, then twisted uncomfortably, and I pulled the mare to a halt.

Why was I doing this? Seeing the place would only make me sad. To be so close but still unable to truly call it mine. And now, with Freddie's news, returning to Hensley seemed a more remote possibility than ever.

But I *had* to come back. I couldn't stay at Aunt El's forever, dependent on her resentful charity. This was home. It had seeped into me. Or perhaps it had been part of me from birth, something passed along by my parents just as surely as height or eye color. Perhaps that's how it was with these old houses: you twined together, and the longer you'd been there, the harder it was to break away. This was where all of our memories lived, sunk into gardens and pets' graves and pleasant rooms my mother had taken such care in arranging.

The mare shifted beneath me, and I absently patted her neck, drawing in deep, shaky breaths. *"Think of a flower, slowly opening,"* Mother had said. But when I tried, all I could see were *her* flowers. Her morning glories and roses. And Father, breathing them in. *"I hope heaven is like this."*

My heart squeezed and my eyes stung. I turned the horse so I couldn't see the roof anymore. I'd see Hensley again when I could walk through the front door and truly call it mine. The thought of seeing it as a visitor was too depressing.

As I guided the mare back down the slope, I saw a rider approaching at a canter. *Dunreaven.* I considered galloping away, not wanting to meet him like this. My mind was everywhere; I'd have no witty exchange to duck behind. My eyes still prickled, threatening tears. He'd know something was wrong. I felt tender and exposed. A shell-less turtle, yet again.

I didn't move. It was too late anyway; he was nearly with me. I tried to pull myself together. Pasted on a wobbly smile.

"You're up early this morning," I observed.

He pulled up a few feet away and tipped his hat in greeting. "Good morning, Miss Davies. I hope you don't mind: the stableboy said you came this way, and I was hoping to catch you up and ask for a tour of the countryside."

"I'm very happy to give it." I nudged the mare forward, away from the house.

He fell into step beside me, glancing my way. "Is everything all right?" he asked after a few minutes of riding in silence. "You don't quite seem yourself. No witty remarks to greet me with?" A teasing grin. "My goodness—have I managed to rattle you?"

"Not you, but . . ." I drew in a ragged breath. "I don't have my wit about me just now." I nodded back in the direction of the house. "Hensley is there."

"Ahh." His face softened into an expression I'd never seen before. It was understanding and sympathy, without pity. "Did you see it?" he asked quietly.

I shook my head. "Too difficult," I croaked, looking away from him as the sting behind my eyes increased. I couldn't cry in front of him. "That must seem weak to you."

"Of course it doesn't," he reassured me in a gentle tone. "It is a hard thing, coming home after a loss. Even when you think the shock has worn off and you've steeled yourself and it'll be all right, it still hurts. Sometimes much, much more than you expect." He looked away from me now, and I wondered if he was swallowing tears of his own. Instinctively, I halted the mare, reached out, and laid a hand on his arm. He smiled a silent thank-you, and said, "You see, I don't have my wit about me either, right now."

I squeezed his arm and retracted my hand. Until just then I had forgotten that he, too, had lost both of his parents. He understood.

"It's a strange thing, being alone in the world," I observed as we began walking again. "Though I suppose I'm not really alone."

"There's a difference between being alone and feeling alone," he said. "I think we both know what the latter feels like."

We looked at each other and smiled, and I realized that now I didn't mind feeling so exposed. I liked it, actually. I felt lighter—that shell had been a burden.

And there was something else: a strange sensation between us. One that was familiar to me and yet at the same time utterly alien. It was a comfortable feeling, a warmth and a security. What you feel when you embrace someone who trusts and loves you, and whom you trust and love in return. I'd never felt this way around any young man before, and it baffled me. Is this what falling in love was like? Did I even *want* to fall in love with him? Oh, he had all the proper requirements: charm, youth, position. But he couldn't help me get Hensley back. And what would he think about Raymond?

And yet, keeping him at arm's length was starting to feel exhausting, and unnatural. Just one more battle when I was already so heavily engaged.

But maybe it wasn't love at all. Perhaps it was only an infatuation, or a friendship developing further. One day I might look back and laugh at my girlishness. My naivete.

Did he feel it too? He smiled at me again, and I sensed that he did.

He stopped his horse again and twisted in the saddle so he was more fully facing me. "At the risk of overstepping my bounds by some miles, may I ask you something?"

My heart sped up. "Of course you may."

"I think we may safely consider ourselves friends?"

I grinned. "I'd say so."

"Then could we dispense with formality and use Christian names? I'd rather just be Jeremy with you."

My smile broadened. "Of course. I'd like that."

He smiled back, and I basked in it, feeling warm all over.

"Now, Jeremy, I believe you wanted a look around the countryside," I said, gathering up the reins and digging my heels into the mare's sides. "Come on. There are some wonderful bridle paths this way."

* * *

The invigorating ride and a hearty lunch back at Elmswood restored me: The sense of lightness held, and I felt energized and even a little hopeful. So much so that I once again settled down in the library and started writing business notes. Things I didn't understand, things I wanted to know, people we could approach, arguments I could use to persuade Porter to return. I worked and worked, and before I knew it, the shadows had begun to slant, and the clock in the hall was chiming teatime. I started to put my papers aside and Alice poked her head in.

"I'm so sorry—no need to wait on me," I told her.

"No, no, it's quite all right. You seemed quite possessed of a *cacoethes scribendi*. I hated to disturb you."

"You're not disturbing me," I reassured her.

"Oh, well," she said, glancing over her shoulder, seemingly afraid someone else was listening. She slipped into the library and tiptoed up to the desk. "I was wondering: What are you working on?"

"Oh, it's—it's some business matters," I answered. "I'm trying to work some things out with a company I'm invested with." I immediately regretted telling her that—surely a friend of Aunt El's would believe that the business world was no place for a girl. I should have just said I was writing a poem or something.

I steeled myself for a lecture, but instead Alice's eyes widened and she breathed, "Really? Why, how remarkable! You young ladies these days— you do so much. How I envy you!" She drew up a chair and sat beside me.

"I'm not doing much at all," I admitted. "Mostly I'm just discovering how little I know."

"Well, you must start somewhere," she said staunchly, reaching out and squeezing my arm. "Keep at it, my dear. You go out and you find people to answer your questions, and you keep at it. You seem like a clever thing; I've no doubt you'll learn quickly."

"That's really kind of you," I said warmly.

She smiled, rose, and went over to one of the bookshelves. She quickly retrieved a small stack of books and returned, spreading them out on the desk. They were all Greek and Latin works: Ovid and Livy and some names I didn't recognize.

"These were my father's. He was a professor of ancient cultures. When I was a little girl, I'd pick them up and try to read them but, well, they were all Greek to me." We chuckled together. "He saw me looking at them, so he sat me down and taught me Greek and Latin. Turned out I had a knack for it. He and I used to converse in Latin sometimes. It annoyed mother and Bellephonica to no end." She smiled mischievously at the memory, then sighed. "I wish I could have done something with it, but it was not to be. There wasn't much a girl could do with such things, back then. But now! There are possibilities, aren't there? At least, it seems like there are. Some. So do pursue this, Miss Davies, if that's what you want. I'm sure your parents would have encouraged you, just as my father did."

Would they? I had my doubts. But then, perhaps if I'd applied myself to something like this while they were still alive, they'd have trusted me to help when Mother fell ill. Hopefully they would have trusted me enough to actually tell me she *was* ill in the first place. Tears burned the backs of my eyes, and my breath was ragged as I breathed in. *Think of flowers! Count back from ten!*

"Oh, oh, my dear, are you all right? I'm sorry!" Alice patted me on the back as if I were an infant to be soothed.

"No, no, I'm sorry," I said as she gently led me to a divan. "I've just been thinking about my mother a great deal recently."

Alice nodded sympathetically. "She was a lovely lady. And she loved you so, so much. She talked about you all the time, and kept all your bits and bobs from when you were a baby. It was so sweet."

I blinked at her. "I didn't know that you two were friends."

"Oh, not friends, really. We visited a bit, but there was . . . a coolness between our two households." Alice shrugged. "The matter with her sister . . . it was to be expected."

"Her sister? Aunt Elinor, you mean? What matter?" The questions came out in a gush, and Alice looked startled. And then something flashed across her face. A momentary flutter. Something like realization.

"Oh. Oh well, there was a disagreement. It passed. Such a lovely place, Hensley! And your mother had very ambitious plans for the gardens."

I closed my eyes and willed myself to remain in control. Alice patted my hand and cooed soothingly. "It's a terrible thing when a girl loses her mother young." She sighed. "You have suffered a great misfortune. But remember: *Ad astra per aspera.*"

I blinked at her. "I don't know what that means," I admitted.

"Oh, of course! Silly of me," she tittered. "'To the stars through difficulties.'" She blushed. "I'm sorry. I forget sometimes. Slipping in and out of Latin became such a habit with dear Papa, I don't seem able to control it."

The door opened and Arthur poked his head in. "Ye'd best get to the drawing room. That man'll not leave ye a single tart if ye don't."

"Bring up some extra tarts for him, Arthur," Alice said as we moved toward the door, arm in arm. "That poor boy. The way he eats, I'm convinced your aunt starves him. Oh!" She stopped and turned to face me. "I nearly forgot: Bellephonica told me she saw your maid out in the garden earlier with someone."

"Did she?" I'd given Reilly the day off, so I didn't see much harm in her being out in the garden. "Is she not supposed to be in the garden?"

"No, no, it's perfectly all right. Only, 'Phonie said they seemed to be speaking quite intently and for a very long time. And she said they were over near some hedges and thought maybe they didn't think they could be seen from the house. It was a woman she was speaking with. Had very red hair, apparently."

The same woman she'd been speaking with in London, perhaps? For an alleged stranger, she certainly had a knack for finding Reilly. Why on earth would Reilly lie about knowing her?

"Did Bellephonica recognize the woman?" I asked.

Alice shook her head. "No. I'm sure it's nothing—just a friend. But you can never be too careful when it comes to one's servants and the people they mix with. I only thought you should know. Come along, the tea will get cold and the tarts will vanish if we don't hurry."

Chapter Eleven

❧

Like many brides, Belinda had assumed her wedding day would be perfectly sunny and glorious. How could it dare rain on such a special day?

Well, it dared.

It *bucketed*. A real drenched-in-seconds, biblical downpour that showed no signs of letting up. I woke to the unwelcome sound of it, and when Reilly pulled the curtains back all I could see outside was a solid sheet of gray.

"It might stop before the ceremony," I suggested, more hopefully than I felt. Even if it did, the roads would be rivers in some places. As I dressed, I wondered how Belinda felt about this. Hopefully she was so blinded by love she wouldn't notice or mind.

Alice, Toby, and I had a quiet breakfast, watching the rain cascade its way down the windows. Toby pouted into a boiled egg and said nonsensically, "This would never have happened in London."

"Yes, it never rains there," I flung back.

"You know what I mean!" he snapped as he angrily buttered a slice of toast.

"Now, now, *omne bene erit*," Alice said.

Toby glared while continuing to scrape butter across his bread like both had personally offended him.

"Surely it will be all right," Alice continued. "She wasn't planning on having the wedding outdoors anyhow."

"There were plans for the wedding breakfast to spill into the gardens," I told her.

Alice's eyes flicked to the windows. *"Amantes sunt amentes,"* she murmured.

"My thoughts exactly." Toby nodded and bit savagely into his toast.

I reached for a slice myself, but then Arthur came in and announced, "There's a man 'ere from the 'all. Says 'e's been sent to fetch Miss Davies. The bride's 'ysterical." Arthur rolled his eyes.

"Hysterical? Why? What's happened?" I asked. Arthur shrugged. "I'd better go, then," I said, setting my toast aside. My stomach was already knotting. Summoned to Rakesburn by a hysterical Belinda the morning of her wedding? Dear lord, had she found out about Hampton's note? Had Millicent, after all, carried out her threat?

"What am I to do?" Toby asked plaintively.

"Finish murdering your toast and then meet me at the church," I answered. "Arthur can drive you. I'm sorry, Alice."

Alice waved her hand. "Never mind, my dear. You are needed. *Amicus certus in re incerta cernitur:* A friend in need is a friend indeed."

I followed Arthur into the front hall, where a uniformed chauffeur was waiting, looking quite put out by all the fuss.

"Can you just give me a moment to change?" I asked, zipping past him and up the stairs.

Reilly was in my room, laying out my wedding clothes.

"I need to go to Rakesburn now," I explained. Without question she began unbuttoning and relacing, and in less than fifteen minutes I was in the car and driving to Rakesburn along muddy, rutted streets that, as I feared, were already starting to flood. I wondered if the Humber would manage by the time Toby was ready to leave.

Everyone was scurrying at Rakesburn, and the air was as rich with anxiety as it was with floral perfume. As I passed one of the drawing rooms, I spotted a clutch of ladies inside, gathered around Belinda's mother. She was waving a handkerchief and calling for smelling salts. I swallowed hard.

Joyce appeared on the first floor and leaned over the balustrade. "Astra! You'd better come up here. None of us are much use at all."

"What's the matter?" I asked, ascending the stairs like Anne Boleyn going up the scaffold. "What happened?"

Joyce shrugged. "I can hardly understand a word coming out of her. She's summoned just about everyone. It's a complete crush in there."

Oh, God, I was going to be facing a mob.

"Honestly," Joyce huffed as we headed down the hallway together, "I can't believe nobody thought to bring some phenobarbital with them. The stuff's as vital to a wedding as a groom and veil! I'd give her one of mine, but I took the last one yesterday."

We heard Belinda long before we saw her: her wails were ricocheting off the walls of the hallway leading to her room. I wondered how long she'd been keeping this up and felt sorry for anyone with a bedroom nearby.

We stepped into her room, which was so crammed with people it was difficult to shoulder in. The heat and mix of perfumes were enough to make you feel light-headed. Someone had drawn the curtains, shutting out the dreary outdoors, but nothing could disguise the sound of the rain thrashing against the windowpanes. I will say, though, Belinda's sobs were making an excellent attempt.

The bride, a perfect picture of complete and utter grief, sat in the middle of her bed in a crumpled pink dressing gown, face red and tear-streaked, eyes bloodshot.

Bridesmaids, friends, and female relatives clustered in concerned little knots, patting her and making soothing noises. A few ladies, having already given this up as hopeless, were scattered on chairs and settees. Everyone looked desperate to escape. I considered slipping back out and hiding downstairs, but then Belinda looked up, and her face crumpled anew. I froze, waiting for the onslaught.

"Look what's happened!" she gasped, pointing to the covered windows. "Just look! My beautiful wedding's ruined! *Ruined!*" She shrieked this last one. Three bridesmaids sitting near her cringed.

I blinked. All this . . . because of the weather? A sudden feeling of hysteria came over me, along with a rush of relief, and I nearly began laughing. I managed to strangle the mirth and wondered what to say. What could I say, really? Or do? I couldn't make it stop raining. What would Cecilia or my mother say if they were here?

"Oh." I shifted my weight from one foot to the other, thinking, then grabbed a brush from the dressing table and hissed at the nearest girl to fetch a cool facecloth. "Belinda," I said in my most calming voice, sliding onto the bed and looking her right in her reddened eyes, "I want you to try doing something for me. I want you to close your eyes and slowly count backward from ten. Or imagine a flower slowly opening."

Belinda nodded and obeyed. After a few anxious seconds, her sobs began to ease. I moved to sit behind her and began brushing her hair, taking long, easy strokes.

"Keep imagining that flower, Belinda. That's it . . ."

She was beginning to breathe normally. The others watched anxiously.

"Now, I want you to think of yourself gliding up the aisle, a beautiful vision in white, on your father's arm. And Georgy standing up at the front, smiling," I continued, still brushing her hair. "Look at all the lovely flowers around you—lilies, is that right? And roses?" She nodded. "Of course. Lilies and roses everywhere. And there's Georgy, smiling at you. And there you are, at his side, and he's taking your hand, and you're thinking, 'This really is the most perfect day.' And it is, Belinda. It's a perfect day."

She glanced back at me, eyes still wet, but no more tears brimming. "I so wanted a sunny day," she whimpered. "I wanted us to be able to walk in the garden."

"You'll have the rest of your lives to walk around in Rakesburn's garden," I reassured her. "And anyway, who needs the sun today? You and Hampton can be each other's sun." Good lord, was I actually saying these words? Joyce was staring at me in absolute horror. But it worked: Belinda smiled. The room seemed to collectively exhale.

"So silly of me," she mumbled, as that wet cloth finally materialized. I handed it to Belinda and she pressed it to her eyes and cheeks. "I must look a terrible mess."

"You'll be all right. A little powder and nobody will ever know," I promised her, though it would probably take quite a *lot* of powder to fix what all that hysteria had done to her face. Hopefully the veil was a thick one.

Someone brought a cup of tea and a plate of toast.

"Eat that," I ordered the bride, replacing the brush on the dressing table.

"Thank you so much, Astra," she said, her face practically glowing with gratitude.

"What are friends for?" I chirped.

The bridesmaids took over, chattering happily as they pressed more tea and toast on her. Joyce and I took the opportunity to slip out and make our way downstairs.

"You have quite the touch," Joyce commented. "Cee's been rubbing off on you."

"That was my mother, actually. I've been thinking about her a great deal lately."

"Ahh, yes, of course. That's to be expected. I feel like a ciggie—do you want one?"

"Oh yes." What I really felt I needed was a stiff drink to firm up my jellied knees, but it was a bit early in the day. Instead, we stepped out onto the front portico and lit up.

Joyce shivered slightly as she leaned against one of the columns. "I wish the Duchess wasn't so fierce about people not smoking inside," she grumbled. "We'll catch our deaths." She turned to me with a probing look. "I heard you and Jeremy had a nice ride yesterday."

"Did you indeed?"

"He had nothing but praise for your bridle paths. Such a gentleman." She smiled wickedly. "Anything else you'd like to share? You may as well: I'll just get it all out of David later, if you don't."

"He can't tell you anything because there's nothing to tell." Not entirely true, of course, but Joyce was not the person to confide in about all that had happened yesterday. I exhaled a stream of smoke in the direction of the rain. "How are things with David?"

Joyce sighed. "Oh, up and down, as with everything. Belinda will discover soon enough that not all days are sunny in a marriage." She shrugged. "You get through it."

I frowned, concerned. "I hope so. If that's what you want."

"It is. Don't mistake me. I do love him to bits. I just think that sometimes I have trouble telling him in a way he understands. We'll smooth off each other's edges and start fitting together better over time." She dropped the finished cigarette, ground it out, and helped herself to another one. "The key to happiness, I think, is to always have a project, and to keep other people around so you don't grate on each other too much. And on that note: What are your plans for the summer? You can come out to Wotting, if you like. We've got Laura coming, and I think I might rescue Cee from months with Millicent."

"I might take you up on that."

"Please do. And don't forget, Midbourne isn't far. I'm sure Jeremy could be persuaded to come around now and again." Another suggestive look, which I refused to acknowledge. Joyce rolled her eyes. "Oh, be difficult, then." She glanced at her watch. "Nearly time for us to be off to the church. Where are the men in my life?" She stamped out her second cigarette just as Porter's Rolls Royce came splashing through the puddles toward Rakesburn. "Ahh, here they are. Do you need a ride, Astra?"

"I'd love one." I certainly didn't relish walking to the church in that rain.

The car stopped and David jumped out, dashing up the steps with an umbrella. "All is well?" he asked his wife.

"All's well that ends well, thanks to Astra. We must always remember to have her around in a crisis." She waved to her father, still seated in the back of the car.

"Is Miss Davies coming with?" he shouted, leaning forward to peek out the door.

"She is!" Joyce yelled back.

"One big happy family," David remarked wryly, holding the umbrella over Joyce's head as they made a run for the car.

Porter smiled greedily and patted the seat beside him. I managed to smile back as I unfurled my umbrella, reminding myself that, thankfully, it was a short drive.

The church near Rakesburn is enormous, nearly a cathedral. My father adored it, and we visited often. He'd relate, again and again, the story of the crusader knight who built it as a thanks for his safe homecoming. Somehow, I never tired of the history. Or of seeing Father brush his hands over the stones, face shining in wonder at the skill, care, and devotion that built such places.

Unfortunately, what you got in grandeur, you lost in warmth. We younger ladies, dressed in frothy floral chiffons, shivered in the creeping chill and longed for hot toddies. The matrons seemed to have got it right: many of them were wrapped up in furs. The lady standing in front of me on the way in was wearing a fox stole that still had the head. Its beady glass eyes seemed to glare in my direction.

Once again, the flowers were just short of completely overwhelming, and Joyce's eyes started visibly watering as soon as we walked in. She mopped at her face with David's handkerchief as the four of us were escorted to a pew.

Toby had yet to arrive, but Cecilia and her family had managed to slop their way through the floods and were seated a little farther up. Cee was watching the arrivals intently, and as soon as we sat, she hopped up and came scurrying over.

"How's Belinda?" she asked. "The poor thing! Such terrible weather for a wedding! Of course I wanted to go to the house, but it took us ages to get here because of the roads, and by the time we arrived, it would have been too late. Is she all right?"

"She'll make it down the aisle, never fear," Joyce answered, her voice thickened by a stopped-up nose.

"Joyce, are you crying? Oh, you really have become a softy, haven't you?" Cee reached over and patted Joyce on the shoulder.

A few pews up, a woman with Millicent's hawkish face and Cecilia's coloring stood and bellowed: "Cecilia May! Come back to your seat this instant!"

Millicent, seated beside the woman, turned and smirked.

Cee rolled her eyes. "We'll talk afterward, dears." She skittered back to her seat.

Other guests flowed in, complaining about ruined hats and shoes. Jeremy arrived with a handful of other gentlemen and smiled at us as he was led to the same pew as Cee and Millicent.

"I wonder how much Millicent paid that usher," Joyce snorted.

Only moments before the organist burst into the wedding march, Toby materialized: limping, sodden, muddy to his knees, face even more thunderous than the skies outside.

I stared at him, aghast. "What on earth happened to you?"

"The Humber *died*," he announced through clenched teeth.

"Oh, you poor thing." Joyce hid a laugh behind David's oversized handkerchief.

Toby looked like he would have happily bludgeoned us all with the nearest vase, but the wedding party began to move down the aisle, and his manners and better nature prevailed. Belinda floated past, resplendent in yards and yards of embroidered lace and a halo-like headpiece. She was smiling beatifically and not looking at all like she had spent most of the morning in tears (hurrah for face powder!). As she reached the groom, Hampton grinned just the way you want your husband to grin at you on your wedding day. He took her hand and things got under way.

A fine ceremony, and at last Hampton and Belinda were officially declared man and wife. I let out a breath I hadn't even realized I was holding, in a great, hot rush.

Joyce shot me a questioning look. "What are you so nervous about?" she asked.

"I'm always nervous at weddings," I lied. "I've seen too many films where someone intervenes at the last second, or the bride runs off."

The bride and groom, smiling almost idiotically, made their way back up the aisle as the organist burst into a particularly exuberant song.

Outside, the men made a mad dash for the cars while the ladies huddled under the church porch until their chariots arrived. Toby took the front passenger seat in the Rolls, leaving me jammed next to Porter again as we splashed back to Rakesburn. There, poor Toby vanished upstairs to see if his clothes could be salvaged while the rest of us fell on the champagne. I spotted Freddie near the stairs, unsteadily raising a glass in my direction, and sighed. He would be no help at all. But maybe *I* could do something to save the company. I had to try, at least. So much depended on it.

"Mr. Porter," I said, sidling up to the man as he reached for a second glass of champagne. "I wondered if I might have a word?"

He grinned. "Of course, Miss Davies. Here, have some more champagne. And have I said how lovely you look today?"

"You're too kind, sir." I took the second glass but didn't drink it. "Well, sir, it's about Vandemark Rubber."

There it was: that freezing look. The hard, steely eyes that poor Beckworth had faced back at Gryden, merely for saying the word "business." But what could I do?

I pressed on. "I know you hate talking about such matters at social events, but this is very important. Could you, perhaps, be persuaded to reconsider taking your business elsewhere?" I smiled sweetly at him. Laid a hand gently on his arm.

He looked down at me. No smiles now. His arm shifted away and my hand fell.

"There's nothing to reconsider. My mind is made up," he informed me in a voice as cool as his gaze. "It was a business decision. That company and the idiot who run it are both rotten. If you're mixed up in it, I'm sorry, but I can't help you."

He turned away as I felt a chilly wave crash over me. Freddie's raucous laughter cut across the room and pounded into my skull. *That idiot who runs it . . .*

Porter turned back, a new expression on his face. Disgust. It was so pungent on him I nearly recoiled. "There's a certain type of woman, Miss Davies, who uses her charms and wiles to get what she wants out of old men she thinks are easy prey," he hissed, so low only I could hear him. "I've met many such women. I didn't think you were one of them." He snapped his glass down on the tray of a nearby footman. "Excuse me." He lumbered away as Cecilia bounded in.

"Darlings!" she greeted us, hugging both Joyce and myself, failing to notice I was shocked stiff. "It was a lovely ceremony, wasn't it? Despite the rain. But, you know, they say rain falls on the head of a happy bride."

"They say all sorts of things, don't they?" Joyce noted. "Cee, I like what you've done with your hair today."

"Do you?" Cee patted her hair lightly (and indeed it was a flattering new style). "It's a bit of a surprise, really. Millicent's maid is looking after me this weekend, and usually she's quite abysmal with hair, but she had an afternoon off yesterday and must have used the time to read some magazines or something, because, well—" she gestured to her head and giggled. "Between us, I think she's in love. She's been in an exceptionally jolly mood lately. Is there anything love can't fix?"

An afternoon off yesterday . . .

My heart knocked uncomfortably. "Cee, does Millicent's maid have red hair?"

"Lord, yes, *ever* so red! Millicent thinks she should do something about it, because she thinks it's a bit flashy, but Collins seems determined to keep it. It'll probably start going gray soon anyhow. Hello, Toby! You look better!"

I didn't hear his response. My palms had gone clammy, and my stomach turned over. All I could hear was Alice, over and over again: *"They seemed to be speaking quite intently. By the hedges, where they thought they couldn't be seen."*

I needed to work my way through that, to ease the rising panic. (What had Reilly told her? Was it possible that my maid, a woman privy to some of the most personal details about my life, was spying on me? And passing that information along to *Millicent*?) But this was a wedding, I was in a crowd. There was no time.

Cee was giggling, chattering. "Ducky's been so sweet ever since Paris. He started sending me a bouquet every week, and wonderful letters! Millicent looks like she'll smoke at the ears whenever the flowers arrive."

"Completely worthwhile, then," said Joyce. "Remind me to congratulate him on a job well done next time I see him."

Cee laughed. "You're terrible, Joyce. Shall we go look at the gifts?" She hooked an arm around my waist and steered me toward the library. I let myself be moved because otherwise I'd have just stood frozen and pale, sweaty palmed and nauseous with anxiety. Toby noticed and gave me a questioning look, but I shook my head and tried to give myself something else to focus on.

Wedding presents! A lifetime's worth of excess, gathered for all to see. Sets of china, paintings (old masters, new cubists), silver, dazzling necklaces and brooches and tiaras, matching desk sets in hand-tooled leather, priceless porcelain, Lalique vases, the keys to a Jaguar roadster (from the Arnold clan, according to the accompanying card). Records and a gramophone, silk sheets, new saddles, a globe with each country carved from semi-precious stone and capital cities marked by diamonds, rubies, and emeralds (from Porter, of course). One quick sweep of my hand probably could have ended my money woes forever. Each gift was accompanied by a small card indicating the giver, so we could all compare and bestow approval (or not) as we saw fit.

"Very nice," Joyce declared, looking over my offering—a length of lace that had been in my family for at least two generations. "I'm sure Belinda will love it." I tried to smile, though the scene with Porter, the revelation about Reilly, and the sight of the lace, which had been a wrench to give up, combined to make me feel like bursting into tears.

Toby eased over to me. "What's wrong with you?" he asked. "You're not getting all soppy over a wedding, are you?"

"No. I'll tell you later," I answered just before a voice in my other ear murmured:

"I do love your lace."

I jumped a mile.

"Gosh, Jeremy, we should put a bell on you or something!" Joyce commented.

"What, and rob me of my element of surprise?" he said, laughing. I turned to glare at him, but the malice dissolved at the sight of his apologetic smile. "I'm sorry. I couldn't resist," he said.

"You'd better make it up to her," said Joyce, winking at me.

"I am entirely at her service," Jeremy declared.

I wished more than anything that I could take him at his word and do something shocking. Throw my arms around him, cry, and have him hold and reassure me that everything would be all right. But it wasn't his job to make that happen; it was mine.

A footman appeared in the doorway, politely cleared his throat to call everyone's attention, and asked that we please return to the front hall.

"Oh, the speeches!" Cee squealed, shepherding us out of the library.

The wedding guests crowded around the base of the stairs, where the newlyweds and their parents stood, uniformly beaming. More glasses of champagne circulated, and once everyone was ready, the father of the bride launched into a long-winded speech heaping praise on "this glorious young couple, who represent all that is best in Britain today!" He thrust his glass triumphantly in the air, and the rest of us followed suit.

"To the bride and groom," we all responded in unison.

I couldn't help but exchange amused looks with Jeremy, standing beside me.

"Here's to the best of Britain!" he murmured. "I've heard," Jeremy continued as the crowd made its way to the dining room, "there's to be dancing later on."

"We must get our information from the same sources," I said, trying to put my worries aside for the time being. We skirted the seven-tiered wedding cake and began scrutinizing the feast spread out along the dining table.

"May I ask for the first dance?" he asked, offering me some angels on horseback.

I declined the angels, realizing I had no appetite at all. "I'm so sorry, but I've already promised the first dance to the groom's third cousin." A shame: Theo wasn't nearly as fine a dancer as Jeremy.

An exaggerated look of concern came over Jeremy's face. "Oh, dear, I'm sorry to be the one to have to tell you, but poor Theo's had a bit of an accident."

"How *awful*! Will he be maimed for life, do you think? Will he ever walk again?"

Jeremy could no longer keep from smiling. "The doctors hope so. It seems some clumsy oaf may have stepped on poor Theo's foot. Hard. Twice. Perhaps three times."

I laughed in spite of myself even as I winced at Theo's pain. "All right, you may have the dance, since you worked so hard for it. Next time, though, ask ahead of time."

"It was foolish of me not to realize you'd be in such high demand," he acknowledged. "I certainly know better now."

His arm brushed against mine as he reached for a canapé, and I felt an electric tingle go straight from my wrist to my head. Both cheeks started to warm.

"The early bird gets the worm, so they say." I pretended to be fascinated by some pastries filled with chicken salad.

"Yes indeed. And it seems I've been lazy," he sighed. "You'll excuse me? I believe there are a few more feet I need to flatten."

"Don't you dare! We can't be seen to monopolize one another. People will talk."

He grinned. "I hope people talk about all the time I'm spending with a beautiful woman."

I swallowed hard, and with difficulty.

"Are you hoping to compromise me?" I asked, trying hard to keep my tone light.

"Of course not. I prefer to win on my own merits."

"And yet you've stooped to sabotage," I tsked.

"Well, everyone needs a bit of help now and again."

"Yes, indeed," I said, and sighed before I could stop myself.

Jeremy cocked his head. "Is there something you need help with?"

"No, it's something I need to sort out myself."

His look was all sympathy. "Another grown-up thing?"

"Very."

He nodded. "I won't pry. But I will do my utmost to amuse and distract you by speaking only of bright, happy things. Did you enjoy the wedding?"

"I did," I answered. "I know it's very expected, but I like all weddings. They're such purely happy occasions. At least, the ones I've been to have been."

"That's lucky," he said. "There are few things sadder than an unhappy wedding. Except, perhaps, an unhappy marriage." His mouth tightened momentarily. "But I think this pair will make a success of it. They seem quite made for each other."

"How lucky for them. It's such a rare thing."

"Yes, it is," he agreed quietly.

We drifted toward the door, but the crowd was too thick to get through, so we were left hovering next to the wedding cake.

"Quite the crush," Jeremy murmured.

"Grand weddings," I sighed, even though I can't say I was too sorry the crowd was pushing the two of us closer together. "Everyone simply must accept the invitation."

He sensed the weariness in my tone. "I take it you prefer something quieter?"

"I hadn't really thought about it," I replied, toying with a vol-au-vent.

"Haven't you? I thought most girls were brought up to spend their time dreaming of the day they'd be taken off the shelf."

His smile was mischievous, and I was about to respond with something equally teasing, but then Freddie came swaying through the door. He saw me and waved enthusiastically, endangering the topiaries flanking the doorway.

"Miss Davies!" he hollered. "Here you are!"

He moved toward me, stumbling into an elderly lord who protested, "Careful!"

Freddie managed to drunkenly tip his hat to the man, then set it back on his head crookedly before resuming his journey. Other guests stared and smirked. One of the Arnold brothers tried to grab Freddie's arm as he passed, but Freddie somehow managed to shake free.

Toby climbed to his feet from a chair where he'd been resting a twisted knee. "Now, now, Freddie, I think some fresh air would do you good. Come on, let's get some."

Freddie shoved Toby away, probably harder than he meant to. Toby stumbled backward, arms windmilling, and was fortunately saved from tumbling into a vase of ferns and lilies by one of the ushers.

"No, no, she wants to speak with me," Freddie announced, reaching into a pocket and whipping out the note I'd sent him. My stomach and throat clenched simultaneously, and I could actually feel the blood leaving my head, hands, and feet. "Isn't that right, Miss Davies?" Freddie continued, marching toward me, waving the note. "Isn't that what you wrote here?" He stopped in front of me and made a production of unfolding the bit of paper. "*Freddie, it's very important that we meet privately and discuss what's to be done. Please advise a place and time. Astra Davies.*' Can't deny you wrote that, can you?" He refolded it and jabbed me in the chest with it.

Jeremy immediately stepped forward and pushed Freddie's arm away. "You need to collect yourself, young man," he told him, drawing himself up and giving Freddie that officer's glare again. "You're not fit for company."

Freddie's look turned surly. "Oh, you're after *him* now?" he asked me. "What, did I not act fast enough? I thought that after the ball the other night . . ." He snorted, and I noticed several people in the crowd exchanging glances. Lady Crayle, the mother of the bride, was so enraged she was shaking. Her ice-blue moiré dress rippled, and the fur trim shimmered with the movement. The two girls who had passed Freddie and me in the hallway at the ball suddenly began whispering between themselves. Millicent, stationed nearby, glanced at them, then back at Freddie and me.

"You're a *tease*, that's what you are! A tease, dangling me and him and—" he threw out an arm, gesturing to the room at large and nearly slapping another Arnold brother, who ducked at just the right moment. "Whoever else. Anyone else had notes from her?"

The room was dead silent. Cee, David, and Joyce were all frozen. Porter shook his head. *A certain kind of woman . . .*

"That's quite enough," Jeremy said sharply. "You aren't behaving like a gentleman. Remove yourself, or I'll do it for you."

"Oh, you will, will you?" Freddie smirked.

But the look Jeremy gave him scalded the smile right off his face. "I *will*."

Even I felt a little cowed. Freddie actually flinched, and when three footmen surrounded him, he went quietly. As he left, a few people shook their heads, muttering, "Disgraceful!" The looks some of them were casting my way suggested they weren't only talking about Freddie. And now a sly smile was slithering its way across Millicent's face.

I had to get out—their judgment was smothering me. The blood was pounding in my ears, and I felt lightheaded. I needed air. I turned and rushed through the nearest door, which opened onto the rose garden.

The rain had slowed from a downpour to a persistent drizzle. It would ruin my dress and straggle my hair but felt so soothing on my hot face I didn't care. My head hurt, and it was strangely painful to swallow. I sucked in giant lungfuls of air, like the victim of a shipwreck who's only just managed to find the surface.

How could I have been so stupid? I should never have sent Freddie that note! And now the place would be abuzz with that scene—five hundred of the country's great and good would come away from this talking not about how lovely the bride's dress was, but what a mess Freddie was and how Astra Davies was no better than she should be. Who would want to do business with either one of us? How could I take care of myself and those who depended on me if I couldn't even get through one wedding without disaster?

The door opened and Jeremy slipped out, unfurling a large umbrella as he came and stood beside me.

"If you'd prefer to be alone, I'll just leave this with you." He offered the umbrella.

"That's kind, thank you," I said, wearily rubbing my forehead. "Freddie got the wrong end of the stick. That note wasn't what it seemed."

"You don't have to explain yourself to me," Jeremy said.

"Yes, I do." It was important that Jeremy not think poorly of me. "I'm stuck with this piece of his family's company. There's been a mess, and I wanted to try to sort it out. But that doesn't seem likely now."

"I wish I could help you," Jeremy said after a few moments' silence.

"I'm not sure anyone can at this point." I had a feeling even Cee would struggle to remain cheerful if she were in my shoes.

Jeremy reached out and gently patted my arm. I sighed and looked out at the sodden roses.

"I keep going to things like this, thinking they'll cheer me up," I commented darkly, "but then I always feel worse at the end of them."

"Perhaps you should be less optimistic," Jeremy suggested.

I glanced at him, and he smiled hesitantly. I smiled back.

"So I should accept Joyce's invitation to spend the summer with her and David, but only expect terrible things?"

"Absolutely! It's a hideous part of the world. The weather will be miserable, the bridle paths dreadful, and by the end of it your aunt's house will seem like a paradise."

"All right," I chuckled. "Your task is set, Jeremy. I'm counting on you to help give me the worst summer of my entire life."

He laughed and shook my hand. "Challenge accepted."

* * *

Another ten minutes and I was fully composed and prepared to face the stares and whispers inside. But as I made my way back toward the dining room, one of the footmen stepped in front of me, blocking my way, and told me Lady Crayle wanted a word.

"She'll want apologies, and she should have them," I said to Jeremy. "I'll just be a moment." He nodded and went along while I was led to the nearby study.

Her ladyship stood in front of the unlit fireplace that dominated one entire wall. A full-length portrait of the second duke, dressed in ceremonial armor, hung just over her head, making me feel like I was being glared at by two people. Lady Crayle held a folded piece of paper in both hands, and she was pale with rage.

"Miss Davies," she hissed, managing to pack an impressive amount of loathing into only three syllables.

"Lady Crayle, I'm so sorry," I began. "Believe me, it was all a complete misunderstanding. Belinda's such a dear, and I would never want—"

"How *dare* you mention my daughter's name, after what you did!"

I had been moving toward her, hoping to at least close the physical gap between us (and make it harder for anyone to overhear), but now I stopped.

"Please, your ladyship, don't blame me because Freddie—"

"Freddie! You know perfectly well this has nothing to do with Freddie!"

"It doesn't?"

"No. It's about this!" She brandished the paper she was holding.

Dear God, Millicent *had* done it. She'd shown someone the mislaid love note.

"Lady Crayle, that's a mix-up! If you just bring in Lord Hampton, I'm sure he'll be happy to explain."

"I think it's best he not know about this," Lady Crayle responded. "Why should we mar his happy day with this evidence of your— your . . . oh, I can't even say it! Girls like you—" She made a disgusted noise.

Bewildered, all I could do was stare. That only seemed to enrage her further.

"You know what you did!" she shrieked. "Sending desperate love letters to a man *engaged* to marry *my daughter*! And pretending *all that time* to be her friend! Cozying up so you could steal him later!"

"What do you mean?" I asked. "I never wrote Lord Hampton any love note!"

"Oh no?" She thrust the paper into my hand and I opened it.

My Darling Hammy (Hammy!),
My heart broke a thousand times over when I heard about you and Belinda. Hammy, my darling, she doesn't deserve you.

I didn't bother to read any more. I could guess the tenor of it. "I never wrote this," I said, folding it and handing it back to her.

She refused to take it, crossing her arms over her chest and stepping away from me as if she thought I was infectious.

"It's your writing—I know it is," she said tightly. "It matches that note Freddie has and the note you sent with that cheap bit of lace you gave as a wedding present."

Cheap bit of lace? That had been in my family for more than fifty years and was made by specially trained nuns at a French convent (or so the story went). Mother and I had always thought that would be part of *my* wedding dress someday. *Cheap bit of lace!*

"Did Millicent give you this?" I demanded, thrusting the letter toward her once again. "I'll admit, it's an excellent forgery, which just so happens to be one of her talents."

"It did not come from Lady Millicent, and how dare you suggest she might be guilty of such a sordid thing?" Lady Crayle's nostrils flared. "We've all seen today what sort of a young woman you are, Miss Davies. Devious and grasping and . . . depraved! As a mother, it's my duty to protect my daughter from influences such as yourself. You will not be tolerated in this house a moment longer. Leave now."

There wasn't much I could do. I gathered up my dignity (what little of it was left), turned, and opened the door. Two footmen were waiting, ready to deposit me back outside in the rain.

*　*　*

Thank God for Tommy Ruckle.

The footmen led me straight to the front door, handed over my umbrella, and left me to sort out how I was going to get back to Elmswood. I was contemplating the prospect of walking through sucking, ankle-deep mud when a cheerful voice to my left said, "Oh, hullo! Are you escaping as well?"

I looked over and saw Tommy Ruckle looking sheepish, with his tie loosened and a half-finished cigarette in one hand.

"Excuse my, uh, appearance," he apologized, hastily doing up his shirt's top button. "Not one for the glad rags, me." He gestured to his clothes with the cigarette, dropping a bit of ash on his right spat.

"Mr. Ruckle," I smiled ingratiatingly, "I'm afraid I'm not feeling very well. I don't suppose you could drive me home, could you?"

"Course!" Tommy stubbed out his cigarette and ran me over to Elmswood, talking the whole time about a really excellent club he and his wife had recently discovered in London. "Do go when you're next in town—their negro band is one of the best I've heard, and I consider myself quite the connoisseur." He peered at the house through the rain-smeared windscreen. "Someone's been pulling an architect's leg, by the look of things."

"I'll let you get back," I said, hopping out under the porte cochere. "Thank you, Mr. Ruckle, that was really sweet of you."

"My, you're early!" Alice exclaimed as I let myself in. "Is Toby not with you?"

"He's staying a little longer," I explained.

Alice looked confused but then shrugged. "Of course, men always have a little . . . extra celebrating to do, don't they? What was the bride's dress like? Please, give me all the details!"

"May I do it at dinner?" I pleaded. "I really could do with a nice hot bath."

"Of course! Of course, my dear. Oh, how silly and selfish of me. You go right on up, and I'll tell your maid you want her." She gently pushed me toward the staircase and disappeared through a door to the servants' hall.

I waited in the green toile bedroom for Reilly, who materialized, smiling, and asked if I'd had a pleasant time.

"I did not, Reilly," I answered tightly. "And I think you know why."

Her smile faltered and was replaced by a bewildered and—dare I say it?—frightened look.

"Miss?"

"You've been spending your days off with Lady Millicent's maid, haven't you?"

A long silence. Then, "I have, miss. We're friends, she and I."

"Oh? And you typically lie about having seen friends, then? In London you told me she was a stranger who asked for directions. You must see that it all looks very odd. It looks — well, what am I supposed to think?"

She opened her mouth, then closed it. Her eyes darted. Then, something seemed to dawn on her.

"Oh, miss," she breathed. "Miss, I haven't been telling tales about you, I swear it! Honest, I'd never!" She stepped toward me, arms outstretched, imploring. "Please, miss, you must believe me. I'd never do anything to harm you, not after what you've done for me. You could've dismissed me months ago, and plenty would 'ave, but you kept me on, and I'm grateful, miss, and I'd never repay that by . . ." She shook her head, looking briefly disgusted. "You remember how Lady Millicent was toward me. She'd 'ave thrown me out in the middle o' the night, wi'out a penny to bless myself with. You really think I'd help *her*? By harming *you*?"

"I don't know, Reilly," I answered, crossing my arms and leaning against the dressing table because I was starting to feel weak and wrung out. "I know your family's in trouble and that desperate people sometimes do desperate things."

"We aren't *that* desperate, miss," she replied stoutly. "I'd never. Please, miss, you must believe me."

I studied her, still suspicious. But her face—there was something in her expression. It was a nakedness, a pleading, and a desperation I recognized from the people I'd seen begging on the streets in London and Leicester. I couldn't say I was entirely ready to trust her, but neither was I prepared to fire her.

"Come help me undress, please," I said, turning so she could undo my dress. "It's been a day; I need to lie down."

Chapter Twelve

～

"Do cheer up, my dear," Toby importuned as our taxi drew up outside Aunt El's. "It wasn't all bad. Alice was charming, wasn't she? And your new frock went over a treat."

I merely sighed as we disembarked. My head felt heavy, and I seemed to have caught a chill from standing in the rain.

"No one listens to Freddie anyhow," Toby continued. "That whole matter will blow over in no time. Everyone will be too busy talking about the favorites at Ascot, and what on earth is to be done about this little rebellion in India, to bother with *you*."

I was less certain than he. The previous day he'd returned from the wedding and burst into my room demanding, "Lord, Astra, what on earth did you *do*?"

As I sat up in bed (I had, in fact, been fast asleep) and tried to reengage my brain, he'd paced the room, giving me a dire rundown of the rumors that were already swirling.

"Freddie wouldn't stop talking about what a tease you were, and said he thought you were trying to make someone jealous. They bundled him off, but word was already spreading about who it might be. There was something about a love letter you sent Mustard—really, Astra? Surely not!—and more than a few people said you'd hoped to be a duchess and now were settling for an earl and playing Jeremy Harris for a fool. Jeremy spoke up for you, good man. Said you and he were really only friends, but I don't think it helped much. Especially not after Tommy Ruckle reappeared, tie askew, and said he'd just driven you home. His wife turned puce—absolutely *puce*!—and marched him right out of the room, and we didn't see them again. I think we're all glad not to be in his shoes tonight.

"Oh, and thank you *so very much* for abandoning me with no way to get home. I had to persuade the Arnolds to take me, so I was smashed into that car with seven—no, *eight!*—of them, all laughing and talking about how they couldn't wait for Booboo Woolten's next party because it was to have a crime and criminals theme, and they have the brilliant idea of dressing up as a chain gang. The only good news I can give you is that everyone kept the whispers to a dull roar so Belinda didn't overhear, so her day wasn't *really* spoiled. You may be able to win her back yet."

But everyone else? That might be another matter. Already, an old school friend had rescinded her invitation for me to join her family at Wimbledon. And Bellephonica had evidently overheard Toby's tirade after the wedding and sent word to the servants that we were to be on the first train back to London in the morning. Alice saw us off, apologizing the entire time for her sister's lack of hospitality. At the station, fellow wedding guests had steered well clear. They'd bunched and gossiped, looking me up and down. *"So that's what a certain kind of woman looks like . . ."*

So as I walked through the front door of Aunt El's and began divesting myself of hat and gloves, I think I could be forgiven for feeling more than a little low.

"Astra Lillian Davies!"

Toby and I both jumped and looked up at the staircase. The sight of Aunt El standing there, clenching her cross, made my heart skip several beats. She was staring at me in such white-hot rage I was amazed my skin didn't melt.

She turned and pointed one trembling finger up the stairs. "Up! Now!"

I slowly ascended, followed by Toby. Aunt El brought up the rear, herding us into a dressing room she'd transformed into a combination study and chapel. On one side was a heavy desk and on the other, a prie-dieu facing a crucifix on the wall. She slammed the door shut behind her and went to stand in front of the prie-dieu.

"You have brought shame into my house!" she accused, pointing to me, shaking. "*Shame!* After I spent more than *twenty years* purifying it!"

"Mother, what on earth are you talking about?" Toby asked, backing away from her as if he thought (with good reason) that she'd gone mad.

"I have had a very upsetting telephone call from Lady Crayle this morning," she said. "She told me all about your . . . activities at Lord

Hampton's wedding. Carrying on with Freddie Ponsonby-Lewis! And making advances toward the groom!"

"It wasn't like that at all!" I insisted, willing myself to find the energy to put up some defense. But every bit of me felt lethargic, and my brain seemed to be full of sawdust. Coherent thoughts were having a hard time swimming through the muck and being found. "I never wrote a note to Lord Hampton, and the matter with Freddie was about business—just business," I gabbled. "He misunderstood."

"You can't believe what Lady Crayle says anyway," Toby added. "She's being fed information by Lady Millicent, and you know what she's like."

"Did you not wear a *scarlet* gown to the wedding ball?" Aunt El demanded. "Were you not seen *brazenly cavorting* with Mr. Ponsonby-Lewis in a hallway by not *one,* but *two* people? Were you not party to a scene that ruined the entire wedding?"

"It was all a misunderstanding," I repeated. I heard a loud, high-pitched buzzing and felt sick. What little I'd eaten that day began to churn. I groped for something to steady myself with and found the edge of the desk.

"She didn't ruin the wedding," Toby argued. "It was a bit of excitement. A wedding without excitement's like roast beef without mustard: acceptable, but a bit dull."

"Enough, Tobias!" his mother barked.

"Don't be angry with Toby!" I cried. "It's not his fault Freddie's an idiot."

"*Freddie's* the idiot?" Elinor's face was incredulous. "*You* are the one making a spectacle of yourself. Your position is precarious, Astra! And you've made everything worse! What man will have you now?"

"I daresay Lord Dunreaven will have her," said Toby.

His mother rounded on him. "Then *you* are the fool, Tobias. Men like him don't give their titles to girls who seem like easy conquests." She turned back to me. "You have brought *nothing* but trouble ever since you came through my door. You and your probing and *utter lack* of respect for decency! I have tried to be patient with you, tried to tell myself that you were young and simply needed a firm hand to guide you, but you clearly don't care at all about me or Toby or our good name or your own.

I'm not sure—not at *all* sure—I can continue to have you here, Astra. No, I really don't think I can."

The nausea built and rushed upward. Was she throwing me out? Where would I go? Would any friend take me in, now that I existed under a cloud of scandal? If I had to pay for a room somewhere *and* pay Rosedale's fees, I'd never be able to save up enough money to go back to Hensley. And if Vandemark collapsed, I might not even be able to afford the room and the fees.

Toby was remonstrating with his mother, saying something about Christian charity, but I wasn't listening. I had reached a crisis, stomach burning and revolting. I stumbled to the nearest vessel—some sort of vase near the door—and vomited into it.

*   *   *

Influenza. Apparently Bellephonica was more contagious than her doctor realized. I spent nearly a week shivering even as I burned, unable to keep anything down. Asleep, I suffered from fever dreams. I dreamt I saw my parents standing in the doorway of Hensley, waving and smiling, even as the house began to shake and writhe around them. I tried to call out, to run to them, but I was stuck in every way. And Aunt El appeared beside me, saying, "Best not to interfere."

I woke to someone wiping my forehead with something shockingly cool and smelling vaguely of lavender. I thought it was my mother but gradually realized it was Reilly holding the cloth. I cried, fell asleep again, and the fever finally broke.

I slept until noon the next day and came around weak and pale. My eyes flickered open, and the first thing I saw was the picture Raymond had painted for my birthday. The joyous smears of color, made in generosity for someone he didn't even know, coaxed a smile from me and made me feel for the first time in a while that there was some brightness in the world.

"Gifts for the invalid!" Toby announced, coming to my room two days later, carrying a small stack of magazines.

I was still in bed, but sitting up, and Reilly had fixed my hair and draped me in a silk and lace bed jacket, so I felt a little more human. A tabletop radio tuned to Radio Normandie was playing Marion Harris.

Dandy was curled up next to me on one of the few spots not covered by old photographs and piles of papers.

Toby processed in, followed by Reilly carrying the mail and a tiny, potted rose plant. Behind her was Jeffries with a massive hamper from Fortnum and Mason.

"You took your time," I chided, grinning nonetheless at the sight of Toby.

"Forgive me, please, for not wanting to join you in your misery."

"You are forgiven. I didn't want to be in my place either."

"Ahh, poor lamb," Toby sympathized. "Just over there, please, Jeffries."

Jeffries set down the hamper and made himself scarce. Reilly handed me the mail. Judging from the addresses, I guessed they were more rescinded invitations.

"Have the rumors not died down?" I asked Toby, reluctantly slicing one open.

"Oh, you know how these things are," he answered vaguely, wandering over to the window and peeking out. "Oh, the milk delivery is very late this morning."

I noticed Reilly giving him a look. "Spill, Reilly, if you please," I prompted.

"I only know what the other servants say, miss, but"—she took a deep breath—"It's very bad. With you having so suddenly taken ill after what happened, it only fed things. Some think you got into trouble and had to have . . . a procedure."

"Others have been more creative," Toby piped up. "They think your note to Freddie was about drugs and say you're hopelessly addicted to cocaine. But that's all right—it's quite fashionable now. They could have said opium, and who does opium anymore?"

"You're all brightness, Toby," I remarked drily. "What does your mother think?"

"She's taken herself off to Eastbourne to steady her nerves. But cheer up, it'll blow over soon enough," Toby said, making room on the bed and sitting down.

"Probably *not* soon enough. Thank you, Reilly."

She set the plant she was holding on my bedside table and departed.

"I'll work on Mother," Toby offered as I went through the mail. Just as I thought, all notes informing me, in clipped tones, that my presence would not be required at the given sporting event or party or country house weekend. What was I going to do all summer? Sit in stinking, boiling London, waiting for the ax to fall and wondering what my maid was up to? And never mind trying to make inroads into business; I doubted anyone worth anything would even be in the same room with me now. If they *were* willing, it would be for all the wrong reasons. I sighed.

"Millicent has done her work well this time," Toby noted. "Though I don't see why she went to the trouble of forging a letter when she had Mustard's note."

"Who knows why she does anything?" I snapped, shoving the mail to one side and crossing my arms. "Maybe she wanted to keep some control over the poor man."

Toby noticed my glum expression and went to fetch the hamper. "Do smile, old girl, you have some friends still." He tugged the hamper a little closer and flipped it open. Inside was a mass of rich foods I could hardly bear to look at. "From Joyce. She telephoned twice to see how you were feeling and asked me to tell you you're still welcome at Wotting Park this summer, if you find yourself at loose ends."

Dear, dear Joyce!

"I suppose at times like this you really do discover who your true friends are," I remarked, finding and unfolding a little note that had come with the rose plant.

Dear Astra,

Toby says you haven't been well, so I thought I'd send a little token to cheer you up. Joyce says she still hopes to have you at Wotting Park. I hope you take her up on that, because I did promise you a terrible summer, and I'm a man of my word!

Your friend, in sickness and in health, Jeremy

"That's very sweet," I murmured.

"He's been championing you," said Toby. "A few chaps were having a whisper about you at the club, but he told them it was all nonsense because he'd never known you to be anything other than perfectly respectable."

"That's nice of him."

"More than just nice, old girl," said Toby. "You know that people are saying you've taken him in."

"Well, he's a man; men can come through gossip unscathed," I grumbled. "And a titled man—well! He can commit murder and still dine with a duke the next day."

Toby was quiet for a little while, then gestured to the strewn bed and commented, "Seems you're keeping yourself distracted. What's all this?"

"I'll tell you, but could you please turn up the radio first?"

He looked confused but obeyed. "I had no idea you were so fond of 'Goodnight Sweetheart,'" he commented.

"I'm not. I just don't want anyone listening in."

"Listening in? Are you serious? Is this fever delusion talking?"

"No," I whispered as he resumed his seat on the bed. "It's just a precaution. I thought I might use this time trapped in bed to learn more about Mr. Porter."

"Oh? Still hoping to talk him round?"

"No. That seems unlikely now. But the man certainly knows how to make money, and they do say you should learn from the best. I'm studying his methods."

"And what do they tell you?"

"That you need money to begin with."

"No rags-to-riches story for him?"

"Not really. His father did well in dry goods and left a tidy sum when he died. Porter bought some land, and not long after, someone wanted it to build tenements on. Porter leased it to the builder, who put up his tenements and paid rent. The land's value went up, and Porter sold for a tidy profit. And he moved into other things and now . . ."

"And now he has his finger in every pie," Toby finished.

"So it seems. And any pie he so much as sniffs becomes valuable."

"Well, best of luck making Vandemark Rubber delectable again, darling. And what's all this?" Toby picked up one of the tarnished christening cups I'd found in my mother's box of mementoes. "Not Porter's, I take it?"

"Of course not." I reached out and took it back. "It was in one of Mother's boxes. I've been going back through them." I rotated the cup in my hands.

"Reminiscing?"

"Something like that. There was something Alice said—it made me realize that my mother doesn't seem to have anything of Raymond's, which is odd. She obviously cared for him, and she kept *everything*. So why doesn't she have any of his bonnets or rattles?"

Toby scrunched his face sympathetically. "Well, if she did have him before she was married, perhaps your father didn't want any reminders around the house."

"I don't think so." I struggled to imagine my father forbidding my mother anything, let alone something so important. "He didn't keep her from seeing Raymond regularly, or supporting him, which she did with Father's money. And he took out that life insurance policy with Raymond as a beneficiary. Even if Mother had been behind that, surely it suggests he didn't bear Raymond any ill will?"

"What explanation could there be? That his things were lost or hidden away?"

"Or given to someone else," I murmured, handing him back the christening cup. I had noticed, just that morning, that each cup had an initial engraved on it. Nearly unreadable, thanks to the tarnish, but I could just make out the *L*, *E*, and *M* that graced each one in turn. *L* for Lillian, *E* for Elinor, and *M*.

"Who's *M*?" Toby wondered, examining the cup.

"Who indeed?" I reached into the box and retrieved the crumbling posy with its initialed card: M.E.C. "M. E. Carlyle, do you think? And there's this too." I retrieved one of the photo albums and opened it to a page with a large photograph of my mother, dressed for her court presentation. Alongside her was another woman, also in court dress. She was willowy and dark-haired, like Mother, but had light eyes. I pointed to the photograph. "Does anyone here look familiar to you?"

Toby briefly studied the photograph. "Your mother, of course. But who's this, then?" He indicated the other woman.

"I believe," I said quietly, "that's our aunt, M. Carlyle."

Chapter Thirteen

~

By late June, the heat and stench made London intolerable, and those who could fled to country piles or Continental bolt-holes. Even Toby went, joining his mother in Eastbourne, which was just civilized enough to suit him. Grateful for the escape, I boarded a train to Wotting Park with Reilly and Dandy. The rumors and general air of disapproval (one dowager actually *hissed* when she saw me at Selfridge's) were making me miserable, and I hoped that being out of the city and near the coast would help.

Unlike many country houses that have remained virtually unchanged for hundreds of years, Wotting Park has a long tradition of being pulled down and rebuilt. The current house, the sixth to stand on the site, was built by David's father just after he came into the title. But Baron and Baroness Merseley had only lived in the house for a year or two before they both departed forever—and separately. She scandalously ran off with a lover (a Spanish sailor, some said), and he retreated to the casinos of Monte Carlo, where he remains to this day. Hopefully Joyce and David would have better luck once, as Joyce said, they managed to rub off each other's sharper edges.

Dandy spent the train ride and drive from the station curled up in my lap, snoring gently. As the car drew up to the house, he suddenly animated, leapt up, and pressed his nose to the glass, his entire body wriggling with the force of his wag.

David, who had come to collect me from the station, laughed. "He knows where he is!" he said, and braked at the front door just as Joyce came around the corner of the house. A garden trug loaded with irises was slung over one arm; a yapping herd of dogs tumbled over one another in her wake.

"Astra!" She lifted her arm in a wave. I waved back, smiling, as I climbed into the sunlight. Dandy spilled out behind me and rushed to join his mother and sisters.

"He's coming along nicely," Joyce observed, indicating Dandy.

"He's glad to be out of London for the summer," I said as we went in. "We both are. Thank you for inviting me." Her support through this disaster meant the world.

"Do you really think I was prepared to face a summer alone with Laura? She'll kill me. Cee was supposed to come but"—she cleared her throat awkwardly—"something came up. What do you think of what I've done in here?" She gestured to the hall, which had been stripped of the overly elaborate baroque furnishings and heavy floral carpets her mother-in-law preferred. Now, the parquet floor was permitted to shine, covered only by a zebra skin and a lion hide ("David shot both on our honeymoon and was *so* proud of himself," Joyce explained) and an oval rug with a simple design of overlapping curlicues worked in black, silver, and buff. Two gently curving cream-colored sofas and a pair of matching armchairs were arranged around the oval rug. The Tiffany lamps had gone, replaced by a large pendant that looked like the Chrysler Building inverted, suspended from the ceiling.

"It's lovely, Joyce," I told her. "Quite fresh."

"I'm glad you think so. Up we go." We headed upstairs, and she threw open the door of a bedroom overlooking the gardens. The windows stood open, and I could just smell the salt on the air, blowing off the Channel. This room, too, had been redone and now boasted mint-green walls, a white suite of furniture, and matching curtains and eiderdown in a simple floral pattern. Over the bed was a faux canopy, the fabric of which was pleated to resemble a sunburst.

"I remember you've always liked this room," Joyce said with a smile as she stretched out, catlike, on the bed. "Hope you don't mind the changes."

"Not at all—it's lovely." I eased my sweaty hands out of my gloves and stood by the window, where the breeze soothed my heat-prickled skin. "Have you seen much of Jeremy since you've been here?"

"A bit," Joyce answered, fixing her eyes on me while she traced the outline of a flower on the eiderdown. "He comes to see David. But now you're here . . ."

I shot her a warning look. "Now, now." Even so, I felt a thrill when she said it.

"Oh, please," she groaned. "He'll come to see you. You have quite the allure. Even Daddy felt it. He'd been talking about spending the summer here, but then after the wedding he suddenly changed his mind and said he'd go off to a spa in Baden. I talked him out of it—Germany's no place for him just now. David and I felt quite uncomfortable when we were there. Like people were staring at me, all the time, just wondering . . . And, of course, if you have money it's even worse. They just assume. Anyway, no Germany: he's taking the yacht to Cannes instead. What did you do to annoy him?"

"I didn't do anything," I insisted. "I only mentioned a business matter—"

"Ahh!" She smiled triumphantly. "There we are! Daddy *hates* talking business at social events—people are always trying to get something useful out of him. He doesn't do well with people who *need* something from him. If anyone should know that, it's me."

She grimaced, and I thought about what her childhood had been like. Full of the best of everything, but I'd never seen her father hug her. Not even on her wedding day.

I sat on the bed and took her hand. "I'm sorry if I've caused trouble with you and your father."

"Oh, don't worry. Daddy'll clear his head at sea, and he's promised to come by later in the summer," she said, withdrawing her hand and fiddling with her wedding ring. "I have other things to worry about anyway. He's got to take second place."

I noticed then the faintly purpling half-moons under her eyes and a tightness to her jaw.

"Joyce, is everything all right?" I asked gently.

"Oh, you know, marriage," she said with another shrug. "Well, you'll know someday. It has its peaks and valleys."

"And what's pushed you into the valley?"

"My husband's Englishness." She rolled her eyes, then pushed off the bed and wandered over to the window, pulling a cigarette case out of her pocket and lighting one up. She offered one and I accepted.

"Can you really fault him for that?" I asked.

She exhaled. "I can when it means he's an utter stick in the mud!"

There was a soft knock on the door, and Reilly poked her head in. "I'll come back later," she proposed, noting the tension in the room.

"No, it's all right—come and get Miss Davies settled," Joyce answered before I could agree and send Reilly away.

Reilly glanced at me, then slipped into the dressing room with a packing case.

"I do so much, you know!" Joyce cried. "And he does so little! I can't seem to get him to pay attention to *anything* important, and then he gets annoyed with me when *I* try to do anything meaningful and tells me I shouldn't meddle. So I thought I'd try being domestic, and I redecorated this whole house, which was hideous, thanks to his mother, and all he does is complain. So then I bought him an airplane for his birthday—"

"You what?" I couldn't help myself. An airplane? Who buys someone an airplane as a birthday gift? Most wives give their husbands a tie!

Joyce seemed baffled by my reaction. "He loves to fly—why shouldn't he have a proper plane? That old one he was rattling around in simply wouldn't do. It wasn't safe: I'm surprised it didn't come apart in midair. Of course, now he spends almost all his time at the factory where they're building the thing. I've hardly seen him for weeks. He may as well have a mistress." She frowned. "Why are you looking at me like that?"

I was thinking of my own struggles. How hard it was for me to keep Raymond in comfort and find a way to just go home. And then, guiltily, I thought of Reilly's brother, with his five hungry children. The people I'd seen in Leicester, the war veteran in London, the men I'd heard about selling apples for a nickel each up and down Fifth Avenue. I wondered how hard their thanks stuck in their throats as women like Joyce, toasty in their furs, bent down, holding a shiny nickel with the tips of gloved fingers, like a distant auntie offering a treat to a young relative. "How much you've grown! Here you are. Now, run along and play like a good boy. And don't spend it all in one place, ho ho!"

"Astra!" Joyce said sharply, recalling me to the here and now.

I shook my head. "I'm sorry. Goodness! An airplane! That's . . . quite something."

"I thought so too. And he seemed pleased enough, for a while, but then bills from the craftsmen working on the house and the couturiers in Paris arrived, and he started in on my extravagance. That hypocrite! I pointed out that he was quite happy to pay his father's gambling debts and keep him in comfort in Monaco—not that the man deserves it—but if I dare to buy myself a few frocks, well! That's the end of the world, isn't it?"

It had, of course, been much more than a few frocks, but I didn't want to make her cross. I crooned and stroked her arm.

"I'm sure he'll come around. The house is lovely. He just needs to get used to it."

"He won't even try." She stubbed the cigarette out hard on the outside windowsill. "He says he feels like it's someone else's home now. I only wanted to make it fresh for us. I don't understand why people want to live in the reek of those who came before."

Her own father had been one of those people. Porter had bought his country estate furnishings and all from a distinguished clan that lost all of its sons in the Great War. Once he had the place, he'd refused to make any changes, living uncomfortably among another family's relics. It was as if he thought societal prestige came automatically with forebearers' portraits and trinkets picked up on grand tours of centuries past. The complete absence of anything personal gave the house the feeling of a mausoleum.

"Perhaps David misses having any reminder of his parents," I gently suggested. "Not all of his memories of them are bad ones. Are there a few things you can change back, just to keep the peace?"

Joyce lit another cigarette and thought about it. "There's a portrait of his mother that used to hang in the drawing room. It's not too awful. I could have that brought back out, I suppose," she offered.

"There you are!"

Her answering look was a withering one. "Don't think you're some sort of matrimonial expert."

"I don't think I'm an expert at anything. And I may be wrong about this, but it's worth a try, for the sake of peace."

"Indeed. I suppose none of you want to spend the summer in No Man's Land. You'll have other concerns: brace yourself—Millicent's in the neighborhood."

I groaned, unable to help myself. I'd hoped to find a little peace, at least for a while, but that seemed unlikely now.

"I know!" Joyce huffed. "She's staying at Lush Wycombe with the Sutton-Cooper-Carters, and I think we can guess why."

I nodded. The eldest son and heir, Lord Scott, better known as Laddie. Unmarried.

Joyce stubbed out her second cigarette. Down in the garden, the dogs were enjoying a game of rough-and-tumble, watched indulgently by their mother.

"I thought better of Laddie," Joyce said, sighing. "But I don't suppose we can blame him. Everyone must sing for their supper, and suppers at Lush Wycombe seem to be getting a bit dear. His father had to dismiss three footman and the chauffeur in the last six months alone. They'll be on a skeleton staff before long. Laddie might have to do his own dusting!" She chuckled at the thought.

I failed to see the humor in the situation. Where would those men go? "What a shame," I murmured.

"Yes, very," Joyce agreed, fussing with her cigarette case. "Imagine doing without a chauffeur.! He's a good one too. We took him on, along with two of the footmen."

I turned away so she wouldn't see me rolling my eyes, and caught sight of Reilly in the dressing room, grimacing as she unpacked a batiste blouse. "I meant—"

"I know what you meant." Joyce snapped the case shut with a punctuating *click!* "I do what I can, but we simply can't hire everyone. Even we only need so many footmen." She sighed, tucked the case away, and turned to face the looking glass at the dressing table. "Laura's taken over the tennis courts," she reported, patting her hair smooth. "So you may want to linger out of sight until dinner. Unless of course you want to be dragged off and put through your paces for several hours?"

"I do not."

"I thought not. See you later, then."

As soon as she was gone, Reilly materialized in the dressing room doorway. "Shall I send for the rest of the cases to be brought up, miss?" she asked.

"Yes, please."

She rang the bell and gave instructions to the footman who answered, then began arranging things on the dressing table.

"If you don't mind my saying so, miss, an airplane factory must use quite a lot of tires," she commented.

I had been sitting at the window, watching the dogs play, thinking, but now turned to face her with eyebrows raised. "Have you been listening at keyholes, Reilly?"

"No, miss."

"You have the hearing of a bat, then."

"Yes, miss."

"I'm not sure that's always a good thing."

"Yes, miss." She withdrew to the dressing room.

I sighed. I'd been thinking the same thing about the factory, but I'd need Freddie to make that happen, and working with him was unappealing, to say the least. Unappealing, but almost certainly inevitable.

I sighed again, lit a cigarette, and smoked, wondering if things were ever going to become easy or if this was just what adulthood was all about.

*   *   *

I went down early for dinner and found Laura pacing up and down the terrace with a cigarette.

"Halloo! Here you are!" she called merrily, waving the cigarette. "You caught me enjoying my one a day!"

"We all need vices—they keep us interesting," I excused, retrieving a cigarette of my own and gesturing to hers. She held it toward me, and I lit mine off the end.

"All the same, don't tell David or Joyce. I'll never hear the end of it. Right, then, let's have a look at you." She stood back and cast an eye over me, shaking her head. "Thin and peaky! Never mind—I'll go to work. You'll be as brown as a bandleader before the summer's out."

"I'm not sure I fancy being your project."

"Find me someone else to improve, then. I can't simply sit around, I'll grow moss. Or become peevish and quarrelsome, like Joyce and David." She rolled her eyes.

I sighed. "I don't know what David says, but Joyce feels unappreciated. Your brother hasn't been appropriately grateful for all the work she's done."

"In all fairness, it *is* a lot of change," Laura observed. "I barely recognized the place when I arrived. Not that that's a bad thing—Mother's taste in furnishings and men were equally bad." She shrugged cheerfully.

Unlike the house, Laura was much the same as she'd ever been: wiry and unadorned. She wore her brown hair in a close Eton crop, fashion be damned, and couldn't be bothered with makeup. Her stark white, slightly rumpled, Grecian-inspired dress was so loose and simple it could have been mistaken for a nightgown. The only jewelry she wore was a plain wedding band and a silver charm bracelet, tinkling musically with a miniature tennis racket, golf club, star, pineapple, and sheepdog.

"Joyce thinks David hates all the change," I told her.

Laura exhaled a stream of smoke. "Some marriages have harder adjustments than others, I've found. It helps to have something to throw yourself into once the race to the altar is done. Joyce is still trying to settle on what that something will be, and David just doesn't understand it yet. When they were in New York on their honeymoon, he and I had lunch, and he kept complaining about how Joyce insisted they go film people living in all these grotty places. She wanted to see the Hooverville in Central Park, but he put his foot down, so she sulked and skipped lunch to go shopping. Dropped a fortune at Macy's, apparently, and David blew his top and there was a row. She sent the bills off to Porter to be paid, and there was *another* row." Laura rolled her eyes. "I knew this would happen. See, he thought she'd turn into a Bradbury, once they married. But she thinks *he* should be a Porter. David doesn't understand that lifestyle: it's not very English, is it? All flash and the latest thing. If you ask me, they need a good long break. Does wonders for Bobby and me."

"No trouble in paradise for you, I hope?"

"Heavens no! We go together like toast and marmalade: the one making the other infinitely better. He's spending the summer sailing down South America. We both thought it was a good time to escape New York for a while. It's so . . . sad there just now." She flinched. "But the voyage over was quite jolly. All the tennis players were coming over for Wimbledon. Helen Jacobs and I kept each other in top form."

"I'm sure we'll all be most grateful to her," I said drily.

Laura laughed, then commented, "You're down early for dinner. Someone you were hoping to see? I'm afraid Jeremy's not here."

"Maybe I wanted to see you."

Laura cackled. "Nobody comes down early to see me. Not even my husband. Joyce says you've got Jeremy wrapped around your little finger."

"Hardly."

"Not interested?" She raised her eyebrows. "Good for you for preserving your independence. If I'd had money of my own, I'd have probably steered clear of the altar."

"Would you really?"

"Oh yes. I'd have had Bobby as a lover instead, so we could both wriggle out if we got bored. Hard to wriggle once you're bound."

"You two seem to be making a good go of it," I observed.

"We are. We've found ways to make marriage work for us. But you, my dear—you stay single for as long as you like. Be modern, and ignore all those vicious rumors."

"Oh." I sighed. "You heard about all that?"

Laura laughed. "Of course I did! You're quite the talk of the town these days."

"Thanks to Millicent," I grumbled.

"Still a magnificent bitch." Laura shook her head. "I almost admire her. Having her aunt give Lady Crayle that love letter: lends credence and provides Millicent with deniability. Poor you. But at least you've got Jeremy in your corner, and that makes for a *very* attractive corner, doesn't it?"

"If you say so." I hoped I sounded nonchalant and that the fading light covered the blush I felt creeping over my cheeks.

"So coy! Have your little secrets, then." Laura stubbed out the remains of her cigarette on the stone balustrade, then leaned against it, spreading her arms wide. She looked up at the house, breathing deeply and exhaling with a sigh. "Coming home as a guest when you're an adult is strange."

"Is it?"

She looked at me. "Have you been to Hensley? You know, since . . ." She grimaced.

I shook my head, swallowing hard against a lump in my throat.

"All in good time, toots." She patted me on the arm, then grabbed my cigarette, took a puff, and handed it back. "You should visit Midbourne while you're here. The gardens there are beautiful. Jeremy Harris has quite a lot to offer the right girl."

"Then I hope he finds her soon," I responded breezily.

Laura rolled her eyes as Joyce poked her head out.

"Here you two are! We're pouring the cocktails." She frowned at the stonework. "Have you been putting out cigarettes on my balustrade?" she demanded as Laura passed.

"What? As if I would ever smoke a cigarette! Must have been Astra." With a cheeky smile, Laura disappeared inside.

Chapter Fourteen

I came down for breakfast the next morning and found Joyce already at the table. A cup of coffee, a half-finished plate of bacon and eggs, the morning post, and the evening's dinner menu were before her.

"Oh, good," she said as soon as she saw me. "Astra, you're better at French than I am: What is this word?" She pointed to the menu.

"Brains," I translated, telling myself to go ahead and skip that course.

"Oh. I wish Monsieur le Chef would send these up written in English, but I don't dare ask. I'm sure he'd just think I was even more déclassé than he already does."

"I'm sure he doesn't think that."

"Don't be silly—of course he does. And I am. We Porters are so *nouveau* we don't even have ancestors: just dead relatives."

Through the open windows came the sound of Laura counting aloud as she did jumping jacks on the lawn.

"I'm surprised she didn't come fetch me at dawn to join her," I commented, sipping my coffee and watching her stretch and bend and twist.

"I forbade it," Joyce told me. "But don't expect her to hold off too long. She's gone and become an actual fitness instructor, with a certification and everything, so now she views everyone as either a future project or a work in progress."

"Talking about me, Joyce?" Laura asked, jouncing into the room with so much energy I expected her to cartwheel her way to the table. "You both *have* to join me tomorrow morning. Nothing like a good run of exercise to get the blood flowing."

"I'll take your word for it," Joyce said drily.

"No, really, Joyce, you should try it," Laura urged. "It'll turn your mood right around. There was a colleague of Bobby's who was heading straight for disaster—drank and smoked too much and just looked *awful*. So I took him in hand and before you knew it, he was a new man. He dropped 15 pounds and gave up all the vices. And it's all thanks to me. So you should really take up exercising, Joyce, before it's too late. You know your family's inclined to stoutness. You should put in a pool. A few laps every morning will get your day started just right."

"There's a river nearby. Why don't you swim laps in that?" Joyce suggested.

Laura grinned. "I'll take Astra with me. We can paddle down to Midbourne and have breakfast with Jeremy in our swimsuits." She dropped into the chair next to mine and squinted at my plate. "Are you really going to eat that?" she squealed, scrutinizing the marmaladed toast and oozing egg yolk. "Honestly, you have no idea how much you're clogging yourself up, do you? All that ghastly stuff is just plugging your pores and arteries. It's why your skin looks the way it does."

I blinked at her and then looked at Joyce, who rolled her eyes over her coffee cup and shook her head before digging into the pile of post.

"I'll fix you right up," Laura promised, clapping me on the shoulder and bounding to the sideboard to retrieve a broiled grapefruit decorated with a maraschino cherry. "Always a light breakfast," she told me in between juicy mouthfuls. "Too much animal protein slows you down from the inside out. Joyce, is there any Melba toast?"

"No, just ordinary toast. This one's for you, Astra." Joyce handed me a letter as, with a wink, Laura lunged to pluck a piece of toast from my plate.

"From Cee," I murmured, tearing into the envelope as Laura munched my toast.

Astra, darling,
I'm so, so, so sorry I can't come to Wotting Park and see you! Please don't be cross with me—I've begged and begged, but my aunt's been on Daddy so fiercely he simply won't budge. I don't know what's possessed him, but he's made it clear I'm not to go, and there's nothing I can do about it. Sorry! Sorry! Sorry! I've missed you awfully and was sooooo looking forward to seeing Laura again. Poor dear, you must have felt so

abandoned—I didn't even inquire after you when you were ill! Terrible, I know, but Millicent was going through all the mail and watching me every time I went to use the telephone, so I couldn't. But she's away now, so I've a bit more freedom. I'll keep working on Daddy, and Ducky's coming up for a few weeks, and I'm sure he'll help me because he's always thought very highly of you. Darling A, please forgive me! –C

I slumped, appetite gone. Cee's sweet father too? Was there anyone left whom Millicent hadn't poisoned?

Laura finished the toast and snatched the letter. She read it, shaking her head, then crumpled it up and tossed it over her shoulder. Dandy and one of his sisters pounced on it and began nosing it across the floor. Laura patted me on the shoulder. "Don't fret, chum, I'm sure it'll work itself out sooner or later. These things do. I mean, really"—she paused to take a large bite of grapefruit—"it was inevitable that something like this would happen. Of course you would end up being a scandal."

"What do you mean, 'of course'?" I asked.

Laura smirked, pointing to me with her grapefruit spoon. "You, my dear, currently defy categorization, and we all love to categorize. It makes us think we understand the world. A loose woman doesn't fit into any of the proper boxes—wife, mother, daughter. It makes people nervous. They don't know what to expect from you. So, naturally, they were only too eager to assign you the one label that was left: whore. Without family or a willing guardian to speak up for you, you had no protection, and that's how these kinds of reputations get made. Sorry, dearie, but that's the world at work." She patted me on the shoulder again, as if that would comfort me.

Joyce gaped. "I think that's quite a stretch, Laura."

Laura shrugged. "You saw for yourself what happened. The only way to reel it back now is to get the women on your side or to find a better label. We all need labels. Or you could embrace it. If everyone who matters thinks you're hopping into any bed that takes your fancy, then do it! What have you got to lose?"

"Quite a bit, I think," I replied.

She smirked. "Like your reputation? Gone now: these sorts of whispers tend to follow you all your days. Maybe you should just come back to America with me. Everyone's more tolerant of the amoral woman there. They took me in, didn't they?"

"You weren't a scandal," I pointed out.

"No, but my mother was, and that's just as bad. These things always follow a family, especially the daughters. Immorality, they think, is passed down in the genes. If I'd stayed in England, I'd never have got married. Not because the boys weren't interested, but because none of their mothers would have me. But America, well! That's a fresh start! We love a notorious woman there: we celebrate them in films and everything! You, my dear, could be the quintessential 'It Girl'!"

"Those are my choices? Be notorious here or make myself notorious in America?" I wondered aloud.

"Oh, you make it sound so dreary. It's loads of fun—really! Have a fling or two; you'll enjoy it."

"That's risky business," Joyce pointed out.

"Oh, hardly." Laura turned to me. "If you want, I know a nice doctor who'll fix you up."

"Fix me up?" I didn't like the sound of that. As if I were a car or misbehaving boiler.

Laura nodded. "He's very nice, this doctor. Fits you for a Dutch cap, tells you how to use it, then sends you on your way. No judgment, no lectures. Much better than resorting to Lysol."

Joyce seemed intrigued. "Does it really work?" she asked.

"Of course it does! Look at me: no squallers. Bobbie and I agreed on that from the outset."

"And where do you come by your vast knowledge of the benefits of flings?" I asked with a wry smile.

"I come by it naturally: we Bradburys are born knowing these things," Laura answered. "We clearly lack sexual hang-ups, isn't that right, Joyce?"

Joyce buried her face in her teacup, which failed to cover her incredible blush.

"So I take it you've had affairs, then?" I asked Laura, somewhat intrigued.

"Only with Bobby, before we were married."

"You never did!" Joyce breathed.

"Of course we did! Three days in a grubby little cabin camp, with spiders and a bed that squeaked and sagged in the middle. Nearly did poor Bobby's back in." Laura winked at me. "And then we decided it'd be fine, and off we went to the courthouse."

Joyce and I gaped at her.

"But—but what if it had been terrible?" Joyce stammered.

"Then we probably would have skipped the courthouse," Laura responded. "You don't buy the car that gives you a bumpy ride, do you?" She took one last bite of toast and bounced back onto her feet. "I think I'll go do a few laps around the garden before tennis. It'll slow me down, so the rest of you can keep up."

"Good heavens, Laura, what sort of drugs are you taking?" Joyce asked her.

"Fresh air's all the drug I need," Laura answered. "Though a friend of mine swears by cocaine when you really need to pep up. Astra, tennis in an hour. Up you get and into the whites. We need to work that breakfast out of you."

"Sounds delightful," I said dully as she galloped out.

"Have another few eggs, just to spite her," Joyce urged, as she perused a letter of her own, frowning.

"Not bad news, I hope?" I asked, nodding toward the letter in her hand.

"No, no, just something from a lovely woman I met when we were in Dresden." She folded the letter and stood. "I'm going to speak to the chef about these brains. I don't care if he does think I'm déclassé, I still want him to make food I want to eat. Ta, darling. Make sure you drink plenty of water—it sounds like you'll need it."

By late morning I was exhausted, hauling myself gracelessly back and forth over the tennis lawn, diving for balls Laura lobbed my way with a serve so deadly it should have been weaponized. It went on and on, set after set. I told myself I was tiring her out, but there's no tiring Laura. By the time a maid appeared with lemonade and biscuits, I was literally dripping wet, my whites sticking clammily to my skin.

"You've barely worked off breakfast; you haven't earned your ca-ake!" Laura singsonged as I stuffed an unladylike number of ginger nuts into my mouth. I told her I was finished and stumbled, colt-legged, back to the house and summoned Reilly. She took one look at me and went to draw a bath.

"I could tell them all you're indisposed this afternoon," she offered, returning to help me peel off the soggy whites.

"I'm not sure Laura will accept any excuses," I said, sighing.

Reilly smiled very briefly and handed me a letter. "This came today, miss," she said, searching for bath salts among the cut-crystal bottles on the dressing table.

I tore open the letter. It was from Toby.

Greetings, cousin mine! Hope Wotting Park is all you wanted and needed. Eastbourne is . . . well, we won't talk about that. I'll never understand the appeal of sea air: it smells of fish, and the seagulls have no respect for new hats or the need for peace.

Rest assured, I have not forgotten my task here. I believe I've made some inroads with Mums vis à vis you continuing to live with us. I actually quoted Job the other day, can you imagine? Remarkable what one can do when called upon in a crisis! I'm sure she'll come around soon. Better news in the next note, I'm sure.

Do be a darling and send cake or biscuits. I know Joyce has that marvelous chef; please, be generous to one in need.

All love, T

"Good news I hope, miss?" Reilly remarked.

"Oh yes, very," I lied, quickly refolding the letter before she could see anything. She noted it and cringed as someone does when you raise a hand against them.

"I'll see to your bath now, miss," she said, holding the jar of bath salts to her chest, as if to shield herself. I noticed, then, that her fingernails were badly bitten, and her eyes were red, as if she'd been crying.

"Reilly," I said, "is everything all right?"

She paused just a few seconds too long before answering, "Yes, of course, miss."

"Reilly, you are the *worst* liar. You might as well tell me."

"You needn't concern yourself, miss. Not when you have so much on your mind."

"Then what's one more thing?" I caught her hand as she tried to move toward the door and gently drew her back toward me. "Is there something you need to tell me, Reilly?" I braced myself for her answer.

"Well, it's—it's my brother, miss," she replied.

I felt strangely relieved it wasn't something to do with Millicent. And then terribly guilty for being so self-centered. "The one with the five children?"

She nodded. "He's lost 'is job, and they're, well, a bit desperate." She looked desperate too, eyes welling with tears. "I've sent 'em all I can, but it's not enough, and there're no jobs to be 'ad."

"Oh, Reilly, I'm so sorry," I breathed. "I wish there was something I could do."

She shook her head. "No, miss, it's all right. It'll come right in the end, I'm sure."

Her optimism was admirable, but still the situation weighed on me. So much so that Joyce noticed at lunch and decided I needed cheering up.

"Why don't I invite Jeremy for dinner tonight?" she suggested.

"Oh yes, Joyce, he brightens a room right up," Laura agreed.

"Well?" Joyce asked me.

I shrugged. "It's your home, invite whomever you like." But I couldn't deny the thought of seeing him again did lift my spirits.

Once again, I was down early and found Jeremy crouched on the floor of the hall, playing with Dandy. He looked up and grinned as I came down the stairs.

"Welcome to my part of the country," he greeted me.

"Welcome *back*," I corrected him. "You forget I've been here before."

"Of course." He straightened. "I promise: no doll kidnappings this time."

I laughed.

"I'm very glad to see you recovered," he said, smiling.

"Thank you, Jeremy." I reached over and brushed some stray dog hairs off the front of his crisp black dinner jacket. "And thank you for the rose you sent me."

He shrugged. "A poor replacement for a real garden, but one can only grow so much in London. And speaking of gardens, would you like a turn in this one before the others come down? I think he will appreci-ate it." He indicated Dandy.

"As would I."

We walked in comfortable silence through the garden as the sunset blazed the sky and Dandy rushed after a ball we took turns throwing.

"So," Jeremy said with a wry smile, "how's life with the Battling Bradburys?"

"You know all about that, do you?" I sighed.

"Of course! When they're off I get regular earfuls from David, and I'm sure you hear plenty from Joyce. Seems they've been off a fair bit lately."

"They should be railing at each other instead of sniping to us."

"Well"—he bent to pick up the ball—"what are friends for?"

"What does David have to say about it?" I asked.

Jeremy hesitated and gave me a sidelong glance. "Strictly between us?"

"I can keep a secret," I reassured him.

He chucked the ball and Dandy sped off. "David thinks Joyce is having an affair."

The idea was so ridiculous I burst out laughing. "Why would he think that?"

Jeremy shrugged. "Apparently she disappears with no warning. Stays away for hours, overnight a few times. When they were up north, Joyce left one morning, saying she was going to Newcastle, which is absurd: Why would she be going to Newcastle?"

"Did he ask her?" I asked.

"Of course he did. She just said she was working on something and he wouldn't understand. She doesn't give him much credit. And there's all this tussling over the cost of redoing the house. David says it could have been done much more cheaply than it was, but she kept insisting on hiring only the best master craftsmen for absolutely everything. Joyce spends money as if there's no end to it."

"That's because to Joyce there *is* no end to it," I pointed out. "Porter could stop making money this instant, and she could still spend what she wants and never run out."

"David doesn't want to be a kept husband."

"Then he shouldn't have married an heiress!"

Jeremy held up his hands in a defensive gesture. "Your quarrel isn't with me!"

"I know," I said, in a calmer tone. "It just seems silly. Joyce is *not* having an affair, and I can't blame her for wanting a nice home. It's not as if she swept away anything of historical importance. *That* would be something to quarrel about. And she did buy him an airplane. You'd think he'd be pleased about that."

"Oh, David thinks that's just further proof of this alleged lover," Jeremy sighed, seeming weary of all this. "He thinks the plane's a distraction, so he won't pester her."

"He really is looking for reasons to be annoyed," I muttered. "She thought she was doing something that would make him happy. She's trying to take some interest in something that interests him. He could try doing the same."

"Don't think I haven't tried to point that out to him." Jeremy shook his head. "It's funny: we think that having a fortune will make us happy and our lives easier, but it doesn't. It just brings a different set of problems."

"And yet we keep pursuing it." I sighed too. Dandy returned and dropped the ball, thick with slime, at our feet. "Laura thinks Joyce needs to settle on a project, and I agree. She always tended to be the arranger, even when we were small. If we can find something to keep her busy down here, there won't be any mysterious journeys to Newcastle or wherever. I don't suppose a village hall needs redecorating nearby?"

Jeremy scooped up the ball and rotated it between his thumb and forefinger for several moments. Dandy whined and spun in anxious, frantic circles.

"There isn't, but I may have another idea," Jeremy said, at last throwing the ball. Dandy sped off. "I think I know just the thing." His smile widened into a grin.

I couldn't help but grin back. "Do you? Gosh, how useful you are! What is it?"

"Let me get everything worked out," he said, "and I'll tell you all about it. Perhaps on a ride later this week? I believe I owe you some bridle paths."

"That sounds delightful!"

The air was cooling as twilight approached, bringing with it a summery mist. The perfume of the roses was as thick and heady as it had been at Belinda's wedding, and the crickets and cicadas were beginning their evening chorus. It was peaceful. A world away from, say, a miner's cottage where the air was thick with desperation.

"Do you think you might be able to help me with something else?" I asked.

"Of course. Ask me anything."

"Do you know anyone in mining?"

He frowned, thinking. "I may, but I'd have to give it a think. Why do you ask?"

I stopped and looked up at him imploringly. "This is a mission of mercy. My maid's brother has lost his job and needs a new one."

He frowned again, puzzled. "Your *maid's brother*?" he repeated.

"The poor man has five children and they're in a very bad way, apparently."

He kept frowning. "Is this the maid who's a socialist?"

"She's not a socialist!" I cried, startling Dandy, who was returning with the ball. "Millicent was just making that up." I wasn't sure how I felt about Reilly, but I did know that much. And it felt so unjust for her brother and his children to suffer unnecessarily.

"Is her brother a socialist?"

"What does that matter?"

"It might matter a great deal to whomever I recommend the man."

"Just because someone's a socialist doesn't mean they aren't trustworthy or a good employee," I argued. "You said so yourself, remember? He's a good man; he's just having a difficult time. You must have heard what it's like up in the north these days."

He sighed. "It's miserable up and down the country." He twisted his signet ring a few times. Then, "I'll see what I can do. Is there anything else you need?"

"No, thank you. I think that's enough for one day." I smiled gratefully and his answering grin made my heart thump. *Hard.*

Dandy edged forward and dropped his ball at my feet. I bent to retrieve and throw it, suddenly thankful for the distraction. Back at the house, the others were spilling onto the terrace, cocktails in hand.

"We should go back," I murmured. "We'll miss Laura's excellent mint juleps."

Jeremy handed me a handkerchief to wipe my slobbery hand. "Well, if we do, I'll make you a gimlet. They're my specialty."

"Of course you have a cocktail you make marvelously well," I said, laughing. "Another of your hidden talents. Do you have many more?"

Again, his smile made my heart do strange things. "I may. It's up to the right explorer to find out," he invited.

"You do intrigue me, Lord Dunreaven," I responded, unable to help myself. "I'm glad I have the whole summer to winnow these talents out."

I slipped my arm through his, and we strolled back to the house, throwing Dandy's ball as we went.

Chapter Fifteen

"You're up with the larks!" Laura declared as I came down dressed for riding. "I daresay it'll be worth it, though. Jem's at the stables. Do have fun and be as naughty as you please."

I rolled my eyes good-naturedly and headed for the stables, where Jeremy was waiting with a pair of grays.

"I have a dreadful morning planned," he promised as a groom gave me a leg up into the saddle. "All ready?"

"Very." I nudged the horse into a trot. "Where are we off to?"

"It's a surprise," he responded, taking the lead and urging his horse into a canter. I let my horse have her head as well, enjoying the freeing feeling of cutting through the damp, fresh morning air. The sun was just searing off a low-lying mist, and a salt-edged breeze had kicked up.

Jeremy glanced over his shoulder with a boyish smile. "Race you!"

He kicked his horse into a gallop, and I crouched down and urged my mount on as well. She responded instantly, relishing competition. We closed in on Jeremy and his gray. He looked over as we drew up alongside and laughed. I did too, momentarily forgetting all my cares, letting summery wind take them away.

We reached a river and slowed to a walk, letting the horses catch their breaths. I spotted a rickety bridge spanning the river and realized I'd been there before.

"We used to pick blackberries near here," I recalled. "There were loads of them over there in the woods"—I pointed to a wooded area nearby—"and we'd come out and eat ourselves into stomachaches and take the rest back for the cook to make jam. She'd reward us with jammy dodgers once we could face fruit again."

Jeremy laughed. "Do you think Monsieur le Chef would do the same?"

"Hardly," I chuckled. "He wouldn't deign to lower himself to jammy dodgers. The berries probably wouldn't be ripe now anyway."

"Well, there are wild strawberries where we're going. We'll feast on those."

"And where is that?"

"Midbourne Abbey," he announced, leading the way to a spot where the river was shallow enough for the horses to cross. As we splashed through the water, he turned and said, "You may be pleased to hear that I have a solution to the Joyce problem."

"Do you? Gosh, you work fast!"

He shrugged. "I'd hate to be thought lazy."

"That's not the first word that comes to mind when I think of you."

"Oh?" he asked teasingly. "And what is?"

"Grand," I replied, teasing as well. "So what are you going to set her on?"

"Joyce is going to plan the annual fete," Jeremy said. "I understand it's quite the undertaking, and I've no doubt she'll make it a fete to remember. She'll soon receive a note from the head of the Ladies' Benevolent Society and then should be on her way."

"That's a really marvelous idea, Jeremy. How clever of you to think of it! Now we just need to find something to distract Laura, before she kills us."

He rolled his eyes. "I'm not sure I can help there."

"Of course you can! With enough of us, we can work out a tennis-playing rota."

Jeremy grinned. "Or we could just keep ourselves out of the way. If she can't find any partners, she can't play."

"And how do you propose we do that?" I asked, arching an eyebrow. "Escape and enjoy a nice spot of fishing, perhaps? A walk through the fields? Country pleasures, as the poets say?"

His eyes slid toward me. "Is that what they were talking about?"

"Of course." I turned to him, all wide-eyed innocence. "What else could they mean?"

He studied me for a few moments with a slightly wicked smile I couldn't help but return. "What indeed?" he murmured, almost too quietly for me to hear.

"Careful, Lord Dunreaven. You'll scandalize me."

"I doubt that," he chuckled. "It would take a lot to scandalize a friend of Laura's."

I laughed. "Very true. She was always a bit wicked. Runs in the family."

Out of the corner of my eye, I saw him make a strange movement. Like a flinch.

"God save us from our families and their unhappy legacies," he said darkly. He noticed my startled look and shook his head. "I'm sorry. Only, like Laura and David, I know what it's like to grow up with parents who weren't well suited."

"I'm very sorry about that," I said quietly.

Jeremy shrugged. "There's no changing it now. I understand things were very different in your family?"

"My parents were certainly devoted to each other," I agreed. "Though there are downsides to that."

He glanced my way. "Such as?"

"They insulated themselves. Kept things from me. Important things, which I should have been told."

He thought about that for a little while. "I suppose everyone's entitled to a secret or two," he finally observed. "Surely you have a few of your own?"

An uncomfortable frisson shivered through my belly. I tried to play it off with a toss of my head. "No woman reveals all her secrets, Jeremy. Not even to her husband. She must preserve some allure, don't you think?"

"You have plenty of allure. You don't need secrets," he said.

Another simmer in the belly, but for another reason entirely.

He turned away from me and gestured. "There." I followed his hand and saw, rising on a slope ahead, the ruins of a magnificent old church and abbey.

We tied the horses at the bottom of the hill and walked up, enjoying the unfurling view over the valley below. To one side was the river, sparkling in the distance; on the other, a thick forest that marked the easternmost edge of Midbourne's park.

Midbourne Abbey, Jeremy explained as we climbed, was once a sprawling complex with a soaring, stately church. But the Reformation came, the nuns were turned out, and the place was left to molder and decay.

"It's lucky follies came into style," Jeremy said. "My great-grandparents turned what was left of the abbey into a showpiece. Both Turner and Constable came out to paint it. Tourists still visit, now and then."

I could see why. What a glorious place! A Wordsworthian fantasy of crumbling pale-gray walls and soaring archways that stubbornly refused, for now, to give in to the abuses of time. Bits of the flying buttresses remained, arching into the sky, still supported by carved figures of writhing sinners and benevolent saints. Ivy and climbing roses twined up the carved columns along the nave, and bluebells grew underfoot.

Jeremy watched me drink in the ruins. He seemed pleased that I liked the abbey and continued telling its story. How centuries ago the order was established and financed by a wealthy and pious countess who was buried in the nave. About a king's mistress who fled there for safety from his vengeful queen. How a brave abbess had hidden the church's vital relics under her gown when William the Conqueror's men flooded in, bent on pillage and conquest. About witches tried and heretics burned. How a piece of the sword St. George used to slay the dragon was said to be buried beneath the altar. I had never seen him so lively and almost childishly excited, gesticulating and weaving stories, pointing out details here and there that hadn't—yet—been worn away by time and weather. It reminded me of my father, breathing life into his favorite haunts through the vibrant histories of the people who lived, loved, and died there.

We walked the footprint of the old abbey, wandering through dormitories that were now just knee-high walls in danger of being grassed over. Feeling bold, we risked the climb up the tower flanking the church's entrance for a better view of the countryside. From there I could see that the river forked, far in the distance, and ran down on either side of the estate, making it seem as though we were on a lovely island.

"Oh, Jeremy," I breathed, "it's wonderful."

He looked out over the estate, a strange mixture of emotions playing across his face. Pride, certainly. And sadness. "We can see the house from there," he said at last, gesturing with his head toward the orchard on the other side of the dormitories. He helped me down from the tower, and we wandered over. The orchard had been left to go wild, of course, but some of the trees were still producing. He tugged a pear off one and handed it to me.

We paused at the edge of the orchard, overlooking a sweep of land that led right to Midbourne, an enormous red brick house glowing warmly in the distance. It boasted a wide central tower with a clock edged in gold that caught the morning sun. Two wings, each comprising three stories, spread to either side, finishing in smaller dome-topped towers. Decorative pinnacles and chimneys thrust upward, turning the roofline into a hedgehog's back. I spotted a large glasshouse and formal gardens basking in the golden light.

"What a lovely old place," I said.

"Do you think so?"

"Don't you?"

He was silent a few moments. Again the strange looks. "I do," he agreed at last.

"Could we go see the gardens, Jeremy?"

He twisted his signet ring a few times. "Not today," he finally answered.

"Why not?" I gave him a teasing look. "What are you afraid I'll find? A mad wife locked up in the attic?"

He chuckled. "Not at all. We keep the wives locked in the wine cellar. The Madeira keeps them quiet, and the walls are less flammable."

"Well, then?" I arched an eyebrow.

He leaned against an apple tree. "You're very eager to see what's under my roof."

"I only want to see where you grew up. What sort of place made Jeremy Harris the man he is today?"

"I don't know that it was Midbourne that made me." He laughed. "Surely it's the people inside rather than the houses themselves that make us what we are? I think you would be much the same whether you grew up at Hensley or in a crofter's cottage or"—he indicated the mansion—"there."

"Possibly. In that case, *who* made you? Your father?"

He barked a laugh. "Not at all. My parents were strangers. Father was with us long enough to teach me to sail and use Morse code, and then I was off to school, and then he died in the war. And Mother . . ." He sighed. "She never liked children."

I tossed the pear between my hands. Thought of Laura's parents and Joyce's father. "Not everyone's suited to parenthood, as you said."

"Your mother was, from what I hear. Joyce says she took all your motherless little friends under her wing."

I smiled, remembering it. Mother always urged me to bring my friends to Hensley during the school holidays. We'd help in the garden and ride ponies and make jam and biscuits. Those were sunny, idyllic days, just like this one.

And then, of course, there was Raymond. Another motherless child, perhaps, whom she took under her wing, even though she didn't have to.

I'd been quiet too long: Jeremy was looking at me curiously. Puzzling me out again. I took a bite of the pear (a little hard and underripe) and perched on the edge of a nearby wall, trying to look nonchalant.

"How long has your family been here?" I asked, nodding toward the house.

"Nearly four hundred years."

"Ahh, then this place is in your bones."

"Do you really think so?" He chuckled.

"I'll prove it! Would you sell it? Have you ever considered selling it?"

"Oh yes, from time to time. It would certainly make my life simpler." He chuckled again, though a little bitterly, I felt.

"But you didn't," I pointed out. "Why not? Surely you could find a buyer for this fine piece of land? It could be the site of more Homes Fit for Heroes."

He paused for a little while. "The thing is, it doesn't feel like it's mine to dispose of," he admitted. "Certainly not so the house and farms can be pulled down and turned into a cluster of soulless semi-detatcheds. I'm meant to care for it until the next generation comes along. It seems wrong for me to get rid of it simply for my own comfort. And it would be a wrench," he allowed. "There are some good memories there."

"Tell me one," I urged, yearning for a glimpse into his life. *What made Jeremy Harris the man he is today?*

He smiled, thinking. "My grandmother used to have the most wonderful parties," he recalled at last. "There was one to celebrate King George's coronation—I must have been around six or seven years old. They put lanterns up throughout the gardens, and I remember thinking it looked like a fairy's paradise. There was dancing in the main hall, and I snuck out of bed to go peek through the banisters and watch. Swirling silks and lace and so many jewels it was blinding. My nanny found me and scolded me for being out of bed, but Grandmother came along and sent the woman away, and we watched the dancers together, she and I. She was wearing a blue silk dress and a diamond tiara. She smelled like"—he closed his eyes for a moment, recalling—"lavender and peppermints. She told me funny stories about all the people below."

He was deep in a reverie now, and I was afraid to breathe lest I intrude. His eyes shone, and he smiled so sweetly it broke my heart. We stood in silence for a while, then he seemed to remember I was there, and pulled himself back into the present.

"I wish you could have seen it," he murmured.

"I feel as if I have," I responded with a smile. "Your grandmother sounds lovely."

His smile turned sad. "She was. I wish I'd spent more time with her."

"Everyone has those regrets. We convince ourselves that the people we love will always be there, because it's too awful to think otherwise. And then they go and suddenly the world seems . . . chillier." I laid my hand on his arm, and he placed his own hand on top of it. My arm tingled a little.

He considered what I'd said for a while. "Perhaps that's what makes us want to start families of our own. Filling up that space and warming ourselves again."

"As much as we can," I agreed. "But they can never really be filled." I looked at the house for some time and murmured, "Nearly half a millennium your family's been here. No wonder you don't feel you can leave: It's hard to ignore roots that deep."

"It is," he agreed. "And I've found it intimidates as many people as it impresses." He looked at me seriously for a few moments, then suddenly asked, "Could you imagine living in a place like that?"

Startled, I answered, "I don't know. It seems like a lot of rooms to fill up."

He nodded. "It is. Room upon room upon room."

Something about his tone saddened me, and I squeezed his arm. "You sound lonely, Jeremy."

"I am." He chuckled. "It's why I wanted to start filling the place up."

I could feel a blush rising up through my cheeks. I looked away and cleared my throat. Tried to clear my head too.

"You can't be that determined," I commented. "If you were, you'd have found a companion by now. I've no doubt you had plenty of willing ladies."

"There are plenty willing," he agreed. "But my bar has been set higher, these past several months. I'm not just looking for someone to choose wallpapers and write guest lists. I want someone who *understands*." He looked at me, and I could see he was hoping I grasped what he meant. I did. He wanted someone who understood *him* and what he needed, and what was important to him and why. He wanted someone who knew his hurts and sore spots and was willing to soothe them, or toughen him, when necessary. He didn't want an ornament; he wanted someone to help make Jeremy Harris the man he'd be *tomorrow*.

And I knew instinctively that he would be that same person to his partner.

I nodded slowly, and his look changed. It heated. I felt the sear of it, as if he wanted to strip everything away, expose me—body and mind. To know it all, and to know *me*. I stared right back at him. I couldn't look away. Didn't want to.

After a long pause of quickened pulses and dry throats, he swallowed hard and said, "We should get back, or the others will be suspicious."

I nodded and laughed a little shakily. "Yes. And I can't go adding more scandals to my name now, can I?"

* * *

I met Laura and Joyce on their way to the tennis court, as I was returning to the house.

"Ahh, here she is." Laura's eyes twinkled wickedly. "I hope you had fun and behaved *terribly*. I'll want a full report later. Onward, Joyce."

"Astra, your lawyer telephoned and said it's important you telephone back immediately," Joyce said as Laura dragged her off. "Hurry up and come *save me*!"

Without waiting to change, I telephoned the lawyer, wondering what fresh hell I was about to face. Or maybe there'd been a miracle, and Vandemark Rubber had suddenly turned around. One could hope!

"I'm glad to hear from you, Miss Davies. There's something important we need to discuss," he said as soon as he got on the line. "There's been an offer to buy Hensley."

"What?" My heart skipped a beat. "But it hasn't even been offered for sale! Who wants to buy it? The tenants?"

"No. The offer came from Mr. Porter. I think you should seriously consider it."

"What"—I lowered my voice as a footman passed—"what would he want Hensley for?" Compared to Porter's country pile, Hensley was like a garden shed.

"He plans to build homes on it and let them out. He thinks the area's ripe for suburban development."

I felt cold as death. Porter wanted to raze my home and put up a bunch of cheap houses so bank clerks could play at being country gentlemen?

"I won't hear of it," I hissed. "I'm not selling Hensley to Porter or anyone else."

The lawyer sighed deeply. "It's a very generous offer, Miss Davies, and I really think you must consider it. The tenants aren't renewing the lease, which means that soon the place will be empty. Vandemark Rubber is on the brink of collapse. When it does, you will have no income at all. You must think clearly, Miss Davies."

No income at all. I wouldn't be able to move out of Aunt Elinor's, let alone go back to Hensley. I would never stand on my own.

I swallowed hard. Imagined life as a permanent dependent, relying on other people's charity and goodwill.

I will not be pitied.

And that's if I was even allowed to stay. Despite the jocular tone of Toby's letter, I didn't have much faith that he'd managed to talk his mother around. Aunt El didn't listen to him; she never had.

And Raymond! Poor Raymond, what would happen to him? Torn away from his own home, unable to understand what was happening. Tossed into some nightmarish place where he knew no one and nobody seemed to care.

And I wouldn't be able to pay Reilly's salary and upkeep, so she'd have to go as well. What would become of her? How would she live, when her family was already in such dire need?

This couldn't be.

"I'll think of something," I told the lawyer. "I just need some time. I'll manage. Good afternoon."

Chapter Sixteen

⁓

What else? *What else?* I begged off lunch so I could pace my room, smoke, and think. It was impossible not to imagine walls being pulled down, gardens dug up, and a young man shivering in a dank cell. I had to find a way to stop it. But *how?*

I only had one thing left: Vandemark Rubber. I had to pull it back from the brink somehow. I needed it. I needed Freddie. Dear God, I *needed Freddie.*

This was the way it had to be. I could no longer rely on other people to act as my protection or to give me purpose. I needed to create my *own* protection. Money would give me that. I needed, as Laura had said, to find a label that people could swallow, even if it made them a little uncomfortable. Not wife or daughter. *Businesswoman.*

By late afternoon I had the beginnings of a plan. I went out to the garden, where Laura was doing some bizarre combination of jumping and running in place.

"Laura, I want to know about this friend of Bobby's you helped turn around."

"Larry? Not much more to tell. He's a good 'un—just needed a positive distraction. We all do. Without it, we fall into bad habits. Really rigorous exercise gave him something to focus on. It was rough at first, of course, but then he felt better and looked better; and the better he looked and felt, the more he wanted to do it."

"Do you think you could do it again?"

"I *have* done it again. And I was thinking of having a go at Father next."

"Would you consider taking on a project for me instead?"

She actually stopped. And beamed. "Lord, yes! I don't want to go to Monaco this time of year. Or see my father again. Who is it?"

"Freddie Ponsonby-Lewis."

She considered that for a moment. "Well, that'll be a challenge," she admitted. "Poor boy's well on his way to being a wreck. At least, he was when I saw him in New York. I don't suppose he's improved any?"

"Doesn't seem like it. Do you think you might be able to turn him around?"

"I don't see why not. Why's it so important to you?" She got a sly look on her face. "Don't tell me—"

"Nothing like that, Laura. I'm just helping out a friend," I answered with a bright smile, hoping she believed me.

She didn't, but she let it go.

"Whatever you say, Astra. Summon the boy, and I'll see about straightening him out. It may take a little while, though."

"Hopefully not too long. He doesn't have forever."

Neither do I.

* * *

Joyce next. I found her curled up at one end of a beige sectional in the morning room, reading *Tatler* while "Dancing in the Dark" spilled from the wireless.

"You beastly creature, abandoning me earlier," she scolded. "How was the ride?"

"It was lovely." It felt like years ago now, but the thought of it—warm sun and cool breezes, soaring arches and Jeremy's smile (and that *look*!)—made me stop just for a moment and grin. "Really lovely. Joyce, I was wondering if you'd do something for me?" I turned down the wireless and sank into the sofa beside her.

"That depends. What do you need?"

"I need you to invite Freddie here."

She looked horrified. "Freddie? *Freddie? Freddie Ponsonby-Lewis?* That idiot, in my house? What are you thinking? Who knows what he'll get up to! Astra, you can't—" Her face switched to serious. "You aren't *really* carrying on with him, are you?"

"Of course not! This is for Laura. If we give her a project, maybe she'll leave the rest of us alone."

"Ahh!" She looked relieved. "Why, you clever girl! I suppose I can put up with him for a little while if it buys peace for the summer. Do you think he'll come?"

"He will if you ask nicely. Feel free to tell him I asked, if you think it'll help."

"Oh, it'll help," she said, chuckling as she rose from the settee. "I hope you know what you're doing, though. If anyone finds out you wanted him here, it'll be fuel for the fire."

Oh, I knew the risks. But I also knew how limited my options were.

I smiled brightly. "Who would tell? And my behavior will be above reproach. Please, just ask him, Joyce."

"All right, dear, but only because it's for you." Her face darkened. "And because if I have to play tennis with Laura once more, I think I'll die. Or kill her. If we bury her in the rose garden, do you think anyone would notice?"

*　*　*

"Ugh! This infernal heat!" Laura snarled, petulantly kicking the newspaper at Dandy. The little dog, spread flat on the floor like a tiny bearskin rug, couldn't even be bothered to move, despite the journalistic assault.

"Don't, Laura," I groaned, pressing a sweaty cup of Pimm's to my forehead. "It's too hot for rage."

A week on from my trip to Midbourne Abbey, and the weather had slipped into a sultry rut that it couldn't seem to escape. We'd been mired in air as thick and sticky as custard for the past two days. It felt like relief would never come. We'd sought refuge in the drawing room, with all the windows open in the dim hope there might be a breeze.

Laura growled and snatched another bit of paper as Joyce sauntered in.

"Save your strength," Joyce warned. "I have dire tidings. Is that Pimm's? Thank God." She went to pour herself a cup.

"Oh no, what is it?" I groaned, bracing myself for whatever she had to say.

Joyce took a gulp of Pimm's and arranged herself on the sofa with a sigh. "We're having the party from Lush Wycombe to dinner, and that includes Millicent."

Laura sprang upright. "Joyce, no! Why would you do such a thing?"

"I couldn't very well invite her hosts and not her!"

"But why invite any of them?" Laura whined. "Laddie's such a wet sock! And his father . . . well, I'll just say I was never sorry our families didn't mix much."

"Because I promised Lord Woolmer we'd show him the films I took during our honeymoon," Joyce explained. "It's all arranged, so there's no use complaining about it now. Don't be angry: I've asked Jeremy as well," she said to me before taking another swig of Pimm's, signaling an end to the conversation.

I sighed. It didn't matter if a dozen Jeremys came; I still wouldn't be able to enjoy myself with Millicent there, staring me down, smirking, reveling in my disgrace. I felt a heat that had nothing to do with the weather build in my chest, and I gulped my Pimm's.

Joyce bent down and scooped up the paper Laura had been abusing. "Ahh, Belinda and Hampton are returning from their honeymoon in August," she reported, scanning the Society column. "I hope they took my advice and stopped off in Nassau. Oh, and Astra? Freddie says he'll come. Promised to be here in time for cocktails Monday."

Well, there was that, at least.

"Thank you, Joyce."

"Mmm. You can keep him entertained, can't you? Because apparently I'm to plan the local fete this year," she said. "I've had a note from a Mrs. Barrett about it."

"Good. You could use a project," said Laura. "Not sure I'd choose something so dull, but I'm sure you'll make it your own."

"Your faith is bracing, Laura, it really is," Joyce said sarcastically.

"Well you can't expect me to have much faith in you," Laura sniped. "You are, after all, inviting Millicent into your home."

I didn't want to think about that any more. I set my cup down on a table and rose. "I think I may go lie down for a little while," I said, as if that would provide any relief.

I had just reached my room when Reilly appeared and hissed: "Miss! Would you mind coming with me, please?"

"All right," I agreed uncertainly.

She led me down the hall to a door cleverly concealed in the paneling. She pushed it open, revealing a cramped, winding stone staircase. Up, up to the servants' quarters. It was so boiling up there I actually felt lightheaded for a moment. Once I recovered, I could see that the ceiling on my right sloped steeply with the roof, while to my left was a row of doors. Reilly opened one and waved me inside. I stepped in, blinking to adjust my eyes to the gloom. The only light came from a small, dusty skylight, and there was just enough space for a dresser with a washbasin and pitcher and two narrow metal-frame beds. A woman was waiting, perched on one of the beds. She was dressed in the all-black uniform of a lady's maid, her orange-red hair pulled into a tight chignon. She stood as I came in. Reilly glanced up and down the corridor, then closed the door behind us.

"We'll need to keep our voices down," she whispered, crossing to stand next to the other woman. "Miss, this is—"

"I know who this is," I said. "This is Collins, isn't it? Lady Millicent's maid."

We eyed each other, Collins and I, while Reilly wrung her hands.

"Miss," she whimpered, "I want you to know—that is, *we* want you to know . . . that you can trust us. Trust me."

"All right," I said warily. "Have you come to tell me that she hasn't been giving you information to pass along to Lady Millicent?" I asked Collins, gesturing to Reilly.

"She hasn't, miss. And I've never asked for it," Collins reassured me, reaching out and squeezing one of Reilly's hands. "I'm not interested in that sort of thing."

"Are you not?"

"No, but . . ." she glanced at Reilly, who nodded. "You should know that you're being watched."

"*Watched?* By whom?"

"I'm sorry, I don't know," said Collins. "Lady Millicent gave me an envelope with no name on it and told me to give it to a maid at the house where we're staying. I looked inside—I know I shouldn't have!—and it was full of money. I gave it to the housemaid, and later I saw her giving it to a man I didn't recognize. I asked her about it later—in a roundabout sort of way—and she mentioned he worked here."

"But you don't know who he is?"

Collins shook her head. "Safe to assume he's someone who works in the house, here. A footman, maybe."

"Mrs. Bradbury did hire two footmen from Lush Wycombe," Reilly reminded me.

Collins continued: "He's brought notes for Lady Millicent, which the housemaid delivers herself, and Lady Millicent has given him at least one more envelope."

"It must be you she has an eye on," Reilly said to me. "Who else at Wotting Park would she want information on so badly she's willing to pay for it?"

No one. Joyce and Laura were married, and therefore mostly untouchable. And their money afforded them even greater protection. It had to be me she was after. Why? Hadn't she already done enough? Or was that forged letter just the first step in some plan? First, isolate and discredit me, and then move in for the real kill.

I sighed and rubbed my temples, unsure what to do. I was being watched by a person or persons unknown. Who knew what information had already been passed along? Did she know about Hensley? Freddie's summoning? Raymond was probably safe, thank God, but he was hardly my only secret.

"Thank you for warning me, Miss Collins," I said. "I know it was a risk to you, and I do appreciate your helping me."

Collins smiled a little, then glanced at Reilly, who nodded.

"Miss, there's something else," Collins said, her voice coming out as little more than a squeak. She began wringing a pair of black gloves in her lap, twisting so hard I thought they'd tear in half. Reilly gently stilled her hands, keeping her own hand over Collins's, and placing the other on Collins's shoulder. It seemed to soothe Collins, who continued: "I-I've been with the family for a very long time. More than twenty years. I used to work as a housemaid." She swallowed hard. "Thing is, miss, the housemaids, no one notices them. We keep out of the way, and no one sees we're there, so people say and do things in our seeing and hearing without thinking about it. They talk the way they would around the furniture."

I nodded, guiltily realizing I probably couldn't have identified most of the housemaids at the homes I'd visited if my life depended on it.

"And did Lady Millicent say or do something?" I prompted.

"Many things," Collins snorted, and Reilly smirked. "But the worst of it isn't what *she's* done—it was her mother. Lady Millicent is not Lord Caddonfoot's daughter."

Chapter Seventeen

~

I gaped at Collins, sorting through what she'd just said. "Then whose child is she?"

"Lady Caddonfoot had . . . unusual tastes, for a woman in her position," Collins answered, shaking her head. "Most ladies took a man in their circle for a paramour, but she let the stableboys touch her legs when they helped her mount. She chose footmen for their looks. And she had a dressmaker she was very fond of. A man who claimed to have dressed the Grand Duchesses of Russia before he was forced to flee with the other Jews during a pogrom. Tall, and thin, and black-haired he was. When his lordship was away, she'd summon him to Gryden to fit her clothes. Hours and hours, locked up alone in her rooms. I was young, but I know what I heard. I found some letters he sent her, when I was tidying, tied with a pink ribbon." A blush crept over her face at the memory. "Some time after one of his visits, I saw her crying. And then Lady Millicent was born." She smiled bitterly. "Lord Caddonfoot sent champagne down to the servants to celebrate. Poor man."

The silence when she was finished was a long one. I was pop-eyed, taking all this in. It wasn't the affair that was shocking—affairs seemed almost de rigeur among a particular set at that time. There were plenty of well-born ladies who were known not to be the children of their mother's husbands: everyone knew that the Countess of Carnarvon was the daughter of a bachelor Rothschild. But there was a world of difference between a Rothschild and a dressmaker, even one who had dressed Grand Duchesses.

Others must know about this, I realized. Then aloud: "This couldn't have been a secret in that house. Surely the other servants noticed something as well and talked."

"They did," Collins acknowledged. "And Society gossiped as well, before moving on to other things. But it still lingers. If it came up again now, when she's trying to secure a husband . . . Well . . ." She raised her eyebrows for a moment. "And I doubt it would sit well with some of the company she keeps. She saw a fair bit of Oswald Mosley when we were all last in London, and I've heard he's no great friend of the Jews."

I cocked my head and studied her for several moments. It was possible she was lying, playing some sort of elaborate trick or game, but to what end?

"Why are you doing this?" I asked. "You're taking an enormous risk. If Lady Millicent knew you were here . . ."

"It's my afternoon off, and Angela made sure no one saw me coming in," Collins said, looking up at Reilly with a smile. "It's unlikely she'll find out I was here. As for why I'm doing this: I saw an opportunity to help someone and I took it. And Lady Millicent is not the sort of person who inspires loyalty."

I thanked Collins and left to make my way back downstairs. The pressing, baking heat of the room made it difficult to think, and I needed to think.

As I reached the spiral staircase, Reilly came out of her room, calling, "Miss!"

I paused and turned. "Yes, Reilly?"

"Miss?" She stood in front of me. "Do you trust me now?"

My heart broke, just a little, thinking of her pleading with her friend to help because her mistress's chill convinced her she'd be sent packing any moment. I reached out and clasped both her hands, looked her full in the face. "Yes, Reilly, I trust you."

* * *

What does one do with a scandal such as this? I was unaccustomed to handling such volatile information. Should I use it? Light the fuse and see what could be salvaged from the wreckage? Or keep it, and risk missing my chance and being left with something useless?

Because once Millicent was married, she'd be safe. Oh, a rumor like this might sting a little. Might make her an object of sly grins over a few dinner and card tables, but that was all. It wouldn't ruin her, by any means. But if it got out now, suitors might think twice about pursuing her. People love a scandal unless it's about their own family.

But heaven only knows how she might retaliate. I still had a spy to worry about. I still had secrets and people to protect.

I was still thinking about it when I came down to the much-dreaded dinner with the Lush Wycombe party. This was all very formal, which meant the Wotting Park crowd was lined up in order of precedence as the guests arrived. I, the lowliest, was last in line, next to Laura.

Joyce and David greeted the arriving guests at the door: Lord Woolmer, Laddie, Millicent, three other houseguests from Lush Wycombe, and Jeremy, who pulled up in his car right behind the others. He shook hands with both Laddie and Woolmer, asking about some horses and commiserating on their bad luck at Cheltenham that year. His greeting for Millicent, I noticed, was cooler. She pursed her lips but then glanced my way, smiled slyly, and slid an arm through Laddie's, whispering in his ear.

The guests were taken down the line and introduced. Lords received a curtsey and a hand to bend their heads over. Woolmer—a rotund, white-haired gentleman with a handlebar mustache —gave me a smile as well as a nod. His son, whose own foray into facial hair yielded a pencil-thin upper-lip fuzz, ignored my raised hand, refused to touch or acknowledge me, and turned away, clearing his throat against his fist. I was so thrown by this blatant snub I actually kept my hand dangling in midair for a moment. Jeremy rescued me from embarrassment by smoothly tucking it into the crook of his arm.

"I hope you'll allow me to see you in to dinner, Miss Davies," he murmured.

I smiled gratefully up at him. "You're too kind."

Laura clapped Millicent heartily on the back. "Hullo, old girl! Sorry to have to tell you there's no babies' blood on the menu tonight."

Millicent remained unnervingly quiet over dinner, letting the others lead the conversation. Joyce had Lord Woolmer talking about his work in the House of Lords and what he thought the odds were of another general election in the coming year ("Oh, there'll be one for sure. Did I tell you Laddie's thinking of standing for Newcastle? A fine thing, I think, for a young man to be an MP. We all owe it to the country to serve."). Millicent spoke only to Laddie, leaning over to whisper to him while laying a hand gently atop his. I watched, unable to ignore it, wondering what she was talking about. She looked at me often when she spoke. Was she talking about me? Telling him lies? *"That wicked girl, you know what she's like. I should never have her at my dinner table."*

I wished I knew how to lip-read.

When she wasn't murmuring to Laddie, she was smirking at me every chance she got, almost as if she knew something. Had her spy passed along something useful to her? He must have, if she was still paying him. What? What did she know?

I watched her, and I watched the footmen circling the table, eyeing us as they removed plates. Was she looking at one of them more than the others? I couldn't tell anymore. Couldn't figure out what was real and what I was conjuring up in my anxiety.

After dinner I escaped to the terrace with a cup of coffee, wishing it was something stronger. I needed to clear my mind, steady my nerves. I saw Jeremy glancing through the open French windows and understood the subtle question on his face. I gestured that it was all right for him to join me.

"Not that I blame you, but you seem very pensive tonight," he observed after closing the window behind him. "Is it simply because of Lady Millicent?"

"It is," I admitted. "But not only because she's here."

He grimaced sympathetically and offered me the glass of whisky in his hand. I took it, smiling my gratitude, and drank. We stood in silence for a little while.

"May I ask your advice in confidence?" I asked.

"Of course you can."

"If you knew something very damaging about someone who had hurt you, would you use it? Or would that just seem . . . I don't know, petty? Or cowardly?"

He took his time answering. "It might," he acknowledged. "I suppose it depends on how widespread the damage would be. One can't ignore the innocent bystander."

I had considered that. This would certainly harm Millicent, but Cee would be caught up in it as well. She seemed to have such a romantic notion of her parents' married life, it would be a shame to damage that. And her father too: how much did he know? He'd evidently thought Millicent was his child when she was born, and he had fond memories of his wife. This wouldn't kill, but it would surely wound.

And Collins was unlikely to escape. Millicent would surely trace the story back to her, and Collins would be dismissed without a reference. She'd be unemployable.

"If I may be forgiven for falling back on a naval metaphor," said Jeremy, "if your ship has been hit and is sinking, it's tempting to ram the enemy ship. And it may be that's the best course: your enemy dies with you. But you can't ram the ship thinking you'll keep your own afloat on the wreckage. There is no salvation here: all hands go down."

I nodded. "That's what I thought too."

He took my hand and squeezed it. "Don't play her game. It's not worthy of you."

"I think you think more highly of me than I deserve," I said. "But thank you."

"Would you be cheered by some cautiously good news?"

"I'll be cautiously cheered," I answered.

"Well, then: I think I have found a mine owner."

"You haven't!" I gasped, feeling my heart lift. Perhaps I could repay Reilly for what she'd done for me.

Jeremy laughed, buoyed up by my excitement. "I have. One of my Dartmouth classmates comes from a mining family. He's stationed at Portsmouth, so I thought I'd go and pay him a visit."

"Oh, Jeremy, that's wonderful! I could almost kiss you!"

His smile teased, a little. "Almost?"

"Sorry to interrupt," said Laura, poking her head out, "but Joyce is summoning everyone. The show's starting."

The library had been set up like a miniature cinema, with a sheet stretched over the bookshelves on one wall and rows of chairs in front. Joyce and the butler fussed with a projector as we all filed in and sat down.

"Nearly ready," Joyce said, placing a record on the gramophone. She then turned off the lights and slipped into a chair between David and Woolmer as "I Wanna Be Loved By You" spilled from the gramophone and a panning image of a mansion flickered onto the makeshift screen.

"Oh, Lush Wycombe!" exclaimed one of the ladies Woolmer had brought along.

"That's right," Joyce confirmed. "Heavens, how did these films get in here? Ah, well, we can still enjoy them!"

The film moved from Lush Wycombe—a Gothic sprawl of a place— to a cottage smaller than the room we were sat in, with moss growing on the roof and two half-naked toddlers cavorting out front.

"You know where this is, don't you, Lord Woolmer?" said Joyce. "This is the cottage the Hastings family lives in on your estate. Lovely people! Two parents, two grandparents, seven darling children, and Mrs. Hastings's sister, all under one roof! I imagine things would be much easier for them if they had indoor plumbing and their roof didn't leak, but these things are *such* luxuries."

Woolmer shifted uncomfortably in his seat and cleared his throat.

The film moved on to another family. An exhausted-looking woman and an alarmingly thin teenage boy were struggling to wrangle some cows.

"Oh, and these are the Mitchells," Joyce went on. "Poor Mrs. Mitch-ell lost her husband in the war, and her brother has terrible shell-shock, so it's just her and her boy trying to work the farm. They're up every day at four o'clock—can you imagine!—milking those cows before the boy goes off to school. They manage to keep body and soul together, but I hear dairy prices are taking a terrible downturn—surely that's not true, Lord Woolmer? Of course you and the other members of the House of Lords would do something about that. Otherwise, how will your own tenants manage to pay their rent?" She turned questioningly to Woolmer, who pointedly avoided her gaze.

Joyce faced forward as we moved on to scenes from a city. "Laddie, you'll appreciate this! Newcastle! Your future constituency!" Up came an image of a mass of men bunched at the tall, spiked gates of a ship-yard. A man came out of the gates, and the waiting workers surged for-ward. "Please don't forget these good men, Laddie, who built England's great ships and are now in desperate want of work. Their wives and chil-dren"—thin-faced women and children hauled heavy buckets of water and waste, queued at soup kitchens and hawked family trinkets—"face terrible need because the dole simply isn't enough. I tried to do what I could, but . . ." She shrugged. "I'm only one woman. But surely you gentlemen have a plan! You always do have a plan, don't you? To fix things?"

The record ended, leaving the gramophone to go, hic, hic, hic, but nobody got up to change or restart it. Nobody seemed to know what to do. The Newcastle images disappeared, and the Arc de Triomphe flickered into view. David pranced into the frame and pretended to heave the distant Arc up onto his shoulder. "Oh, *here* are the honeymoon films," said Joyce in a "silly me!" tone. "Paris was enchanting, but it was nothing to Germany! You know, we were there during the election, and I'll say this for the Nazi party: they do like a parade, and they *do* celebrate. I've never known anyone to be so excited to come in second place!" This was accompanied by images of a frantic, swastika-flag-waving crowd at a rally, and then shops and businesses with their windows smashed. In one shot, a man with a beard, wearing a skullcap, picked through the debris of his ruined livelihood.

"Apparently there was quite a bit of celebrating the first day the Reichstag reconvened," Joyce told us. "I believe we have India next."

Lord Woolmer jumped to his feet. "Heavens, how late it is!" he said stiffly. "You'll forgive us if we see the rest of this some other time, Mrs. Bradbury?"

"Of course, Lord Woolmer," Joyce purred. "We'll see you out."

As soon as the front door closed behind the guests, David turned on his wife.

"You did that on purpose!" he sputtered.

"Dear me, there must have been a mix-up with the editing," Joyce responded disingenuously. "What a silly goose I am!"

"That was outrageous, Joyce!" he continued, even in the face of his wife's cool-eyed indifference to his rage. "Those are our *neighbors*!"

"For God's sake, David, if you're going to scold your wife like a child, at least have the decency to do it in her dressing room, out of sight of the guests," said Laura.

David shook his head, sputtered, and stomped off toward the billiards room.

"I think I'll go see if I can smooth things over," Jeremy offered.

Laura smiled wryly at Joyce. "You sly sausage. I'm glad to see I've taught you a thing or two."

Joyce pretended to be very interested in a bracelet. "Don't know what you mean."

"You have a member of the House of Lords—two, if you count Jeremy—*and* a possible future MP to dine so you can trap them into a shame-filled social lecture. Brava, dearest. Honestly, I always thought it'd be Cee who'd have the do-gooder streak."

Joyce shrugged. "I filmed what I saw. Everyone can draw their own conclusions."

Laura planted both hands on her hips. "Don't be coy with me, missus. That day we were meant to lunch in New York, you went to the Hooverville, didn't you? And then you ran up an astonishing bill at Macy's. I'd bet good money most of the people in the park received a very welcome parcel from a mysterious benefactress that day."

Joyce left off the bracelet and looked up at us. "Have you been through there, Laura? All those people—*decent* people, who've worked hard for years and lost it all through no fault of their own—in shacks and threadbare clothes, cooking tinned beans over open fires, if they're lucky enough to even have that. Winter was coming on, and they needed coats and blankets. I could give them that."

I felt deeply ashamed of myself for failing to do anything to help anyone other than myself, and for failing to give Joyce the credit she was obviously due. I glanced at Laura and saw her bite her lip, the only sign that she, too, was thinking the same.

"I'll be sure to tell David he's a heel if he gives you grief over this," Laura said.

"Don't bother, he'll get past it," Joyce told her. "I'm to bed. Good night, ladies."

We watched her go up, admiring her boldness in silence.

"If she achieves nothing else, she at least enraged Millicent, and I support that," said Laura. "She was practically steaming at those films from Germany." She glanced at a nearby clock and bit her lip again. "I have some phone calls to make now." She strode toward the telephone, and as I ascended the staircase, I heard her say, "Yes, I need to schedule a call to Albany, please, and then there'll be three to New York City."

Chapter Eighteen

Our host and hostess were no longer on speaking terms. He spent his days shut up in the billiards room or out somewhere. Joyce shrugged it off and threw herself into preparations for the fete with an enthusiasm that actually surprised me.

"Good heavens, Joyce, it's just a little village fete," Laura commented after Joyce had filled us in on her increasingly elaborate plans.

"It's *not* just a little village fete; it raises funds for the Ladies' Benevolent Society," Joyce countered. "Do you know what they do?"

"Munitions distribution?" Laura guessed.

Joyce rolled her eyes. "They provide support for those in the neighborhood who find themselves wanting. And it's becoming dashed difficult for them just now because so many more people are in need, and fewer people have extra money to give. So this fete is important! If you paused in your jumping jacks or whatever it is you're doing, you'd realize this. Lord! You're just like your brother: can't be bothered to care about anything that's important or doesn't directly affect you."

"I resent that," Laura protested. "Do you have any idea how many charity auctions I've been dragged to this past year? And I'll have you know: I *always* overbid."

I helped Joyce as much as I could, reining in some of the more extravagant ideas and planning for Freddie's arrival. I needed to move things along there as quickly as possible, to neutralize the threat from Millicent. I was already anxious, looking over my shoulder constantly, wondering if my mail had been read, speaking to Reilly and most of the others in whispers. ("What's wrong with you?" Laura demanded. "Speak up!")

Jeremy left for Portsmouth the Monday after the dinner party, and that afternoon I went to the station to collect Freddie.

"Miss Davies!" Freddie called, hopping onto the platform as soon as the train stopped. He bounded over, flushed and sweaty, and grabbed my hand. "Glad to see you! Gosh, you are the cat's pajamas, aren't you? Not the sort to hold it against a fellow when he's been at the champagne. I mean, it *was* a wedding, and you did send that note—"

"Enough, Freddie." I steered him into the station's tiny (and thankfully empty) waiting room and sat him down on a bench. I stood over him, hands on hips, giving my best schoolmarm glare. It must have worked, because he visibly shrank.

"First of all, Freddie, I want to make it *very* clear that you've put me in a terrible spot. You know that now, don't you?"

He nodded.

"My aunt is scandalized. She's going to throw me out of her house. I may be *homeless* because of you, Freddie!"

He whimpered. "Listen, I'll talk to her. She's all right, isn't she? She'll listen."

"No, you most *certainly* are *not* going to talk to my aunt, Freddie. You're going to talk to *me*. Are you sober?"

"More or less."

"Well, is it more, or less? Say 'indubitably.'"

He blinked up at me. "In-dewb-it-a-blee?"

I sighed. "That'll have to do. Tell me straight: Is there any hope at all for Vandemark Rubber?"

"Oh, well, there's always hope, isn't there?" He retrieved a handkerchief and began mopping his glistening forehead. "Show's not over until the fat lady sings, right?"

I clenched both fists, longing to smack him. "Freddie . . ."

Something about my blazing eyes, or tone, knocked the joking out of him. "It's not hopeless," he said. "There were one or two others who thought of leaving, but I think I've convinced them to stay." He beamed, pleased with himself. "The sisters didn't think I'd manage it, but by gum I did! They always did think I was a sap." He glowered.

"So you've stemmed the tide—for now—but what about replacing Porter's order? Your father made it sound like the whole company rested on it."

"Yes, that was a blow," he admitted. "And I'm dashed if I know what to do about it right now. We'll have to find someone else who needs tires. Lots of them!"

"I might have something. But I need to know that anyone who orders from Vandemark will get their tires. Why were Porter's orders so late?"

He swiped at his face with the handkerchief again, then twisted it between his hands. "See, Dad's not been well. Things slipped. It's why Mams thought I should come home and take over. The man in charge at the factory is all right, but some of 'em under him are just flat tires. Ha! Flat tires!"

"Freddie . . ."

"Well, they just got behind." He shrugged. "Happens sometimes, right?"

"They can't fall behind," I said. "This is a business. If some of the men aren't doing their jobs, they need to be replaced by those who will. The man in charge—"

"Raines! Oh, he's the berries, Raines is. Loves that company like it was his own."

"He's trustworthy, then?"

"Oh, yeah. Straight and square as a house."

"I'll just see about that. I want to talk to him. You, meanwhile, need to clean up and get straight yourself. You won't be getting any major new orders if you're drunk all the time and making a spectacle of yourself. David's sister is going to help."

"What, Laura?" He looked panicked and started to rise. "Now, now, that's just not on, Miss Davies! I never agreed to that!"

"Freddie!" I pushed him back down with one hand and redoubled the glare. "Do you want the company to go under? Well? Is that what you want?"

"No," he answered meekly.

"Do you want to be a failure?"

"No?"

"Then do this thing, Freddie. I'll make sure Laura doesn't kill you. You need to straighten up and show all these people that you can apply yourself. Remember how happy you were to prove your sisters wrong? Do it again! *Prove yourself*, Freddie!" I grabbed him by both shoulders and gave him the Full Glare right in his face.

Eyes wide, he nodded. "Right you are."

"You'll do as Laura says?"

"Sure."

"Good boy. Now come on, off we go."

*   *   *

Laura took one look at Freddie and shook her head, clucking. "This'll be harder than I thought. But we'll get there, don't you worry," she added, patting me on the shoulder. "Right, Freddie! Into your tennis whites. We need to sweat out all that alcohol."

He looked desperately at me, but he was getting no sympathy from that quarter. "Remember, Freddie, this is for the good of us all," I reminded him. "Prove to me that you can make something of yourself."

Astonishingly, it worked. Laura took him in hand, and Freddie actually did as she said, from jumping jacks at daybreak to going completely dry. Even David, who had moaned about having Freddie to stay, seemed impressed.

"I didn't think he had it in him," he commented as Freddie finished a round of lunges and looked toward me. I smiled and nodded encouragingly.

"He may just surprise us all," I said. But it had only been two weeks. No telling whether Freddie would be able to keep this up for long.

I, meanwhile, got on the telephone with Raines to try to get a handle on things.

"Some of the men are a problem," he admitted. "They're young, but they've got no drive. They do just enough to earn their pint at the pub on a Friday night. And there have been issues with the rubber supply too. A lot of it comes from India and, well, things haven't been so peaceful there. The disruption drives the price up."

"Is there anywhere else where we can get the rubber?" I whispered, looking around to make sure no one was near. Was that a flicker of a shadow on the landing overhead?

"Sure. But most rubber comes from parts of the world that are . . . troubled."

I sighed, wondering what to do, with so many obstacles beyond my control.

"I'd not lie about any of this, miss," Raines said, clearly mistaking my silence for disapproval. "I need this company. I'm not a young man. If I lose this job, I'll not get another. If this place goes under, I'll be homeless."

That makes two of us.

"I didn't think you were lying, Mr. Raines," I reassured him. "Could you please send the company's accounts and start weeding out these men who aren't working out?"

"Yes, miss. I'll do that."

To keep myself busy, I turned back to writing poetry, something I hadn't managed to do since the day my parents died. I had a good run one day and as I finished, I glanced up and saw Jeremy hovering in the doorway, watching me with a fond smile.

"You're back!" I noted stupidly, as a warmth that had nothing to do with the weather traveled right through me.

"Am I?" he asked, coming into the room. "Or have you just conjured me up?"

As he approached me, I reached out and pinched him lightly on the arm. "You seem real enough," I said decisively. "How long have you been standing there?"

"Not long," he answered. "I didn't want to interrupt. What's this you're doing?"

"I'm writing a poem."

"Are you?" He claimed a nearby seat. "That's a charming hobby."

"I wouldn't call it a hobby. It's quite hard work."

"And you, of course, are not interested in simply being a lady of leisure."

"Not at all. As Laura says, if we sit too long, we grow moss. And green's not my color."

He laughed, then asked, "Will you let me read it?"

"Perhaps, when it's done. I'd hate to leave you suddenly wanting more."

He smiled wryly. "That would indeed be a tragedy. But now my curiosity is piqued. *'Wilt thou leave me so unsatisfied?'*"

I leaned toward him. "*'What satisfaction canst thou hope for tonight?'*"

"What indeed?"

227

"Lord Dunreaven, if I didn't know better I'd think you were trying to proposition me." I tried to ignore the heat creeping up my neck. And a dangerous tingle, deep down.

"I wouldn't dare."

"No? Why not?"

"Because I'm not sure you want me to." He frowned slightly. "Do you?"

Did I? If I told him to persist, what would he do? Where would it lead? I thought of Laura, laughing: *You should take Jeremy as a lover.*

I swallowed hard and changed the subject. "How was Portsmouth?"

His face fell, the tiniest bit. But he rallied, smiled, and responded: "The same as ever. Full of sailors and one very promising lieutenant commander named Peter Whelan. Unfortunately, I have to report that I've failed you. He says his family's reducing staff at the mines, not adding. I'm very sorry."

"Oh. What a shame." I tried not to think of a man with five children growing more desperate by the day. "Thank you for trying."

"I'm sorry I couldn't do more." He seemed almost as disappointed as I.

"You did more than most," I told him warmly, reaching across the desk and squeezing his hand. "And I really do appreciate that."

He smiled. "Have I missed anything while I've been away?"

"Not much. Joyce has started planning the fete, and thank you very much for that as well. And Freddie's come for a visit."

Just like everyone else, he was taken aback by that. "Freddie? Why is he here?"

"A project for Laura," I answered blithely. "It's going quite well so far."

"I'm amazed she hasn't killed him. It doesn't seem like it would take much."

"Perhaps he's made of sterner stuff than we all give him credit for." God, I hoped so. "Everyone's outside playing croquet. Shall we join them?"

He smiled warmly. "I was rather enjoying myself here."

"Well, I'm afraid I've run out of clever things to say. Do be a gentleman and let me hide behind a mallet for a bit while I think of more?" I playfully batted my eyelashes.

"All right," Jeremy chuckled. "But only because I'm *such* a gentleman."

* * *

Vandemark's accounts arrived three days later: two huge ledgers that I hauled into the study and thwacked down in front of Freddie. His eyes dilated at the sight of them.

"You and I are going to comb through these and find out exactly what's going on," I announced, opening one and taking a seat next to him. "We need to know everything."

"But I don't know anything about any of this," he said, thumbing the pages of the unopened ledger. "Afraid I'm hopeless at sums." He chuckled.

"Well we *have to learn*, Freddie! Do you really think I know anything about running a business? But like it or not, here we both are, and we need to do something, or loads of people are going to be jobless and penniless, including us. Do you want that?"

"No. Sounds unpleasant."

"That's right. So let's get stuck in."

I thought it would be an impossible task, making head or tails of the rows and rows of numbers, but it wasn't. Oh, it was hard going for a while, but eventually it began to make some sense. The practice I'd had with my own accounts helped. And when we got really stuck, Joyce was unexpectedly able to help explain a few things.

"I used to look at some of my father's account books," she explained when she noticed how surprised I was by this talent of hers. "I thought he might be impressed if I learned a little something about his business, but he didn't think much of my suggestions. Mind, I was only twelve, and they were probably silly. We'll see if his opinion on my abilities has changed any—did I tell you he's coming for the fete? He thought it sounded too charming to miss. You know how he is about these very British things."

I was only half listening, keeping one eye on the ledgers and the other on a footman who seemed to be lurking just outside the study door. When Joyce mentioned her father, though, something popped into my head. I scrawled *Play along* on a sheet of paper and showed it to Joyce and Freddie as I loudly said, "Joyce, that's excellent! It'll give Freddie and me a chance to discuss our new business deal with him!"

Freddie seemed completely lost. Joyce frowned but responded, "Oh yes. That's actually one of the reasons he's coming. He does like to manage business himself when he can, especially with an order this large."

"Did Raines tell you about this?" Freddie asked me.

"Yes, he did!" I replied jovially. The footman was obviously listening in: he was just standing there with the afternoon post clenched in one hand. "Isn't that wonderful?"

"Yes," Joyce put in. "An enormous order for–for—" She looked desperately at me, and I mouthed, *fifty thousand.* "Five hundred thousand!" she finished.

Freddie's eyes popped.

"Won't it be a laugh when everyone finds out that Porter never intended to take his business elsewhere?" I said. "These rumors, they get so out of hand."

"Yes, very," Joyce agreed. She glanced through the door and said, "Melville, are you finished with that post yet?"

The footman skittered off.

"Thank you both," I murmured.

Poor Freddie deflated. "Oh, so there's no order, then?" he asked. He seemed so forlorn I felt badly for having misled him.

"No, Freddie," I answered, patting his hand. "I'm just hoping word gets out now that the company's stable. It'll make other clients less likely to move elsewhere and may attract some new ones." *Any pie Porter so much as sniffs becomes valuable.*

"Are you finished with me, then?" Joyce asked impatiently. "Because I do have things to do." She headed for the door, then suddenly stopped. "Oh, Astra: Jeremy telephoned to remind you about going riding with him tomorrow morning."

"I can't." I gestured to the ledgers. "Would you mind telephoning him back?"

"Cancel your own spooning sessions," she snapped. "As I said, I'm busy!"

She marched out, and I followed as far as the telephone, where I asked to be connected to Midbourne.

"Midbourne on the line," a sonorous voice weighted with self-importance informed me.

"Yes, is his lordship in? This is Astra Davies."

"I'm afraid his lordship is out at the moment, miss. May I take a message?"

"Yes, please. Could you tell him I won't be able to go riding tomorrow as I'm quite tied up just now? I'm terribly sorry."

"I say, Astra," Freddie said, coming to the door of the study and leaning against the frame, "I'll be dashed little use to you the rest of today: you've plumb worn me out. Can we pick back up tomorrow? Maybe somewhere more private? I can't make any decent headway with Joyce and Laura and the servants darting in and out all the time."

"Yes, all right, Freddie!" I hissed.

There was a long pause on the other end of the line, then: "I'll see he gets the message, *miss*," and the punctuating click of the receiver being put down.

I glared briefly at Freddie as I hung up the telephone and pointed back to the study. "Work, Freddie!"

He slumped back to the ledgers, sighing. "Far as I can see, it's like old Raines says, there's trouble with the supply. That is right, isn't it?"

"Yes, you're right," I agreed, resuming my seat. "All the upheaval is making the price go up and the supply unreliable. But I don't know what we can do about that."

Freddie scrunched his face and pondered. I was amazed he didn't break a sweat with the effort. "You know," he said slowly, "when I was in America, I met a fellow who worked for DuPont. He said they had a sort of rubber that they were making without rubber from trees. Synth-something, he called it."

"Synthetic?"

His face brightened and he nodded. "That's the one! Synthetic. Maybe we could try that. I doubt America's going to rebel anytime soon—they already did that once!"

I blinked at him, shocked. "Freddie, you surprise me!"

He shrugged. "I knew Father would want me to run the business someday, so I did *try* to learn a little along the way. And things are coming through a bit clearer now I'm off the sauce."

"Good for you! Do you remember the man's name? Could you speak to him?"

He beamed, warmed by my approval. "Sure could! I'll do it today, if you want."

"I do want."

Freddie smiled, nodded, and turned back to the ledger.

I watched him for a little while and then said, "I'm proud of you, Freddie. You've been applying yourself and doing really, really well."

"Aww, shucks," he grinned. "You'll make me blush."

I reached over and squeezed his arm. "I mean it, Freddie. You've exceeded my expectations." No need to tell him how low those expectations had been.

"Well, I can't very well see you out on the street, now can I?" he said. "Chivalry and all that, right?"

I smiled. "You're very sweet when you want to be."

"We've all gotta have something to offer, I guess," he said. "My family never thought I had much of anything to give. They'll be shocked out of their shoes to find out I'm not hopeless"

"Of course you aren't hopeless," I reassured him. "Surely they know that."

"Aww, you can't blame 'em. I've never been much good at much. At least, that's what all my sisters say. Lord, they gave me an earful when Porter went!" He rolled his eyes. "We had to sell the country pile. We would have had to anyway, probably, but that was the last straw. They said it was my fault." He shrugged. "Guess it was."

"I'm sorry," I grimaced sympathetically. "That must have been difficult."

He thought about it for a little while. "Dunno," he said at last. "The place was drafty, and the nursery had mice and spiders in it. The hard part is all of us cramming into the London house. Quite a squash and a squeeze, with all the sisters. I've four of 'em, you know. All older."

"Good lord! And they're mean to you? I thought older sisters usually doted on their little brothers."

He chuckled. "No, no, they don't dote. You think they'd be fonder of me, though: they love a good gossip, and I give them so much to work with!"

Laura appeared in the doorway. "Freddie, you're five and a half minutes late for your prelunch exercises." She eyed the ledgers. "What's all this?"

"We're doing business!" Freddie excitedly announced.

Laura crooked an eyebrow. "Are you? Well, far be it from me to interfere. I'll leave you to it. But you're not getting off easy, Freddie. Tomorrow will be twice as hard."

He looked alarmed and I patted his hand. "Don't worry—I'll talk to her."

Chapter Nineteen

~

After days of wrangling and puzzling over numbers, working out more sums than I had in my entire life up to that point, telephoning Raines four more times, and hovering nearby (glancing about nervously) while Freddie shouted down the telephone on a long-distance call to DuPont, it finally felt like we were getting somewhere. This marvelous new rubber could be supplied regularly and in large enough quantities to keep orders filled.

"The smell is a problem," the DuPont man apologized, "but we're working on it."

"It's for tires, my good man! No one expects them to smell like roses!" Freddie reassured him. "Maybe airplane tires. They'll get aired out, won't they? Ho ho!"

Raines was already at work on his purge, and he reassured me that, yes, they could make airplane tires if they had to. Now we just needed to secure the order.

"You seem happier these days, miss," Reilly observed as I dressed for dinner.

"I am, Reilly. Things are looking up!"

She smiled briefly. She'd been subdued ever since Jeremy's unsuccessful Portsmouth trip. I felt terrible for having even mentioned the possibility of a job for her brother, but now, I realized, I had a solution.

"Reilly," I said as she fussed with the hem of my dress. "Do you think your brother might adapt to factory work?"

She looked up, puzzled. "I suppose so, miss, if he had to." Her face turned hopeful. "Do you know of something?"

"As it turns out, I happen to know of a rubber factory looking for new managers," I answered. "Reliable men who are willing to work hard." I guessed that five children and extended unemployment would be plenty of motivation for him to do an exemplary job.

Reilly burst into a smile, a real one, and the largest I'd ever seen from her. "Oh, miss!" She covered her mouth with both hands. "Would you really?"

"The job's his if he wants it. I'm afraid he'll have to move nearer to the factory."

"He'll do it," she promised immediately. "There's not much for 'em where they are now. Thank you so much, miss!"

"Don't thank me just yet," I warned her. "Let's see if all of this is a success first." After all, the man may have no aptitude for the job. The company may yet founder. But at least he'd have work for a little while.

The dinner gong rang and I headed out. I was halfway down the hallway when Laura appeared, strung her arm through mine, and drew me into her room.

"Here you are, you little sneak," she said good-naturedly, pointing to the bench at the foot of her bed. I gingerly moved a sweaty pair of exercise shorts and a sleeveless vest aside before taking a seat. "Now," said Laura, crossing her arms and leaning against a dressing table scattered with hairpins, "you are going to tell me just what's going on." She dug underneath a pile of magazines and rumpled handkerchiefs on the bed-side table until she found a cigarette case. "Why did you bring Freddie here?" she asked, taking out a cigarette, tamping it down, and lighting it. "It wasn't to give *me* something to do. You two have been holed up for days now. What's happening?"

"It wasn't for you," I readily confessed. "It was for him and me. My father bought a stake in Freddie's company, and now it's in danger of going under. I brought Freddie out here so you could sober him up, and he and I could save the company."

"Why on earth didn't you just say that to begin with?"

"I don't know." The subterfuge did seem a little stupid now. "Maybe I was afraid you'd think I was just using you."

"You are. But that's what talents and skills and connections are for. To be used."

"True. But people can get funny about mixing business with friendship. And they especially don't seem to like it when women are doing business."

"Oh pooh!" She flapped her hands and dropped onto the bench beside me. "Have you forgotten that I'm a woman in business myself? It's only sensible, really: we can't always rely on men to support us." She sat up a little straighter. "A friend of mine, Megsy Rillington—her husband lost nearly everything in the Crash and then shot himself. Left her holding the bag completely. Poor dear had to sell everything, right down to her little girl's china tea set. It was dreadful watching Mona Lewis cart that off for her little brat." She rolled her eyes. "Right after that, I started taking those fitness courses, so at least I'd have something to fall back on if it ever came to that. So of course I wouldn't disapprove. Good for you, I say! Tell me, what plans have you two cooked up?"

"We're hoping to convince the owner of that airplane factory where David's having his plane made to order tires from us."

"How thrilling," she observed drily. "You really think Freddie's up to it?"

"I don't know," I sighed. "He'll have to be."

"He's not. We'll need to get his confidence up." She patted me on the knee. "Fear not, darling, we'll start work on him tomorrow. But now we ought to go down. Jeremy's here tonight, you know."

I didn't know, and the news made me tingle all over. I'd missed him. It felt like a long time since I'd seen him last, even though it had only been a few days.

We went down together, and found the others just coming in from the terrace.

"Have we missed cocktails?" I asked Jeremy, with a bright smile. "I was hoping you'd make me one of your famous gimlets."

"Sorry to have to disappoint you," he responded in a cooler tone than I was used to.

"I'll make you something," Freddie cheerfully volunteered. "You deserve it after the week we've had!"

Jeremy shot me a questioning look, and his mouth tightened a little.

"It's all right, Freddie, I don't want to hold everyone up," I said, feeling strangely annoyed at the feeling that Jeremy thought I owed him an explanation. "Let's just go through."

"Right-o. Onward!" Freddie crowed, taking my hand and leading me into the dining room. He plunked down beside me. Jeremy raised an eyebrow and sat next to Laura, at the opposite end of the table.

Freddie was ebullient, clearly feeling as happy as I'd been at our successes, and I have to admit, I got a bit caught up in his jolly mood. The two of us joked and teased like siblings even as I sensed Jeremy's mood darkening a bit. I seemed to feel every glance he sent my way. They stung and pierced like thorns.

After dinner, we all returned to the drawing room, where I left Freddie and Joyce sorting through gramophone records and joined David at the piano. He was tapping random keys with one finger, provoking the dissonant sound of boredom.

"Do you mind?" I asked, gesturing to the instrument.

"Please do," he invited, sitting back and smiling warmly.

"Joyce tells me you have a new airplane, David," I said as I began playing "Rhapsody in Blue." "You must be so excited! Is it nearly finished?"

His face brightened. "Yes, nearly. She'll be ready to fly in the next few weeks!"

"Really? How wonderful! Could we go and see it, do you think?"

He looked surprised. "I didn't know you were interested in airplanes."

"Of course I am!" I gushed. "They're *wonderful*. And the people who fly them are so brave!"

I heard a snort behind me and turned. Jeremy was seated on a nearby sofa, his back to me. He had a book open in front of him, but was clearly listening to David and me. I chose to ignore him for now.

"Do you know who else loves planes? Freddie. Freddie! Come here for a moment," I called.

"What? Oh, right-o!" He handed the records off to Joyce and bounded over. "What's the news? What's the word? Love your playing, by the way," he told me. "Really puts a spring in the step, eh?"

"Freddie, David and I were just talking about his new airplane." I turned to David with a conspiratorial smile. "Freddie was telling me the other day how much he loves planes and wants to learn how to fly. Isn't that right, Freddie?"

He looked alarmed at the prospect but quickly covered it. "Oh—oh yes! Clever little things, planes! How they stay up in the air, without even flapping their wings!"

"David and I were just discussing paying a visit to the factory where the plane's being made," I told Freddie. "And of course you must come along."

"Oh yes, Freddie, you must," Laura seconded, sidling up to him with a cup of coffee. "And you should meet the owner too. I'm sure you'll have loads to talk about, manufacturer to manufacturer. You two can talk all about the challenges of business." Laura dropped her voice slightly. "Did you know, David, that Freddie recently showed Porter himself the door?"

David frowned, glancing between the three of us. "That's not how I heard it."

"Well, of course not," Laura said. "Porter wouldn't very well admit to having been given his walking papers, especially after behaving so disgracefully. But the man was an absolute heel, David. He insisted that Freddie's company cut corners for him. But, of course, Freddie simply wouldn't make a shoddy product, so in the end, Porter had to go elsewhere. And good for you, Freddie, I say!"

"Yes, good for you!" David said, nodding vigorously. "That man—" He dropped his voice, checking to make sure Joyce was nowhere near. "He thinks he can get away with anything and buy his way out of anything. Well done, showing him otherwise!"

"Thank you! Thank you!" said Freddie, almost seeming to believe this story was true. "What a weasel! A regular John D, wouldn't you say?"

"If you say so," David chuckled. "I know I've plenty of my own stories to tell."

"Then do tell, do tell! I am here to listen."

I abandoned the song and slid off the piano bench so Freddie could take my spot. Jeremy had left the book and the sofa and was now standing by the fireplace, tapping the mantelpiece while giving me a look that sent a chill down my spine. I gradually picked up the Morse code he was tapping. *What's your game?* I strolled over to him, looked him straight in the eye, and said loudly, "Why, Jeremy, I'd love to see the first editions in the library. How nice of you to suggest it."

I looped my arm through his and steered him out of the room and into the library. He once again took up a spot by the cold hearth.

"We are not going to be like David and Joyce, letting things fester," I told him as I closed the door behind us. "We'll have this out right now." I crossed my arms. "Something you'd like to say? You've been freezing me all night. Another few minutes and they could chisel cubes off me for the cocktails."

"There *is* something I'd like to say, but I almost feel as if I need an appointment," he answered, twisting his ring.

"What does that mean?" I tightened my arms across my chest and frowned.

"Just that you've seemed very unavailable ever since Freddie showed up." He spat Freddie's name as if it tasted bitter.

"You aren't jealous?" I scoffed.

"Perhaps I am. I've liked having you to myself."

"Well, that's too bad. You don't *own* me. You have to be a good boy and share!"

"You don't make Freddie share!"

"Oh, honestly, Jeremy! You can't possibly think that Freddie and I have something going on, can you?" I actually laughed, but he was not amused.

"I didn't, until you sent me off on a fool's errand. And while I was gone, you summoned him here and lied about him being a project for Laura."

"A fool's errand?"

Now it was his turn to scoff. "Really, Astra. Finding a job for your *maid's brother*? I should have known that was ridiculous. Who cares that much about finding employment for the relative of their servant? I should have seen through it, but I didn't because all I saw was an opportunity to please you, and now this is my reward!" He was pale with anger, and I found myself wanting to back away from him. But I held my ground.

"After I stuck my neck out for you!" he continued. When everyone was saying such vile things about you, I told them no, you'd never. Not with Freddie, of course not! I've never had any reason to think your character was anything but impeccable. I knew they were laughing at me behind my back, saying I'd been taken in by some adventuress, but I ignored it, because I thought I knew you better than they did. But now, have you made a fool of me, Astra Davies?"

"Why on earth would you think that?"

"Why shouldn't I? You're doing the same with David in there." He gestured in the direction of the drawing room. "So I'll ask again: Have you made a fool of me?"

A rage had been steadily building as he spoke. It started in my belly, which clenched and churned and sent up something that boiled and surged and made my whole body feel fiery.

"Oh, you *poor thing*!" I hissed. "With your wounded pride! Just like all the others, so eager to assume the worst of me. And why? Because Freddie's here and I'm trying to help him make something of himself, and make something of *myself*?

"And you, you talk about a reward," I sputtered. "Your *reward*! Just what were you expecting, Lord Dunreaven? For me to fawn all over you? Worship at your feet because you did one good deed? Or did you expect payment of some other kind, since you clearly, like the others, think I'm that sort of woman?"

He blinked, taken aback. "I would never—"

"Wouldn't you? Why? Because you're such a *gentleman*?" I spat. "Perhaps you don't care enough about other people to help them simply because they need it, but it seems you and I differ there. No, I don't know Reilly's brother, but I do know he's in dire straits." I spread my arms, indicating the room, with its leather furnishings and thick carpets and expensive paintings. "Is it so outrageous that I should look around and see that we all have so much, when so many others have so little, and to want to do something? I can do precious little in this world, but I could do this one thing! Help this one man! And so I asked if you knew anyone because that's how these things are done. I didn't ask you to go and beg on my behalf—you did that all on your own. And you didn't even manage to get the man a job. I did! That's right—*I did!* So I don't know what sort of reward you were expecting, because in my experience, failure never warranted anything more than a pat on the head and a 'good try, better luck next time!'"

He wasn't twisting his ring anymore. He was just staring at me, shocked. I was a little shocked too, but I wasn't quite done yet.

"As I told you before, Freddie and I are in business together. We've been working. I need to work because my parents left me almost nothing. Freddie's business is the only thing standing between me and utter penury, and we both know he can't manage things alone, so *I* have to do it. I know talk of business and money is common and disgusting to the great and titled of this land, and if that's how you feel, then you can just go back to your *palace* and stew about it!"

Now I was done. I spun and marched out, slamming the door behind me.

* * *

Upstairs, I dipped my entire face in a sink of cold water before turning myself over to Reilly.

"Could you come brush my hair please, Reilly?" I asked once I was dressed for bed. I needed soothing. My face still felt hot. My heart was hammering away like a bird throwing itself against the bars of its cage. Reilly sat me down, picked up my silver hairbrush, and drew it through my hair. Slow strokes, just like my mother used to do.

"You have such beautiful hair," Mother had commented the very last time she ever did it. "When I was young, a woman's hair was thought to be her crowning glory. We never would have thought of cutting it all off. Well, except for Diana Cooper, but she was always an odd duck."

"I can't blame her," I said. "Long hair takes ages to wash and dry and comb. It doesn't seem worth it."

"Oh, you young people," Mother had sighed, setting down the brush and coming to rest on the bench beside me. She was pale and tired looking, and I had felt guilty about goading her. "You're all in such a hurry."

Perhaps we were. But then, we had to be. No race was ever really won by a tortoise, was it? The world moved fast, and we all had to scramble to keep up, or be lost in the slipstream.

What would Mother make of me now? Diving into business and shouting at a lord? Manipulating friends and scrabbling to get ahead? Would she be proud? Mortified?

I missed her so much just then. I felt it, a hard physical pain in my chest and behind my eyes, which smarted. I wanted to lay my head in her lap and have her stroke my hair while I cried and complained about how unjust things were and how unfair Jeremy was being. She'd have advice right when I sorely needed it. Mothers always do, if you have the sense to ask. She'd be able to tell me if this was all right to fight with someone like that, to feel such rage. Would that go away? When? Tomorrow? Next week? Next year? Would *he* go away and never come back? Did I want him to come back?

I thought about it, now that the rage had ebbed. I was still angry, but the thought of Jeremy disappearing made me feel cold—and lonely. And it suddenly felt like a very real possibility. I'd told him about the money. In my anger I'd told him I had nothing. He couldn't marry a pauper. Surely he'd turn his attentions elsewhere now. He'd have to.

The idea made me want to burst into tears. Was that normal? Was I in love? Or just some silly girl with a persistent crush? How could you tell the difference?

Mother would know. She'd tell me what it felt like to find the person you wanted to share yourself with so completely. She could tell me, in the way only a mother can, how to navigate from a fond kiss on the doorstep at the end of the evening to showing yourself in all your glory at bedtime: face smeared with cold cream, hair in curl papers, downing the cup of cocoa you simply can't sleep without. But you're not meant to sleep, are you? Should you have coffee, to stay alert?

These were the things—the terrifying, mysterious things a girl was supposed to ask her mother in those last desperate hours before the veil came out and the satin engulfed her. When the girl was supposed to be cramming herself full of the knowledge that was to serve her for the next fifty years. But who was I to ask now?

I stopped fighting and let the tears come. I choked them out, sitting there, staring at my reflection in the looking glass. Watching my face crumple and go all blotchy.

Reilly laid the brush down, handed me a handkerchief, and patted my shoulder.

"Thank you, Reilly," I said in a wobbly voice. "I'll see you in the morning."

"Good night, miss." She gathered my laundry and jewelry, but as she reached the door, she turned back. "I know it's not my place, miss, but my mother used to say that a proper fight now and again was a good thing. Clears the air, like a thunderstorm."

I managed to smile. "Thank you, Reilly," I repeated.

She nodded, smiled sympathetically, and left.

I remained at the dressing table for a while, toying with the hair-brush as the tears eased, then wandered over to the window, hoping to catch a breeze.

The air was still as heavy as midday, pregnant with the possibility of a real storm. It pressed suffocatingly close. Crickets droned, a deep buzz that vibrated through me and rattled around. The rising moon carved a shimmering path down the center of the rectangular pond that ran from the back terrace to the espaliered fruit trees on the opposite side of the garden. As children visiting Laura during the school holidays, we had used it like a pool on hot summer days. Stolen away from Nanny long enough to climb in and splash about, slip-sliding on the slime that gathered at the bottom. Pity the poor footman enlisted to help drag us out of there.

Did Joyce and David still steal into the garden on hot nights like this one? Shed their layers, dip into thigh-deep water? Did the servants spy, catching a glimpse of their mistress's moon-pale skin gleaming in the wan light as she frolicked with her husband?

And could any maid or footman serve bacon and eggs the next morning without blushing? Surely it was impossible to look at someone the same way again after you'd seen them in the altogether?

Or maybe it didn't really matter. Maybe it was just like looking at a Greek statue. After all, we've all got the same parts, so one naked person was probably much like another. And yet, I couldn't help but think it wasn't really like that. Surely if I ever saw Jeremy naked, I'd never be able to look at him the same way again.

I blushed and tried to force myself to think of something else. But of course once something like that's fixed in your mind you can't get it back out again.

Jeremy must have joined us for those childhood swims sometimes. But hard as I tried, I couldn't remember him being there. He'd made less of an impression in those days. Now, however, I couldn't help but imagine him ducking under the water, coming up slowly, rivulets running down his face, arms, and legs, clothes plastered to his body.

Or perhaps no clothes at all . . .

You should take Jeremy as a lover.

I went to douse my face in water again, and when I returned to the window, I saw one of the men walking around the pond, smoking. I could just make out his outline and the occasional flare of orange from the tip of his cigarette. I couldn't tell who it was: any of the men in the house might have had reason to need a late-night stroll to calm his thoughts or cool down. But I laid my forehead on the glass and watched him for a while anyway, wondering if he saw me. After a few moments, he flicked his cigarette away and headed into the house.

I crawled into bed and tossed until I managed to find a cool spot. I pressed my face against it and clenched my hands so they wouldn't go wandering where perhaps they shouldn't. I fell asleep like that and dreamed of Jeremy, coming out of the pool, dripping wet and gleaming. But when I reached out to touch him, he turned into marble. Hard and cold, like Galatea in reverse.

Chapter Twenty

❧

"She's ready!" David crowed, galloping into the dining room at lunch-time the next day.

The rest of us blinked at him until Joyce said, "Oh! The plane! Of course. I might have known he'd never be so excited about an actual woman."

"Don't ruin it," David scowled, taking his seat.

"Same goes for you," Laura said to him.

"When do we get to see it?" I asked. "Or *her*. Why *her*, anyway? Why are ships and planes and things always women?"

"We men like being reminded of lovely things, and what's lovelier than a woman?" David responded with an ingratiating smile toward his wife.

"Hear, hear!" Freddie crowed.

"Besides, airplanes and ships tend to be staffed with men," David continued. "There aren't too many men who want to spend all their time in another man."

"I don't know that that's true," Laura remarked.

Freddie guffawed. "You sure take the cake, you know that?" he said to Laura.

"So when do we get to see her, David?" I asked again.

"End of the week?" he suggested. "Thursday?"

"No, not Thursday," Joyce protested. "I've got the Ladies' Benevolent Society coming about the fete on Thursday, and I need Astra."

"You do not," I argued. "Can't you face them down yourself?"

"Let her go with the boys, Joyce, if that's what she really wants," said Laura. "I'll help you manage the Benevolents. With a name like that, how bad could they be?"

"Huh," Joyce grunted. "Just you wait and see."

*　*　*

Now that we were under a ticking clock, Laura and I took Freddie off to the study immediately after lunch to try to work some backbone into him. But after a good hour and a half, it was starting to feel hopeless.

"Honestly, Freddie, you couldn't convince a rabbit to take a free carrot from you right now," Laura groaned. "Have some verve! Find your vim!"

His forehead puckered. "I'm trying. Vim's dashed hard to find sometimes."

"Try again!" she ordered. "Convince me to buy your tires, Freddie."

I wasn't much help. A sleepless night and overcrowded mind left me flaccid and easily distracted. I drooped, unable to come up with anything useful to say. Worrying one moment about the company going under, the next about Jeremy never wanting to speak to me again. And then wondering what sort of notes Millicent was receiving today.

"Astra! Are you listening?"

I started and sat up. "What's that?"

Laura shook her head in disgust. "You're both hopeless. Astra, go and finish thrashing things out with Jeremy will you? Purge your mind of this nonsense so you can get down to the business at hand." She waved toward the doorway, where Jeremy was waiting, with a smile both kind and apologetic. I'd been so lost in thought I hadn't even noticed him arrive. My heart lifted even as my stomach knotted. He'd come back! But what would he say?

"I'm sorry to interrupt," he said.

"No, please do." Laura waved us both off. "Take her away and have another ripsnorter, you two. Make sure the air's well and truly cleared."

He looked questioningly at me. An expression that said, *"Could we talk?"*

We returned to the library, and I went to stand next to the windows, where there seemed less risk of us being overheard. I wasn't sure what to say; every time I looked at him, all I could see was that dream. The rivulets of water trickling down a perfect Grecian body. And that body going hard and cold. Unreachable under my touch.

He, too, seemed uncertain. He cleared his throat several times, went to the fireplace, then joined me. "I've come to beg your forgiveness," he announced.

"I don't like the thought of you begging me for anything," I quickly rejoined.

He smiled momentarily. His posture eased a little. "All the same, I overstepped last night, as you so rightly pointed out. I had no business making claims on you or your time. I'm very sorry. And I'm sorry that I accused you of having ulterior motives for wanting my help in finding that man a job." He looked away from me and flinched, looking disgusted. "I can't imagine what you must think of me. As if I couldn't imagine helping someone simply because it was in your power to do so."

I touched his arm. "I think you were upset and speaking purely in anger."

"You're generous and kind. More so than I deserve."

"Not at all," I said, sighing. "I haven't been blameless. The way I've been behaving with you, of course you'd think . . ." I took a deep breath. Tried not to think of the dream.

"But you've been very clear from the beginning that you aren't interested in anything more, and I should have respected that." He cleared his throat again and stepped back. My hand fell from his arm.

No!

"Good heavens, Jeremy, who's still keeping their New Year's resolution in August?" I asked with a shaky laugh.

He looked up at me and blinked. His expression turned the tiniest bit hopeful.

"I'm sorry, I—I don't know what this is!" I burst out. "I don't know what any of it is! I don't know how to be with you, and there are so many things happening for me just now and so many . . . complications. I don't know how to manage it all, so I'm just making mess after mess." I threw up my hands. "And who am I to ask for advice? My mother can't help me. Joyce is miserable and, now, too busy. Cee would just turn gooey and romantic, and Laura says I should just take you as a lover!"

What was I saying? I felt the blood shoot straight up from my neck to meet the roots of my hair. I could have made toast on the heat coming off my face.

Jeremy was taken aback but then burst out laughing. "Did she really?"

I couldn't help it. I started to laugh too. It was like turning a faucet: neither of us could seem to stop. We laughed and laughed until tears came.

"Well," he said, once we were spent and starting to regain control of ourselves. "You know what everyone else thinks. What do *you* want?"

"I don't know," I admitted. What did I want? To be friends? Yes, but more. There was more there—I could reach out and just brush it with my fingertips. I wanted to grasp it and hold it, pull it close. I wanted to sit by the fire or in the garden with him. Tell him all my adventures and hear his and have some together. Make plans and tease and comfort. Take his hand as the fire died and the sun went down, and go upstairs . . .

Did I want the surety, the finality of marriage? To know that he was mine, and mine alone, forever? Or should I cling to my freedom and be his lover, as Laura said? Shock the world and make a scandal? Become the woman they all thought I was?

"I don't know," I repeated, feeling stupid, childish, helpless. And angry with myself because of that.

Jeremy smiled that beautiful smile of his. As always, it went straight through me. He stepped forward and gently brushed one of the lingering laughter tears off my cheek.

"We may be getting ahead of ourselves," he said. "We don't need to make any decisions about anything just now. We can . . . just be, for a bit."

"Probe and winnow out all our faults and foibles?"

He chuckled. "If that's an invitation, I'm happy to do a bit of foible probing."

My heart sped up. His hand was still on my cheek, cupping my face now. I saw him swallow hard, and then he lowered his head and kissed me. Soft and sweet, like a summer's rain. But I tingled all over and my heart went *pit pit pit* and my face felt hot and I thought, Yes! Yes! *Yes!*

And then it was over, and we were looking at each other and smiling.

Then Laura was there, saying, "Sorry to interrupt, but Astra, I'm about to say 'uncle.' Freddie's hopeless."

I concentrated very hard on not killing her with the nearest blunt object.

"Yes, all right, Laura," I said tightly.

"What is it you're trying to do?" Jeremy asked.

"Freddie and I need to convince the owner of an airplane factory to start buying tires from us," I explained.

"Could I help?" Jeremy suggested.

"You know what? I think you could!" said Laura, grabbing him by the arm and hauling him back into the study. She stood him in front of Freddie, stepped back, and said, "Now, Jem, show Freddie your best 'I'm in charge, and you'll do as I say' glare."

Freddie already looked terrified.

"I don't think that will help," said Jeremy. "Freddie, why don't you and I go somewhere? Change of scenery will do you good."

"Right-o!" Freddie was out the door like a spaniel after a rabbit.

"Back in a while," Jeremy promised.

"Don't get him drunk!" Laura bellowed after them. She turned back to me with a sigh. "Well, now I'll be bored and you'll be jumpy. Distraction is needed. Tennis?"

I let her put me through my paces for a solid two hours, until we saw Jeremy's car coming back up the drive. Freddie leapt out as we approached and dashed toward the house, but Laura was too fast for him. She grabbed his arm as he passed and turned him to face her. "Alcohol," she declared in the voice of a detective inspecting a dead body and proclaiming, "Arsenic."

"Oh." Freddie's eyes darted to Jeremy, who rolled his slightly. "Just a little pint. A half pint! Not even a full half pint. I think the barman was cheating us."

"My fault, Laura," Jeremy said. "One drink at The Fox. Just the one, I promise."

Laura released Freddie, who fled inside. "You'll undo all my good work," she growled at Jeremy, waggling a finger menacingly at him. "All of it. And *she* won't thank you for that." She jabbed the finger in my direction, then stomped off toward the tennis lawn, muttering about thankless tasks.

"I thought the poor boy needed some release," Jeremy apologetically explained.

"It's all right. He's earned a little something. Did it help?"

"Oh, enormously. I've seen plenty of others like him, meek and bullied. They just need a little building up. Those sisters of his have spent their whole lives haranguing him. Putting him with Laura was hardly going to build his confidence. But I can keep working on him, if you like."

"I do like, if you don't mind," I answered, trying to pour all my gratitude into the look I was giving him. "I need him in top form for the factory visit. Are you coming?"

"Yes, I think I might. David's talked about this plane so much I feel as if I know it already. It'll be nice to see it all put together."

I smiled at him. "Good. It'll be quite the excursion, then."

He smiled, then reached out and very gently pulled me closer, lowering his head so his lips were next to my ear. "I don't want to alarm you," he murmured, "but I have reason to think someone here is keeping an eye on you."

"I know someone is," I told him. "How did you find out?"

"Lady Millicent has shown her hand," he answered. "She telephoned me this morning, quite out of the blue, and asked if I might show her around Midbourne Abbey. Some of the things she said suggested she knew that you and I had quarreled."

"And she thought she might strike while the iron was hot?" I shook my head. "She certainly knows an opportunity when she sees one, and takes it."

"Well, she'll be disappointed, then, because there's no opportunity here." His voice had a hard edge to it. I looked up at him in surprise, and he explained: "I know what she did to Mustard. And to you." Off my shocked expression, he continued, "Mustard had a glass or two of brandy the eve of the wedding and spilled, but swore me to secrecy."

"He hardly needed to do that. You're too much of a gentleman to slander a lady," I observed. "Although it doesn't serve me well in this instance, it's one of the things I admire about you, Jeremy."

"I hope you don't think less of me for not doing more to defend you," he said, looking embarrassed.

I reached out and took his hand. "You did what you could. I know that. And I appreciate it, I really do."

"Well, I want you to know that Millicent has no hope with me. I made that very clear to her. As you know, I'm not one to suffer bullies."

"That's very good to hear." We grinned at each other, still holding hands. "Are you staying for a while, or must you rush back home?" I asked.

"I have nowhere to be but here."

"Well, then," I said playfully, "I'm going to take a bath. And afterward, why don't we go back to the library and give that spy something *really* interesting to report?"

Chapter
Twenty-One

Off to the airplane factory, where the lads and I were greeted by a box-shaped man with thinning hair who smirked at me and said, "Who brought the wife?"

"I'm not anyone's wife." I offered a hand to shake. "I'm Astra Davies."

He very delicately took my hand, as if he thought it might shatter, then gave David some backslaps and the other men hearty handshakes.

"How're things, Dicky?" David asked him. "Everyone, this is Richard Linklater. Owner and airplane builder extraordinaire!"

"Too kind," said Linklater. "You'll want to see your little lady, I suppose?"

"Of course!" David replied.

Linklater glanced at me. "Want her to wait with my secretary?" he asked David.

I felt Jeremy, standing beside me, stiffen. I answered with a tone and smile equally bright, "Oh no, please, I want to see the plane too!"

Linklater finally lowered himself to address me directly: "It's very loud inside."

"I think I can manage," I replied, my voice cooling even as my smile widened.

"She's a tough bird is Astra," Freddie piped up.

"All right," Linklater grumbled. "Come on."

He wasn't lying about the noise: the machinery clattered and clanged deafeningly. Shiny bits of airplanes moved past on conveyor belts. Men with tools swarmed them, and away came wings and propellers. In a corner, the more delicate work of building an engine was underway.

Linklater pointed this way and that, talking, but none of us could hear. Freddie nodded mechanically and tried to look like he knew what was going on.

We were taken through a back door, to a long drive where the finished planes were lined up. Linklater continued talking as we passed them, and now we were out of the din of the factory, we could actually hear him.

"We specialize in racing airplanes, but we're doing some passenger carriers as well," he explained. "Loads of orders coming in for that. People have gone off airships since that crash last year, and they love that they can get places so much faster by air. Only a week to get from Croyden to Karachi now. Imagine that! We're just about to sign a contract with Empire Airways. They want to start a London-to-Moscow route next year and add more Paris flights. For the ladies, you know," he added, smirking at me.

"You'll be building quite a lot of planes, then," I commented, already noting how large their output appeared to be.

He seemed a little surprised to hear me speak but just shook his head and stopped in front of one of the planes. "Here's David's baby!" he declared with a flourish.

"Ahh, yes! Yes!" David murmured, leaping toward the shining, bright yellow biplane. He ran his hands over the body, along the wings, down the wheels, his face glowing. "Isn't she beautiful?"

"A modification of the Cirrus III Avian," Linklater explained. "One of 'em cinched the King's Cup just last year."

"Flown by a woman, if I'm not mistaken," Jeremy put in, with a smile my way.

"Yeah, well . . . This one'll win next year for sure, won't it, David? That's if the wifey lets you fly!" Linklater chuckled.

David paused to roll his eyes, then swung into the cockpit.

I glanced at Freddie, who was shifting his weight from one foot to the other, squinting at the plane, then sliding his eyes to Linklater, then to me. Both Jeremy and I nodded to him, and Jeremy drew himself up straight. Freddie nodded back, stiffened his spine, and walked over to the plane and began kicking at the tires.

"Not sure about these, David, not sure at all," he said.

David looked down from the cockpit, frowning.

Linklater was taken aback. "What's wrong with 'em?"

"Well, they're . . . they're not really well reinforced, are they?" Freddie was beginning to dip into some of the knowledge Raines had managed to cram into us.

"The tires are perfectly fine," Linklater reassured David. "I've never had a problem." He looked at Freddie. "What do you know about it?"

Freddie's eyes widened, and he looked panicked.

"Oh, Freddie knows so much about these things," I gushed, hurrying to stand beside him. "Don't you, Freddie? He's so very clever about it, even *I* can understand what he's talking about!" I tittered like an idiot. Jeremy's face was a mixture of horror and bafflement. I ignored that and patted Freddie on the arm. "Go on, Freddie, tell him. How do you know they're not strong? It's something about the color, isn't it?"

"Y-yes! Yes! You can tell by the color. See how they're grayish?" Freddie grinned, pleased with himself. "See, we use carbon black in our tires. Makes 'em much stronger. Less likely to burst under pressure, and they last longer." He kicked at the tire again.

"And didn't you say that tires like these are all right on a light aircraft but would be trouble for something heavier?" I prompted.

"That's right." Freddie nodded. "You use an unreinforced tire on something like a passenger plane, and you'll have 'em bursting up and down the runway. And passengers won't like that." He and I both solemnly shook our heads. "No siree. Not at all."

"Oh," said Linklater, now bending down to poke at the tire.

"Why don't we go somewhere and talk about it some more?" Jeremy suggested.

"Yes, I'm sure there's plenty more Freddie can say about it," I added, patting Freddie on the arm. "He really is *so* clever."

Freddie puffed his chest out a little and grinned.

"All right," Linklater agreed. "How about a round at the pub? We can wet the head of David's new baby." He reached out and patted the plane's nose. Then he glanced at me, and his face fell. "Oh. Um—" He brightened. "There's a Lyons Tea House just across the street," he recalled.

My answering smile was as brilliant as it was false. "How lovely!"

*   *   *

I sat for over an hour in that teashop. As my unwanted cup of Earl Grey cooled before me, I worried and wondered about what was happening in The Noisy Cricket. Was Freddie keeping himself together? Or had a succession of pints undone him? At least Jeremy was there and could rein him in, if necessary. But what if he intervened too late? What if he didn't offer the encouragement Freddie needed? What if Freddie couldn't properly answer any questions? What if Linklater refused to even discuss the tires?

Then I started to think: What if Freddie succeeded? Would my troubles be over?

No. Not by any means.

The income I'd received from Vandemark before Porter left had only been a few hundred pounds. Barely enough to cover taxes on Hensley, let alone basic upkeep. There would be nothing left over for repairs or even for me to live on comfortably. I'd been so consumed with the idea that Vandemark Rubber needed to be saved, I'd failed to consider any of this. Just keeping it from going under wasn't enough to make me independent—the company needed to expand. We needed more orders. Large ones. And we couldn't just rely on tires alone forever. What if cars and airplanes no longer needed them? Diversifying was a key to prosperity. I'd learned that from studying Porter.

Agitated, I beat a teaspoon against the starched tablecloth. Two elderly ladies at the next table glared at me, and I dropped the spoon with an apologetic smile. I tried to take a sip of my tea, but it had overbrewed and was bitter, which at least seemed to fit my mood. This waiting! This helplessness! Being shoved aside so the men could manage things! I dug my nails into my palms and pursed my lips.

A waitress in a frilly bonnet came bustling over. "Are you finished, miss?"

"Yes, thank you."

"I believe that gentleman is here to collect you." She nodded toward the doorway, where Jeremy was waiting. To collect me. Like a hat left at a theater cloakroom.

"Thank you." I paid for my tea and joined him. "Did you enjoy your drink?" I asked hollowly.

"I would have enjoyed it more with you there," he answered. "Freddie has news."

Outside, Freddie was waiting by David's car, beaming and hopping up and down.

"Astra!" he cried, throwing his arms wide. "I've done it! I've actually done something! Linklater's going to order our tires. We're saved!"

* * *

I should have been pleased—and I was—but it was hard to be excited when the very thing I'd done all this for was still out of reach. And Linklater's dismissive behavior toward me and the way I had been shut out of everything made me feel a little sour. Still, I let Freddie have this triumph, even if he had exaggerated it a bit (Linklater had only agreed to try out the tires, and if he liked what he saw, would put in an order). Freddie had done well. Even Laura was willing to allow him one cocktail before dinner.

"I couldn't have done it without you—especially you, Jeremy!" Freddie toasted, lifting his glass to me, Laura, and Jeremy.

"Don't get too sloshed—you've got calisthenics in the morning," Laura warned.

Freddie sighed, then shrugged. "Best make the most of it, then!" He downed his drink, then darted inside to turn the radio on. When he returned, he grabbed Laura around the waist and began dancing her up and down the terrace. "C'mon, Laurs, let's show 'em all the Hoosier Hop!" he urged. Laura laughed and protested simultaneously.

"Suppose I ought to make sure I get those new tires fitted on my plane," said David. "And then she'll be perfect."

"Will she?" I asked.

"Of course! She's an absolutely top-notch plane."

"You're pleased with her, then?"

"Very." He frowned at me, confused.

"And have you told Joyce that?"

David was taken aback. "Well, I—of course I thanked her for the plane," he finally answered.

"Your flying terrifies her, but she bought you a plane because she knew you would love it. She did over the house so you two would have a comfortable place to start your lives together. She's planning the local fete. She's doing everything a wife is supposed to do, but all you do is complain."

"What's got your back up?" he demanded.

I turned slightly, so I was fully facing him. "Women work hard, David, but we get almost no credit. Give your wife some credit now and again."

He opened his mouth as if to answer, but Jeremy shook his head.

"I wouldn't," he warned him. "She's absolutely right, and you know it."

David blinked at the pair of us and then, without another word, went back inside.

I released a lungful of air in a rush, then turned to Jeremy. "Could you please make me one of your gimlets?"

"I think you could use one double strength," he observed, mixing one up and handing it over.

"I wouldn't mind," I admitted, taking a sip. "I suppose I was a little harsh."

"No, no, that was exactly what he needed," Jeremy reassured me. "I thought you'd be happier tonight, though."

"I know. I shouldn't be sulking. I got what I wanted. Nearly."

"*Freddie* nearly got it," Jeremy corrected, making a drink for himself. "You spent the day playing the giddy goose. I never thought I'd see that."

"And I wish you hadn't, but what was I supposed to do? Do you really think Linklater would have listened if I'd talked about reinforcing tires?"

"We'll never know now, will we?" He shrugged. "If you want to be in business, and make a success of it, then *be in business*. Don't stand by and leave it up to Freddie to get things done. Engage! You've just shown me how good you are at it."

"Oh, that's easy for a man to say," I snapped. "Everyone assumes that men can do anything, and they listen to you. They see a woman and all they think is that she's a pretty face or entertainment or a brood mare." I took a good swig of my drink.

Jeremy regarded me quietly for a few moments. "Women fly around the world and set world records. They serve as MPs and cabinet ministers. *And* they run businesses. They work hard. Don't tell me all men think women are useless creatures. We don't. But they have to prove they're not useless, just as men do. No one ever won the day by staying well behind the front lines. Think of your ancestor, fighting alongside the Conqueror. Get out there and be bloody, bold, and resolute."

I set my empty glass aside, crossed my arms, and stood in silence, thinking. Jeremy patted me on the shoulder and left me to it. He was right, of course. I'd known it even before he spoke. I couldn't just rely on Freddie. I needed to act for myself.

Chapter Twenty-Two

⁓

The Humber heaved itself over the hill, crawled up the semicircular drive, and stopped at Hensley's front door. Arthur slowly climbed from behind the wheel and opened the door so Alice and I could alight.

I stared up at the house, at its red brick facade glowing in the midafternoon sunshine. The swing my father had hung from the weeping willow drifted in a lazy breeze. I half expected to see my mother at the door, smiling and welcoming me home.

But of course there was no Mother. There was no one. The tenants had left, and as I stepped inside, the silence seemed to press down on me. Even the presence of Alice, following close behind, couldn't lighten the atmosphere.

Divorce. The chorus girl from *Rio Rita* had apparently not been the first, or the last. The fed-up wife had taken the children and gone home to her mother. The husband had gone off to wherever men go when they're abandoned by wife and mistress, facing bad press and a damaging settlement. Was it their unhappiness that seemed to hang in the air like a mist? A miasma of misery that now infected my home? Or was it the sense of betrayal I still felt toward my parents? The knowledge that my blissful, carefree life here had been bought and paid for with secrets, lies, and the hiding away of inconvenient people?

I moved through rooms, past furniture draped in cloths that made bulky ghosts of innocent tables and armchairs. In Father's study I uncovered the desk and chair and sat. I skimmed my fingers over the gleaming ash-wood surface—no heavy walnut for him! "A woman's desk," Edgry had sniffed, when he saw it that day he brought the ledgers. Was that really only a little more than a year ago? It smelled faintly of the beeswax furniture polish Mother scented with lavender.

I thought. About things I had never wanted to think about.

* * *

The morning after our trip to the factory, I'd sat Freddie down for a serious talk. Convinced him that the company needed to branch out and grow.

"That's all right," Freddie agreed, "but we'll need money to do it, and I haven't got any. I'd scare it up if I could, but my family hasn't got anything left to sell."

And who did have ready money? I tried probing David and Laura, but neither of them were eager to sink cash into an uncertain company, even for a friend. A talk with my lawyer suggested most people were being cautious now, and no wonder: every day seemed to bring some new calamity. The world was heaving. Banks were collapsing, countries rebelling or falling more deeply into disturbing extremism. Businesses failed. People clung to whatever they had, and who could blame them?

So any investment in Vandemark would have to come from the inside. Freddie had nothing, but I did.

Could I? Could I really face giving up the dream I'd clung to the past year and sell Hensley? My home? The last place I'd seen my parents? The place where I'd grown up, scraped knees, learned to ride and garden, cried and laughed? Could I bear to let it go, relinquish its memories and secrets to someone else? Wouldn't that be a failure on my part? Or perhaps it would be a strange sort of triumph because doing so would set me on the path to true independence. Because I'd be selling on my own terms, to start my own life. My grown-up life.

I'd mentioned the idea to Freddie, who seemed pained at the sacrifice.

"I could try talking to some people," he suggested, though clearly even he knew that would get us nowhere. "Or—or maybe we don't need to expand right away. We can see how Linklater's order goes—maybe we'll get lucky there and he'll buy more than we expect. And it's not . . . you're not in such dire straits, are you? Really? Would your aunt really toss you out? Have I ruined things for you so badly? Can't I fix it?" His distressed face reminded me a little of Dandy's when he sensed I was upset.

"Oh, Freddie, that's sweet of you," I said earnestly. "But it's not just the trouble with my aunt—which isn't all your doing, believe me. We need to get ahead and strike while the iron is hot."

He nodded slowly. He'd already known all that. We sat there, looking at each other for a little while, and then he patted my shoulder and said, "I guess you want to be alone for a while and think about things."

"Yes, Freddie. Thank you."

I sat for a long time in the gloom of the library at Wotting Park, turning things over and over in my mind. The thought of selling Hensley didn't horrify me enough to shout, "No!" immediately, as I once had. But I couldn't shrug it off and say, "Yes" either.

It was a relief, really, when I looked up and saw Jeremy in the doorway, head cocked, watching me.

"Puzzling me out?" I asked, gesturing for him to come in.

"I hope you don't mind," he responded, taking a chair near mine. "You seemed quite far off, just now."

"I was. Miles away. In Leicestershire."

His face was sympathetic. "Dreaming of home?"

"Not dreaming. Thinking." I sighed and looked out the window.

"I hope I didn't upset you yesterday," he said quietly.

"No, of course not." I turned back to face him. "I'll never be upset with you for being honest with me."

"And I promise the same," he said solemnly.

I studied his face. Did he mean that? Would he see it through, once he knew the whole truth? I had to risk it. It had to come out sometime if we were to move forward together. And these secrets and emotions were all starting to wear on me.

"There's something I want to tell you," I said quietly. "Nobody outside my family knows it. There's a man I'm responsible for. His name is Raymond. He lives in a home called Rosedale. I don't know if he's the son of some vanished aunt or a secret brother, but I know that he's my responsibility."

Releasing that into the world lightened me somehow. Secrets are such heavy things. I watched Jeremy absorb what I'd just said. Heard Aunt El screeching, "Tainted blood!"

There was no judgment, only concern on his face. He reached out and took my hand, lacing our fingers together. I drew in a shuddering breath.

"I feel like my life used to be so clear," I said softly. "Everything seemed simple and straightforward. There was no question what would become of me. But now. . ." I shook my head. "It's all become so uncertain. There's so much confusion; so much puzzles me. I feel like there's so much I don't understand, and what I thought I knew was all wrong, and I'm sailing through a mist, hoping I don't wreck on the rocky shoals." I looked at him, yearning for him to know. Would he think I was talking nonsense?

He squeezed my hand and said quietly, "I understand."

And I said, "I have to go back to Hensley."

* * *

And here I was. Visiting my own, lonely house.

I stood and walked over to the window, looking out at the garden. "I hope heaven is like this!" Father used to say.

Well, Father, is heaven like this?

Probably not: it was impossible to ignore the signs of neglect. There were weeds in the paths, and the bushes were overgrown. The morning glories around the windows sagged, needing water.

Without tenants or more money, this place would fall to pieces. Autumn and winter were coming, with their freezing rains and battering winds. Slates would loosen, water would seep into cracks, turning them into dangerous fissures. Could I really watch that happen?

What would I do here, anyway? Live by myself, rattling around? Alone, with only my ghosts and memories to keep me company? A house needed life in it! Would I be like Alice, so desperately grateful for even a reluctant guest?

Dear Alice: she'd been so excited when I'd telephoned and asked if I might come and stay for a day or two (Bellephonica was too ill to object).

"It's been such a dull summer—you've no idea how happy I am to have you here to brighten things up a little!" she'd gushed as soon as I stepped off the train. "I made an embarrassing number of jam tarts!"

I had smiled and asked if she wouldn't mind an excursion to Hensley. Her answering smile had been sweet, and she'd clasped both my hands and said, "Oh yes, my dear girl, of course!"

I heard her come into the room behind me, and turned.

She sighed. "Still a lovely place. But quiet."

"Too quiet," I agreed, finding it more oppressive than ever. I heaved one of the windows open, so I could at least hear the birds and air out the room, which had the close, neglected feeling of Uncle Augustus's study.

"You seem troubled," she observed, taking my hand.

"I am," I confessed. "I'm thinking that I'll have to give this place up. My home, and all its memories with it!" Tears smarted and my throat swelled. It felt like something had reached into my chest and squeezed my heart.

"Oh, my dear," she crooned. "How very, very hard for you! You poor thing." She sighed. "Though surely you can take all your memories with you? You shall not forget the important things. *Tempus fugit, non autem memoria*: time flies, but not memory."

I smiled weakly. "Could you ever bear to leave your home?"

She sighed again and was quiet for some time. "I did want to leave, once," she finally whispered. "Many years ago. I was to go away and study, but it seemed like such a change from what I knew that I panicked. And when my sister became ill, I clung to that as an excuse not to go. But I regret that every day and wonder what my life would have been." She smiled and shrugged. "I suppose we'll never know."

"Do you resent your sister for holding you back?" I wondered.

"*I* held myself back," she replied. "And though she and I may have our difficulties, she is my sister. Blood is thicker than water."

I mulled that over. "Alice, did you know anything about my mother's and Aunt Elinor's sister?" I asked.

Alice shifted uncomfortably. "None of that is for me to say."

"Alice, please, I need to know!" I turned her so I was looking her in the face.

Her eyes darted, and she shook her head. "No, no. We promised Elinor we'd never breathe a word. She was so insistent! The scandal of it! She couldn't bear any of it, and who could blame her? Poor woman! To have a thing like that happen . . ." Alice pressed her lips together and shook her head again. "I'm sorry, I can't say anything else about it."

I sighed and turned away, afraid that if I didn't distract myself I might throttle her. The answers were there—so tantalizingly near, and yet I couldn't reach them. Would I ever? Did I want to?

I did.

I walked into the hall, picked up the telephone, and asked to be connected to Rosedale.

Chapter
Twenty-Three

❧

I hardly had time to drop my bag at Wotting Park before I was in a car borrowed from David, motoring down to Dorset.

I'd had a very illuminating conversation with Miss Kitt, the woman in charge of Rosedale. She had been kind enough to keep me informed about Raymond these last several months, but she'd been surprised when I asked if it would be all right if I visited.

"Yes, yes of course, Miss Davies!" she'd said. "I'm so happy you'd like to come—so many families don't visit at all."

I felt ashamed of myself for not visiting earlier. I had considered it and broached the topic with Toby.

"Do as you like, of course," he'd said, "but isn't it likely to be distressing for you both? Who knows how he would manage with a complete stranger inserting herself into his life? Perhaps that's why your father never visited."

And so I hadn't. But I should have asked Miss Kitt instead of Toby.

I brought Dandy with me. During our conversation, Miss Kitt had mentioned that Raymond loved animals, so I'd asked if it would be all right if Dandy visited as well.

"Raymond would love that!" she'd said. "Yes, please do, Miss Davies."

Dandy barked and wagged his tail, excited to be on an adventure. My own emotions were confused; I couldn't quite tell if I was apprehensive, upset, or elated. Perhaps all three. But as we drove into West Lulworth, with its squat cottages peering sleepily from beneath their bushy thatched roofs, my heart lifted. I thought of the Cove as I remembered it when Grandfather Carlyle and I would go sailing. Of its bright blue water and encircling rocky arms seeming to embrace us as we set out in the little boat. The echoing caves and romantic stories of dark and daring deeds in those wicked days past. This was always a happy place. No wonder Mother had brought Raymond here.

Rosedale was a long, low brick building spangled with climbing roses and surrounded by a very tall wrought-iron fence. Inside was bright, the walls cheerful yellows and soft blues. Miss Kitt, a woman with gray streaks in her hair and smile lines around her eyes and mouth, met us in the front hall and bent to pat Dandy on the head.

"It was so sweet of you to bring him," she said, gesturing to the dog.

"Anything to make this easier on everyone," I replied with a nervous smile.

"Oh, Miss Davies, there's no need to be worried. Raymond is a dear boy. I'm sure you'll love him as much as we all do."

My smile strengthened. "I'm sure I will. You'll excuse me—I know so little about him. How long has he lived here?"

"Nearly his whole life. He was brought here when he was just a year old."

"And when was that?"

"In September 1908. A very fine autumn, I recall."

He was only four months older than I. He couldn't possibly be my mother's child.

"Did my mother tell you he was hers?" I asked.

"She did. And she certainly treated him as if he was."

"That sounds like her," I murmured, remembering the way she clucked over my friends. Comforting and cajoling and correcting them just as she did me. "Did anyone else ever come to see him? Another woman, perhaps, who looked like Mother?"

Miss Kitt shook her head. "No, no one else came. But your mother was here as often as she could be. It was difficult, sometimes, for her to get away, but she was always here for Raymond's birthday, and she sent gifts at Christmas. When she couldn't visit, she'd write or telephone."

Difficult, sometimes, for her to get away. Because she was too busy tending to Father and me, and Hensley. We made it difficult for her to see him as often as she'd have liked. And the secrecy meant I couldn't contribute visits when I was older.

"Do you know why his name is Carlyle and not Davies?"

"I'm afraid I don't. But it's not unusual for families to want to distance themselves." Her mouth tightened.

"And he's happy here?" I asked hesitantly.

"He's quite happy," Miss Kitt reassured me. "We're his family. And he keeps quite busy. He likes to go down to the beach when the weather's fine. And he spends a great deal of time out in the garden. Raymond loves flowers and growing things."

I smiled. My mother's son in spirit, if not by blood.

"Does he know?" I asked quietly. "About Mother?"

Miss Kitt nodded solemnly. "He does."

"He understands that she's dead?"

"Raymond understands death. He's like a young child in his understanding. He knows simple, basic things. It's the complex ones that escape him."

Well, he certainly wasn't alone in that.

"And he knows about me?"

Miss Kitt smiled and nodded. "Your mother spoke of you often. She said you loved gardening as well. He's curious about you."

I absorbed that in silence. Thought about my mother telling him all about me but telling me nothing at all about him.

Miss Kitt said, "I'll take you to him now, if you like."

"I would, very much."

Dandy and I followed her down a corridor to a corner room washed in sunlight. A young man sat expectantly on the edge of a bed with a lemon-yellow coverlet. He grinned as soon as we appeared and came over to greet us. His gait was jerky and awkward, but the expression on his face was so warm and happy I hardly noticed anything else.

I stared, unable to help myself. Took him in, this unknown kinsman. He was tall—a little taller than me—and lean, with dark hair like the rest of the family. It wasn't slicked back, like most men's, and so fell across his forehead in unruly waves. He managed to brush it back with his palm, chuckling. His eyes must be his mother's. They were a clear, clear blue, like the water in the Cove.

Dandy yapped and Raymond looked down at him. His face brightened even more as he dropped to his knees and patted the dog.

"Da! Da!" Raymond cried, grinning up at Miss Kitt and me while Dandy good-naturedly endured the somewhat heavy-handed petting.

I laughed and nodded. "Yes, that's Dandy." I knelt on the floor with Raymond and found myself telling him all about the dog—how he snored so loudly at night he vibrated the mattress, and when he was happy he spun around and around in a tight circle. Raymond laughed and clapped his hands with delight, then gestured to the wall, where he'd pinned my Christmas card and hung the pastel from Paris.

"I'm so glad you liked them," I said to him.

He pointed to something else and I walked over to look at it. It was a watercolor painting of bluebells the same color as his eyes. I recognized it: undoubtedly my mother's work. Father's study had been full of her delicate horticultural paintings.

"Ma," he said, joining me at the painting. He smiled for a few moments but then hung his head. "Ma," he repeated, softly.

I reached out and took his hand, squeezing it. He looked up at me, and there was a sadness in his eyes that reached in and touched me. Here was someone else who had loved my mother in a way no one left alive had. He understood the pain of losing her. The emptiness it left behind. I quickly blinked away tears and nodded, squeezing his hand a little harder. He patted me sweetly on the head.

Dandy whimpered, and Raymond's smile returned. He bent down and scooped up the dog, then gestured wordlessly to the windows.

"He wants to show you the gardens," Miss Kitt explained. "He's very proud of them. He and your mother did quite a lot of work on them."

Of course they had.

"I'd love to see them," I said to him.

He led me outside to a beautiful space filled with brilliant color and floral perfumes. There were morning glories around the door, just like at Hensley, and a border of roses and lavender that grew like a hedge. A lilac shaded a bench where another patient worked earnestly at some crochet. Richly colored marigolds turned their sunburst faces upward, examining us as we passed. There were small lemon and orange trees in tubs, brought out to catch the warm sun. Raymond plucked an orange off one of them, held it to his nose, and inhaled deeply before passing it along to me. I, too, smelled it and thought of Christmas mornings, finding one of these in the toe of my stocking.

Raymond set Dandy down and led me to a privet hedge, gesturing for quiet. We both bent, and he pointed out a nest where three tiny baby robins chirped, flapping helpless wings, wanting food and their mother. Raymond's face lit up as he watched them.

"Oh, Raymond, have you done all this?" I asked him, looking back at the garden, a lush paradise, where one would never expect to find it.

"He had a hand in most of it," Miss Kitt confirmed. "There wasn't much here before he and your mother took it in hand. Whenever she visited, they both came out here first, whatever the weather, so he could show her its progress."

"This is wonderful," I told him, wrapping an arm around his shoulder. "Really remarkable." He blushed a little, then led me to the herb garden.

I stayed until it was time for him to go rest. As we parted, he threw his arms around me and hugged me tightly. I returned his embrace, promising to write, to telephone, and to visit again soon. As he was led away, I turned back to Miss Kitt.

"I'm so sorry I didn't come before now," I said. "He must have felt abandoned."

"No, not at all. As I said, we're a family here."

"Well, I promise he won't lack for my attention from now on."

Miss Kitt smiled encouragingly. "That's good to hear, Miss Davies."

"Thank you so much for everything, Miss Kitt," I said, shaking her hand. "You've been very helpful, and it's clear Raymond is well taken care of here."

"We do try, Miss Davies."

"You do an excellent job. Thank you again. I'll be back soon."

* * *

I took Dandy down to the Cove and stripped off my shoes and stockings so I could walk in the surf. Dandy ran up and down the shoreline, barking and scuttling away from the water as it hissed along the sand. I smiled, wishing my life could be so simple.

But that was adulthood, wasn't it? A messy, complicated knot that would not come untied no matter what you did. And nothing simplified it. Not having money or good looks or connections. As Jeremy had said, those things just brought their own sets of problems. All we could do was muddle along, let the current take us or fight our way through it so we could keep our course, however difficult it was to hold.

And my course? What would it be? To retreat to Hensley and wrap myself up in the past? Or move forward?

The only way to move forward, that I could see, was to sell Hensley. That one thing, which had been so unthinkable only a year ago, was now the only possible choice. I couldn't keep it and grow the company and make something of myself. I couldn't build something, with the old place holding me back. I couldn't take care of Raymond.

I couldn't have Jeremy.

The chilly water tickled my ankles, dragging the sand from under my feet. I watched it wriggle backward toward the sea. It calmed and cleared my mind. It always had. I'd always thrived near the water. I thought of Leicestershire, with its suffocating factories. My past was there, but my life now was very much down south. Here, in Lulworth, and a short distance away, at Midbourne.

*　*　*

I spent a restless night thinking, and an equally restless morning circling the gardens, making plans. I skipped lunch and ducked Joyce, who was overseeing last-minute preparations for the fete the following day. By the time I returned to the house, marquees had popped up like mushrooms across the pristine front lawn, and Joyce looked tired and frazzled, hair escaping combs and falling in wiry waves to her shoulders.

"Where have you been?" she screeched at me. "I have *so much to do* and you simply *disappeared*! Daddy's arrived, and I don't have time to entertain him right now. Go make yourself useful and amuse him, will you? He's in the drawing room."

I crossed briskly to the drawing room, where Porter was holed up, reading the newspaper. "Good evening, Mr. Porter," I greeted him, clear-eyed, my voice crisp. "I hope you enjoyed your time in Cannes. There's something important we need to discuss."

Chapter
Twenty-Four

Porter drummed his fingers on the top of the desk, regarding me, sitting opposite. Sizing me up. I kept my back straight and my chin up and met him look for look. At last, he folded his hands and shook his head. "You've changed your tune," he observed. "Not long ago your lawyer told me you weren't inclined to sell. What changed your mind?" he smirked. "Has Freddie let you down at last? Surprised it took this long."

"Not at all. We've recently secured a new client and are thinking of expanding."

He fussed with some of the pens on the desk, to hide his surprise.

"I don't want you to think I'm coming here with a begging bowl out," I continued, remembering Joyce telling me how he hated it when people needed something from him. "But as you have expressed interest and we are on friendly terms, I thought it only right to give you first refusal. We British are sporting that way."

He pursed his lips. "What sort of price did you have in mind?" he asked. "My original offer was quite generous. It won't be so again."

"That's all right, because I'm not selling. Not the land anyway. I'll offer the buildings for sale at a good price. You can"—I swallowed hard—"salvage them and keep all the profits from that. The land will be offered on a ninety-nine-year leasehold." I held my breath, hoping he wouldn't notice. Would it work? Would he storm out of here in a fury?

"Why on earth would I want that?" he asked. "I want to build there."

"And you may. You'll have every right to do as you please to the property, as long as you pay your rent on time. It'll be far less of a financial outlay for you than buying outright, and less risk ultimately. If anything should happen to prevent you from completing the project, you won't be left with a useless plot of land." *I would.* But risks need to be taken in business. Nothing ventured, nothing gained.

"Why shouldn't I be able to complete the project?" His eyes flashed as he perceived some unintended threat.

I refused to be cowed as he clearly expected. "There's no reason, Mr. Porter. I'm sure you have everything well in hand. But these are uncertain times. None of us know what's around the next corner. Isn't it best to protect yourself as much as possible?"

"As you are? Securing a regular rental income instead of simply a lump sum?"

"Surely you of all people can see the wisdom in that."

He nodded, and I thought I saw the tiniest, most fleeting smile dash across his face. "A leasehold," he murmured, drumming his fingers again. "Tricky business. Bringing in extra people never simplifies things. Perhaps I'll go find someone willing to sell up entirely."

"You certainly could do that," I agreed, ignoring my pounding heart, my drying mouth. "But it would take time for you to find another suitable property and to negotiate the sale. Hensley is very well situated, and your interest in it has already brought attention from others. I'm sure I wouldn't have trouble finding someone else willing to strike a deal." I hadn't the faintest idea if there was any interest in Hensley from other buyers. But even if there wasn't now, if I put the word out that Porter had been sniffing around, surely I'd get another bite. Surely. Hopefully.

"There's something else I can offer," I continued, thinking fast. "I know the people who live there and serve on local councils, issue permits, that sort of thing. They're a tight-knit bunch and don't always take kindly to outsiders. You know how these country people can be, especially up north," I added with a "we're-in-this-together" sort of smile. "I could help pave the way, to ensure your project runs smoothly from beginning to end."

A wry smile from him. "You'd do that? Out of the goodness of your heart?"

"No, not at all, sir. This is business. My services in that line would be entirely separate from the leasehold and negotiated accordingly."

"Ha!" He sat back, steepling his fingers over his belly, shaking his head again. "You're one cool creature, Miss Davies," he observed in a tone that suggested it wasn't entirely a compliment. "I never would have guessed."

"One has to be. It's a harsh world, and I'm alone in it."

We stared at each other for several moments, and then, "Have your lawyer draw up the papers," he said. "He knows where to send them. You have your deal, Miss Davies."

A gush of relief washed over me, and my knees jellified. Nevertheless, I stood and solemnly extended one hand. "I'm glad we could do business, Mr. Porter."

He looked at the hand for a while, then took it in a firm grasp. "Never thought I'd be doing business with a woman. One young enough to be my daughter, at that."

"Well, sir, we pilot airplanes, serve as cabinet ministers, and, yes, run businesses now," I responded. "So you may just have to get used to it."

*　*　*

Had I really done this? Had I really managed it? Was I, at last, taking those first difficult steps toward complete independence? I was so stunned I couldn't (yet) feel the sting of losing Hensley. I would. Oh, I would!

But a distraction came almost immediately.

As I left the study, Reilly rushed over, face pinched with fear, hissing, "Miss, please come with me!"

As my heart pounded in alarm, she took me back up to her room, where once again Miss Collins was sitting on the bed, strangling her gloves. She was crying.

"My goodness! What happened?" I asked, sitting beside her and taking her hand.

"Miss, I'm so sorry to bring this to your door, but Lady Millicent, she—she's dismissed me! No notice or reference or anything!" Collins blew her nose on a handkerchief the size of a dinner napkin.

"Dismissed you?" The poor woman! Cast out, just as Reilly thought she would be. And at her age, with no reference, she had no hope of finding employment. "Why? Did she find out about what you told me?" I felt awful for being the cause of this.

"No, miss, not exactly." Collins paused to mop at her face. "She found some letters that Angela—that is, Miss Reilly here—wrote to me. She accused me of spying on her, even though the letters indicated nothing of the sort, and told me to go."

"Oh, dear," I murmured, patting her on the back. "That's awful, Miss Collins. And so terribly cruel! Here," I handed her a handkerchief of my own (hers was sodden) and thought for a few moments. "Right. Tidy yourself up, and we'll go talk to Mrs. Bradbury about this. I'm sure she can help." If Joyce wanted to help others, she may as well begin under her own roof.

Miss Collins looked up at me, barely daring to hope. "Do you think she will?"

"I'm sure she will," I patted her on the back again.

Once the woman had composed herself, I took both her and Reilly downstairs to the morning room, where Joyce was discussing the following day's schedule with Laura.

"Oh, here you are, Astra, at last! I—who's this?" Joyce had finally looked up from her papers and noticed Collins.

"Joyce, this is Miss Collins, Lady Millicent's maid," I explained. As Joyce's eyes narrowed, I hastily added, "Her *former* maid."

"Oh, that's all right, then," said Laura.

"The thing is, Joyce, Millicent's turned her out on her ear without a reference, simply because she's friends with my maid, Reilly."

Laura shook her head and uttered an unbelievably crude word under her breath.

"I'm very sorry to hear that," Joyce said sincerely. "But I'm afraid I already have a lady's maid, and even I couldn't justify having two."

Crestfallen, Miss Collins nodded. "Of course. I understand, ma'am," she said, edging toward the door.

"Joyce, don't you know of anyone who needs a maid?" I asked.

"I don't," she admitted.

"I haven't got a lady's maid," Laura suddenly volunteered. "How would you like to come to America, Collins?"

"Oh, I, uh . . ." Collins glanced at Reilly, who flinched but then subtly nodded.

There seemed no other solution. I felt terrible for Reilly. And Collins.

"There we are, then," said Laura briskly. "It won't be so bad, Collins. I don't require much upkeep. And I can test out some of my new exercises on you."

Collins looked alarmed but nevertheless managed a brave smile. "Thank you, ma'am. That would be . . . nice."

"I'm not sure where she'll stay," said Joyce. "The housekeeper says we're full up."

"She can stay with me," Reilly offered.

"If you're sure you won't be too crowded," said Joyce.

"Oh no, it'd be just fine," Reilly reassured her.

I smiled. "Settled, then! Back in two ticks, Joyce."

I led the two women out and murmured, "I'm sorry, Miss Collins. If I knew any other way, I'd suggest it."

"It's all right, miss—you've done more than I could expect," she said as Reilly blinked in that way people do when they're trying not to cry. I reached out and patted both her and Collins on the arm, feeling helpless.

"Miss," Collins said, dropping her voice to barely a whisper, "there's something you should know: Lady Millicent knows about Rosedale."

Chapter
Twenty-Five

I drove to Lush Wycombe in the blaze of the setting sun, careening dangerously around corners but unwilling to slacken my speed. *"Lady Millicent knows about Rosedale."* And she would use it. I knew she would. I might have restrained myself, but she never would. She'd dismissed poor Collins, ruined my reputation, and now she was going to drag Raymond down into the mud as well. I could not allow that.

According to Collins, Millicent's spy had overheard me talking to Jeremy just before I went to Hensley. All they'd heard was the name, Rosedale, not the bit about Raymond. But Millicent had taken that one clue to her aunt, who remembered that one of her housemaids had worked at Hensley years ago and had heard Rosedale mentioned. It would only be a matter of time before they sorted out what it was and who lived there.

I raced up the drive in front of the mansion and banged on the door.

"I have an important message for Lady Millicent," I said to the startled butler when he opened it. "It can't wait. Which room is hers?"

"Third on the left," he replied. "But, miss, wait!"

I ignored him, rushed up the stairs, and pushed open the third door. Millicent, arrayed in a yellow silk dressing gown, was sitting at the looking glass, struggling with her hair. I yanked the door closed behind me, and she looked up, startled.

"You are a sordid, wicked creature," I snarled, marching right up to her, emitting waves of wrath. "You have *some* nerve, calling *me* a devious woman while you cultivate your spies and your gossip and hatch your sad little schemes. You think I'm alone and vulnerable and won't fight back, but you have touched my last nerve, and I'm finished tiptoeing around you and sitting back while you slander me."

I leaned down, so I was looking her directly in the eye, and jabbed a finger at her. "Do you really believe you're so protected this won't all come back on you? Well, it has already. It has lost you Hampton and Jeremy, and it has made me your enemy and *that*, mark my words, is something you will regret, Millicent. I see you and I know what you are. You are cruel and worthless, and I know that you are *not* your father's child."

Very slowly, she put her comb and pins down and stood. I rose with her, holding her gaze, face stony. She would not bring me low.

"How *dare* you make such a ridiculous assertion?" she hissed, but I could see the flicker of fear in her eyes. Her voice shook, just a little.

"You may think it's ridiculous, but I'm sure others won't," I replied. "They must be tired of talking about me now; they'll want another distraction. Someone else to chew up and spit out. And *what* a story this will make! Your mother carrying on with some dressmaker, in her husband's house! Grand Lady Millicent—no noble lady at all, but the daughter of some East End tailor. So afraid of anyone finding out that she built herself a fortress of monumental snobbery and keeps everyone good and scared of her so they never ask questions. In her fear, dismissing a maid of more than twenty years' standing."

She opened her mouth to protest, but I kept on in a low, dangerous tone. "Yes, I know all about that. She came running to us for help after you cast her out as if she meant nothing! People *do* frown on that sort of thing. And they ask questions. Oh! What a story she can tell! Don't think you've discredited me too much for it to stand. I am not friendless, and I have learned from your methods. I will send this out into the world, and *everyone* will look at you and look at your father and think, 'I always knew there was something not right there. Cecilia is the very picture of her father, but Millicent? No.' This will grow far beyond your control, believe me. It will ruin your chances for a grand marriage. Lords don't want the risk of the daughter of a loose woman. They don't want mongrel blood in the line."

She drew in a sharp breath. She was trembling. The fear was much more than a flicker now.

"Someone I care about lives at Rosedale," I told her. "And he *will not* be used by you. If you want to fight with me, then you fight with *me*. You are not to drag innocent bystanders into this sordid mess. You can let this feud die here and now, and I won't tell anyone what I know. But if you so much as telephone Rosedale or mention the word to anyone, I will unleash a scandal on you that you will *never* recover from. Do. Not. Test. Me. I am a creative thinker, and you've given me a great deal of material to work with."

* * *

Had David felt this way as Goliath lay at his feet? Elated, frightened, dazed? Or was it more than just the scene with Millicent that left me feeling this way? Was it everything that had happened over the past day, month, year piling up and now finally sinking in? And adding to it, the knowledge that my fight wasn't nearly over. My fight—or fights, because now I realized they were legion—were likely to last the rest of my life.

This strange mix of emotions carried through to the following morning as the fete got underway. It seemed everyone within eight miles of Wotting Park put on their Sunday best and came to play, see, and be seen. They wended their way through tents filled with fruits and vegetables ruthlessly chosen for their aesthetics and uniform sizes. Cakes, tarts, cloudy meringues, and jams and jellies gleaming like treasure jostled for the attention of judges and public alike. Pigs, chickens, and calves, penned up downwind, were examined by farmers looking to add to their stock. The house was opened for tours, gallons of tea and lemonade served, barrels of beer and cider rolled out. Joyce had even hired a band to come down from London so there could be dancing.

We all had our tasks. David led tours. Porter refereed the tug-of-war. Laura, bizarrely, had been assigned to help judge the handmade lace and knitwear. As I passed the tent on my way to oversee a three-legged race, I saw her holding a crocheted baby's bonnet upside down, plucking at the ribbons with a befuddled look.

I duly refereed the three-legged race, smiling as I handed out prizes to flushed and pleased village children. As I finished pinning rosettes onto the winning pair (freckled sisters in matching floral cotton dresses and enormous hairbows), I looked up and saw Jeremy watching me as he applauded along with the parents.

He smiled, and I smiled back, but I must not have been very convincing because as I approached him, he cocked his head and murmured, "Something on your mind?"

"Lots of things," I admitted in a quivering voice, throat tight and eyes stinging.

"Here." With a hand at my back he guided me toward the gardens, which were quieter. I sank onto a stone bench near a high shrub. He sat next to me and waited.

"I went and saw Raymond the other day," I began, smiling genuinely at that memory. "And it was lovely—*he* was lovely. I've been neglecting him terribly." I tried to take a deep breath, but my chest wouldn't have it. "Jeremy, I-I sold Hensley!"

It had taken this long for it to completely sink in. I had done it. I'd sold my home. The place would be pulled down, the gardens ploughed under, and a line of soulless semi-detacheds would spring up instead. *No, Father, heaven is not like this.*

I burst into tears.

Jeremy wrapped his arms around me and pulled me onto his shoulder. I cried and cried. For my parents, gone too soon, before they could teach me all I needed to know. For Raymond, left alone and unvisited for so long. For Hensley and all it represented: my easy, carefree, simple life, which I would never have again.

But I had other things now. Things I might never have had if not for that terrible day in February. Those things made it all easier to bear. Thinking of them eased the tightness in my chest and stemmed the flow of tears.

I sat up and accepted Jeremy's offer of a handkerchief.

"I needed money to keep Hensley," I explained. "But in order to get the money I needed, I had to sell it." I chuckled mirthlessly. "The center could not hold."

"You did what had to be done," he agreed. "But I'm sorry it hurts."

I drew in a deep breath with some relief. "A very nice lady told me recently: *Ubi bene, ibi patria*: Where you feel happy, there is your home. I think 'home' in that case was really 'country', but all the same, I'll just try to think of that."

"And find a place where you feel happy."

I smiled and he smiled back, brushing a few errant tears away with his thumb.

"Here you are!" Joyce's shrill voice was like a bucket of ice water thrown over the pair of us. We jumped and leapt apart. She was storming our way, looking murderous. "What are you doing? I have jobs for you, Astra Davies! Jeremy Harris, you can make love to her some other time!" She stopped in front of us, hands on hips, panting with all the effort of shouting.

"I'm sorry," I said, getting to my feet. "I just needed—" I squinted into the distance, frowning. "Is that Cecilia?"

Joyce spun and shaded her eyes. "Cee? What on earth is she doing here?"

Sure enough, Cee was barreling toward us from the driveway, with Belinda following close behind. As soon as she was within earshot, Cee shrieked, *"Astra Davies! Explain yourself!"*

Chapter
Twenty-Six

∾

Cee drew up beside Joyce. Her yelling had attracted Freddie, excited by all the drama, and Laura, who jogged over asking, "Cee, what's got into you? What's Astra done?"

"Astra Davies, I want the truth right now," Cee panted. "Has my sister been *blackmailing* you?"

I blinked at her in shock. Freddie hooted, and Laura clapped a hand over her mouth. Joyce's jaw actually dropped.

"I—who told you?" I asked Cee, glancing at Belinda, who had taken up a position between Cee and Joyce and was shaking her head.

"Georgy told me all about it when we were away on our honeymoon," she burst out. "Poor, poor Georgy—and poor you! He told me it was all a silly misunderstanding—and of course it was! I wouldn't have thought any different! He said Millicent was making all sorts of trouble. And right after we returned, we heard all those rumors about you, and I simply couldn't believe it! I spoke to my mother, and she showed Georgy and me the letter, but he said there's no way you would have written that because it was never ever like that between you two. So I showed it to Cee, and she realized it was a forgery."

"Millicent still spells 'importance' wrong," Cee chimed in. "It was just like back at school. Oh, Astra!" She threw her arms around me. "I'm so, so sorry. I didn't think you'd done any of those things, of course, but Aunt Constance convinced Daddy and said I wasn't to speak to you until this was sorted, and there wasn't much I could do. But it's all right, because Belinda and I told Daddy what had happened and he was absolutely apoplectic! He told me I could come to speak to you, and then he got on the telephone with Millicent, and—well, I don't think she's going to have a pleasant end to her summer."

"My mother was none too pleased either," said Belinda. "She feels she's been played for a fool, and she's very sorry for what happened and wants to apologize, Astra. She and my mother-in-law don't intend to have Millicent on their guest lists for a good long time, and I, for one, will *never ever* invite her anywhere." Her face darkened. "She should never have upset my Georgy like that. Poor lamb was beside himself!"

"Well, that'll all help, Belinda," said Laura, settling her hands on her hips. "You remember, Astra, I said clearing your name would be a task for the ladies."

"Ladies?" Freddie piped up. "I can get you ladies!"

"Not *those* kinds of ladies, Freddie," Laura said witheringly.

"No, no, *proper* ladies—and excellent gossips!" We all looked at him curiously, and he shrugged. "What? I've got four sisters. May as well use 'em."

"We'll talk later," said Laura. "But before we embark on anything, Astra, is there anything else we should know?"

I sighed. "Oh, girls. So many, many things."

* * *

Joyce took Laura, Cee, and I up to her bedroom, where I spilled every last thing they didn't know. I told them about my nonexistent inheritance and how Vandemark seemed like the only way to hold onto Hensley. I told them about Raymond and this mysterious aunt who must be his mother. About Aunt El's hostility, Edgry's cheating ways, and Hensley finally going. The only thing I didn't spill was the secret about Millicent. Despite my threats to her, I hoped never to tell that particular story. It felt too sordid and low. But I did mention the spy Millicent apparently had at Wotting Park.

"God," Joyce grumbled. "A spy in my own house! I'm never taking on anyone else's servants again. I'll hire local kids and train them up." She took a cigarette out of her case and lit it only to have Laura grab it and start puffing away herself.

"I think I'll allow myself two of these today," she murmured. "Did Millicent really say she compared the handwriting on your note to the signature in the guestbook? Nonsense!"

"She knows Mustard's handwriting," Cee chimed in. "He wrote her loads of letters, and I think she kept them all."

That made me look at Millicent a bit differently. Keeping his letters suggested she actually cared for him. Perhaps that's why she hadn't shown anyone the note that reached me by mistake. She wanted to discredit *me*, but not at the risk of Mustard's happiness.

"Oh, Astra," Cee sighed, clucking, shaking her head, looking at me with an expression of deep sympathy. "What a terrible time! And you had to keep it all to yourself. What a dreadful burden!" She hugged me tightly. "I'm sorry I abandoned you."

"Cee, darling, you didn't. You didn't have much choice."

"All the same . . ." She gestured with her hands, and we all saw something glittering on her left ring finger.

"Care to explain this, young lady?" Laura demanded, grabbing the hand.

Cee's blush deepened, and her smile widened. "Ducky's been at Gryden this summer, and just the other day, well . . ." She giggled and we squealed and piled around her, all arms and love.

"Why, Cee," I said, once the obligatory questions about details and wedding plans had been asked, "you'll be needing a lady's maid now, won't you?"

"I suppose I will," she agreed.

I raised my eyebrows and looked questioningly at Laura, who shrugged.

"Cee can have her," she said carelessly. "I don't have much call for a maid."

Joyce had gone quiet just after Cee's announcement, and now she rose and walked into her dressing room, waving her cigarette case and muttering something about it being empty. I slid off the bed and followed, quietly closing the door behind me. She had taken up a position at the window and was looking out at the fete she'd created.

"Joyce," I murmured, laying a hand on her shoulder.

She slipped away from me and exhaled some smoke. "You are quite the planner. You put me to shame. You've even managed to maneuver Collins into a better position."

I didn't know what to say to that, so I waited.

"You didn't trust me," she said at last. "I asked you once in Paris if there was anything you wanted to tell me, and you said there wasn't." Her face wore a hard expression, but there was a wounded look in her eyes.

"Joyce, it wasn't just you—I didn't tell anyone," I reminded her. "Not even Cee!"

"Well, we both know Cee can't keep a secret," Joyce hissed. "But I . . ." She toyed with a cigarette. "Was it because you didn't think I would care, or were you afraid I'd poison my father against you? Ruin all your neat little plans?"

"Neither," I answered stoutly. "And there was nothing neat about them, believe me. It was messier than that time we accidentally let the jam overflow. Remember that?"

A smile flickered. "Part of the stillroom floor here is still dyed red." A long silence, then: "I'm so glad I could provide you with an entrée to my father, Astra. It's good to know I have some use in this world. I can't believe I actually thought you were romantically interested in him." She rolled her eyes. "How stupid of me."

"Joyce Bradbury!" I took her by the shoulders and turned her to face me. "Don't you dare try to say that you're useless or some kind of fool! We both know that's not true at all. Look what you've done here!" I gestured to the tents and crowds outside, and then waved a hand to indicate the whole house. "And you planned our marvelous fortnight in Paris and your father's ball. And you're being very clever about playing politics and trying to do some good in the world. You are a marvel, Joyce, and it was wrong of me not to trust you. You'd probably have found a way to solve all my problems in about a day if I'd only given you the chance." How stupid it had been for me not to tell all of them what was going on from the outset. How could I condemn my parents for concealing things from me, protecting me, when I'd been guilty of the same?

Joyce stared at me for a few moments, and then smirked. "It *was* wrong of you—very wrong," she agreed. "Don't go making that mistake again, all right?"

"I won't," I promised, relieved that we seemed to be reaching some even ground.

"Good." She looked out the window again and finished off the cigarette. "What on earth am I to do now?" she wondered. "I'll need a new project. Do you think Cee will let me plan her wedding?"

"She may let you help, but we both know Cee's been planning her own wedding since she was four."

"Yes, yes, I know." Joyce sighed. "I'll just have to find something else."

"Whatever it is, I'm sure you'll do it marvelously," I said warmly. "Should we go join the others? Enjoy the last few minutes of your fete?"

"Yes, let's."

* * *

The fete was winding down as we reemerged. Parents packed sleepy children into cars and wagons, admiring prize cups and raffle winnings as they headed home.

Jeremy lingered, of course. He and David were out front, waving people off. As soon as we ladies joined them, David caught Joyce around the waist and hugged her.

"It was a brilliant fete, Joyce, really," he said warmly. "The best we've ever seen, isn't that right, Laura?"

"Oh, certainly," Laura agreed.

"Thank you," Joyce said, surprised by her suddenly effusive husband.

Jeremy grinned, turned to me, and murmured, "All is well?"

"As well as can be," I answered.

"I'm glad. Do you feel lightened now everything's out in the open?"

"I do. Very much so."

He took my hand and laced his fingers through mine. "I was wondering if you might like to come to Midbourne for tea. If you still want to see it, that is."

"I would love that, Jeremy."

He smiled briefly. A sad smile, I thought. "All right then. Thursday, let's say?"

Chapter
Twenty-Seven

～

"Where are you off to?" I asked Laura, coming upon her in the front hall as I came down to breakfast Thursday morning. She was—astonishingly—wearing a dress and high heels and a neat turban-style hat and *pearls*. I hadn't seen her look so smart since . . . I wasn't even sure. Her court presentation, perhaps? And it had been a fight to get her into the obligatory train and feathers for that.

Laura looked up at me while yanking on a pair of gloves. "I'm off to London with Freddie. Never mind why. I'll tell you all about it later, if it's a success. Oh, here, a telegram came for you." She held out a yellow envelope and I took it.

COUSIN MINE—WHAT ARE YOU DOING? JUST RETURNED TO LONDON WITH MUMS TO FIND A LETTER WAITING. UNSIGNED, BUT TOLD HER ALL ABOUT YOU HAVING FREDDIE TO STAY AT W-P. MUM'S LIVID, SAYS YOU'RE NEVER TO COME BACK. ALL MY HARD WORK THIS SUMMER DOWN THE DRAIN. STAY IN THE COUNTRY UNTIL I TELL YOU IT'S SAFE.

—TOBY

PS: I QUOTED JOB FOR YOU!

"Good news? Bad news?" Laura asked, frowning into the hall looking glass and adjusting the turban.

"Expected news," I answered. There was too much on my mind to fully absorb this now. I'd have to think about it—and make plans about it—later.

Laura finished with her hat, cupped one hand around her mouth and bellowed: "Freddieeeeee! Come on!"

Freddie skidded out of the dining room, still munching a slice of toast. "Sorry, sorry! Coming! Morning, Astra!"

"Morning Freddie. Have fun in London today," I called after them both as Laura collected a handbag and hustled out the door to a waiting car.

*   *   *

It was a nice enough day to walk to Midbourne, so Dandy and I set off just after lunch, ready to enjoy the last burst of summer and pick some blackberries along the way. As I plucked the sun-darkened fruit, I noticed the air had an autumnal edge to it now. Dull still, but it would sharpen soon. The afternoon sunlight was turning richer and more golden as we slipped into September.

We crossed the river at the rickety bridge, and soon the Abbey came into view, seeming like an old friend. *"Welcome,"* it seemed to say. *"I've been expecting you."*

Just beyond the Abbey the ground sloped toward the mansion, glowing in the sun. The gardens beckoned, dressed gaily in their late-summer colors and looking, from a distance, like gorgeously rendered embroidery.

Dandy yapped and dove down the hill, with me following. As I descended, I could see what appeared to be a knot garden with a fountain at its center just beyond the house's back terrace. Trellises draped with wisteria and climbing roses arched over white-stone pathways on either side of the elaborate hedge knots, and benches set deep into shady arbors invited someone to enjoy a good book outside on a fine day, or a couple to steal a few naughty minutes together in private during a ball.

This was a garden designed for lovers. A garden of the previous generation, before it was laid to waste by war and economic ruin. Ladies with parasols should be strolling down those paths, glancing devilishly at young men over the brilliant rosebushes. Making their plans for the slow hours between teatime and dinner. It was glorious.

But as I came closer, I couldn't help but notice the signs of neglect, just as there were at Hensley. The untrimmed hedges had a grizzled, unkempt look. There were rust spots on some of the roses, which had also been chewed by insects. The fountain was still and empty. The trellis supporting one of the wisteria arches was beginning to rot.

I stood by the fountain and took it all in. Clearly, Jeremy was having to economize on garden staff. Changes would have to be made here, to keep it from running to ruin. Hardier plants should replace the more delicate flowers in need of constant care. Perhaps succulents and mosses could be introduced, to add interest without effort. And the wisteria, I saw, looked sturdy enough to support its arch without the trellis. Metal poles—less pretty but more durable—could be used to prop up any bits in danger of falling. The roses should be culled, the sickly ones taken away so the others could thrive.

Yes, there were possibilities if action was taken quickly. It would be sad, of course, to lose some of the graceful old designs, but everything must evolve to survive.

As I looked around, hands on my hips, mentally replacing trained box hedges with holly shrubs and wondering what should be done with the magnificent glasshouse near the kitchen garden, an enormous bull mastiff emerged from the house. It trotted up to the edge of the terrace and let out a single bark. Not an aggressive one, but one which definitely said, *"Who are you and what are you doing in my garden?"*

Dandy yelped and sprang toward me. "Oh, Dandy, don't be such a coward," I admonished him as, from inside, Jeremy called, "Hector, what's all the fuss?" and came out to join the dog. "Ahh. I might have known you'd come by way of the gardens," he said when he saw me.

"I hope you don't mind."

He joined me, followed by Hector. "I invited you here to see it," he said. "What do you think? Not quite what you imagined, I suppose?"

"It's a beautiful garden, Jeremy," I told him. "It needs a little love and care, is all. A few readjustments, to fit with the times. You could say that about any of us." I smiled up at him and he grinned back.

"I would love to hear what you think. But first, shall I show you the house?"

"Please do!"

He led me first into a long gallery lined with windows on one side and ancestral portraits on the other.

"The Harrises, in all their glory." He waved an arm in their direction. "The first earl—" He indicated one man in a slashed doublet and hose, hand on the rapier slung at his waist. "A boon companion of Henry VIII, who gave him this land when he dissolved all the monasteries. He's the one who built Midbourne." He turned and pointed to biblical scenes in the stained-glass windows. "He took these right out of the abbey church and installed them here. Most of the lovely decorative bits around the house are from there. He was a looter extraordinaire. Made most of his money through funding privateers." He smiled mischievously and moved down the line. "This man, the third earl, hid the future King Charles II from the Roundheads on his flight to France. Tucked him away in a hidden cupboard in the library. I'll show you . . ."

We moved down the line of great Harrises past, Jeremy detailing their histories—romantic, funny, tragic. They stared down their noses, over snowy ruffs and frothy laces, in mute judgment of the girl walking beneath their gilded frames. *Does she belong here? Would she be one of us?*"

Jeremy paused and gestured to the last portrait in the hall. "This is my father."

I looked up at the man, a tall, russet-haired, pencil-mustached exemplar of his class and time. He was dressed in a ceremonial naval uniform and wearing the family signet ring on his right hand, just as Jeremy did. Unlike many of his forebearers, who stared directly (some even accusingly) at the viewer from their canvas perches, he was gazing off into the left distance, as though looking ahead to some future he would never experience. It seemed that most of Jeremy's looks came from his father's side. I wondered what, if anything, of his mother there was in him.

For two hours we toured Midbourne, climbing twirling staircases with dusty, elaborately carved banisters. I saw state bedrooms draped in dark brocades and heard about the dukes and princes who slept there. I crawled into the tiny closet that had once concealed a king and felt terribly jealous of the magnificent two-story library, with its shelves and rows of books, soft chairs to bury yourself in, and a fireplace big enough for Jeremy and I to stand in together. In the dining room, I heard more stories about the parties his grandmother had hosted, taking the place of Jeremy's mother, who had avoided company. There was a dinner for fifty, with Kaiser Wilhelm and the Prince of Wales as joint guests of honor, and a masquerade ball that Jeremy insisted had rivaled Porter's.

We ended in the morning room, where tea was already laid out along with a plate of jammy dodgers filled with blackberry jam.

"I thought you might like some," Jeremy said, offering me the plate.

I laughed and helped myself, placing my little basket of freshly picked blackberries beside the plate.

As I nibbled my biscuit, I toured the room. It was at a corner of the house and caught the sun for most of the day. It was paneled in light oak, with a mantelpiece thickly carved with shells and leaping fish surrounding a heraldic sea lion. The furniture, upholstered in a fading floral brocade, had a dainty look to it. A portrait over the fireplace depicted a warmly smiling woman with soft gray hair, in a blue dress. She wore a beautiful diamond and ruby ring on her left hand. Jeremy had inherited her chin and nose.

"Your grandmother," I guessed, indicating the portrait. Jeremy nodded, smiling fondly. There was something comforting about her, even in portrait form. "You're right, Jeremy, she's lovely."

I turned my attention to a collection of photographs on the writing desk. There was one of Jeremy as a child, dressed in a sailor suit and clutching a toy boat. I laughed and held it up. "A sailor from the start!"

"Family tradition dictated it," said Jeremy with a slight roll of his eyes.

I replaced the picture and picked up the next one. Five little girls in ruffles and curls, posed stiffly for the camera.

Jeremy poured two cups of tea and joined me, handing one over. "My mother," he explained, pointing to the youngest girl, "and all of her sisters."

He sighed, stirred his tea, then stared at the tiny vortex he'd created in the cup.

I set my tea aside and reached for his hand, wanting to ease this hurt. He took a deep breath and put his teacup down. Looked at me finally and held both my hands.

"My father was a coward," he announced. "They hushed it up, but he was a coward. The war came and he was off with the navy, but when he saw action, he didn't have the stomach for it. He wrote my mother a letter, telling her he was going to refuse to fight. Then he went to his superiors and told them he couldn't manage. The ship was at sea, and there wasn't much they could do except lock him up in his cabin. He drowned in there when the ship foundered. He and seven hundred other men. Worthy men," he added bitterly. "My family had enough influence to keep it all quiet. Officially, he died in battle, and we were spared the humiliation. But my mother"—he shook his head—"she never tired of telling me about it. About what a disappointment my father had been."

"Good lord," I breathed. "Why would she do that?" He'd been so young! A child—who does such a thing to a child? How can any mother hate her child so much?

"She could be erratic in her moods," he explained. "And the marriage was not a good one. She didn't want a husband or a child, but there was nothing else for her. Her family had more daughters than money and couldn't keep her, so that was it. She couldn't vent her frustration on Father, so she did so on me instead." He swallowed and a pained look spoke volumes of days he had spent as a terrified child, hiding from his mother's wrath. At the Dower House, when he could. Or in a closet that had protected a king.

He closed his eyes for a few moments. I reached out and embraced him, hoping it conveyed what I was thinking. *I'm here. I'm on your side. I understand. I love you.*

"Jeremy," I murmured. "Jeremy, I'm so sorry. So, so sorry."

Hector, lying on a rug at the hearth, lifted his head, cocked it, and whimpered, upset by his master's distress. Even Dandy forgot to be nervous about Hector for long enough to paw at Jeremy's leg and wag his tail.

Jeremy sighed and patted Dandy on the head. "No one else knows any of that," he told me. "Not even my aunts."

I nodded. "It's safe with me."

"I know." He squeezed my hand, then looked around the room and sighed. "I think about my father and what he did every time I think of selling up. It feels like I'm doing the same—running away—but I don't see what else I can do. The estate isn't profitable anymore, and I haven't the faintest idea how to turn it around. I'm a navy man," he added with a self-mocking smile. "What do I know about the land?"

"Then *learn*, Jeremy!" I ordered him. "If you don't want to just give up as your father did, then don't. If I could learn all about rubber manufacturing, then surely you can learn a thing or two about farming."

"Ahh, but you forget that you are an exceptional creature of rare talents," he said.

"I'm nothing of the kind. I did what had to be done, and you can and should too."

"And what would you suggest, then?" He crossed his arms, stepped back, and looked at me. Head cocked, smiling, inviting me to take the challenge. And oh, I would.

"Use your imagination. Joyce opened Wotting Park to visitors during the fete and charged a few shillings for the privilege. They went through in crowds; she raised a mint for the Benevolent Society. And that's just Wotting Park, a place of no real significance at all. A place like this, with its stories . . ."

"Tours once a month, led by a real-life earl—" he mused.

"—who just so happens to look like a movie star? They'd come from far and wide, Jem, mark my words! And you could charge more than a few shillings for that, too." I trotted over to the window and pointed out into the garden. "And that marvelous glasshouse—put it to work!"

"Growing a cash crop to ship to London!"

"Or points beyond! Start small, and build outward! *Engage*, Jeremy!"

He laughed, ran over, and kissed me. "I do love you," he declared, cradling my face in his hands.

I rested my forehead against his and looked him in the eye. "And you love this place too, I can tell. And you *should*, Jeremy. It's magnificent. And you have a responsibility here. Hensley—much as I loved it—was just a house and a garden, but this is an *estate*. You have farms and tenants and people who rely on you. What will become of them if all of this goes and becomes some suburb? Where will they go?"

"I'm well aware," he said. "It's nearly the only thing keeping me here."

"The house too," I said, "it's part of history—yours and the country's. We can't lose that. Too many of these old estates are going nowadays. Soon there'll be nothing left and nobody to remember what once was." I took a deep breath. "Your family's been here for hundreds of years. Your past and your future are both in this place. Jeremy, be the sort of man

I know you are. Don't sit around waiting for a miracle. Go use all your advantages and *save Midbourne*."

He grinned, a glowing, delighted smile, and I realized he hadn't needed me to tell him that. He had already resolved to do it. I think he just wanted to see how I felt about it. Find out if I had that same determination he did. The same protective instinct and affection for the place that was difficult to fully explain or understand. *Yes,* I silently told him. *I am your partner in all this. I understand.*

"Since you seem full of ideas, how do you feel about a walk around the gardens?" he suggested. "I'd very much like to know what you think."

* * *

Laura returned after dinner, clattering into the hall, groaning, "Lord! Must remove all this nonsense!" as she stripped off her gloves and kicked off the high heels.

"Did you lose Freddie?" Joyce asked.

"'Course not. He's spending the night in town. Now don't worry," she added, noting my alarmed look. "He's under strict instructions to behave, and he wouldn't dare disobey. Astra, come with me."

I collected the shoes and gloves before following her upstairs. By the time I arrived, she was already tossing aside the turban and wriggling out of her dress, which she left in a forest-green puddle on the floor.

" Help me, will you?" She gestured for me to undo her brassiere. "Ahh," she breathed, sending it to join the dress. "Freedom." She wrapped herself in a silk kimono, lit a cigarette, and reclined on the bed. "I hope you appreciate all that I've done for you," she said, waving the cigarette toward the discarded clothes. "Only the greatest love could get me into the glad rags and up to London on a day like today."

"And what did I have to do with it?" I asked, joining her on the bed.

"It was all for you, of course! While you were off gadding about Midbourne—I hope you were really wicked there, by the way, and you'll have to tell me all about it—Freddie and I were off saving your reputation!"

"Were you, indeed?"

"We were! You remember our former deputy headmistress?"

"How could I forget?" Dear Miss: savior of the sweetshop.

"Well, she and I have kept in touch over the years. Christmas cards and the like. So I phoned her up and asked her to meet me for tea. And she agreed, so we met, and wouldn't you know it: Freddie and three of his sisters just happened to be there for tea as well! What luck!" She smirked. "He brought them over for introductions, and I *happened* to bring up that trick Millicent pulled at school. You remember, when she tried to make it seem as if you were cheating? It was like tipping a bucket with Miss—all manner of stories about the things Millicent did spilled right out. Freddie's sisters were aghast. The story'll be around half of London by now, I'll wager. So we'll see if this bears fruit."

"Oh, Laura!" I was so touched I nearly cried. "Laura, that's so awfully sweet!"

She waved her cigarette case. "What are friends for? Now"—she smiled wickedly at me—"tell me *all* about your afternoon at Midbourne."

Chapter Twenty-Eight

⁓

Summer was over, and we'd slipped into an amber-colored September rich with the tang of autumn. Laura and Freddie had both gone home, and Wotting Park seemed empty and quiet without them. I would have to go before long too. Joyce had shrugged and said I could stay as long as I liked, but I couldn't be a permanent guest. She and David (who were doing much better, it seemed) would be off on the shooting party rounds soon, or away on some holiday. I couldn't very well putter around their house while they weren't there.

And I should really be back in London, to attend to business. I'd put some of the money from the sale of Hensley's buildings into Vandemark in return for a larger share of the business. I owned half of it now, and Freddie, Raines, and I were planning our expansion. We were moving on to product areas we could exploit with our current clients. Gaskets and hoses for the engines in cars and airplanes. We hoped to try other things eventually, but it seemed best to start here and build up gradually.

So, I needed to be back in London. The question was: Where would I go? I waited for Aunt El to get over her tantrum and for Toby to give me the all-clear, but so far, nothing. And did I even want to go back to that place? Wouldn't it be best to make a break now?

I was thinking about it over breakfast one morning, perusing the "rooms to let" section of the newspaper and noting some possibilities, when Joyce came into the dining room with the morning post and announced she had a new project.

"Do you? And what is it? Village Christmas fair?" I asked, smiling.

"No, something more ambitious." She sat down, put the post aside, and looked straight at me. "It's Hensley, darling."

I blinked at her, confused. "What about it?"

"It's my new project, like I said. It occurred to me that there's quite a lot of hardship up that way—I saw plenty when we were there for Belinda's wedding. And a lot of the trouble comes from people not being trained up in areas where they might be able to get good jobs. I mean, if a girl wants to become a secretary or something, she has to go off to secretarial school and pay for the course and for her room and board while she's taking it, and all the while she's far from her family and probably in a city, which is expensive. So I thought, why not bring the training to them? Hensley's in the perfect neighborhood for that. So, I'm going to turn the house into a training school for girls. I thought we'd start with courses in dressmaking and office work and branch out from there. All offered for free, of course. What do you think? Oh, and I think I'm going to preserve the bit of the garden closest to the house, so the girls and the people in the houses around have somewhere to get a bit of fresh air."

I stared at her for a little while, thinking, *Hensley won't go! The gardens won't go!*

"Will your father agree to it, though?" I asked apprehensively. "It'll disrupt his building plans, won't it?"

"Oh, I've already gone to work on Daddy and gotten him to agree," she answered with a shrug. "It wasn't so hard, really. Apparently taking old buildings down is a bother, and between you and me, I think he's quite fond of Hensley—thinks of it as quite the lovely little jewel box of a place, just like an illustration out of a charming novel. He'll still put up his houses; they'll just be built around it."

"Oh, Joyce," I squeaked, as grateful tears stung my eyes. "Joyce, you are the loveliest!"

She smiled, then started leafing through the post. "I'm glad to be able to do something for you and for the greater good. Two birds, one stone." She paused, looking at the address on one envelope: "This is yours." She handed over a letter. I tore into it and saw it was from Alice Horshaw.

A Bright Young Thing

My dear Astra,

I'm very sorry to begin a letter with ill tidings, but I fear I must: my sister, Bellephonica, passed from this life three days ago. As you know, she's been in poor health for some years, and I believe death came as some relief to her. Forsan miseros meliora sequentur.

My sister's passing has given me much to think about, as well as the time to do so, and, my dear, I have been thinking a great deal about you. I regret terribly holding things back from you, things which so closely concern you and which, I believe, you have a right to know. With Bellephonica gone, there is one less person to share this story. Someday, not long from now—yes, it must be said!—I shall be gone as well, and then who shall answer your questions? No, best to tell you everything now.

You were very correct that your mother and aunt had another sister. Mary was her name. (That much I knew already: the day I'd visited Raymond I'd gone to my grandfather's old parish and consulted the christening records. There it was: 29 March 1887. Mary and Lillian Carlyle, Daughters of Rev. Edmund G. S. Carlyle and Elspeth M. Carlyle. Not just Mother's sister: her twin.) *She was a very dear, vivacious girl, much like your mother.*

Shortly after your parents were married, Elinor produced young Tobias. I'm afraid she found motherhood a struggle, so Mary was sent to stay with her, to help.

Mary was with Elinor in London for three months, and then suddenly she left and joined your mother at Hensley. A visit to her sister would not, of course, have seemed remarkable but for the fact that your parents immediately canceled all their engagements, refused invitations, and had the doctor around a great deal (naturally, he and Bellephonica saw each other often, and he happened to mention having frequently been called to Hensley). And then, hardly a week after Mary arrived, Elinor left London as well and went to Hensley. When she discovered Mary already there, however, she refused to stay and instead came here, to Elmswood. She told Bellephonica that she simply couldn't bear to be in her own home, which she said had been polluted and ruined. She couldn't be near her husband either, she said. It was very clear to us that Mary had got herself in trouble.

Your mother came, to try to reason with her, but Elinor wouldn't have it and told your mother that as long as Mary was under her roof, Elinor would have nothing to do with her. Your mother argued that Elinor should help their sister and take some responsibility for the child. There was a terrible row, and your poor mother left in tears. Your father was in quite a temper when he heard of it. He came and gave both Elinor and Bellephonica such a piece of his mind, and rightly so, I think.

A day or two later, your father was back, accompanied by his brother-in-law. Mr. Weyburn sat and talked with his wife for nearly an hour and convinced her to come home. Elinor left us the following day, by the early train, and never mentioned any of this again. I believe she quite put the whole thing out of her mind.

Was such a thing possible? Could someone really forget an event that had shaken and sundered their life, forcing them to rebuild from and on what was left? Could you lock your pain away, until something came along that burst that door open again? My aunt's behavior, which had seemed outrageous to me, suddenly made a little more sense.

Not long after Elinor left, your mother did too, along with Mary. We never saw or heard from Mary again, and I didn't dare ask after her. As I said before, there was a coolness between Hensley and Elmswood after that, though I dearly wished to be friends with your lovely mother. We saw each other once or twice after you were born, but then the invitations to Hensley ceased, and mine were politely refused. I can't say I blame them, really. Bellephonica's behavior toward your parents during and after this crisis was quite shocking.

I have now told you all I know of the matter, my dear, and I hope this helps set your mind at some ease and answers some of your questions. I am very sorry for keeping this from you for so long. It feels wrong to have concealed it, and right, now that I've told you. It seems it's true what they say: Veritas vos liberabit: *The truth shall set you free.*

And one more thing, my dear, if I may: please do not judge your parents too harshly for keeping this from you. I realize, of course, it has pained you to discover their secrets, but you must know that they meant no harm by it. They loved you more than you can imagine, and they wanted you to be happy and unburdened by this painful history. Perhaps, if they had known what would happen, they would have done differently, but of course there are things in our lives we can never anticipate.

My dear, I shall leave you now with this. I hope you can now find some peace and that your business dealings are coming along.

With the very best and warmest wishes,

Alice

I sat for a long time with that letter in my hand, letting my mind unknot and order everything. There was little here that I hadn't already guessed for myself, but as Alice had noted, there was something calming about knowing it all for sure. It is, after all, best to know things—you can't go into the world blind. Part of growing up is feeling real pain that comes from discoveries, and learning to breathe through it. How much had I learned in the past year? About love and friendship, desire, compromise, compassion, strength, and family? How much did it hurt to learn some of these things? How rewarding had it been learning others? The person I had been the previous year—wailing and moaning about finding a way to pay for train tickets and party dresses—seemed a stranger to me now. Would Porter have done business with that child? Would Jeremy have kissed her, said he loved her, shared his own secrets, hopes, and desires?

No. Nor should they have.

My parents had been afraid for me. They knew, keenly, how painful and terrible adult life could be. And so they swaddled me up, protected me from the bumps and jars of life, even though they knew adulthood was about to intrude. It lurked at the edge of my comfortable bubble, brandishing pins and needles. They couldn't know how I'd manage, and so they'd held off preparing me. They lacked faith, but really, who could blame them? I was, after all, entirely untried.

Alice had given me answers, and I was deeply grateful to her, but there were still some questions that nagged, some suspicions that needed confirmation. I wanted everything out in the open. These secrets had haunted the family long enough. Time to throw open the windows and air out the shuttered room.

"Astra!"

My head snapped up. Joyce was looking at me in alarm.

"Is it bad news?" she asked. "You're pale as death!"

"Not bad news," I answered, folding the letter and shoving it back into the envelope. "Joyce, can you drive me to the station? I need to catch the next train up to London."

* * *

I arrived at Gertrude Street and found Toby dozing on the sofa. He sprang up as I came in, and his eyes widened.

"Oh, hello," he said. "Didn't you get my telegram?"

"I won't be long," I promised, heading for the stairs. "Is your mother at home?"

"Dressing room," he answered, trailing me up the stairs.

I knocked briskly on the door to her dressing room and entered without waiting for an answer. She was at the desk, scribbling away at something. As I walked in, she looked up and actually recoiled. "My God! You're *brown*!" she cried. "You must have *lived* in the sun!"

I stood in front of her and took a deep breath. "Aunt Elinor, I want you to know that I know who Raymond's parents are: Mary and Uncle Augustus, is that not right?"

Behind me, Toby gasped.

I gave her a look that I hoped conveyed both sympathy and understanding. "Aunt Elinor, I'm so sorry."

She slowly laid down her pen and sat up straighter. Her gaze was as hard and cold as granite. "And who told you about Mary and Augustus?"

"So it is true, then? Your husband and your sister . . ." I grimaced, reaching for her.

With a violent thrust, Aunt Elinor shoved my hand away. She shook and her eyes now blazed. "She was always a wicked, wicked girl!" she declared.

Toby actually backed away several feet, as if he were afraid of being incinerated. I couldn't help but stare at her, as though mesmerized.

"She always wanted what someone else had," Elinor growled. "She would even steal my dolls as a child, and my parents indulged her. They let her do as she pleased, and look what happened! She brought shame on our family and she—she . . ." Elinor clenched her jaw and both fists.

Now *I* leaned away slightly, wondering if she might try to hit something, and if that something might just be me.

"She got her *reward*, didn't she?" Elinor continued. "Both of them did. The Lord's judgment made flesh. That *cursed creature*."

My heart seized at the words. "That cursed creature?" I repeated coldly. "You mean Raymond? Your *nephew*? Toby's *brother*?"

"Don't speak of it," she spat.

"It?" Toby echoed faintly.

"How can you speak of him like that?" I wondered. "You don't even know him!"

"You're just like your mother," she scoffed. "She was soft too. Harped on me to forgive Mary, said I should take the thing in. And later, when she became ill, she came to me *again* about it. It needed to be cared for. She'd done it because Mary went off God knows where to try to hide her shame. I wouldn't allow Augustus to put one *penny* toward it."

"Mother *was* ill, then? What was wrong with her?" I asked.

"Nobody knew. Some malignancy eating away at her. A punishment, I say, for her part in all this. She knew Mary was a flirt, but she said nothing. And she kept the *thing* around. Visited it. Gave it our family's name, even. She exposed us all to danger and then expected me to make it *my* problem. Well, she was bitterly disappointed in that."

I nodded. "So my father took out the insurance policy to help provide for Raymond. And then you and Edgry stole the money."

"There is no stealing from an idiot," Elinor informed me. "Mr. Edgry and I agreed that, as you were incapable, I should take charge of the money when the policy was paid. I should use it as I saw fit, to provide for the creature's needs."

"But you stopped paying for his upkeep at Rosedale," I murmured, horror stirring and blossoming. "You were hoping they'd toss him out."

"Of course I did! Does that *thing* deserve to live in some *palace*, when there were others in such need? It should have been left to the care of the state, like other stray animals."

"Mother!" Toby moaned in horror.

"I suppose I spoiled your plans, then," I observed in a frigid voice.

She snorted. "It was only a matter of time before you tired of paying for him. It would interfere with your clothes and your parties and trips to Paris! You're a frivolous creature, just like Lillian. Always on about her flowers and her paintings. And Mary—well, she was a fool, and wicked, and you're her *all over again*!" She was puce with rage. "At the very least, if you kept paying that money, you'd never go back to Hensley! And why should you have everything you want? You ungrateful girl, why should you go off and live a life of bliss after what your parents did to me?"

"Good Lord, Mother," Toby breathed. "Visiting the iniquity of the fathers—"

"Don't you dare!" She flung one trembling, pointing finger in his direction. "Don't you *dare* try to quote scripture to me, Tobias Weyburn! You are a *godless* man!"

"And you call yourself a god-fearing woman?" I cried. "Stealing from a helpless person?"

"I stole nothing!" she shrieked. "Why should he be my burden, anyway? Where is his mother? Gone, run off to live her life free from this shadow. She should be *punished*! And by God if she's not here to take her punishment, then someone else will! You or he, I do not care which!"

A chill settled over me as I looked at this woman who was my blood, but more cruel and vindictive than anyone I'd ever known.

"Don't you look at me like that," she snarled. "You don't understand. You—your parents coddled you because it was *so* important for Astra to be happy all the time. Happy and empty-headed and giddy. You don't know *anything*. And you came into my house—*my house*—which I opened to you out of charity when you had nowhere else to go. You probed and asked your questions and couldn't leave well enough alone. And then you brought shame upon it once again. Well, are you happy now?" She coughed violently.

I looked at her for a long time, ricocheting between rage and pity. This woman with her demons, hidden deep inside. Tamped down, locked up, until their unexpected release by my parents and then by me. Taking out her grief and fury on the most innocent target.

"You will return that money," I told her in a low, firm voice. "A check for the full amount will be sent to my lawyer within the week. If it doesn't arrive, I'll instruct him to issue a criminal complaint for theft against you."

She blanched. "You wouldn't dare," she breathed between coughs. "And it wouldn't matter. I could fight it in court."

"Yes, you could," I agreed. "But think of the scandal that would be. All these secrets spilling out; the press and the public eating them up. *Everyone* would know *everything*. I don't think you want that, do you?"

Her skin went from pale to mottled as an intense rage built within her. I calmly watched it until it came spewing out.

"Get out," she rasped. "Out! *Get out! Get out of my house this instant! Out!*

I rose, still outwardly calm although my heart was racing. I slowly walked out of the room, glad to be leaving.

Toby was frozen by the door, staring at his mother as if he'd never seen her before. Or as if she'd suddenly shed her skin, revealing a Gorgon who'd been inside this whole time.

Chapter
Twenty-Nine

The thing was done: I had cut myself free. A sense of calm came over me as I left Gertrude Street that last time. This was what I needed—one big push right out of the nest, to see whether or not I was ready to fly.

I returned to Wotting Park for a few days, then accepted Cecilia's invitation to stay with her in London. She and her family were there for a few days en route to France to meet Ducky's mother and start shopping for Cecilia's trousseau.

"Darling, of course you must stay for as long as you like," Cecilia told me, a sentiment that was heartily seconded by her very apologetic father.

But of course not everyone was so welcoming.

"You!" Millicent hissed, meeting me as I was making my way downstairs the evening of my arrival. Some of Ducky's friends were hosting a celebratory dinner for the engaged couple. Millicent had not been invited.

Laura's scheme had borne fruit: news of Millicent's antics had spread quickly, fueled by Freddie's sisters, and Belinda and her mother, who had put more effort than I'd ever expected into setting the record straight. Lady Crayle had even telephoned me to apologize and invite me to tea, to make a show of how acceptable I now was.

As they had with me, the stories around Millicent quickly grew uglier. Society, bored after weeks in the country, had taken to telephones and monogrammed letterhead to spread ever more malicious tales of Millicent's jealousy. They said she'd poisoned me at the wedding because I knew something about her. But what did I know? They had theories about that too.

Laddie dropped her, saying he needed to concentrate on his election campaign. She hadn't received a single invitation to a house party when the grouse season began. She was in for a long, cold winter, and I felt a bit guilty about how far this had gone. But, in all fairness, she had brought this on herself.

"Yes, me," I sighed, unwilling to dip back into this poisonous well.

She looked terrible: her coloring was off, and she had a haggard look about her. "I don't know how you can show yourself here," she said, drawing herself up. She probably hoped she'd look like a viper ready to strike, but she reminded me of an old hunting dog putting on a good show: dragging itself to its feet because it knows it has to or risk being shot.

"Why shouldn't I be here?" I asked. "I haven't done anything wrong. I warned you that your lies would come back on you, and they have. That's not my fault."

She practically bubbled with rage, trying to think of some way to devastate me, bring me low, so she could feel high. I watched her, weary of this. I thought of my aunt and how she had let her own bitterness twist and warp her. We are all shaped by our tragedies, Jeremy had said. How very true.

"It must be hard for you," I said quietly as she seethed. "To see your sister so happy while you're shut out. I'm sorry for that and for what happened. But people will find another scandal to claw over soon enough, and you'll be invited around again. Until then, keep your head down and emerge humble. And smile. Nobody loves a sourpuss."

I turned away and moved toward the stairs.

"My mother used to say she was glad I was a girl," she said, in a hollow voice.

I stopped and faced her again. Her head was turned to the side, away from me.

She continued, "I used to think she was just happy to have a daughter. But then I grew older and realized she was simply relieved that the title and estate wouldn't be passed down on the wrong side of the blanket." She took a deep, shuddering breath.

How sad, to be so unloved. To be the embarrassment in your family. This is the hand Raymond might have been dealt if not for Mother's care and my determination.

I returned to stand near her. "I won't tell anyone what I know," I promised, reaching out and laying a hand on her arm. There had been enough damage done already.

Her face hardened. She shook off my hand and stomped into her room.

* * *

Within the week, Reilly, Dandy, and I were installed in a set of rooms in a respectable place on Clarges Street in Mayfair. Once settled, Reilly redoubled her efforts to upend the Trade Disputes and Trades Union Act and seemed to be gathering a fair bit of support from fellow servants. I recruited Joyce to the cause, and the two of us sought out friends with influence. We painted vivid, heartbreaking pictures of hungry, ragged children and desperate, decent fathers. Our friends teared up and promised to have a word with the right people.

It seemed that things were more peaceful in the Bradbury marriage. Joyce had her projects, David had his plane, and there was some talk of David standing for Parliament because, as he said, "Joyce is right: things really are a bit of a mess. Something needs to be done, and we certainly can't rely on the likes of Laddie to do it."

Happily, Reilly's brother was settling in well at Vandemark; Raines had nothing but praise for him. His wife had found work as a house-keeper for an elderly couple, and the children were all at school instead of facing a lifetime down the mines.

Freddie, also permanently in London, was pleasantly surprising us all with his commitment to success and sobriety. Apparently, his sisters were so shocked he'd managed to secure Linklater's business they'd actually been rendered speechless, which was enough incentive for him to go out and drum up more business. The pair of us visited the factory often, learning what we could and making further plans. We pursued new clients, some of whom were attracted by that rumor I'd started about Porter keeping his business with us. Freddie was no angel—he allowed himself to be tempted by his gadabout friends now and again—but he was far better than he had been, and even kept up with the exercise regimen Laura had planned for him before he left Wotting Park.

Edgry's trust was finally undone, and my portion of the life insurance was released. Some I invested in government bonds; the rest was saved. Raymond's money, too, was paid back on schedule. That was placed in a trust for Raymond, with myself and Toby as executors. Toby, once he recovered from his shock, had shown enormous interest in this unknown brother. On Raymond's birthday we both went to Rosedale, taking Dandy and a cake and a gift of new paints.

Toby took to spending most of his days at Clarges Street, reclining on the sofa, lazily scratching Dandy's favorite spots. He was there one blustery day in November, blowing smoke rings at the ceiling while Dandy snored and I scribbled away at some paperwork.

"Mother's been talking about you," he told me.

"Has she? I thought for sure she'd never mention my name again. That's what she does with people who displease her, is it not?"

"Come, now."

I sighed. The rage I had once felt toward her had died down and was now just a simmering animosity. I couldn't ignore the terrible things she had done, but I couldn't entirely condemn or hate her either. We are all shaped by our tragedies.

"What does she say?" I asked.

"Not much. You know she wouldn't confide in me. But she wishes you'd visit."

"She could visit me. She knows my address."

He looked up at me. "You know she'd never do that."

"Then we're at a stalemate. I won't reward her with my tacit approval, Toby, and my going to see her would be just that."

"Would it? Or would it be a kind gesture to a sickly old woman?" He propped himself up on his elbow so he could look at me. "We should be angry with my father and this Aunt Mary. They're the ones who misbehaved and then abandoned their child."

"And I am angry with them, believe me. I'm angry with many people in this situation. It was terribly handled by our elders."

"I don't disagree, old girl. But we're such a tiny family now, do we really want to hold each other at arms' length?"

"I suppose not. I'll see her again sometime soon. We can try to find some neutral ground somewhere. Tea at the Savoy, or something."

"She'll complain about the extravagance, but I'll come if there's cake."

I chuckled as the bell rang. "Get that, will you, Toby? Reilly's out."

Toby groaned, hauled himself to his feet, and wandered into the hall. As I finished one sheet and turned to another, I heard the door open and Toby say, "Why, Lord Dunreaven, what a not terribly unexpected pleasure!"

I set the pen aside and stood, face warming and hands tingling. I hadn't seen Jeremy since I left Wotting Park, though we had exchanged letters and telephone calls.

"Butler's day off?" Jeremy guessed.

"Oh no, I'm training for a new career," Toby explained.

Jeremy chuckled. "I should take advice from you, then. And please, call me Jeremy. I hope we've reached the point of using Christian names."

"Have we? I'm starting to wonder if there's some news my cousin hasn't shared."

I poked my head out of the drawing room. "Toby, stop teasing him."

Toby bowed deeply. "As you wish, Madam. I shall go put away his lordship's coat and hat and hide myself away in the kitchen."

I sent him off with a withering look as I ushered Jeremy into the drawing room.

"I'm interrupting," he noted, nodding toward the papers on the desk.

"You are, but it's a very welcome interruption," I said happily, taking his hands and leading him to the sofa.

"I'm glad to hear that." His smile was soft. "How are you? It's been quite a challenging few weeks, by the sound of things."

"I'm all right. Or nearly all right. The dust is settling, and things seem to be spinning less frantically."

"Oh? I'm glad to hear it." He gently ran his thumbs over the tops of my fingers. "I'm sorry I've not been to see you before now."

"It's all right. I've been busy, anyway. Did you know Ford's opening a new automobile plant near London? Freddie and I have been chasing down contacts."

"Have you, indeed?" Jeremy grinned. "You are bold, the pair of you."

"Nothing ventured, nothing gained."

"Quite. Which is why I've been forming some ventures of my own."

"I don't doubt it! And I'm pleased to hear it, Jeremy."

"I'm pleased you're pleased. The pleasing of you is a pleasure to me," he said, playfully. "I've missed you terribly," he confessed.

"And I've missed you too," I replied, squeezing his hands.

He grinned. "I wonder, now that things are settling, how you'd feel about someone coming along and kicking the dust back up? Complicating things?"

"Well, that would depend on the person and on the complications."

"If the person were me?" There was a devilish look about him now, and a warmth—no, *heat*—flowed through my hands, making my blood boil.

"You know you can ask me anything. And if you keep looking at me like that, I can refuse you nothing."

"I'm glad to hear it because I have a proposal for you."

I always thought that when this moment came I'd feel nervous or giddy. That I might burst into tears of joy or perhaps even panic. But although my heart sped up and my face warmed, I felt perfectly calm. Because I knew: *This is right. This is how it should be. This is what you want.*

I grinned and asked, "Business or pleasure?"

"Can't it be both?"

"Normally I'd say no, but I make exceptions for exceptional people."

He laughed and shook his head. "I won't claim to be anywhere near exceptional. But you are, and you've made me feel ashamed of myself."

I hadn't expected that. "Did I? I certainly didn't mean to!"

"It's all right—I needed to be made ashamed," he continued. "You see, some of us are taught from our earliest days that things will simply come to us because of who we are and how we look. So, we wait for them. And we atrophy, sitting around, wondering why everyone else's chance has come and ours hasn't. But I met you and I saw *you* refusing to sit by. You're beautiful; you could have snapped up a rich man and lived in comfort."

"A spoiled little pet?" I snorted. "Decorative and discontented? Not for me."

"Exactly! It wasn't for you, so you did something about it. You saw a challenge and you met it and you—you're extraordinary!" he burst out, face shining with pride. "I realized that I couldn't simply wait for some solution to my problems to drop like manna from the sky. I had to do something, and I am! I've been busy, making plans and sorting things out. We're going to grow strawberries at Midbourne, and sell them at select grocers here in London. A premium price for His Lordship's Berries! The dower house is to be a little hotel for the tourists visiting the area, and the house will be opened for tours. And there are other things, too, that may come about. I am *not* going to be one of these useless men living on their titles and dreams of the past. I am going to *deserve* you." His excitement and energy were palpable, tingling in the air around him. I knew that if anyone could save Midbourne, he would.

"Oh, Jem," I breathed, reaching up to stroke the side of his face.

"The thing is," he went on, "as much as I love Midbourne, it's a dashed lonely place to be right now, and this seems like hollow work to be doing alone. I've hated not being able to see you every day. I keep thinking, 'I should ask Astra what she thinks about this,' but you're not there. I imagine someone else holding your hand or kissing you, and I don't even know who he is, this poor man, but I want to rip his arm off."

I couldn't help but laugh.

"I love you," he said solemnly, looking me full in the face. His expression was so soft and touching, my heart hurt just looking at him. "I love you. And I want to show you how much I love you every day. If you don't want to hear any of this, just tell me to go and I will. I'll never darken your door again."

"Don't you dare!" I choked, clinging to him. "Don't you *dare*, Jeremy Harris!"

He grinned, and it felt like sunlight flooded through me. "And now, since you are a businesswoman, here is my proposal." He sat up and cleared his throat. "Miss Astra Davies, I am here to offer you a house in West Sussex, an excellent private library, a garden to do with as you please . . . and me. Every last piece of me. And all my love and support, whatever you want to do. I promise never to treat you as a bit of decoration or to touch a penny you earn. And I offer this"—he reached into his jacket and retrieved a little velvet box, inside of which nestled his grandmother's diamond and ruby ring, winking at me and urging, *Say yes! Say yes!*—"if you agree to be my wife."

Another warm wave poured over me, and I smiled up at him. But first: "All cards on the table. I don't come alone. Raymond is still very much my responsibility and one I have no intention of giving up."

"Of course. And I look forward to meeting him when you feel the time is right."

"And you should know now that I'm a fright first thing in the morning. I'm beastly when I have a cold or when I haven't had my morning coffee."

He laughed. "These are risks I'm willing to take."

"Good. Because I'm excellent with strawberries. And I love you, Jeremy. I love you *so much*. So put that ring on me, and let's decide on a date!"

He laughed, sounding almost astonished, and slid the ring onto my finger. I grinned at it, glittering on my hand, then looked back up and kissed him.

If our first kiss was a summer shower, then this one was a proper autumnal storm: fierce, wild, and lasting. Oh, how *delicious*! We twined together and my heart was going like an express train, and his was too—I could feel it through his clothes as we pressed close, melding, unwilling to separate. I thought, *He's mine! Mine! Always! And I'm his—always!* I would see him every morning and take him to bed every night. Have his children and watch as he aged into a magnificent, silver-haired gentleman. I would know his secrets and have him know mine. I would tease and comfort, make plans, and love him every single day.

Every single day.

I felt giddy, happy, and warm all over. Every part of my body he touched felt hot, and now I understood Cee's blushes and Laura's and Joyce's knowing looks. All these little secrets of women in love. You can't know them until you've been.

The kiss tapered off, but we stayed clasped together. I traced the curves of his face—lips, cheeks, jawline—with my thumb. Memorizing him inch by inch.

"I love you, Jeremy," I murmured. "I promise I'll try to make you happy despite all my faults and foibles."

He chuckled. "There are still a few I need to probe out, if I'm not mistaken."

"That's right," I purred. "And you have the whole of the rest of your life to do it."

He stayed until the shadows lengthened outside, then departed with kisses and promises to return the next day. As I closed the door, Toby appeared in the doorway of the miniscule kitchen, a bottle of champagne in one hand and two flutes in the other.

"Dandy and I went out and bought these on Mother's account," he proudly announced. "Congratulations, darling! Sorry for listening in, but it's a tiny place, this, and it was impossible not to. Gosh, you really are silly over him, aren't you?"

"Very silly, and I wouldn't have it any other way," I said. "It's been quite a year, and I'm happy to be ending it so happily."

He handed me a glass of champagne and clinked it with his own. "I'm happy you're happy. You've earned it. Now, please do me the favor of telephoning Millicent and telling her all about it. And hold up the receiver so I can hear her shrieking."

I smiled a little but shook my head. "No. She'll hear soon enough, and you'll hear her bellowing in rage all the way in Chelsea. I don't want to spoil this by being petty."

He rolled his eyes. "Suit yourself. Now, what do you say we send Reilly to fetch some lobster for dinner? What would Mother say to that?"

"I think her shrieks would surpass even Millicent's," I said, handing him my empty champagne glass. "Do as you please, Toby. I'm back to business now."

"All work and no play makes Jill a dull girl," Toby warned, waggling his finger.

"I play plenty," I reassured him. "Go on and order your supper, if you must."

He bowed and meandered back toward the kitchen. I retreated to my desk, picked up the pen, and returned to my work.

Acknowledgments

As ever, my first and greatest thanks must go to my incredible, supportive, loving, and extremely tolerant family, who have always encouraged and believed in me. Without them, I probably would have thrown in the towel on this whole writing thing ages ago.

I'd especially like to thank my husband, Adam, who manages the day-to-day realities of living with a (sometimes moody, sometimes distracted) working writer. Honey, I don't know where you find your patience, but I'm very grateful that you do!

Thanks also to the Rogue Writers of Edinburgh, who first read this story. Their honest feedback and enthusiastic responses were invaluable. Write on, you lovely people!

And finally (but certainly not at all least!) I'd like to thank the splendid team that helped bring this book out of my head and into the wider world. Thank you to my agent, Steven Chudney, my wonderful editor, Faith, and the rest of the lovely people at Alcove Books. You've all made a nearly 20-year dream of having this book published become a reality, and I will be forever grateful.